LANGUAGE OF LOVE

Maria thought she was alone, bathing in the secluded pond. She had no warning of Cheyenne's approach until his muscled arm seized her bare waist. She only had time to register the shock of his hard torso pressed against her nakedness before his mouth swept down to plunder hers.

Maria shivered as her lips parted and his kisses seared a path to her soul. His fingers found the tip of her breast and caressed it into a ring of fire that rapidly spread throughout her body.

"Maria, *mi carina, querida.*" His words whispered through her senses as if no one had uttered them, caressing her in the same manner as his hands . . . as her whole body melted against his. . . .

CHEYENNE'S LADY

Patricia Rice

AN ONYX BOOK

NEW AMERICAN LIBRARY

A DIVISION OF PENGUIN BOOKS USA INC.

Copyright © 1989 by Patricia Rice

SIGNET, SIGNET CLASSIC, MENTOR, ONYX, PLUME,
MERIDIAN AND NAL BOOKS are published by New American
Library, a division of Penguin Books USA Inc., 1633 Broadway,
New York, New York 10019

First Printing, December, 1989

1 2 3 4 5 6 7 8 9

PRINTED IN THE UNITED STATES OF AMERICA

*To my mother, who is not only responsible
for the Irish eyes in the family,
but the talents, both good and bad.*

Author's Note

The small towns depicted in this narrative do not exist. They are composites of towns that once existed and are no more, victims of the same progress that for one brief moment in history brought them to life.

The descriptions of Santa Fe and other historical details are as accurate as I could make them. If anybody doubts the likelihood of one man controlling an entire town or group of men controlling a territory, they need only read the history of Billy the Kid and the Lincoln County Wars, which occurred only a few years after the time of this tale. Truth can be as fascinating as fiction.

To challenge love
is to venture all.
A game of hearts,
a woman's call,
tempting onward,
but to what fate?

Nothing ventured,
nothing gained.
Life's too short
for living tamed.
Do you wish to
play once more?

Prologue

Dust blew off the mesa and swirled around the hooves of the sure-footed stallion as it eased down the rocky incline to town. The horse's rider scarcely swayed with the motion as his dark gaze swept over the old Spanish mission and the cluster of weathered wood and adobe buildings ahead. One hand firmly gripping the reins, the other resting casually on a muscular thigh, he approached civilization cautiously, his gun hand near his holster.

From the town's lone street, the sheriff eyed the stranger's approach with cynical skill. Along with the bedroll tied to his saddle hung an old Spencer rifle, unprepossessing in appearance but a weapon with the ability to fire seven rounds in nearly as many seconds, not the kind of weapon a rancher needed.

A black, low-crowned Stetson shadowed the stranger's face from view, and his heavy sheepskin vest hid the powerful breadth of shoulders and the agile leanness of a man accustomed to long hours in the saddle, but the sheriff read the way he rode his horse and wasn't fooled by the disguise. If he needed further proof of the man's occupation, the dual Colts riding at the stranger's hips confirmed any doubt. No cowboy needed two such expensive deadly weapons, nor would he wear them as the stranger did—low and within a flick of a finger.

A few other bystanders drifted into the street to follow the sheriff's gaze. A rancher in a wide-brimmed sombrero gave a low whistle at the sight, and a storekeeper in dark vest and suspenders jerked his gaze ncrvously as the lawman spat a long wad of tobacco into the street.

"Reckon he's one of Vasquero's men?" he asked, barely hiding his fear.

"Won't know until he gets here," the sheriff replied laconically.

"Sure as hell none of the rest of us can afford him." With a cynical grimace the rancher swung on his booted heel and strode back into the saloon.

As if that summed up the situation, the others followed his lead, and the stranger arrived to the whistle of a cold wind down an empty street.

BOOK I
Spring, 1876

1

Camille Maria Francesca Connolly glared in frustration at the gaping gray moire bodice. She had no difficulty fastening the buttons at her waist, but in the three years since her sixteenth birthday her bosom had filled out, and there was no earthly way she could make the gown fit in time for the pageant.

"What am I going to do, Pieta?" The cry was one of wounded femininity as well as disappointment. Once she had had closets full of silks and satins she seldom thought to wear. They were little but a nuisance when she preferred riding the ranch with her father. Now she dreamed of enchanting the town with her womanliness for a change, and she had nothing that fit.

The fact that she had known she had nothing to wear when she accepted the part of Mary Magdalen in the Easter pageant had no effect on Maria's disappointment now. She had wanted to wear something besides these infernal denims and faded work shirts for a change, and she had jumped at the opportunity. There was always the heavy black bombazine Pieta had cut down to fit her for her father's funeral, but that ugly, shapeless excuse for a dress wasn't what Maria had in mind. She had worn that to church every Sunday since his death; it was even less feminine than Jose's Levis.

"Maybe if you use a shawl . . ." Pieta began doubtfully, but her employer's vigorous shake of disapproval silenced that suggestion.

"It will fall off or slide down or something equally disastrous, I know," Maria announced derisively, continuing to glare at her slender figure in the tarnished

mirror at the back of Jesse's storeroom. She had slim
hips and a waistline so small she needed no corset, so
why did she have to be cursed with her mother's full
bosom?

The dress rehearsal was only half an hour away. She
couldn't go like this. She would have to surrender the
gown to someone else and back out, make some excuse, tell them an emergency had arisen at the ranch.
And never show her face in town again.

Pieta sighed at Maria's mutinous expression. The
child had never learned to take anything lightly. Each
day's delights were exhilarations beyond measure.
Every disappointment was a catastrophe. She came by
her mercurial temperament naturally, the servant supposed, but it did not make living with it any easier.
Even now she could read Irish Connolly's devastating
temper boiling in those emerald eyes, and the wide,
passionate mouth of Maria's Spanish mother had set
in a grim line only that fine woman had managed
gracefully. The combination was deadly, both physically and emotionally. The mother's aristocratically
haughty features and vivid coloring, the father's brilliant eyes and cutting tongue, and a double dose of
both passionate natures—*Madre de Dios!* It was
enough to make grown men weep. Pieta had surrendered any attempt at control shortly after the death of
the girl's mother. Only Irish Connolly could control
her, and now he, too, was gone.

Not wishing to think about that tragedy, Pieta lifted
a tortoise-shell-backed brush to Maria's heavy black
tresses. Loosed from their usual braid, the silken
lengths fell past Maria's hips, more like a wild Indian's
than a young lady's. At least she could fashion some
feminine coiffure instead of the usual braid.

But Maria had other ideas. With the sudden brilliance of the sun after a storm, her expression changed,
and she swung from her faithful friend's hands.

"Consuela! Consuela will have the kind of gowns
Mary Magdalen would have worn! Why did I not think
of it before?"

Laughing delightedly at the wickedness of her

thought, Maria began to shrug off the ill-fitting bodice, much to the horror of the older woman.

"You cannot! What will Father Díaz say? The gown of a—" She choked on the word, unable to utter it.

"A whore?" Maria finished derisively. "And what was Mary Magdalen?" Stepping out of the gown, she determinedly reached for her old work shirt. "Who am I to judge? Consuela is my one and only friend. She will help."

With that, she was gone, leaving the older woman to stare after her in dismay.

Freshly shaved and bathed after days of dusty travel, Luke Walker pulled a fresh shirt from his bedroll and shrugged it on with careless ease. Bronzed shoulders rippled lightly with the movement, giving some hint of the muscular strength behind the gesture. Shirt laced and topped with a leather vest that left his arms free to move swiftly, Luke reached for the gunbelt that never went far from his reach.

A quick glance in the looking glass over the shaving stand assured him the barber had left the mustache trim, though the golden-brown edges of his sideburns still looked a little rough. The chances of finding a decent barber in these desert outposts were slim, and he had long ago given up any vanity concerning his looks. He had no use for impressing ladies and men seldom gave his square jaw a second look, in any case. Brushing the irritating wave of sun-scorched hair from his forehead, he strode toward the door, a parched throat uppermost in his thoughts.

Stepping into the narrow back hall of the saloon where he had found lodging, Luke cautiously attuned his senses to his surroundings before going farther. Too early in the day for a crowd, the saloon produced only the usual noises of clinking glasses and low murmurs. That was not the direction of the sound that caught his ears now.

Hand already halfway to his hip, he swung to watch the stairway. Then with a slow grin he relaxed and lounged against the doorjamb, admiring the vision materializing above him.

Garbed in a vivid red satin that would have shamed the devil in hell, black hair streaming in wanton abandon over dusky, bare shoulders and half-concealed breasts, an enchanting young witch flew toward him. All she needed was a broomstick. Forgetting any thought of thirst, Luke positioned himself in the shadows at the foot of the stairs. He had not expected to find this kind of luck out in the middle of nowhere. Perhaps doing good deeds had other than monetary rewards.

Aware only that she was late for rehearsal, Maria raced down the back stairway without thought to danger. The men of San Pedro had long ago become accustomed to the coming and goings of Irish Connolly's hot-tempered brat. Fear of her father's ire had taught them to keep their hands to themselves; inertia kept them from realizing Connolly's wrath had died with him. Maria wandered in and out of this man's world with impunity.

So she had no warning, no inkling of danger until she reached the bottom of the stairs and collided with the stranger's solid chest. Steel-like arms wrapped around her, stopping her in mid-flight and taking her breath away. Even then she was only mildly irritated, not in the mood for horseplay while she kept Father Díaz waiting. Not until a stranger's deep voice murmured passionate phrases in her ear and heated lips sought her own did Maria realize the trap she had entered.

"Bruja bonita, mi cariña, let me see if you are real and not a mirage in this desert."

The man's words whispered warm and lovingly against her ear, not words to fear. Though they drew her like a moth to a flame, Maria was no fool. Strong arms did not mean safety, and she squirmed in his tight embrace, heart pounding erratically as the smooth chambray of his shirt brushed the bareness of her breasts. Realizing she had no hope of escape, she opened her mouth to scream. As if waiting for that moment, his lips closed over hers.

The sensation was not unlike that of drowning. Maria went under, gasping for air as his hot breath filled her nostrils and his tongue penetrated the opening between her parted lips. Trapped against the stranger's chest, her hands clawed at his shirt, finally clinging to the loose folds as her knees threatened to collapse under her. Never before had she been kissed like this, and foggily she found herself responding, drawn to the urgency of his demands. Her lips moved beneath his, growing soft and welcoming as he gave a guttural growl of pleasure.

She had been kissed before, but never like this, never with such a hungry yearning that it touched a chord in her soul and sent shivers down her spine. All the fears, all the loneliness, all the pain of these last months dissolved beneath the need of his lips. It was an impossible sensation, a caressing of two lost souls, but she did not have it in her to deny what she found there. She wanted it too much.

Not until she felt long fingers slide to her hips and press her against the hard bulge of his loins did Maria react with an instinct born of self-preservation. Fist knotted as her father had taught her, she swung viciously and with all the strength that she possessed.

Her blow missed the mark and landed solidly against an abdomen made of steel, but the surprise caused her attacker to take a step backward, and that was all the leeway she needed. With swift grace Maria dodged beneath his arm and flew out the back door, the stranger's muffled curses flying after her.

At the sound of feminine chuckles from above, Luke hesitated, swinging from his intended pursuit of the elusive witch to glare up the stairway to a more earthy beauty.

"That one was not meant for the likes of you, gringo. If you must burn your hands playing with fire, why not play with me for a while?"

And because he had a need that could not be satisfied otherwise, the stranger took the stairs two at a time and swept this second dark-haired beauty through the open door behind her.

He had little respect for women, but this one was good at what she did, and for a while she eased his mind as well as his body.

2

Gazing up at an unreasonably cold March sky, then back to the rippling, stirrup-high grasses of this New Mexican valley, Luke Walker found himself pondering a destiny he had never planned, a future that did not exist. The loneliness of the empty plain rose up cold and aching within him, and he wondered—not for the first time—why he continued this existence.

"Because you can think of nothing better to do" came the usual reply, spoken with its usual bitter irony inside his head. The challenge kept his blood circulating, his senses alert, and it was only at times like these that he felt fully alive. The only substitute was liquor, and he had seen what that could do to a man. If he courted death, he preferred it to be a swift one.

The news he had received in town had engendered this dismal train of thought. He had few friends left from his youth, few ties left with his family. One of those fragile ties had just been severed, and he felt the loss with curious intensity. It had been years since he had thought of Irish Connolly, almost a decade since he had seen him last, but the image of the older man still lingered strong in his memory.

The Connollys had been neighbors and friends of his family years ago. Some of them still lived back there on the Kansas plains, others had returned East. He knew little of them except from talk of his parents. Only Irish stood out in his mind—a more bull headed, hot-tempered man than he had ever known, and broken with a grief stronger than any eighteen-year-old could ever imagine. He had never seen a man cry before, but that burly, blustering cowboy had sat there at

the kitchen table and cried that night as he spoke of
his wife's death. The next day Connolly had risen and
rode with the rest of them to capture a band of raiding
Kiowas, all trace of tears gone except in Luke's mind.

Luke remembered the image to this day, had reason
to remember it because it corresponded with his determination never to let another woman under his skin
again. If a woman could reduce a man like Irish to
tears, they had no place in his life. That Irish Connolly
would have violently objected to this reasoning had
nothing to do with why he was here today.

They had told Luke back at the ranch house how to
find the little cemetery where Irish lay beside his wife
and the babies that had never lived. The least he could
do was pay his last respects before turning toward
home. He hadn't been home in years, with good reason, but it was time. Luke felt it in his bones even as
he found the small picket fence with its lone tree and
weathered crosses.

A horse grazed inside the fence and a boyish figure
knelt beside the newest cross. Luke hesitated, not
wanting to disturb a stranger at his prayers, but his
sense of trouble had already aroused his curiosity, and
he spurred his mount over the last few yards remaining.

With her long braid wound up and pinned beneath
her father's old felt hat, her slender figure enveloped
in one of Jose's discarded shirts and her hands as rough
and chapped as any boy's, Maria appeared little more
than a young lad from a distance. She had cultivated
the look from an early age, ignoring the silks and satins her father had once purchased for her. Of late, it
had been cheaper to continue this costume, and her
boyish clothes were second nature to her now, a
chameleon-like protection in a man's world.

Even in her grief she reacted swiftly to the approach
of a lone rider. Rising and whistling softly for her
pony, she placed the animal between herself and the
newcomer, shielding the rifle strapped to the saddle.

The Stetson disguised him until he was almost upon
her, but the mustache lingered in Maria's memory with

a revulsion and a fury she had no intention of controlling. The rifle slid out of its scabbard smoothly, and the saddle served to prop the bore as she took deadly aim at the broad, furrowed brow beneath the brim.

"One step closer and you're a dead man," Maria warned in a voice trained to carry in the vast distances of her surroundings.

Luke had already come to a halt when he saw the barrel of the Winchester, but the almost musical quality of the words thrown at him took him by surprise. Slowly sweeping his hat from his head and propping it over the saddle horn, he tried to get a closer look at his adversary.

"I apologize for disturbing you." He hesitated over "ma'am," deciding against it. "I came to see Irish Connolly. I didn't expect to be paying my last respects."

"What would Irish Connolly want to do with a gunslinger like Cheyenne Walker? My father was a law-abiding citizen. He wouldn't want the likes of you on his land. Now go, get out of here before I put a bullet between your ears."

Her father! A ripple of shock coursed through Luke as he realized this little hellion must be Connolly's only child. He remembered now a mention of a daughter, a subject he had carelessly disregarded at the time. It had never occurred to him that a female could grow up to be as deadly as a male. How she came to know his name remained a mystery, but that wasn't his major concern at the moment.

He squinted against the sun for a better look. "Your father sent for me. I've got the letter right here in my pocket if you want to see it. I'm sorry to hear about his death."

Suspicious, Maria kept the rifle trained on the gunman as he swung down from the saddle. She felt certain he didn't recognize her, and she aimed to keep it that way.

"Well, I reckon you came a little too late, Mr. Walker. There ain't no use lingering now."

The rifle barrel hadn't lowered an inch, and Cheyenne eyed it warily as he rested his hand on the gate. From this angle he could see a little more of her, although that abominable hat she kept pulled over her face hid any charm her features might possess. Still, he could read the straight, grim line of full lips, and he made no effort to advance farther.

"What do you mean by 'too late'?" He stalled for time, hearing something in the way she said those words that sent ugly warning signals through his brain.

"Too late to help him, too late to help me, too late to help any of us, if you're telling the truth about that letter. Now just go away, back where you came from. We don't need any more of your kind around here."

Maria cursed silently at the way he just stood there, the wind whipping that odd-colored hair of his into his face while he studied her. A glint of sunlight played on his amber-colored eyes, giving them an almost sympathetic cast before they narrowed and grew hard.

"Your father was a friend of my family's. I'd like to pay my respects," he announced in a voice that brooked no further argument.

Before she could refuse, he swung the gate open and entered.

A single shot carried his hat away. Annoyed but not afraid, Cheyenne swung on his boot heel, hand reaching for his Colt to prevent any further incursions upon his limited wardrobe. To his surprise, the little witch was breaking the rifle and returning it to the saddle. The little witch! His eyes narrowed suspiciously as she swung up on the horse and he retrieved his hat.

Maria caught his glare and spoke coldly. "I will respect my father's peace if you will not, but next time the bullet will be aimed a little lower."

The gunfighter moved quickly, grabbing her reins before she could maneuver the sturdy pony from the cemetery.

"You haven't told me how he died."

That was the last thing Maria had expected from this stranger, and surprise prevented her from reacting with her usual caution. Instead of applying the quirt to the back of his hand, she replied vehemently, unable to conceal the unshed tears in her voice.

"He was killed, shot in the back, on his own land, for money he never had. Now, if you'll let me go, I'll let you pay your respects in peace."

It was her all right. Somewhere beneath that godawful checkered shirt and decrepit hat was the passionate little beauty who had bewitched him the morning before. Curiosity and the pain of those unshed tears kept Luke's hands on the reins.

"He wrote to ask for my help. I don't like to let a friend down. Have they found his killer?"

No longer caring if he recognized her or not, Maria glared at this hired gunman with scorn. "My father would never ask help from the likes of you. Let loose of the reins."

Cheyenne shrugged, releasing the reins to reach for the letter in his coat pocket. "He didn't sound as if he wanted a friendly visit to me."

Mesmerized by the sight of his gloved hand reaching inside his buckskin coat for the correspondence her father must have written before his death, Maria forgot her intention to spur her pony to freedom. She wanted to see her father's words, starved for just that small communication with the man who had meant everything to her. The aching emptiness his death had created had left her hollow and brittle for too long. She needed this touch of familiarity from beyond the grave.

Cheyenne stood aside as she grasped the crumpled letter and read it avidly, not once but several times. He didn't know what had possessed him to give it to her. He didn't trust women, and this one was no exception. In fact, he was more wary of this deceptive bundle of femininity in boy's clothing than of any man he'd ever known. He could have turned around and rode out of here and been home by month's end. Why in hell had he passed that piece of dynamite to that tinderbox who called herself Connolly's daughter?

Watching the shadows darken under high cheekbones as her lips tightened into a grim line, Luke knew why he had done it. He had wanted to see what she

was made of, and he had a good inkling of it now. No
tears coursed down those smooth cheeks. No apologies crossed her lips. She merely folded the letter and
handed it back to him.

"I can offer you the job, but I can't pay you. The
bunkhouse doesn't leak and the food's good, if you're
inclined to stay awhile."

Luke made up his mind in that moment. If she had
fluttered her lashes or wept or promised him the moon,
he would have rode off and thought nothing of it. But
she had replied as her father would have done, and the
decision was made.

"I left my gear in town. I'll be back by sundown."
Luke moved toward his horse, but the soft voice behind him stopped him.

"Find my father's killer and you'll find the man responsible for these attacks he wrote about."

Luke shoved his hat brim up with his finger and
stared directly into the greenest eyes he had ever
known. "I already reckoned on that, Miss Connolly.
My father didn't raise me to be a stupid man."

Sleek black brows arched in disbelief. "I don't
imagine he raised you to be a hired gun, either, Mr.
Walker, but I'll accept your word for it, for now. I'll
have Pieta keep your supper warm for you."

She rode off before he could mount, and he stared
after the rhythmic sway of the narrow hips, a silent
whistle on his lips. Damned if the Irishman's spirit
didn't live on, but what a hell of a package to put it
in!

Unconcerned with the opinions of a man whose gun
could be bought and sold, Maria rode back to the ranch
with new fire in her eyes. Why had her father never
told her his suspicions about the series of "accidents"
and disasters that had befallen the ranchers this side
of the river? Roving bands of renegade Indians could
be blamed for the deaths and fires at the Sumner and
Smith spreads. The poisoned cattle at Otter's could
have been locoweed or alkali water. Merle Roberts
had a wicked temper and that horse could have thrown

him. What had made her father put all those incidents together and write to this gunslinger for help?

And why choose a man like Cheyenne Walker? She knew nothing about the man, but she had seen his type before. You didn't live this far from civilization all your life without running into the breed who preferred to carry the law in their hands. Yet her father had written to him as if he were an old friend, a trusted friend he could rely on. That wasn't like her father. He was much too shrewd to rely on a man who lived by his guns.

The puzzle fired her curiosity, but the knowledge that someone may have deliberately burned those homes and poisoned those cattle fired her anger. The pointlessness of her father's death took on a whole new meaning. Perhaps he had been too close to the truth; close enough for someone to murder him.

The defeat and the hopelessness that had overwhelmed Maria these last few months were replaced with grim determination. A cowardly thief could be any drifter passing through, impossible to chase, but a murderer—! That would have to be someone who lived right here, who knew he would be riding home alone that night and who knew his victim well enough not to approach him from the front. Irish Connolly would have blown his killer's brains out with his dying gasp if he could have seen him.

Since her father hadn't had that chance, Maria would have to do it for him. She didn't know how long she could expect this Cheyenne Walker to hang around without pay, but she didn't intend to put much faith in his help. Now that she knew her father's suspicions, she would start her own investigations. If she had to spend the rest of her life searching, she would see the bastard swing.

Pieta looked up from the stove as the back door swung open with a forceful slam she recognized well. How anybody could come back from placing flowers on her father's grave in a temper like that, she did not want to know. What she wanted to know was how a pint-sized termagant like Maria Francesca could terrify all those man-sized cowboys out there into following her wishes.

"Charlie said to tell you he's got the fences up along the ridge, but he'll quit before he rides herd on no sheep," Pieta repeated the message calmly as she removed the bread from the oven. She was thankful she hadn't started the cake yet. The explosion to come had been known to make cakes throughout the valley fall.

To Pieta's surprise, Maria only flung herself against the long wooden bench lining one adobe wall of the kitchen and began to tug at her boots.

"Charlie can go to hell. I'm sick and tired of babying these prima donnas who think their manhood will fall off if they get down off a horse and do something besides drive cattle. Manuel can deal with them after we're married. In the meantime, I've got a new foreman coming in who will make them carry out my orders."

Pieta's eyes grew wide with surprise as she wiped her hands on her apron and turned to stare at her petite and much-too-young employer. Not only did the mention of the new man startle her, but Manuel's name had not been heard around here for months. What had prompted this sudden change of heart?

"Manuel? He is returned from Santa Fe?" she asked casually. Too casually, for Maria turned a suspicious glare on her as she massaged her aching toes.

"Of course. Did you think he would leave his precious father forever? I'm to have dinner at the hacienda next month." Suddenly remembering something, she slammed her feet back on the floor. "Damn, I won't have anything to wear but that crow's black. How in hell am I going to greet Doña Vasquero in boots and jeans?"

"Better you should mend your language than your wardrobe," Pieta scolded, stirring the embers in the stove before sliding the cake batter on to the rack. "The ladies at the hacienda will faint if they hear such words from the heir's fiancée."

The French word rolled oddly on Pieta's Spanish tongue, but Maria didn't take time to notice. Pieta had been mother, friend, companion, cook, and maid to her for as long as she could remember. Part Indian, part Mexican, part almost everything, she had never had a formal education, but she learned quickly and mercilessly from those around her. She had learned to read with Maria and had devoured every page in Señor Connolly's well-worn library since then. The active minds and education of the Connolly family had fed her eagerness for learning until her lore of knowledge came only as a surprise in its wide variation and odd tangents. That she used the French word instead of the Spanish failed to shock her mistress.

"How am I supposed to practice my feminine wiles wearing your son's hand-me-downs? They've not seen me since last summer when I could at least decently wear your blouses. But I can't wear white and embroidery and ruffles while I'm in mourning. And I just can't wear that awful black again. I'll have to tell Manuel I can't go."

Since secretly that would please Pieta thoroughly, she made no immediate reply. Manuel was the only son of one of the richest ranchers in the valley, the scion of an old and noble Spanish house. That he had deigned to look upon the mixed-breed daughter of a cattle farmer spoke of the changing times, but Pieta harbored no good feeling about the match. There was no love between the two, of this she was certain. They only pleased their selfish needs by agreeing to this marriage, and what old man Vasquero hoped to gain by bringing it about was anybody's guess. Certainly nobody else in the valley was eager to take on Irish Connolly's hot-tempered, ill-bred hellion.

"We will take apart the gray bodice and make it work," Pieta finally said, knowing that was what Maria wanted.

"Oh, Pieta, you are a dear!" With an enthusiastic swing of mood, she hugged the older woman, then scampered in bare feet toward the door. "I'll find Carmelita and Pedro and help them with their chores so you can teach them the multiplication table or whatever tonight."

"You put on your shoes—" The door swung closed before she could finish her warning, and Pieta sighed. That was why she put up with the incorrigible *brujita*. Her laughter and her love were as vibrant as her tempers, more so perhaps in the good times. It was just a pity the señor had to die before the good times could come again.

That evening Maria heard the new foreman ride up, heard Charlie's greeting, and Pieta's recalcitrant mutters as he presented himself at the kitchen door. Charlie and Pieta had been around long enough to know how to take care of the itinerant hands who came and went like tumbleweed through the valley. There was no need to stir herself from the desk in her room, where she pored over the ledgers and sorted out the mounting stack of unpaid bills. It did little good to organize the numbers in neat little columns on one side of the page when there were no matching columns on the other side, but it comforted her to carry on as she had when her father lived. When she was done with that task, she scribbled out her weekly letter to her uncles as her father had insisted that she do.

But when she retired to her bed that night, columns of figures didn't dance through her head as she drifted into the first foggy stages of sleep, neither did Manuel nor dreams of revenge. No, the last thing Maria remembered as sleep closed the door upon her day was the hard, unyielding chest of the stranger beneath her hands, and the sensation of drowning in a whirlpool of heat while the fresh scent of shaving soap perfumed the night.

3

Maria lifted a shapely dark brow at the sight of the dust rolling beneath the flock of sheep heading down the trail to the newly fenced field. Alongside the flock ran two barefoot, brown-skinned boys and a dog acting as a team to keep the animals on the move. With a cynical twist of her lips, she watched as two of her younger ranch hands whooped and hollered and chased the odd stray back to the flock, acting for all the world as if they were on a cattle drive. Behind this scene, as she had known he would be, rode her new foreman. Lazily walking his horse and keeping an eye on the ragtag collection of sheepherders and would-be cowboys, he appeared to be at peace with the world.

Spying Maria watching him from the ridge, Luke flung a few instructions at the boys and eased his mount into a canter up the trail. He still wore the disreputable Stetson pulled down over his eyes, though it now sported a new hole in the low crown, but the Colts weren't in evidence this day. He almost looked innocuous riding up the hill toward her, but Maria knew better than to believe in appearances. She had seen him shoot the head off a rattlesnake from sixty yards with that rifle slung to his saddle. Innocuous wasn't the word for a man like that.

"I can't feed the men I have." She took the offensive as soon as he was within hearing. "Who gave you the right to take on a couple of hollow-legged boys?"

Showing no sign that her reproof had reached him, Luke slowed his horse to a halt beside hers. She wore her hair in a single thick braid this morning, and her eyes slanted slightly with the sun, giving her an almost oriental appearance as she glared at him. The loose white shirt she wore did little to hide the woman beneath, however, and his gaze lingered a moment too long at the tanned *V* above her first shirt button. Maria made an angry gesture and jerked her neckerchief around to conceal herself.

Only then did Luke lift his eyes to meet her angry green ones. "You wouldn't have to feed anybody if I'd tried to make your men ride herd on a bunch of woolies. They would have quit."

"And I suppose you feel the same way, too," Maria replied in disgust, turning away from his stare to watch the dust of the sheep roll up the trail.

"Well, you surely don't need grown men to ride herd on the likes of them, if that's what you mean. But if you mean about keeping sheep, no, I don't have any objections to them. Cattle market being what it is, it's a damn good idea."

He caught her by surprise, and she turned back to face his inscrutible expression. This wasn't the first time he had surprised her. She should be growing accustomed to it by now.

"Thank you," she answered with as much dignity as she could muster beneath his unblinking stare. "Have you found out anything yet? I know it's only been three days, but . . ."

Luke fought his stallion's impatient, tossing head while formulating a reply. His gaze drifted consideringly over her petite stillness. "Tell me how you knew my name before I even knew who you were."

A small smile formed on her lips as Maria contemplated the reason for that question now. "It's a small town. There are ways."

"I'm serious. I'd just arrived, and I sure as hell didn't go spreading my name around town before riding out here. Where did you hear it?"

Maria shrugged and the smile disappeared. "I had to return the gown to Consuela before I came home. You didn't waste time in finding her."

Luke considered that matter from behind narrowed eyes, watching her warily. It seemed highly unlikely that the daughter of a man of Connolly's position in the community would be acquainted with the town whore, but admittedly, he had first met her on the back stairs of the saloon. Perhaps there were a few things he would keep to himself until he knew more about Miss Connolly.

"Consuela talks too much, then. You'd better remember that. People are suspicious enough of me as it is. It will take time to learn what isn't being said in front of me."

"Consuela doesn't talk too much. She barely even talks to me. She just thought I might be interested in the name of the man who molested me. Maybe she thought I'd shoot you down." Maria tugged on her horse's reins to turn him around, but Luke's reply followed her.

"You almost did," he called after her, and if she had turned to look, she would have seen the beginnings of an admiring grin on his taciturn features.

She had never referred to the incident in the saloon before, and Luke had kept his mouth shut about it. Perhaps she was having second thoughts about her earlier rejection, but whether the thoughts were good or bad, Luke didn't care to hang about and question. He had set himself a task and he would accomplish it. Then he would go home and face the past.

Maria ignored the sound of Luke's horse following her down the path back to the house. She had lived among men most of her life and was more comfortable in their company than a woman's. She had small problem dealing with overzealous admirers or drunken lust. Most of the men around here knew by word or experience what would happen if they looked at Maria Connolly the way a man looks at a woman. She was never far from a weapon of some sort, and she knew how to use them as well as any man, or better. But her sharp tongue could cut a man's pride to ribbons faster than any knife, and her father's temper had always emphasized whatever point she made. She didn't need to worry about men she knew; strangers, however, were another problem.

She dismounted and Charlie ambled out to take charge of her horse. A small figure apparently clothed entirely in dust came rolling across the paddock, stumbling and falling and picking himself up with a merry gait accompanied by joyous cries of "Frankie!"

Maria grinned and waited for Pedro to reach her on his own before kneeling down in the dirt and catching him up in a bear hug that made the little boy squirm with happiness as he buried his grubby self in her embrace.

"Frankie! Frankie, you gotta come see! Puppies! *Mucho* puppies. *Andale!*" Pedro whipped from her embrace to tug her hand in the direction of the distant barn. Brought up in a household of mixed Spanish-Americans, he spoke both languages without distinguishing between them, neither of them clearly or grammatically.

Maria laughed and let him go. "I will be there in a minute, *chico*. Go think up names for them while I speak to Charlie."

Pieta's youngest took off on chubby legs for the far barn, where one of the hounds had crawled off to have her litter. Maria turned from the sight of his stocky body scrambling under the paddock fence to search for Charlie's ancient and angular frame.

Charlie had been with the Connollys off and on since Irish had pulled up his roots in Kansas and settled down in New Mexico. Breaking his leg in several places on a roundup a few years back, Charlie had taken a dislike to that wandering life. Bunking with the Connollys at the time, he had settled himself comfortably into their lives. The arrangement suited everyone nicely.

Charlie limped out into the sunlight at Maria's call, his eyes blinking after the darkness of the stable. His gaze swerved from her petite figure to the approaching one of the rider behind her, and his eyes narrowed shrewdly. He said nothing, however, as Luke dismounted and joined them.

"Frankie?" With a skeptical lift of his brow, Luke questioned the child's cry of earlier. Hard as Connolly's daughter seemed at times, he had watched her tumbling in the hay in a melee of arms and legs and laughter with the ranch youngsters and knew that was just one of the intriguing little witch's many facets.

"Maria Francesca," she replied shortly, turning away from the hint of laughter behind golden-brown lashes. "Charlie, they're taking the sheep up the ridge. Luke's picked up a couple of kids to herd them. They'll need a place to stay."

Before Charlie could open his mouth to reply, a scream of pure terror rang across the open yard. At the same time frightened shouts erupted in the far paddock. Heart leaping with fear, Maria swung around to find Pieta wailing and knotting her apron near the back door, her face a portrait of terrified anguish as she stared at some sight beyond the yard.

Following the direction of Pieta's gaze, Maria swung back to face the paddock that Pedro had toddled into just minutes before. With a small cry Maria grasped the danger, and she broke into a run across the yard. Luke had already grabbed the rifle from his saddle and was racing with long lopes toward the paddock railing.

For some reason beyond Maria's comprehension, the gate between the paddock and the bull's enclosure was open. The sight of the little boy toddling innocently across the field had attracted the attention of Old Red. Irish had once threatened to butcher the old bull for his meanness but his progeny was needed more than his meat, and he'd been left to grow meaner by the year. Irritated by the shouts of the ranch hands on the far side of the field, the animal switched from a wary stance to full attack even as Maria watched.

Maria screamed for the men to be quiet, but they were already foolishly crossing the fence with lariats in hand, mindlessly angering the bull into a full rage. She cursed as her boot heel caught in a hole, and tears threatened to spill over as she stumbled. She would never reach the little boy in time, and her screams only served to attract his attention. Pedro stopped in the middle of the field to turn in curiosity at the sounds of excitement behind him.

Luke reached the fence rail first. A lariat without a

horse was useless at a time like this. He lifted the long barrel of his rifle to gauge the bull's speed and direction, judging the distance to the child with bone-chilling accuracy before he picked his point and pulled the trigger.

The gun exploded three times before the animal finally toppled to a halt. Pieta's frantic screams filled the sudden silence following the gun's report.

Maria limped to the fence and climbed over as Pieta stood, trapped by her weight and age from reaching the boy in the field. Maria could sense Luke climbing over after her, but her one thought was for the paralyzed boy standing terrified and alone beside the dead bull.

She caught Pedro up in her arms, burying her face against his small neck as the first waves of horror washed over her. So close, *Jesu!* So close to losing this warm little body that had yet to learn what life was all about. Holding Pedro close, she lifted her tear-stained face at Luke's approach.

"Thank you," she whispered, choking on a sob. She had not cried at her father's funeral or in the months since, but she could not help herself now. Death had come much too close, too often, and a new horror took root in Maria's heart as she stared up into the gunman's knowledgeable bronzed features.

Luke read the growing understanding of death's nearness in Maria's eyes and gave only a curt nod of acknowledgment to her gratitude.

"You'd better take him back to his mother," he said gruffly before turning back to bark orders at the incompetent fools running toward them. Luke already knew the bull was the most valuable piece of livestock on the place, but she said nothing of it. The horror in her eyes he had seen before, a horror of death and of the person causing it. But in this case he did not think she blamed him. Mentally churning these fractured pieces of fact, Luke stared down at the steaming carcass at his feet, then turned his gaze thoughtfully toward the open gate.

Pieta reached gratefully for her youngest as Maria carried him out, and as soon as she had him in her arms, she characteristically began to scold. Wearily Maria climbed over the fence and wiped the dust from her brow, staring bleakly after Pieta's retreating form. The incident had shaken her more than she cared to admit, and her hand trembled as she tried to stuff the neckerchief into her pocket.

"Damned handy he is with them guns," Charlie ruminated speculatively as he watched Luke swing from the fallen animal in the direction of the gate.

"It's a good thing." Maria couldn't turn to watch, but braced herself against the fencepost, giving her heart time to slow its pace.

"Maybe it is, maybe it ain't." Laconically Charlie followed the action.

Maria sent him a suspicious glance. "What do you mean? If Luke hadn't killed that animal, he would have torn Pedro to pieces." Her cheeks paled beneath their tan at the thought.

"But's it's almighty handy he was right here when that gate was left open for the first time in years. Nobody uses that gate. Didn't know it still worked."

Maria swung around just in time to watch Luke slam the gate closed and examine the lock. It couldn't be. Someone couldn't have deliberately left that gate open. Everyone in the county knew Old Red was the meanest animal this side of the Pecos. Anyone could have been in that paddock.

Feeling a cold chill, Maria managed only a sharp reply: "Keep an eye on him, Charlie, and any other strangers. I'm not going to lose any more livestock."

Straightening her spine, Maria stalked toward the house. Even if Luke hadn't been there to shoot the bull, the men would have killed the animal if it had mauled anyone. The result would have been the same, except there might have been one dead child besides the bull. Either way, the ability to improve her herd had ended. She had no cash to buy another. The whole town knew it. The deviousness of the plan was almost as breathtaking as its cruelty. Someone wanted her out of the business and didn't care who got in the way. Her father had been right.

* * *

She didn't have the patience left to argue with Manuel when he rode up later with a retinue of his *vaqueros*. She felt the scorn in his dark eyes as he gazed down at her rumpled, dusty apparel, but she was accustomed to scorn. Coldly she watched Manuel dismount and come toward her.

"What is this I hear of your stocking sheep?" Incredulity laced his voice as his eyes swept with vague mockery from her head to her foot. His own tall, well-built frame was garbed immaculately, as if the dust did not dare land upon him.

Maria rolled her eyes heavenward and prayed for the strength to hold her hasty tongue. She had no wish to offend Manuel. As arrogant as he might be, he was the only damned man in the valley to offer for her, and she had to assume he had some reason.

"Sumner offered his herd for the promise of payment when I sell the first flock. He was anxious to be quit of this place. It was too good a deal to turn down." Maria twitched irritably at her soiled neckerchief, wishing she could look as cool and laundered as Manuel in his snowy white shirt and skin-tight black *calzónes*. His dark hair lay neatly slicked back from his bronzed forehead as if he had just stepped from a cool shower.

"A woman's foolishness." Manuel shrugged away the impending argument. He had known Maria most of her life and knew her moods as well as his own. "You should not concern yourself in a man's business. Have you asked Father Díaz about lifting your mourning so we might set a date? Then you will no longer need to worry over such nonsense."

The irritation did not go away with the removal of one subject for argument but increased with the introduction of this new one. "I can manage, Manuel. I will not dishonor my father's name by acting hastily. We can wait."

Not satisfied with this reply, Manuel would have argued the point further, but a glance told him too many eyes followed their confrontation. A frown formed upon his noble brow as his gaze fell on the stranger leaning against the paddock gate. So it was true. She had hired the gunman.

Not bothering to conceal his irritation, Manuel signaled for his men to mount. As they did so, he reminded Maria, "You will dine with us on my father's feast day as promised?"

"I will be there." Maria watched in relief as he rode off. Not until she turned back toward the house did she note Luke's presence, and an odd sensation shivered down her spine as their eyes met. Without considering the cause, she hurried back toward the house and a bath.

Later, when the moon was full and the coyotes wailed in the distance, Maria stood at her window and looked out, basking in the cool breeze off the mountain. She could not sleep. Too many problems thundered through her brain when she closed her eyes, too many memories came sneaking in when she shoved the problems aside. She only wanted to feel the caress of the breeze against her skin, feel the freedom of the stars as they floated overhead.

From somewhere the first chords of a guitar whispered to her senses, and she felt a curious sense of pleasure at the sound. A voice followed the chords, a low voice of haunting melancholy, appealing to the time and the mood, opening up other worlds outside hers. The song and the voice filled her with a longing she had never known, stirred feelings she had yet to understand. The emptiness of earlier filled with unfamiliar yearnings as the spring breeze blew the music through her open window.

Cursing beneath her breath, Maria slammed the window closed. Tomorrow she would send word to Manuel, invite him to dinner. She would show him she could be as much a woman as any other, banish all doubt in her mind and his. To hell with foolish love songs.

4

Luke broke away from the huddle of men at the back of the feed store as Jesse carried out his order. In the last few weeks he had made himself a fixture around town, and the men were growing accustomed to his presence. He had carefully cultivated relationships with several of the ranchers and men like Jesse who owned business interests in and around San Pedro. What he had learned gave room for thought, but brought him no closer to Connolly's killer. For that he would need outside help.

As Luke reached to help with the sack of grain, the older man cautiously lowered it to the counter instead of passing it on. With concentrated thoroughness Jesse scratched out a bill of sale, then wiped the ink from his fingers on the greasy leather of his vest before looking Luke in the face.

"Sorry, Cheyenne, it's gotta be cash." Sticking the thick pen behind his ear and leaving a smear of ink in his graying hair, Jesse waited nervously for his customer's reaction.

Luke reached for the bills in his back pocket while eyeing the storekeeper narrowly. "New policy, Jesse?" he drawled casually, peeling off the necessary cash.

The storekeeper shrugged. "I gotta pay for this stuff myself. I can't bankroll Connolly's place any longer."

Raising an eyebrow but not inquiring further into the ranch's finances, Luke shouldered the bag of feed and strode out, leaving the storekeeper to stare after him with amazement and a touch of admiration. Not many cowboys would hand out their hard-earned cash to pay an employer's bill. Not many men would have taken his announcement without insult. That made this Cheyenne Walker a rare breed, indeed. Either that, or Maria Connolly held something over the gunman that no one knew about yet.

While Luke deposited the feed in the wagon, Maria finished her purchases at the dry goods store and stopped to linger admiringly over a selection of hats left over from Easter. Most of them were much too grand or ornate for her tastes, but a simple straw hat with yellow streamers of silk caught her eye and she could not resist reaching for it.

Setting aside her bag of practical purchases, Maria donned the delicate straw, perching it daringly at a tilt above one eyebrow. The wide brim and small crown was meant to be worn by a woman with upswept hair and curls and not a long, black braid, but the silk trailed fetchingly over her shoulder and contrasted strikingly with tanned skin and the flashing green of her eyes. Even Maria had to admit it looked handsome as she admired the effect in a mirror.

Entering the dry goods store to see if Maria needed help with her purchases, Luke halted in the doorway at the sight of the little witch preening her feminine feathers in the window. Without the filthy slouch hat pulled down over her face, the exotic slant of her eyes behind sooty lashes held his attention. The girlish hat emphasized her youth and accented the soft texture of rose-hued cheeks. Even her mouth seemed softer, fuller, less grim than her usual expression. For the first time since he had entered her employ, Luke caught a glimpse of the lovely woman who had flown into his arms that first day.

Realizing she was being watched, Maria blushed and hastily returned the hat to the shelf. Dusting off the old felt, she grimaced and clutched it in her hand as she gathered up her bags and prepared to leave. She glanced up in surprise as Luke approached.

"You ought to buy it. It looks good on you," he ventured, watching her face. He didn't understand women, never had, never would, but this one intrigued him more than any other he had known lately. All fire and tempest, she did her best to disguise anything womanly about her. Yet he had seen and kissed the woman in the red dress and knew there was more to her than the grim-faced, boyishly dressed figure before him.

"If I had that kind of money, I would pay the bills," Maria scoffed, attempting to brush by him and be on her way. Luke didn't budge, and though he was leaner and not so broad as most of the men she knew, she still felt his masculine presence with an impact akin to running into a wall. In these close quarters she could not avoid him.

Luke's narrow lips quirked upward at one corner, and the golden glints of his brown eyes twinkled with an almost boyish mischief as he regarded her set expression. She wanted that hat so bad she could taste it, he ventured to guess, and impulse directed his next action.

"I know how to get you that hat and win me some spending cash at the same time," he offered laconically, disguising his sudden eagerness to pull this off.

Maria sent him a suspicious look, but could discern nothing behind his studiedly unconcerned expression. "How?"

"Cracker Jack out there bet me the other day you didn't own a hat besides that filthy thing of your father's and that you wouldn't know how to wear one if you did. I'll buy you the hat, and the wager will pay for it and then some. We'll both come out ahead."

Maria continued to look suspicious as she tossed the idea around in her mind. There had to be something wrong with it, but she wanted the hat so badly she could not see the harm. She offered only one weak protest: "That doesn't seem fair. Cracker didn't mean for you to go and buy me the hat so you'd win."

"It serves the scoundrel right to go talking about you that way. Besides, you do know how to wear a hat. I just saw you. Seems fair enough to me."

Luke watched the flash of anger in her eyes and knew he had won. Now all he had to do was steer poor

Cracker out of her way for a few days until the insult
was forgotten. That shouldn't be difficult. She'd have
found half a dozen new things to rankle her ire before
day's end.

Jesse's wife gaped in surprise as Maria slapped down
the hat and the coins to buy it, but Luke had already
wandered back out to the wagon by then, and she saw
nothing wrong in the child falling for a little feminine
finery for a change. With a smile she helped Maria pin
her braid up and arranged the new hat attractively on
top. If the yellow silk looked slightly incongruous with
the white linen shirt and boy's denims, she said not a
word.

Proudly sporting the pert straw with the streaming
yellow ribbons, Maria consented to sit beside Luke on
the wagon seat as he whipped the team out of town.
As they passed Cracker leaning against the corner of
the saloon, whittling a stick into nothing, Luke made
a thumbs-up gesture that Maria pointedly ignored,
turning her nose up in the air. Cracker stared after
them for some while, scratching his head in bewilderment.

Once out of town, however, conversation lagged,
and Maria regretted not riding ahead on her pony,
hitched now to the wagon gate. The man beside her
seemed quite content in the silence, but his proximity
made her nervous. He always wore his guns to town,
and she was very aware the strong, capable hands
managing the reins could move with lightning-like rapidity. Maria wasn't at all certain that was the cause
of her uneasiness, but unaccustomed to thinking things
through, she sought the easiest action to put an end to
her jitters.

"You're certain Cracker will pay up? I'd hate to be
obligated to you for the cost of the hat." She stared
straight ahead at the swaying rumps of the old mules.
The proud carriage horses had been sold long ago,
when things had first started going bad.

Luke slanted her a look askance. "That's a damn
fool question. Got any others you want to try?"

Maria bristled, but he was right. What man would

be fool enough to dispute a simple wager with a man wearing Colts? She just hated being obligated to anyone. "You needn't be rude. I was just trying to make conversation. Did it ever occur to you that you could talk with people and not just at them?"

Luke clicked his tongue and whipped the reins, urging the mules to a faster pace. "Far as I can see, women are the ones that do the talking at. I never had much trouble conversing with men."

Maria grew tight-lipped for a minute at that, but refusing to be baited, she tried another tactic. "Maybe your problem is refusing to think women capable of conversing, so you talk at them as if they were objects. That way you only get the same in return."

Luke grunted, unconvinced, and changed the topic. "You'd better be planting one of those pastures to grain if you're going to feed your animals come winter."

Maria glanced up at his square-jawed visage, surprised by the comment. "I haven't got a plow to turn that sod, even if there was enough growing season. My father never had to grow his own."

"Your father must have paid his bills. Jesse is cutting off your credit. Beef prices being what they are, it would be a shame to sell off the stock. Your only other choice is to sell off some of the sheep."

Maria stared sadly out over the high plateau. From this angle, it blocked all sight of the ranch and the valley below. She had one other choice, but it went against the grain to admit defeat. "I've got to pay Sumner first if I sell the sheep. They won't be worth anything this time of year. It's not your problem, anyway. You just look after the man who killed my father. I'll look after the ranch."

Luke ignored her protest. "How long's it been this bad? Looks to me like you got a pretty good spread here. Bad prices shouldn't wipe you out that quickly."

Maria shrugged, refusing to look at him again. "Bad prices, bad health, bad luck, you name it, we've had it these last few years. I've never seen my father discouraged before, but those last few months . . ." She let the sentence trail off, not wanting to describe the awful helplessness she had sometimes caught in her father's eyes when some new disaster struck. Irish Connolly was a fighter, and he had fought until his dying breath. It was better to remember him that way, not as the broken man he would have become had he lived to see his ranch sold off piece by little piece.

"Don't you have any relatives you can call on? Why keep struggling? Why not pack it up and get out of here?"

Her green eyes lost their sadness and flashed defiantly as she turned to confront this arrogant man who so confidently arranged her life.

"My mother's brother lives in California. He washed his hands of her when she had the temerity to run off with a peon like my father. My father's brother moved back East years ago. I barely remember him and my cousins. I keep in touch with both of them, but my home is here. I don't wish to leave."

Luke made a rude noise. "You don't want to leave dry water holes and starving cattle and a town that thinks you're loco or worse? You know what I think? I think you're scared to leave. You don't know anyplace or anyone else and you're scared to face what you don't know."

"That's not true! A lot you know about me. I'd be off in a shot if I had any reason to go, but I'm no quitter. I know what they think about me back there. My mother's people look down on me because my blood's not blue, and my father's people think I'm little better than an Indian, but I'm going to show them! One of these days I'll walk down that street with my nose in the air, wearing gowns straight from New York and Paris, and they're going to beg for my attention! Now shut up and leave me alone."

Luke grinned then, a wide grin that reached his eyes as he gazed down at the stubborn little witch in her foolish streamers and haughtily tilted chin. She was a tiny thing, too slender by far, but the structure of her face warned she was no frail wisp. A proud, straight nose and high cheekbones revealed her aristocratic heritage, and a round, stubborn chin revealed the feminine image of her father's pugnacious nature. The dark, arched brows and slanted green eyes behind a fringe of thick lashes were entirely her own, though, and her best feature should she ever learn to use them wisely. Instead, they flashed warning signals instead of welcoming lights.

"Are we done conversing, then?" he asked wickedly.

Heaving a loud sigh of exasperation, Maria crossed her arms and stared toward the ranch, purposely ignoring him. He was undoubtedly the most annoying, overconfident male she had yet to encounter, and she had known plenty. Still, she couldn't hide a flicker of a smile crossing her lips.

Luke guided the animals into the cool darkness of the barn, where he could unhitch the team and unload the grain out of the heat of the sun. At this hour the place was deserted, and he was strangely reluctant to let the moment end like this.

Maria, too, regretted her sharp words. He had bought her a hat and treated her as an intelligent human being, which was more than many men had. And he certainly had no reason to stay and help her if she insulted him too much. She sought for words to soften the confrontation.

"I apologize if I was rude. I just resent everyone assuming I cannot take care of myself just because I'm a woman. And I thank you for the hat. I hope you don't have too much trouble collecting your wager."

Maria stared straight ahead as she made these admissions, and the vulnerable curve at the nape of her neck struck Luke with unusual intensity as he gazed down at her. He wondered what she would do if he kissed her there, but he had no intention of finding out. She might consider herself a woman, but she was barely more than a girl. Climbing down from the seat, he circled the wagon to help her out.

"That hat's worth whatever it takes. I like it. And I'm not a fool. I can see very well that your father taught you to take care of yourself. I'm just not so certain that you want to.'' With that enigmatic remark he reached up to swing Maria down from the wagon.

Hurriedly Maria attempted to scramble down by herself, but it was too late. Powerful hands circled her waist and lifted her into the air, setting her down directly in front of Luke, where she could not avoid his gaze.

The shock of this touch vibrated through both of them, and helplessly they continued to stare into each other's eyes. Luke's hands lingered at the soft curve of Maria's waist, and her eyes remained fixed upon the unguarded look on his face as they both remembered a similar intimate encounter. Never had she seen him with his mask of indifference down, and Maria had the sudden wild urge to touch his taut cheek.

The opportunity vanished with Charlie's shout as he entered the barn. Luke immediately dropped his hold as if burned, and Maria nervously began brushing herself off as she moved toward the door. Charlie cast them both a suspicious glance as they parted without a word, but it was none of his business, and he reached for the bag of grain.

That night as the lonesome strains of the guitar again played through the chilly night air, Maria stood at her window and stared out into the darkness with perplexity. She had never known any of her men to play a guitar before. There could be only one man, one stranger who could be making this mournful music, but it did not fit the man as she knew him. Luke Walker was a hired gun, one of that merciless breed of killer who could shoot a man for money. Men like that didn't sing odes to the stars or lost loves.

Too restless to sleep, she drifted out onto the tiled patio, drinking deeply of the cool air that would soon be laden with the scent of roses. This had been her mother's favorite spot, a reminder of the home she had left behind when she had allowed the brash American to sweep her away from all she knew and loved. Maria had only been nine when her mother had died in giving birth to a stillborn son, yet she could still remember her mother's pleasure in the brilliant flowers Irish sought out for her, carrying them from any garden he chanced upon. A love like theirs could only be the work of fate, and the world had done its best to destroy it.

Sadly Maria slid her fingers along the low adobe wall, listening to the music well up inside her. She wondered if her mother had ever regretted giving up the sheltered, aristocratic life of her Spanish family for the raw, new one of her American husband. The life out here was crude and often lawless; her mother's family had learned that the hard way. The land they had claimed had been stolen from them, Maria was never certain where or how. She only knew the Valencias had lived out here long enough to lose their land and daughter before returning to their home in California. Occasional letters passed back and forth across the mountains, but her mother had never returned to her ancestral home. Surely there must have been regret for letting the years pass without trying to mend the broken ties.

Maria stared at the dark ridge of mountains in the distance and wondered if Luke were right. Should she conquer her pride and attempt to locate the family she had scarcely known? She knew more of her American cousins than her Spanish ones, but they were half a continent away, beyond her ability to imagine. She knew there were trains that could take her there, but they had yet to reach this far into the wilderness. The mountains she could see. They were much more accessible to her imagination.

It mattered not. She couldn't lower her pride to appear penniless and homeless on anyone's doorstep. Her father would turn in his grave if he thought his only daughter reduced to that. No, she would continue as she was, and one day she would marry Manuel. Then the people of the town would have to look up to her. She would have position and family and all the pretty dresses she could ever wear. Manuel did not love her, but he had chosen her over all the other available women in town. That must mean something. Perhaps with time they would learn the love that marriage brings.

The music changed its note, as if the musician laughed at his own mournfulness. Unable to contain her curiosity any longer, Maria drifted to the edge of the patio overlooking the outbuildings. Out there, leaning against a wagon wheel, she could see the outline of Luke's lanky frame, his head bent over the silhouette of a Spanish guitar. The music that came from his nimble fingers was amazing, but it was the sensual low notes of his mellow baritone that held her captivated.

Luke sensed her presence immediately, as if a ghostly specter had brushed against him, but he did not lift his head to acknowledge her presence. It took little stretch of the imagination to see her slender grace silhouetted against the moon, to know the feel of her against him. He had seen her silken hair streaming about her shoulders, watched her eyes flash with fire and fill with tears, and he did not want to see more. She was a powder keg more lethal than dynamite, and he had tired of playing with fire.

Tomorrow he would go to town and visit Consuela.

5

What with one thing or another, the trip to Consuela was temporarily postponed, and Luke had forgotten his intention several nights later as he pounded a nail into the sagging foundation of the front porch. He grunted in disgust as the wood disintegrated, and wonder what in hell had possessed a sensible man like Irish to build a porch on an adobe ranch house.

The sound of the front door opening interrupted his disgruntled thoughts and he glanced up in anticipation. The little spitfire would have a few words to say when he mentioned the fact that the porch would have to be hauled down before someone fell through. He rather enjoyed her spirited reaction to his opinions.

He was doomed to disappointment on this subject, though. The rose trellis surrounding the porch hid the occupant from sight, but Luke immediately ascertained that Maria was not alone. Two sets of footsteps echoed against the floorboards, one of them decidedly heavier than a female's.

Setting his mouth in a tight line, Luke picked up his tools and prepared to leave, but the whispered promises drifting from above trapped him in an embarrassing predicament. Anyone on the porch would see him walk away and know he had been within hearing. The little witch would never forgive him for that. On the other hand, if he remained where he was, the darkness would conceal him.

Unaware of Luke's presence, Maria deftly avoided Manuel's wandering hands and stepped to the porch stairs, hoping he would take the hint. It had been a

long and tiring day, and she simply wasn't in the mood
for countering Manuel's provocative lovemaking.

Determined to elicit some response from the evasive
female he hoped to woo to his bed, Manuel refused to
take the hint. Maria had dressed for him tonight, and
his hands slid over the gray moire with appreciation.
It had been a long time since he had seen her in anything feminine. He had forgotten how beautiful she
could be when she put her mind to it. The bodice of
the low-cut gown strained across her full breasts with
every breath she took and he was eager to sample more
than words this night.

Maria caught her breath in annoyance as Manuel
once again enclosed her in his embrace. His darkly
handsome face leaned over her, but she could summon
no passion to meet the flash of his ebony eyes. Why
could she not just relax and let him have his way? It
would please him, and he would go away happy. That
was important to a man like Manuel. She must learn
to enjoy these moments if she would be a good wife.

His kiss pressed insistently against her mouth, and
Maria tried her best to respond. Her thoughts, however, drifted to the passionate hunger and unyielding
arms of another encounter, and she could not help but
compare. Why couldn't she react to Manuel's arms as
she had to a total stranger's? Just the thought of Luke's
kiss aroused a more ardent response from her, and
Manuel's arms tightened appreciatively.

When his hand came up to stroke her breast, Maria
relinquished the game. With a gasp of surprise she
tried to push away, but confident of success, Manuel
did not heed her resistance.

"*Cara,* do not fight me. It is time you let me hold
you in my arms. Let me show you how it can be between us."

His hand squeezed her breast as his kiss ravaged her
mouth, and Maria felt an overpowering urge to scream.
The tactics she would use on another man she could
not use on Manuel. As her *novio,* he had a right to
expect this, and in her present confused state of mind,
she could not summon her defenses easily.

Jerking her mouth away, Maria shoved ineffectively against Manuel's chest. "No, Manuel, it is not right. We must wait. Please, stop it!" This last came out with a little cry of anguish as she could feel the straining seams of her gown giving away beneath his rough fingers. All of Pieta's hours of work were ruined by just a moment's resistance.

Not hearing the words so much as Maria's cry, Luke could control himself no longer. Not bothering to examine the rage simmering beneath his surface, he rose from his hiding place and slammed a booted foot against the bottom stair.

Both occupants jumped at the sound, and sufficient light gleamed through the windows for Luke to note Maria's gown falling from her shoulders and the strands of hair escaping from her carefully arranged coiffure. Contempt flashed briefly in his eyes as he turned his gaze to the man beside her, then back to Maria.

"Did you need anything else before I retire, ma'am?" His drawl held a barely concealed note of sarcasm as his gaze boldly caressed her dusky pale shoulders and bosom gleaming above the sagging gown.

"What in hell were you doing down in those bushes?" Manuel didn't give Maria time to reply, but angrily confronted the intruder.

"The lady wanted the post fixed," Luke replied, not taking his gaze from Maria's. He could not tell if she were relieved or angry to see him. She seemed to retreat to a distance beyond them all.

"Thank you, Luke. I didn't mean for you to do it yourself." Nervously tugging at the torn shoulder of her gown, she turned to Manuel. "Luke will have one of the men bring out your horse. It is late, and you should not be out alone."

"I can find my own horse. Call off this hired dog of yours. I want to talk to you," Manuel's eyes burned fiercely as he glared at the gunslinger.

"I'm too tired to talk, Manuel. Maybe tomorrow." The situation was bordering on dangerous, Maria judged as she sensed the tension straining between the two men. She had flinched at Manuel's insult, but Luke had taken it with remarkable aplomb. She couldn't rely on that lasting for long. She didn't know much of Luke's temper, but Manuel's was notorious.

Possessively Manuel grabbed Maria's arm and drew her to his side. His other hand reached around her, intimately rearranging the torn bodice of her gown. "I am not ready to leave, *cara.*"

Luke raised his other foot to the next step and, resting his arm on his knee as if talking casually with his men, he warned, "The lady asked you to leave, señor. I'd suggest heeding her words."

With an explosive curse Manuel dropped the mockery of his embrace to step forward and meet Luke directly. "The lady is *mine* and she will do as I say."

Neither man missed the unladylike word escaping in a hiss behind them. The quick tattoo of heels on the wooden porch followed by the slam of a door came as no surprise.

Luke shrugged and straightened. "I wouldn't wager on that if I were you, señor." He sauntered off, leaving Manuel no one to take out his rage on but himself. With a string of explicit curses he went after his horse. He would own the lady one day, and then let her try barring the door to his face!

Maria assiduously avoided Luke the next day, and her new foreman did his best to aid her. Maria wasted no time on pondering the logic of her behavior, but Luke understood only too clearly the reason for his. Every time he looked at Maria's slouch hat and boy's shirt, he saw bare shoulders and thick, silky strands of hair, and it was all he could do to keep from touching. Better yet, he wanted to swing her over his shoulder and carry her to the bedroom, fling open her closet, and demand she put on a decent dress for a change. He would not think what he would do once she appeared as a woman again.

In that frame of mind Luke rode to town after the day's chores. His progress in even developing a motive for Connolly's death had not made great strides. A little socializing might give him the opening he was looking for so he could wrap this up and get the hell

out of here. Besides that, his need for Consuela's services had become overpowering.

Entering the saloon, Luke ordered a drink and
looked around. On a week night business was relatively slow, and Consuela could usually be found at
one of the tables. Not tonight, however, and he
scowled. Waiting for another man to finish with her
took the edge off his hunger.

He joined a card game with several of the other
ranchers, but though they welcomed his money, they
still regarded him with suspicion. Luke pondered this
while he waited, one eye on the back of the saloon.
They all knew he worked for Connolly's daughter.
They had all suffered from various "accidents" as had
Connolly. Why could they not trust him to side with
them on whatever issue was dividing the valley? Perhaps he looked in the wrong direction. Maybe he ought
to go looking for ranchers who had not suffered these
past years if these didn't trust him.

Impatiently he ordered another drink and when the
bartender brought it, Luke nodded toward the hidden
stairs. "Where's Consuela tonight?"

With an uninformative shrug the bartender replied,
"She don't want to see nobody tonight."

Luke raised a cynical eyebrow. "That's one for the
books. She got someone paying her way, then?"

The bartender gave him an odd look before walking
off. "You might say that."

Not satisfied, Luke began to push himself from his
chair until one of the other card players caught his arm
and held him back. "Leave it be, Walker. It's Consuela's business."

Any other day he would have left it alone. In another
time, another place, he would never even have questioned it. But this was here and now, and something
was going on in this town that he didn't know about,
leaving him suspicious of every word, every motion.
Luke didn't like the way the other men were looking
at him, and he didn't like being fobbed off with weak
excuses. Everybody in this room knew what was going
on but him, and he meant to find out.

"She got anyone with her?" he demanded, glaring at the man who held his arm until he pulled his hand away.

"You heard the man. She don't want to see nobody. You gonna play or not?"

"Not." Slamming his cards down, Luke rose and headed for the hall leading to the back stairs. No one tried to stop him.

Luke pounded on Consuela's door, noting the weaknesses in the rotting paneling as he did so. It wouldn't be a major struggle to remove it if necessary. He had discovered a long time ago it was always best to be able to carry through a threat.

Receiving no reply, Luke hollered, "Consuela, you in there? I want to talk to you a minute."

Silence was his only reply, although he heard a rustle of movement within. The sultry Consuela was not one to hide behind closed doors without reason, and Luke's nose for trouble began to twitch.

"Consuela, I know you're in there. Either open the door or I'll break it in. Which will it be?"

A resigned voice gave answer. "It is already open."

Testing the latch, Luke found she spoke the truth, and he quickly shoved the door aside. Only one lamp gleamed in a corner, and Consuela had retreated to a shadowy distance, keeping her back to him.

"Are you satisfied? Now you have invaded what little privacy I possess, what do you want? Is it Maria? Does she need something?"

"Turn around," Luke commanded, not answering her question. Black hair hung in thick, coarse lengths over a surprisingly simple robe of red cotton, but he detected an odd slump to the shoulders thus concealed. He had seen Consuela enough times in the bar to know she held her broad shoulders straight with arrogance. Tonight he saw only a defeated woman.

"Go away, Cheyenne Walker. If Maria did not send you, I have no need of your company."

The small room offered no barrier to a determined man. In two quick strides Luke crossed the room and spun her around. When she flinched away, he caught her shoulder in a powerful grip which grew tighter as he stared in horror at Consuela's battered face.

"Who did this?" He touched a gentle hand to a livid bruise along one high cheekbone, not daring to come closer to the swelling that shut one eye.

"It comes with the territory." Jerking her head away, Consuela retreated from his hold. "Now get out of here."

"Why in the hell didn't someone stop him?" Anger bubbled to the surface as Luke realized every scream surely must have been heard below. His fists clenched in rage.

"Why don't you ask them?" Bitter sarcasm tinged Consuela's reply. "What business is it of yours, anyway?"

"I'm making it my business. Tell me who it was."

"I ought to, I really ought to, and then they can find your rotting carcass out in some ravine with buzzards flying over it by this time next week. You're just lucky I promised myself never to make that mistake again. Go back to Maria. Take care of her. She needs you and I don't. I can take care of myself."

"I can see that," Luke said acidly. "What makes you think Maria needs any more help than you do? She's all in one piece. You're the one in here hiding behind closed doors."

"And you think she's not?" Consuela swung on him with the first real sign of emotion she had displayed since he entered the room. "You're a bigger fool than I thought. Get out of here. I don't want your help or anybody else's. Go back to where you came from before you wake up one morning with your small brain blown out."

The blaze of anger in her eyes convinced Luke that, if nothing else, her arrogance had returned. She knew something he needed, but he didn't know how to get it from her. He couldn't threaten her like a man, and he sure as hell couldn't beat it out of her. He despised dealing with women. They didn't play fairly.

"It might help Maria if you told me whatever it is you're keeping from me." Luke took one last stab at reason. Perhaps if she knew for certain he intended to help the girl . . .

Consuela glared at him with contempt. "There's only one way you can help Maria. Get her out of here. Now go, and if you breathe one word of this to her, I'll slit your throat. *Madre de Dios,* I hate dealing with stupid ones."

She turned away, and with a curse Luke accepted her rejection. Women did not deal in logic, he had learned before. What he wanted to know now, he could get from men below. He slammed the door behind him and his boots made furious thuds against the wooden stairs as he headed for the saloon.

No man looked him in the eye as he approached the bar, though Luke sensed every ear in the place was turned in his direction. Instead of ordering a drink, he demanded out loud, "Who is the bastard in this town who beats on women?"

"If Consuela didn't tell you, it ain't none of your business," came the bartender's laconic reply.

Luke's next words were delivered in a deliberately ominous tone, carrying to every corner of the room though he did not raise his voice. "I'm making it my business. If this damn town is so full of old women that nobody dares put a stop to a chicken-livered woman beater, then I reckon it's time for a man to do your work for you."

The loathing and hostility in his voice made every man listening cringe, and the insult raised their hackles, but Luke strode out the door without anyone rising to his challenge.

Luke drank deeply of the cool night air, letting some of the rage seep out. It didn't do to think through temper. He needed his wits about him. But as he recovered his wits, he also recovered the reason he had come here in the first place, and he began to curse softly to himself.

Finding the flask in his hip pocket, Luke took a deep drink and set out to the stable to find his horse. Tomorrow he would apply his wits. Tonight he felt the need to drink himself to a stupor.

He had almost reached that happy state by the time he

returned to the ranch. Even engulfed in a sea of liquor, Luke managed to stable and unsaddle his horse, rubbing the animal down before returning to the bunkhouse. A horse was man's best friend in these parts, and a good one could not be neglected. By the time Luke had finished his task, much of the liquor had evaporated.

Debating whether to refill his flask from the supply under his cot, he strode across the deserted yard, kicking up puffs of dust. A shotgun gleaming from the shadows brought him to an abrupt halt, and his hand instantly shifted to his hip.

A slight figure stepped forward, the barrel of the gun still aimed directly at Luke's belly as Maria gazed with contempt at her half-drunk foreman.

"What in hell are you doing out here this time of night?" she inquired derisively.

Relaxing his stance but still keeping a wary eye on the gun, Luke replied in kind. "I might ask you the same thing. Is it the custom hereabouts for ladies to wander the yard in their nightgowns?" As the liquor fumes began to clear from his head, Luke's gaze wandered from the gun to the woman behind it. The thin linen nightshift had been meant to hang loosely over a girlish figure. Instead, full curves pulled the thin material tight, revealing the full outline of her generous breasts. Luke felt his body stir at the sight, and the liquor in his blood did nothing to quench his desire.

In the darkness Maria could not read his expression. She lowered the gun, but continued to glare at him. "It's the custom for *everyone* to protect their property. I didn't know I had rats still roaming the stables."

Luke laughed softly at this thorny reply, and because he could not help himself, because he needed a woman to ease the evening's pain and a lifetime of loneliness, he reached for Maria.

Maria gasped as a strong arm encompassed her waist and the gun was ripped from her hands. Before she could even put up a struggle, she was caught against Luke's solid chest. His hands held her firmly in embarrassing places, and she could feel the heat of his palms through her thin shift. She dodged his mouth as he lowered it to hers, but Luke didn't allow this to deter him. He buried a heated kiss along the soft flesh joining throat and shoulder, and Maria gave a slight cry of surprise at the sensation.

Desperately she squirmed in his hold, trying to tear away, but Luke's kisses continued undisturbed, rising higher and higher until they caressed her ear, her cheek, her eyelids, finally settling on the frightened quivering of her lips.

Maria's struggles increased. Unheard protests fled her tongue as Luke's mouth moved over hers. He robbed her of her senses, stole her soul, and filled her with longings she instinctively knew were dangerous. As his mouth moved insistently over hers, she felt her resistance weaken, and her fingers wrapped helplessly in his shirt. The yearning hunger of his kiss trapped her more surely than his arms.

As Luke's hands began to roam down her back and sides, Maria shivered, pressing closer to his warmth, completing her own capture.

Luke began to relax, pleasuring himself with the feel of her firm curves resting gently against him, the soft scent of roses filling his nostrils. He did not stop to consider the odd innocence of Maria's kisses, but drank deeply of their passion. When she would not part her lips to deepen their kiss, his mouth began to roam again, seeking the spot that would bring her surrender.

Maria felt Luke's hand cupping her breast at the same time as his lips found the hollow of her throat, and the alarm clamoring in her brain finally reached her senses. The fire Luke's touch had kindled did not have time to ignite as she threw herself from his loosened hold.

"You bastard!" she gritted out between clenched teeth. Then spinning around, she ran for the safety of the house.

Stunned, Luke stood holding the cold night air, the heavenly warmth of a moment before dissipating into a familiar ache. He had lost his wits after all.

6

Maria felt his shadow in the barn doorway as she reached for the smallest hound pup. Holding her breath, she prayed he would not see her, but the fates were not kind. Luke's keen eyes found her at once, and he approached without hesitation.

"We've got to talk."

His gruffness so close behind her nearly caused Maria to drop the pup, but calling on reserves of poise she had not known she possessed, she rose gracefully, still holding the tiny dog but unable to meet his eyes.

"I can't think what about. You obviously aren't any closer to finding my father's killer than before." Haughtily she pushed past him, blessedly unaware of the straw tangled in her long, loose braid.

"You can't take that pup away from its mother, it's too young." Luke felt himself angry all over again. There was no rhyme or reason why he should lose control every time he found himself around Maria, and he took his rancor out on her.

"It's too small to push away its bigger brothers to nurse. It will die if I leave it." Maria didn't turn around, but continued striding across the paddock where Pedro had almost lost his life if not for the man behind her. She had to be grateful to Luke for that, but she sure as hell didn't have to do anything more. Memory of the prior night burned fiercely on her cheeks.

"How are you going to feed it?" Luke demanded, following her up the back steps into the kitchen. He didn't know how he had gotten into this conversation, but he wasn't going to let her out of his sight until he'd had his say.

"Pieta, do we have some warm milk?" Grabbing a towel from the warming bar next to the iron stove, Maria wrapped it around the shivering pup, cuddling it to her breast as Pieta dipped milk from the pail Pedro had brought in earlier that morning.

The pail had not yet been placed in the icy well that would keep the milk all day, and Pieta poured the contents of the dipper into a small wooden bowl. "It is still warm. What are you going to do with that pup? Don't we have enough animals around here?"

Her tone was more kindly than her words, and Maria ignored them. Taking the bowl from Pieta's hands, she dipped her finger in it, then offered it to the tiny pup. The dog sniffed eagerly at the nourishment and opened its mouth, but the drop or two clinging to Maria's fingers didn't satisfy. He whimpered and squirmed pitifully against Maria's shirt.

Luke watched as Maria tried to teach the pup to lap at the bowl, then surrendering his objective in seeking her out, he offered, "I've got something we might try. Give me a minute."

Maria looked up in surprise as Luke's broad shoulders disappeared out the door. She had expected him to walk out in disgust and leave her alone. She had not expected him to help with the runt of a litter. Men tended to be impatient with things like that.

The sun caught in his hair as he came back through the door, and Maria would have succumbed to admiration at the sight had not Pedro's chubby body followed Luke, distracting her. She hastily turned her attention to keeping the little boy from overturning the bowl in his eagerness to get closer to the puppy.

Luke's big hand caught the bowl and swept it from the table, pouring the contents into an unsightly bag roughly resembling dried leather. Maria watched in fascination as the gunslinger took the pup from her hands, cradling it in one large palm while poking the tip of the bag between eager jaws with the other.

Within minutes the pup was suckling happily at this

imitation nipple, and Luke was able to hand the animal over to the little boy solemnly holding out his arms for the prize.

"Now, he's not going to drink much at first, *poquito*, but he will need to drink often. Are you going to remember to come feed him?"

Pedro cuddled the animal in his arms and looked up at Luke with idolatry in his eyes. Maria watched in amazement as Luke smiled and chucked the boy under the chin. Was he a magician who could turn himself from frog to prince and back again?

"What is that thing?" she demanded to know as Luke straightened and turned toward her, the smile already gone from his face.

"You won't like it if I tell you. It's just an old trick I learned to use when calves lost their mothers on the range." Luke watched her with an odd expression as she absorbed this information like a little sponge. He'd like to know what went on in that busy little mind of hers, but he was probably just as well off not knowing.

Maria contemplated demanding the truth but decided against it. From the shape of the ugly bag, she could almost imagine, and she didn't want to know how he came by it. Not daring to look at Pieta, she strode toward the back door. "What did you want to talk about?"

Luke waited until they were outside and out of hearing before coming to a halt, forcing her to turn around and acknowledge his presence. "I want to know what's going on around here."

Not understanding, Maria watched his face. The breeze lifted his unruly cowlick, blowing his hair across his brow, and she decided his mouth would almost be sensual if he did not insist on turning it down in a frown every time he looked at her. Why in heaven's name did he keep trying to kiss her if he disapproved of her so much? Maybe he liked any woman who crossed his path when he was drunk. Remembering he had shared Consuela's bed, she managed to quell her senseless curiosity.

"I thought that's what you were supposed to be tell-

ing me. I can't say that you've been of much help.
Guess I'm getting what I paid for.''

Her green eyes glinted angrily in the morning sun,
and Luke fought with his old foes of lust and admiration, striving to maintain the detached demeanor
needed to deal with women. He'd had enough of conniving, ambitious women for a lifetime. He knew better than to get close to this one.

"Why don't you go to your Mexican rich boy for
help, if that's the way you feel? You're so damned
close-mouthed with me that I can't learn a thing.
Maybe it takes money to make you talk.''

Maria resisted the urge to slap the grim line of
Luke's jaw. He was larger and faster, and she would
never win in a physical confrontation. Experience had
taught her a crueler way of fighting.

"Manuel is Spanish, not Mexican. His father is the
younger son of a noble family. Why should I bother
my fiancé with my concerns when I have a professional
gunfighter to take care of the matter? You were the one
who volunteered for the position. I sure as hell didn't
invite you.''

"Your fiancé!'' Cold anger washed over Luke as he
contemplated this news and the two-faced little witch
before him. Not two days before she had used him to
drive off that arrogant Don Juan, and now she had the
audacity to call the man her fiancé. Women were all
the same everywhere. "That bastard wouldn't look
twice at you if you didn't have the biggest spread left
along the river. Don't kid yourself about his noble an-
cestors. Behind their long noses they're every bit as
greedy as anyone else.''

Maria's ire lashed out at him before thinking.
"That's ridiculous! Manuel's family owns half the territory around here. What would they do with more
land? I could sell it all tomorrow and it would make
no difference to Manuel.''

As soon as she said it, she regretted it. The sudden
gleam in Luke's amber eyes warned her of what was
coming, and the coldness stealing through her insides
warned of her foolishness. Manuel didn't love her any

more than she loved him. They had a mutually satisfactory arrangement. Why had she never considered what it was that he wanted out of that arrangement?

"Try it, *chiquita*. Tell him you're exchanging the land in payment for your debts and see what his reaction is. Do you really think our noble Spaniard wants to marry a half-pint tomboy with a slouch hat and straw in her hair?"

He was better at this game than she, and Maria wanted to rip his throat out. How dare he! If she had the money, she could dress as fancy as any lady he could compare her to. And he certainly was a fine one to talk! A gunfighter with nothing to his name but fancy sidearms and a hat with a hole in it! Maria could barely spit out her reply to his challenge.

"I'll prove it! You and Charlie come with me to his father's fiesta next week. I'll show you it is me that Manuel wants, not this damned land. And then I will demand your apologies."

"That's no way to wager. I'll buy you another hat if I'm wrong." Luke didn't even know the man, had no idea of Manuel's motives, but he'd wanted to get under the girl's skin, and he had succeeded better than he had hoped. He didn't mention the price he would make her pay when she lost.

"You're lucky I do not ask to slit your throat if you are wrong." Maria stalked away without satisfying Luke's wishes or his questions. The damnable man had been a thorn in her side since he had first set foot in town. She would have to show him who was boss for once and for all.

The day of the fiesta, Manuel sent the carriage to carry her, and Maria sank down among its soft cushions as if born to such wealth. The gray moire gown had been discreetly mended, and a lace insert had been added to ease the strain on old seams. Pieta had cleverly added matching gray streamers to her new hat and a fashionable yellow sash to her gown until the outfit looked almost new. Maria felt quite pleased with herself as the carriage lurched forward.

Manuel's driver had given her companions a look askance, but he had no authority to order Luke and Charlie away. Garbed in their holiday finery, they rode a wise distance from the carriage's dust, but their presence had its effect. Maria might have no chaperon, but she had brought along a much more effective bodyguard.

At the walled courtyard of the hacienda, the crowds were such that the addition of two more cowboys created little notice. Colorful lanterns hung from the trees in preparation for the evening's entertainment, and musicians already played in one far corner of the garden. Maria drank in the festivity with excitement, her eyes shining more brightly than the setting sun as she waved at friends and acquaintances in the crowd.

Charlie and Luke had discreetly disappeared by the time Manuel made his way through the crowd. Maria climbed grandly from the carriage as if it were a royal coach, bestowing a blinding smile upon her fiancé before glancing eagerly around.

"The decorations are marvelous, Manuel! Your father must be proud to see all that has been accomplished for him."

Manuel shrugged his handsome shoulders. "He has some businessmen in from Santa Fe and has not been out of his study all day. Come, I will take you to my mother and aunt. They are eager to get to know you better."

Maria felt all eyes follow as she took Manuel's arm and stepped from the courtyard into the cool interior of the Vasquero mansion. Few of the partygoers were honored to be guests inside these walls, and she knew just her entrance had publicly announced Manuel's intentions. The thought frightened her slightly, hurrying her into a future for which she was not yet prepared, but the tide of envy behind her carried her in without further qualm. One day she would stand at Manuel's side, mistress of all she surveyed, and all would know she was the lady her mother had raised her to be.

But for the moment Maria felt only awe for the

woman who currently held that position. Doña Vasquero was a short, stout woman with flowing black silks and a permanent frown etched into her noble brow. She turned that frown upon her towering son as he bent to kiss her cheek, then back to Maria as the younger woman bobbed a polite curtsy. Her dark eyes held nothing of warmth as she addressed her audience.

"It is kind of you to attend our fiesta while you are still in mourning, Señorita Connolly." She made the greeting sound like a reproval as her gaze swept over Maria's colorful hat and ribbons.

"Manuel was most insistent and I did not wish to disappoint him," Maria answered softly, her eyes darting quickly to Manuel for approval.

The aristocratic lines of his lean face betrayed no emotion, but his hand squeezed hers warmly as he spoke up to his mother. *"Maria es mi novia, Madre."* He lapsed into Spanish, emphasizing his possession. "If we are to be married, she must learn to be welcome here."

The admonition apparently struck some raw nerve, and the older woman nodded her head in sudden acquiescence. "Of course, my son. She will be the daughter I never had."

Beckoning Maria to follow, Doña Vasquero led the way to a lovely tiled room of arched windows and doorways. The setting sun sent long shadows across the room and buried the corners in darkness, but Maria could see the beauty without need of the sun for which it was built. Only her nervousness at being left alone with Manuel's family prevented full enjoyment of the room's loveliness. This was apparently the women's chamber. Manuel had stayed behind, and several severely dressed females rose from the shadows to greet her.

To Maria's dismay she discovered the women had no intention of joining the rabble outside the cool adobe walls. They sat stiffly in the high, arched windows, drinking tea and talking softly, if somewhat derogatorily, about the crowds in the courtyard below. They waited only for Manuel's father and various uncles and cousins to join them before going on to the private dinner awaiting them. The festivities outside were only a show for the hired hands.

The occasional drift of music had Maria's toes tapping, and she barely concealed her impatience at being thus confined. She loved music and had not had the opportunity to dance since before Christmas, before her father had died. She would persuade Manuel to take her out after dinner. Surely he could not wish to live forever like a ghost in these catacombs.

When the men finally arrived, Maria had all she could do to maintain her composure. She had met Señor Vasquero before, but this night his attention was purely on her, and the intensity of his gaze made her awkward. Where his attention fell, so did all others, and she was soon introduced to every male relative and connection in the family. Curiosity predominated in this parade of eyes sweeping over her, but Manuel's possessive protection and his father's preoccupation with her gave her acceptance into their closed world.

"Manuel tells me you will not allow a public announcement of your betrothal until your time of mourning is over, señorita." Alfonso Vasquero held her elbow as he guided her toward the dining hall. "Perhaps you would forgive an old man his happiness and allow me to announce it to just this, our family, this evening?"

Maria felt trapped, unable to evade his proprietary tone as he took away her choices by playing upon her respect. Her mother had come from this world and she knew her place in it. A woman had no right to object to a man's wishes, and a young woman had no authority whatsoever over an older man. To tell him no would be tantamount to slapping him in the face.

"I would think family should be told, señor." Maria spoke softly, bowing her head to his wishes. She would have to learn to deal with this man if she were to live here. Surely she could learn to do that. Irish certainly had never been the easiest man to live with, but they had reached an understanding easily enough.

That this understanding was tempered by love did not occur to Maria at the time.

Manuel stood proudly at her side as his father made the announcement of their betrothal and glasses were raised to their happiness. Maria glanced apprehensively into his strong face, seeking some reassurance that her decision had been a right one. A gleam of satisfaction brightened his dark eyes as he glanced down at her, and her breath caught a little in her throat as she understood the fire flaming in his gaze as it swept over her. Nervousness twisted in the pit of her stomach as they sat down and Manuel's hand captured hers beneath the table.

Maria could scarcely eat beneath the stares of seemingly a hundred eyes. She knew many of these people by name or reputation, but they had never accepted her in their small community. She had always been an outsider looking in. Now she recognized the bitterness in the eyes of those who had hoped to marry their daughters into the wealthy Vasquero home, and she read the envy in the eyes of others who had settled on lesser husbands. All wondered why a man as handsome and rich as Manuel had chosen an outsider, and as the evening wore on, Maria's thoughts increasingly turned in the same direction.

After dinner, Maria had little difficulty in persuading Manuel to take her outside. Darkness had finally descended and the lanterns sent colorful shadows dancing across the terrace and the gravel walks. Couples were already embracing behind the shrubbery, and Maria shivered slightly as Manuel's arm circled her waist. Now that he had had his way in this announcement of their betrothal, he would not be easy to deny again. She could feel his confidence as he steered her away from the lighted terrace and the dancers.

"I want to hear the music, Manuel," she complained as his path became clear.

"The mariachis will be next and you will hear them from here to the next county," he replied scornfully, leading her toward the darkness of the garden wall.

"It is not often that a man chooses a wife. I wish to celebrate with you awhile."

She had to do it. She had to learn to invite his embraces if she were to be the kind of wife she wished to be. But Luke's taunting words kept her from complying easily. First she would be certain he had chosen her and not her land. But she needed witnesses if she were to prove herself to Luke.

In the shadows it was not easy to distinguish one person from the next, but Maria anxiously scanned the crowd of dancers and observers as Manuel led her through the garden. She suspected Luke would have already imbibed his fair share of drink and would now be one-half of one of the entwining couples in the shrubbery, but surely Charlie would be looking for her. He had not wanted to come here at all and had only agreed out of concern for her protection. Where would he be?

To Maria's surprise, she discovered Luke's lean frame first. Shoulders propped against a tree just beyond the terrace wall, he had a clear view of the dancers and the gardens. He stared right at her as if he had watched her from the moment she left the house. He had agreed to leave his guns behind, but the way his arms bulged as they crossed his chest warned he was not completely harmless. Maria felt as if amber eyes burned through the darkness and straight through her skin.

Steeling herself, she gave a slight nod in the direction of the garden wall, then returned her full attention to the man at her side. If Luke had not seen or understood, he had only himself to blame. She certainly couldn't scream her destination to the world at large.

Manuel's hand grew bolder as the darkness closed in around them. The shrubbery provided a perfect screen for a warm spring evening, and it did not take much to excite his passions, as Maria quickly discovered. As his hand immediately rose to fondle her breast, Maria stepped out of his embrace.

"Manuel, you go too fast. We have no time together, no time to talk. You must have patience." Somehow she had to give Luke time to cross the garden and find them. He damned well better hurry, she thought irritably as Manuel reached for her again.

"Do not worry, *cara*. I will bring you virgin to our marriage bed, but there is no harm in learning a little of what to expect before then. You shy away like a little sparrow when I know you burn as I do. Come here, let me teach you what you need to know."

Luke came too late to hear the words, but recognized the action well enough as he settled himself comfortably against the bark of some sturdy tree. It was like watching a play silhouetted against the garden wall, he decided cynically. There the heroine held up her hands protesting her innocence, backing away until she could go no farther. Then the villain moved in, murmuring promises, and the heroine swoons into his embrace. Only, of course, Maria would never swoon. She went to the bastard willingly enough. Luke could almost taste her kisses as Manuel bent her into his embrace.

Disgusted, Luke decided not to linger. If she wanted an audience to prove she could have any man she wanted, she didn't need him. She had only to snap her fingers and every man in here would be at her feet, had already been at her feet for all he knew. Or cared. Luke pushed himself from the tree and prepared to leave until the sound of Maria's voice carried to where he stood. He hesitated.

"Manuel, you do not understand. You have such wealth, you do not know what it is to be without. How can I come to you with no dowry, not even a proper trousseau? You must give me time. I had hoped to bring the ranch out of debt so I could at least have that to offer to you, but you are in such a hurry, I must find some other way."

She was talking breathlessly now, and Luke's eyes narrowed with suspicion as he watched their shadows against the wall. Maria had not managed to put Manuel off. His hands freely roamed her slender curves and would be inside her bodice soon if she did not extricate herself. Other than talking more rapidly, this did not seem to deter Maria, and Luke settled back to the performance again. Knowing women as he did, Luke assumed she had plenty of experience in dealing with men like Manuel, probably preferred them. Hot-blooded as they both were, they had probably been tumbling in the hay since they were youngsters. Why should he worry if they preferred an audience? He would only wait and hear his wager won. The performance that would follow should bring the house down.

Manuel's murmured protests went unheard. Maria pushed one hand away only to find the other straying higher. Hastily she continued her monologue, cursing Luke and all men in general in her thoughts.

"I have found someone who has agreed to pay all my debts and give me enough for a suitable trousseau. Manuel, are you listening?" Maria averted her face as his lips sought hers. She suspected he had not paid one iota of attention to a word she had said. She felt his hand fumbling at the lace insert of her gown and her cheeks flushed at the thought of Luke standing there in the shadows watching all this. She wanted to smack his face as much as Manuel's.

"Of course, I am listening, *cara*, but you worry too much. I will take care of your debts and your trousseau and anything else you need. Just name the day, *mi novia.*"

Maria gasped as his fingers found the tip of her breast straining against the thin material. Struggling to free herself, she continued to talk. "You are not listening, Manuel! I cannot come to you empty-handed. If you will only be patient. I will tell this man he may have the ranch if he will do as he promises. Then I can go into Santa Fe and buy my trousseau. I cannot come to your home with nothing but this one dress."

Something of her words finally sank into Manuel's impassioned brain, and he set Maria back a foot, star-ing down into her heated face. "You will do *what?*"

"I will sell the ranch, Manuel. It is worthless as it is. I want you to be proud of me when we marry—"

He shook her before she could finish. "You little idiot! The ranch is all you have. Sell it and you are nothing! Nothing! Do you understand me?"

Maria stared up into the contorted features of his face with terror. His fingers dug into her shoulders, leaving her painfully aware of his greater strength. "Manuel! You are hurting me. Stop it, at once."

He did not release her, but did cease shaking her. "Tell me you will do nothing so foolish as to sell your land to strangers."

"What difference can it make to you, Manuel? You have more land than you can possibly need. No one wants our cattle anymore. I thought you would be pleased."

From his position in the trees, Luke admired this little touch of class. She played the humble female so well for the macho bastard, but even from this distance, he could read the angry flare of her green eyes when the light caught them. Manuel was about to reap the whirlwind.

"Land is valuable for more than cows, you silly goose. That is why we must marry soon, before you do something foolish. The land is all the dowry you need. Promise me you will let no one have it but me."

"And if I don't?" Maria's eyes flashed dangerously, but Manuel knew the upper hand was his.

"Don't threaten me, *cara*. You will get everything you want and more when we marry. The land will be ours, for our children."

Maria jerked from his grasp. "Fine. Then I shall sell my mother's jewels to buy my trousseau and you can make love to a tumbleweed. I'm tired, Manuel. I want to go home."

She stalked off in the direction of the lanterns, passing so close to Luke he could smell the scent of her perfume and see the glint of tears in her eyes. He did not mistake them for tears of sorrow or self-pity. They were tears of pure, hellish rage that she had to contain to get out of here. In that moment he almost felt sorry for her. Almost.

Maria did not wait around for Manuel to order the

horses harnessed and the carriage brought out. Finding Charlie's horse in the stable, she tugged off her wilted crinoline and pulled the hem of her skirt through the yellow sash at her waist. Let them think what they would. She wanted out of here.

Luke barely had time to leap out of her way as the horse crashed through the open stable door and flew down the drive, driven by the devil on his back. With a curse Luke whistled for his own mount. She would break her fool neck out there at that speed.

Ignoring the shouts and yells from the yard, Luke spurred his stallion into pursuit. Manuel's livid face glared up at him from the drive, but Luke had no intention of swerving for the bastard.

Recognizing the gunman's deadly intent, Manuel leapt to safety at the last minute, and Luke sped down the drive without further barrier. Let them think what they would. That little girl up ahead needed him more than she knew.

7

Luke caught up with her on the ridge, where Maria had sense enough to slow down and watch for loose rocks. She refused to look at him but rode in silence, gazing firmly at the road ahead.

"You're missing the dancing." Luke came up beside her, forcing her closer to the main trail and away from the more treacherous path at the ridge's edge.

"Go to hell."

That not being an easy gambit for conversation, Luke remained silent.

As the cold chill of the evening began to seep through the heat of her fury, Maria was forced to more logical viewpoints. She had been humiliated in front of the man beside her, but she had done it to herself. She had asked for it. At least he wasn't gloating openly. What hurt most was her foolishness. Why had she been so blind? Why hadn't she realized there had to be a reason Manuel had chosen her over all the other women in the valley?

"Why does he need my land?" she cried in frustration. It wasn't pure blindness. Even though she understood what Manuel wanted, she could not figure out the why.

"Greed, maybe." Luke pulled a small cigar from his pocket and stopped at an outcropping of rock to strike a match.

Maria didn't wait for him but continued down the path. Lighting his cigar, Luke had time to contemplate her question. It was a good one. Men have always acquainted land with power and coveted their neighbor's. Connolly's spread was a good one with a strong current of water coming down the mountainside and feeding the bottomland, a precious commodity out here. But whatever Connolly had, Vasquero had three times over. It wasn't enough to sacrifice an only son for, not when the land came mortgaged to the hilt. He was missing something here.

Luke spurred his horse to catch up with Maria's. She still didn't look at him, but the stiffness had gone out of her shoulders. He shrugged off his buckskin jacket and flung it over her silk-covered shoulders.

"Why don't you sell it to him? If he wants it that badly, he can pay a fair price."

"I'm not twenty-one. I can't sell it without my uncles' permission."

Her reply came so quickly Luke realized she had already covered this territory. There were more questions left unanswered, however, and if she wouldn't volunteer the answers, he would have to pull them out of her.

"He must have made an offer to your father. Why wouldn't he sell?"

Maria shrugged, pulling the coat more securely around her. It smelled of old leather and tobacco, but the musky male scent underlying those stirred her senses more. "If you knew Papa at all, you would know he took strong dislikes to some people. Señor Vasquero was one of them."

Luke needed to ponder that less than half a minute before asking, "Why did he agree to your marriage to Manuel?"

"He didn't." Maria didn't elaborate. Remembering the heated arguments of last summer, she felt the pain return. She had acquiesced to her father's decision to wait until she was older before agreeing to marry, but it had left a rift between them that had not been there before. They had mended the hurt as much as possible, but there hadn't been time for true healing when he had been taken from her. It wasn't fair. She had loved her father more than life, far more than Manuel. Why had she hurt him over so insignificant a matter? Why did he have to be taken from her before she could show him how much she loved him? Tears welled up in Maria's eyes, but she refused to let them fall.

Luke's less emotional thoughts had taken a different direction, and he turned a thoughtful gaze on Maria's haughty posture. She had left her new hat behind, and the moon gleamed along the ebony tresses polished into an elaborate chignon and teased into curls. Her high cheekbones strained at the fragile covering of her skin, and he was aware for the first time that she was not made of old hickory and leather. He had thought her as tough as any man, but that toughness did not even go skin deep. Perhaps it came from within, but from without, she was as breakable as fine china.

If Manuel and his father wanted that land and Connolly stood between them and having it, he had just found one motive for the killing. It didn't make much sense yet, but Luke had the feeling he was finally getting somewhere.

They continued their ride in silence, each lost to their own thoughts. The moon rose to light the night more spectacularly than artificial lanterns, and the music of the breeze played a song along the grasses. The faint scent of roses wafted through the air, drawing Luke's attention to the slight figure in front of him, and a restlessness not easily quelled stirred his blood. He wondered what it would be like to take that tiny waist in his hands and dance her across the terrace in the moonlight. Would those green eyes focus warmly on him then? Or would they continue to wander over the crowd, seeking better pastures?

The path of his thoughts annoyed him, and Luke broke the silence to put an end to them. "You must have a dozen other suitors to choose from. Why did you settle on the one your father disliked?"

Maria made an indelicate noise and turned to stare at her companion as if he were completely witless. Her eyes formed enormous pools in the shadows of moonlight as she faced him.

"I grew up around most of these men out here. I can outshoot, outride, or outsmart the lot of them. They think I'm one of them most times. Women are those soft-spoken, silly creatures who gaze up at them in adoration and promise a lifetime of pure, unadulterated happiness. I'm a burr under their saddles in comparison.''

Luke gave a hoot of laughter which brought a stiff frown to Maria's brow. She jerked her gaze back to the path ahead. He could at least have argued the point, protested a little, but he seemed quite in agreement with her explanations. Why, then, did she carry the image of moonlight shimmering in golden streaks through his tousled hair as she looked away? He had no right to be so damned attractive. He was naught but a hired gun and by all rights should stink of unwashed clothes and sport a belly hanging over his belt and two blackened teeth behind an unshaven jowl.

''Now that you know my life story, why don't you tell me yours? If you're so bright and fearless, why are you out here wandering the plains of nowhere instead of carving out a place of your own with one of the gorgeous women undoubtedly swooning at your feet?''

The sarcasm was less than subtle, but Luke ignored it. The question hit too close to home and consequently he answered evasively.

''Guess I wasn't born to be satisfied in staying in one place with one woman. The grass is always greener someplace else. Seems to me, once you give up striving for something new, you give up living.''

They had reached the stables and Maria slid silently from her horse before replying. As Luke grabbed the reins to both mounts, she leaned against the door frame and eyed her broad-shouldered foreman with a measure of disdain.

''Spoken like a man with woman trouble. One thing you learn living out here surrounded by men is to recognize all the excuses men use to run from women. You're a coward, Cheyenne Walker.''

She offered a challenge he couldn't resist. Without petticoats to hold it stiff, the soft gown had fallen in clinging folds around shapely legs and hips, and the bright sash emphasized a tiny waist meant for holding. Full breasts pushed temptingly at the tight confinement of her bodice, and the vision of Manuel's arms around her loomed tauntingly before Luke. Hell, why shouldn't he try his luck when she was obviously ripe and ready?

Wrapping the horse's reins to the hitching post, Luke moved with swift purpose. Planting a hand on either side of her head, trapping Maria against the stable door, he answered provocatively. "Not a coward, *poquita*, just too smart to get caught."

With the lean length of his body trapping her against the unyielding wood, Maria had nowhere to run. She wasn't at all certain that she wanted to run. Manuel's kisses had stirred nothing in her, but just Luke's proximity brought a rush of heat flooding through her body. Before she could reply, he lowered his head to catch her lips with his, and she was lost.

This kiss was different from the others. Before, he had kissed her with an urgent hunger that had stirred and terrified her at the same time. He had demanded more than she knew how to give. This time, however, his mouth moved slowly, almost teasingly across hers, and she was the one who wanted more.

Her hands lifted to his chest to push him away and lingered instead, absorbing the sensation of heat and hardness as he pressed closer. She could feel the beat of his heart beneath her palm, and it seemed to measure the pounding of her own.

His kiss deepened when she did not fight him. Slowly Maria allowed herself to respond to the gentle insistence of his lips. Beneath his pressure her lips parted, and a burning pleasure swept through her as his breath mixed with hers and his tongue taught her a lesson in surrender. Maria's fingers wrapped in the soft folds of his shirt as Luke's tongue took possession and threatened to conquer her very soul.

Taking advantage of her willingness, Luke moved his hands to her waist, encompassing it easily. She bent like a willow into his embrace, and his body was suddenly on fire with the need to have all of her. He had learned self-control long ago, he was no green youngster, but this woman in his arms inflamed him with a desire almost beyond his ability to dictate. He clasped her tighter, telling her what he wanted with his lips and hands.

In some dark corner of her mind Maria understood his message, but refused to acknowledge it to herself. What he did was exciting, more exciting than anything she had ever known, and she wanted more. She wanted his strong hands to caress her breasts as Manuel had done earlier. She wanted to feel the hard length of Luke's body closer to her own, touching those places that ached for his caress. She wanted his kiss to go on forever, and she wanted whatever he asked of her now. Her bruised pride healed under Luke's yearning caresses and her young body responded vibrantly to his desires.

Not until Luke's mouth moved persuasively over hers, murmuring tender phrases as he lifted her easily against him did Maria register the import of her actions. Her father had not been a churchgoer, but Maria had clung to the religion of her mother and knew the church's teaching on the sins of the flesh. Never before had she understood the compulsion to fall into this sin, but she knew the danger now. The devil had nearly drained all resistance from her, but before Luke's hand could unfasten the barrier of her bodice, she reacted hastily.

"Don't, Luke!" Maria squirmed in his embrace, surprising him into returning her to her feet, though he made no effort to release her. "Let go!" She jerked from his hold, still trapped between the door and Luke's long-limbed frame, but momentarily free of his magnetic touch. "Let me go," she whispered, her eyes pleading where her words would not.

"Just like that?" Luke asked flatly, staring down into her pale face glimmering in the darkness. "Just pretend it never happened, pretend there isn't an ounce of desire in my body and that you never came into my arms like a woman with needs to match my own? That's not only cowardly, *querida*, it's downright ridiculous."

"Then call me a ridiculous coward and let me go,

Luke. Call me anything you wish, but I cannot be
what you want me to be. I wasn't brought up that
way.''

He could feel the heat of her body, see her breasts
rise and fall with the passion he had stirred in her, and
knew her honesty pained her as much as him. And it
was an honesty of a sort, Luke had to admit grudgingly. Other women would have given in to their needs
and then turned their back on him in the light of day,
pursuing their more ambitious interests. She at least
had the guts or the innocence to tell him now that he
didn't fit into her plans. For they all had plans; Luke
had learned that the hard way long ago.

''All right, little witch, I will believe you this once.
Just stay out of my way from here on out. I'm not
always so noble.''

With that, he turned his back on her and, gathering
the reins of the horses, disappeared into the blackness
of the stables. Maria's knees felt as if they would melt
into the ground, and she clung to the sturdy door frame
for support as she watched him go. She must be mad.
She must be out of her mind. What could have induced
her to a duel of the sexes with a man who had no
honor, no character, and nothing to lose? She was
clearly teetering on the brink of insanity.

Recovering her breath, Maria strode rapidly toward
the house, though her whole body shook with the effort of it.

No love songs caressed the night air as the moon
lowered behind the hills this time. But Maria didn't
need to hear the sound of his voice to know Luke was
out there, lying in the bunkhouse just beyond the garden gate, staring at the ceiling just as she was doing
now.

It was an impossible situation. Somehow she would
have to overcome it, but at the moment all thought
failed her. Even her fury with Manuel paled beside the
fiasco of that scene in the stable. Instinctively Maria
knew Luke would not leave until he had found his
quarry. She had learned that much about him these last
few weeks. He never left a task unfinished. She just

prayed she hadn't become one more item on his list of things to do.

So it was with utter disbelief that she heard her own words the next day when Luke announced his intention of going to Santa Fe.

In the morning sunlight his shoulders seemed even broader than she remembered from the night before. Maria refused to think of how those hard lips had touched hers or of the way those strong, brown hands had so easily claimed her body. She saw only the amber spark in his eyes and heard the impact of his words.

"Santa Fe? Why should you go into Santa Fe? Not giving up already, are you?" Maria couldn't help the flash of anger in her words. She had counted on his help, and just the knowledge of this made her angry. She knew better than to count on anyone.

Luke watched the dangerous gleam of her eyes behind that dark fringe of sooty lashes and kept his distance. "If I'm going to finish up this job before summer gets here, I'm going to need some help. I've got a few friends in Santa Fe who might be interested." And the sooner he got out of this one's dangerous proximity, the better for everyone concerned, he added to himself.

The devil in Maria made a leap for freedom. She had been buried too long in sorrow, caught in a web of poverty and work for which her past had not prepared her. The future loomed dismally repressive whether she chose to marry Manuel or not. Just once she would like to see a piece of the world beyond this one. She hadn't been outside the valley since her mother died and she would most likely marry here and die here. She was too young to contemplate such a fate without rebelling.

"I want to go with you," Maria heard herself saying. Her surprise was no less than Luke's, but she covered it smoothly, repeating her phrases to Manuel from the prior night. "I still have a few pieces of my mother's jewelry to sell. It will fetch a better price in Santa Fe than here." When Luke continued to stare at her as if she had lost her wits, Maria put her hands on her hips and let the words fly. "I want to wear skirts again. I want to hold my head up and smile at the people I meet. I want to see the city and dance to the music. I'm tired of the dust and the cows and the fools and this whole damned valley. Just once in my life I want to be on my own. When I've done that, I'll buy the material for my trousseau and come home."

Luke raised an incredulous eyebrow. "Go with me and you won't need a trousseau. Even Manuel won't buy your reputation then."

Nothing would stop her now that she had made up her mind, and she could almost feel freedom in her grasp. Maria threw her long black braid over her shoulder with a gesture of defiance. "Don't go getting ideas. Carmelita will go with me. She's never seen Santa Fe. We'll take the stage. You can meet us there and show us where to stay. Then you can just go about your business as usual. Don't let us stand in the way of your plans." Her voice added a hint of scorn as if knowing his plans did not include pure business.

Luke hid his impatience. He already knew the point-lessness of arguing. She would do what she wanted regardless of reason. He would just have to see that it was under his own terms. With that in mind, he shoved his hat on his head and started for the stable.

Over his shoulder he threw, "I'm leaving in the morning. You'll need to be on the nine o'clock stage if you're going to make it."

Maria stared at his retreating back and cursed his arrogance and her insanity. Pieta would carve her heart out when she heard the news.

8

Pieta protested long and violently in several languages and emphatic gestures until Maria mentioned Luke would be riding with them. For some reason beyond Maria's comprehension, that pacified the older woman, and she looked Maria up and down warily.

"You said you wanted to buy wedding things. Why is it not Manuel who takes you?"

Because she fully intended to make Manuel sweat before she gave him anything, but Maria knew better than to say that to Pieta. She shrugged casually. "That would not be proper. Besides, it is bad luck for the groom to see the bride's gown before the wedding." That would appease the superstitious Pieta faster than anything.

Pieta still watched her with suspicion, but conceded, "You will be able to buy the goods for your gown more cheaply in Santa Fe."

Maria relaxed and smeared a biscuit with jam. "I will buy yard goods for all of us. Carmelita must stand up with me and she should have a new dress for that. And you will be the closest thing to family I have. You must have a new gown, too."

Though her suspicions did not disappear, Pieta grew more malleable. "I have the coins for Carmelita and myself. You must buy new petticoats and chemises, lace for a mantilla, new shoes . . . I will make a list while you pack."

Maria gulped down the biscuit and headed for the attic, where the trunks were stored, feeling as if she were walking on air. "Nonsense! We will all have new shoes and mantillas. I have not paid you any wages in

months. Soon we will not have to skimp for anything.''

She disappeared down the hallway and Pieta shook
her head slowly in dismay. Maria had a sensible head
on her shoulders, but too often she let her emotions
think for her. She did not know what had set off this
nonsensical adventure, but perhaps Maria would gain
her senses once away from the valley for a little while.
A few days in the company of Cheyenne Walker might
teach her more than she needed to learn, but it was
time Maria grew up.

Carmelita was both terrified and ecstatic at the
thought of leaving home for the first time. Two years
younger than Maria, she appeared older. Inheriting her
mother's sturdy frame, she towered over Maria by
some inches, but her broad shoulders were the only
part of her that had yet filled out. With her hair pulled
back in a severe chignon and covered by a black shawl,
she had the appearance of a lanky duenna but the wide-
eyed innocence of a terrified youngster.

Luke gazed upon Pieta's attempt to produce a proper
companion for Maria and smothered his laughter. It
would be akin to escorting two children through the
evils of the city to take this pair with him, but the only
other choice would be to let them go alone. The fire
in Maria's eyes told him that much.

Unwilling to travel with her and unable to allow her
to go alone, Luke found himself driving the buckboard
with his two severely garbed companions and their
trunk the next morning. He had his own mount tied
behind, but he felt as tethered as the stallion as the
two girls chatted in excited Spanish at his side.

Not letting on that he could understand every word
of their conversation, Luke drove in silence through
the dawn's rising heat. Maria had wrapped herself in
her black bombazine Sunday dress and bonnet, but
even that awful combination did not disguise her
youthful beauty. In fact, it emphasized it, Luke decided as she directed a question toward him and he
gazed down into sparkling emerald waters. Black
lashes and arched black brows accentuated the

smoothness of dusky rose cheeks, and the black of her mourning became only a backdrop to those devastating eyes.

Damn! What had he got himself into? He always traveled alone. Taking these two was the height of idiocy. It was almost as if the little witch had guessed his intention of seeking a more willing woman to slake his frustrations and had set her mind to circumventing it. Well, she'd picked on the wrong man. She wasn't his wife, she wasn't even his boss, and she wouldn't get in the way of his plans. Lashing at the reins, Luke hurried them toward the freedom of the city.

The stagecoach had few riders through this corner of the country, and Maria breathed a sigh of relief as she and Carmelita settled into the front seat reserved for ladies. There was enough room on the back platform for their one valise, and no cigar-smoking strangers crowded the middle drop seat. A couple of traveling drummers in their suave derby hats and fancy vests eyed them speculatively, but when Luke looked in to be certain they were settled safely, the salesmen quickly lost interest. Luke's leather vest scarcely concealed the Colts on his hips, and the authority in his hard amber gaze as it swept over the interior warned the two women traveled in protective custody.

The driver offered Luke a seat beside him, but Luke refused the honor, preferring the freedom of his horse to the confinement of company. As the faded colors of the once gaily painted stage pulled away from the station, a small, brown hand pulled aside the leather shade and waved a cheerful farewell. An odd loneliness blew over Luke like a cold wind from the north, and old wounds took up a familiar ache. He spurred his horse into a gallop.

By noon, the coach had added a few more passengers, all male, and the interior began to grow crowded. Accustomed to the odors of unwashed male bodies and tobacco but unaccustomed to this proximity, Maria kept her nose to the hot, dry air drifting in through the closed shade. Opening it had raised a wail of protest over heat and dust, so she suffered in the semidarkness, wishing she had ridden a horse as Luke had done.

One of the male passengers clinging to the leather strap on the awkward middle seat tried to strike up a conversation, but Maria disliked his placid, oily face and the way his knee kept rubbing hers, and she did not reply. She heard him make several snide comments in English to the other men as if she were not capable of comprehending, but she ignored this, too. She was determined to transform herself into a lady on this trip, and a lady would not curse a fool. She held her temper and kept a tight rein on her impatience as she peeked out the window to the endless plain beyond.

The stage stopped every ten miles or so to change teams, take on passengers, deliver mail bags, and give everyone a chance to stretch their legs and get drinks of water from the rain barrels provided. Maria kept a lookout for Luke, but he apparently rode on ahead of the lumbering stage. If she felt a little frightened at being thus left alone, she made no admission of it to herself or to Carmelita, who was already terrified beyond speech.

By the time they reached a station where they could stop and rest for the night, Maria had grown tired of the unctuous fat man squeezing her knee, felt sick to her stomach from the stage's swaying motion, and wished heartily for a wad of tobacco she could spit back at the filthy old man in the far seat. Her temper had reached a flaring edge and all vows of patience had disappeared with the daylight.

Peremptorily claiming her right to descend first, she nearly fell into Luke's arms as he stepped forward to help her down. Glaring at him in disbelief, she failed to release his hand until the passengers behind her began to complain of the delay. Without a word she dropped his hand and swept into the small adobe hut, her petticoats rustling across the planked porch.

As usual, Luke said little when the conversation over their hot meal became a rowdy argument. Maria sensed Carmelita's relief at Luke's presence, but she refused to admit any fear of her own. The drummers had stopped at an earlier station. Their replacements were hard-eyed men who had suffered through these last years of hard times and known many more before them. They argued now with the paunchy bank teller and the driver over the benefits of hard money versus the greenback, an argument Maria had always found pointless since you could eat neither gold nor greenbacks but both would buy food. When you didn't have either, their worth mattered little.

Somehow the discussion drifted to the railroads and the role their overexpansion played in the economic collapse, but Maria could scarcely stifle a yawn of boredom. She felt Luke's eyes watching her, and she moved her shoulders restlessly beneath the heavy material of her gown. The company and the conversation depressed her, and she felt the overwhelming need for sleep. She had never seen a railroad and could imagine no benefit of having one beyond escaping the tedium of stagecoach travel. She could do that more cheaply with sleep.

She rose from the table, and the argument threatened to continue undiminished until both Luke and the fat man politely rose from their seats at the same time. The others grudgingly did the same as Carmelita hastened to join her, but they quickly returned to their discussion as soon as the two women left the room.

Their sleeping quarters were crude, the only acknowledgment of the possibility of female travelers being a curtain around the two bunks stacked against the back wall. Carmelita pleaded for the top one and Maria threw her bonnet on the bottom. After a day of travel she wished heartily for a bath, but apparently the wash bowls along the wall would have to suffice.

Whispering quietly to each other, they disrobed behind the curtain, appropriating one of the washbowls for themselves and giggling over the consternation of the men when they discovered they would all have to share the other one. Somewhat relieved by the familiarity of Carmelita's foolish jokes, Maria drew on her long night shift and settled in among the covers. If nothing else, the absence of the stage's steady swaying made her peaceful.

She must have slept, for she heard nothing as the men complained their way to bed. She didn't know what woke her, but she heard heavy snores at the far end of the room when she turned over. Apparently everyone slept, though she suspected several of the men had chosen to take their bedrolls outside rather than endure the heavy atmosphere in the station. The heat and the smell and the noise served to waken her more fully.

A movement outside the curtain caught Maria's attention. Perhaps that was what woke her. Someone seemed to be groping carefully through the dark, but not doing a very good job of it.

Irritated more than frightened, Maria pushed aside the curtain and searched for the source of the sound. A sigh of relief exuded from the bulky form hovering uncertainly on the other side.

"I wasn't certain which bunk was yours, ma'am, but I'm happy to see you waited. I knew we would suit from the first moment I climbed on the stage."

Maria gasped and shrank back against the wall as the banker's plump hand caught the curtain away from her. She stared into his beaming white face with disbelief as he bent to look in.

"Well, now, that's a might pretty gown you got on," he whispered, but his eyes did not focus on her cotton gown or even the long rope of black hair lying against it. Glazed with lust and a little too much alcoholic fortification, they gazed upon the full curve of Maria's breasts and the small gap of her nightgown where it tied at the throat.

When he began to reach for what he wanted, Maria quickly recovered her senses and smacked his hand hard enough to echo in the momentary silence between snores.

"Get your grubby paws away from me, you filthy bastard," she stated firmly and in a voice that threatened to grow louder if not obeyed.

The intruder looked visibly startled at both her language and her action, but apparently rejection had not occurred to him and he had no other plan in mind. He sat down heavily on the bed's edge and again reached for Maria in the darkness.

Before she could scream, an ominous click sounded just outside the curtain, and a tall silhouette loomed against the room's single candle light.

"I think the lady made herself clear, mister. You'd best find your own bed while you can still walk."

Luke! Maria retreated further against the wall as the fat man tried to stand up and banged his head, then sat back down hard, clamping his hand to the sore spot and glaring at the intruder. Anger built inside Maria as the man continued to protest.

"This ain't none of your business. The lady and I have come to an understanding. Now put your toys away and go rope some cattle."

Maria heard the amusement in Luke's voice as he made some reply, and she had the urge to kill both men as she placed both feet in the center of the stranger's fat back and shoved. "Out! Get out and stay out and never get in my sight again!"

The man went sprawling across the floor at Luke's feet and Maria pulled the curtain back in time to watch Luke add his own kick to the man's upended posterior.

"I protect what's mine, mister, and the lady is mine." Luke's drawl followed warningly between the cacophony of undisturbed snores.

Whether it was this threat or the sight of two Colt revolvers aimed at his belly when he turned over that convinced the man, Maria couldn't tell. In either case, she was too furious even to laugh as he scrambled away on all fours.

"You addle-pated, ignorant, lying, conniving, two-faced sore on a coyote! Why didn't you scare that bastard away *before* he nearly frightened me out of my wits? And what do you mean, *your* woman? I'm not about to be branded your woman for every lickspittle in the territory to gloat over."

Luke's grin grew broader with each curse Maria threw at him until she finally ran out of breath and

curses and he could get a word in edgewise. Holding
the curtain back and staring admiringly down into her
flushed features, he spoke quietly and forcefully.

"For all I knew, you had invited the jackass in here.
He's probably just as wealthy as Manuel and isn't bur-
dened with a pompous family. And if you really mean
to keep out of trouble, then the easiest way to do it is
to be branded my woman. There isn't a man in the
territory who will come close to you that way."

Having said all he meant to say, Luke dropped the
curtain and prepared to return to his bedroll at the foot
of her bunk. An angry groan of frustration and fury
issued from behind the curtain and a second later a
high-toed shoe came flying at his head, whizzing past
his ear with amazing accuracy.

Chuckling, Luke located the ammunition and tucked
it under his pillow. Let her figure out what to do about
it in the morning.

9

By the time Maria waited for all the men to dress and disappear into the dining hall for breakfast so she could come out and hunt for her shoe, the banker had time to whisper words of caution in everyone's ear. When she finally got dressed and appeared at the table with Carmelita at her side, she felt the silence and the speculative glances like an invisible wall between herself and the others.

Not quite understanding at first, she sat in an empty place at the table and helped herself to a bowl of hominy and cold piece of toast. Carmelita's fears had returned and she sat shyly and silently, taking whatever Maria put on her plate. If she heard any of the prior night's ruckus, she gave no indication.

Maria knew the instant Luke entered, though her back was turned to the door. A couple of the men looked up and watched with interest as Luke approached the table. The banker kept his gaze firmly on the bowl in front of him. Maria lifted her head and daringly turned to meet Luke's eyes.

He had obviously just come in from scrubbing himself in the wash basin outside. He still sported a stubbly growth of beard, but his hair was wet and combed neatly out of his face, though it wouldn't remain there long once it dried, Maria surmised. His eyes were dark and uncommunicative as they met hers this morning, but his step didn't hesitate as it turned in her direction.

Wearing his Colts strapped low on his hips, his eyes hooded and threatening as he entered the room, his booted heels making distinct thunder against the floor, Luke created an aura of danger around him as thor-

ough as a rattler's warning. When he stopped to place
a proprietary hand on Maria's shoulder and murmur a
few words of greeting for her and Carmelita's ears
alone, every man in the hall understood the message.

With amazement Maria watched as eyes dropped
around the table and the speculative glances disappeared. Even when Luke found himself a place in the
corner, away from the others, the men went out of
their way to be polite, urging more coffee on her and
offering to heat her toast over the fire.

By the time she found her seat on the stagecoach,
Maria could barely contain her amusement. She had
wanted to be treated as a lady, but if last night were
any indication of how a lady was treated, it just might
be more interesting to be thought a gunman's fancy
lady. Even her slight cough at the whiff of a cigar resulted in the offending weed being thrown from the
window.

Understanding nothing of these undercurrents, Carmelita began to smile and chat more easily in this
friendlier atmosphere. By the time the coach reached
Santa Fe, both girls were ready and eager for adventure.

The coach rattled around the dusty plaza and came
to a stop in front of one of Santa Fe's leading hotels.
Several hands quickly went out to help Maria climb
down to the covered walkway. She never noticed whose
hand she took once her gaze located Luke leaning lazily against the hotel's adobe wall, following the whole
proceeding. An odd sensation rippled through her as
she met his cynical gaze and realized he had no intention of leaving her to her own pursuits. She wanted to
be angry, but it wasn't anger she felt when he pushed
through the crowd to claim her.

With one hand on Luke's arm and the other lifting
her skirts from the dust, Maria entered the hotel feeling like a prim and proper lady. Carmelita followed
behind her, someone else carried her valise, and the
hotel clerk leapt to his feet at their approach. Even
knowing Luke compromised her beyond the bounds of
propriety, Maria couldn't resist the charm of being

treated with this old-fashioned elegance. Her soul hungered for this recognition, and if she must gain it on the arm of a gunman, so be it. She would confess this sin of pride later.

To her astonishment the hotel clerk addressed her as ''Mrs. Walker'' and hurried out from behind the desk with a key dangling in his hand as if he had been waiting for her. From beneath her slat-brimmed black bonnet Maria threw Luke a questioning and decidedly suspicious frown, but he acted as if the man's behavior were normal and guided her toward the stairs.

The clerk threw open a door to a sunny, whitewashed room. A brilliantly colored blanket decorated the room's one large bed, and a cheerful blue and white pitcher and wash basin waited on the bleached wood of the bedside stand. The arched wicker of the low headboard matched the woven basketry of a cushion-covered chair in the corner, and Maria felt instantly at home.

The only complaint lay in the man at her side and as if guessing the path of her thoughts, Luke finally spoke. ''My room is right next door, through there.'' He pointed to a door other than the one they had entered by.

The relief on Maria's face must have been plain to see. When she glanced up at him, she read the mockery in hard amber eyes. She met their challenge coolly. ''That was thoughtful of you. Now, if you don't mind, Carmelita and I would like a little time to wash and recuperate from our journey.''

She acted the part beautifully, and Luke grudgingly admired her swiftness of thought under pressure. He had half expected a temper tantrum, but it seemed she only indulged in those after the fact. Once the clerk left, she would in all probability skin him alive with that vicious tongue of hers, but she had already offered him the opportunity of escape. With a suppressed grin Luke bowed in obedience to her command, murmured a few polite phrases, and left.

Carmelita stared in astonishment at Maria's satisfied expression as maids hastily filled her water pitcher with warm water and returned with huge, soft towels. Not until all the strangers were gone, however, did she dare to speak.

"I do not understand, Maria. Did that man think you were Luke's wife? Why did you not correct him?"

Maria threw off the dreadful bonnet and shook the pins out of her hair. Pins always tormented her. That was one part of being a lady she could do without. As she ran her hand through thick strands of ebony hair, she replied to Carmelita's puzzled inquiry.

"Luke is getting even with me for making him take us along." Maria bent to grin at her reflection in the mirror over the washstand before whirling around the spacious room with happiness. She had sense enough to know she would never have been given a room like this if she had arrived alone. If Luke had intended to make her angry, he had lost. "But I think I shall disappoint him by thanking him graciously. Isn't it lovely, Carmelita? They must think we're rich."

Since thoughts of money didn't make her happy, Maria brushed them aside and danced to the lovely lattice doors opening onto a wrought iron balcony. She unfastened the onyx buttons at the neck of her bodice and breathed deeply of the fresh air, enjoying the sensation of sunshine on her throat and chest after being confined in the hated bombazine for two days.

The shots, when they came, were so beyond her present state of mind that Maria didn't register their significance until Carmelita screamed. Then the tinkling of glass and the sound of running footsteps on the balcony outside came together, and she threw herself to the floor. Two more shots rang out, and the beautiful water pitcher shattered into a million shards, spilling water all down the polished stand.

The adjoining door burst open, and Maria had a brief glimpse of the terrifying sight of Luke's Colts drawn and ready, but Carmelita's screams continued and her one thought was for the younger girl. Keeping to the floor, Maria crawled back to where she had left Carmelita, while Luke searched for the source of the shots.

Cursing as the noise ceased and no target came to

sight, Luke hastily slammed his guns back in the holster and reached to lift Maria from the floor. Hair streaming in black rivers over her back and shoulders, she struggled wordlessly against his proprietary hold, and after quickly running his hands down her back and ascertaining it was fury and fear that illumined her eyes instead of pain, Luke let her go.

By this time Carmelita had ceased her hysterical cries, and running footsteps and shouts outside the door could be heard. While Maria rushed to embrace her maid, Luke threw open the door to confront the hotel clerk and a small crowd of curiosity seekers.

Once certain that Carmelita was terrified but unharmed, Maria turned her attention to the commotion in her once lovely room. Luke's square jaw was thrust forward in grim fury as he surveyed the angle from which the bullets had come, and the hotel manager wrung his hands nervously, clucking his dismay as he alternately watched Luke and chased people from the room. He purposely avoided meeting Maria's eyes, and she wanted to fling something at him to force his attention to Carmelita's terror, but she forced herself to remain calm. Luke's hard-eyed expression would be enough to terrify anyone.

"He got away over the roof. I can't follow him without getting my head blown off." Luke stifled his curses as he turned back toward the room and read the warning in Maria's eyes. His explanation was for her and not the banty rooster clucking at his side, but he had forgotten Carmelita. The child was near hysteria already.

"Why?" Maria demanded, knowing he would understand the single word without stating the entire question.

Luke would have preferred to have answered in privacy, but he had to take action now, and explanations would be necessary before he could enforce them. He kept it as brief as possible.

"I've made a few enemies in my time. If it's who I'm thinking, he didn't aim to kill, but I'm taking no chances. Gutierrez, we'll need rooms without a balcony.''

Luke's quiet command startled the hotel man, and he pursed his lips and stalled until he had collected his thoughts. Then shaking his head, he admitted, ''There are no others, señor. The judge is here and the town is full. These are my best rooms. I save them for those willing to pay. The others are filled up.''

''My wife could have been killed, Gutierrez.'' Even his quiet tones seemed menacing as Luke stared down the nervous clerk. ''You will have to move someone in here and let us have their rooms. That shouldn't be so difficult.''

''But señor.'' The clerk threw a pleading look for reasonableness to the gunman's pretty lady. With her lovely throat and shoulders visible through the silken veil of hair, Maria seemed very vulnerable, and he sought her assistance. ''The other rooms, they are not like this. The beds are small, and there is no door between''—he gestured toward Luke's adjoining room. ''I do not think I can even get two together. It is very difficult—''

Luke cut him off. ''I can't leave two women alone with varmints running through the streets shooting at them. Give us one room, without a balcony, and get us the best one you can find. Someone surely won't object to trading for one of these.''

Maria opened her mouth to protest, but the words didn't come out. She couldn't subject Carmelita to a room that might be dangerous, but she had trapped herself by allowing Luke to masquerade her as his wife. One room, indeed! She shot Luke a look of fury that should have blistered the hide off a rhinoceros.

Luke shrugged it off without a qualm. She had asked to come with him and now must pay the price. As the harassed clerk offered his own room as the next best room available, Luke extended his arm for Maria to take. Her fingernails dug painfully through the cotton of his shirt, and he reminded himself to take his coat out of his bags for pressing. With this one, the extra protection was necessary.

After the clerk had removed his own possessions from the dark room at the back of the hotel and left his guests to settle in, Luke closed the door and waited for the tirade to come. There was no point in putting it off and letting it build to even greater proportions. He lounged against the wooden door, his gaze settling on the tempting *V* of Maria's open bodice.

His gaze unnerved her and Maria swung away to examine her new surroundings before venting her ire. "You and your little games! So much for your protection. I would have been safer if I came alone."

"As long as every man was stupid enough to turn his back on you," Luke agreed wickedly.

Carmelita quickly hurried out of the way as Maria flung herself around to confront this arrogant beast. "I didn't need your help last night. I can take care of myself. It was the insult I objected to, and you allowed me to suffer that and offered more of your own. Get out, Luke Walker! Take yourself and your narrow-minded prejudices to some whorehouse and leave us alone! At least then we will only suffer insults and not be targets for your friends."

"Are you finished?" Luke calmly crossed his arms over his chest and waited for her reply.

Maria wanted to wrap her fingers in the tousled lengths of his hair and jerk it out by the roots, but she suspected such devastating proximity to Luke's lean strength and dangerous lips would wreak havoc with her intentions. She kept her distance.

"Just go, leave us alone. There is nothing more to be said."

Luke's gaze traveled insolently from the magnificent mane of ebony hair to tanned cheeks flushed with rage and down the slender frame that contained so much pent-up fury. The first thing he intended to do was get rid of that abominable black cloud covering her from head to tiny toe.

"Then I'll give you two choices. I can put you on the next stage back to San Pedro, or you can wash up and be ready to go into town in half an hour. Just let me know when I come back which it will be."

He didn't give her an opportunity for reply. Maria staggered under the sting of his mocking look and didn't react in time before he strode from the room. When she recovered her equilibrium, it was only to erupt in rage at his high-handedness. A string of Spanish epithets followed him down the corridor.

Carmelita looked to her employer in perplexity. "Why does he say these things, Maria? Can you not tell him he is fired? How can he do what you do not want him to do?"

Because he did what she wanted him to do. Because he knew she wanted to stay and because he knew she was terrified. He seemed to know everything and she hated him for it. Mostly she hated herself for allowing him to see her weakness.

"I cannot fire a man I do not pay, 'Lita. He does as he pleases." Maria felt a sudden cold chill as she realized the import of this simple phrase. Luke did do as he pleased, and she had no power to stop him. She had invited a man-killing animal into her home, and now she had no means of throwing him out. Heaven help her, what had she done?

10

The problem did not seem so great later that afternoon
when Maria walked the sunny streets of Santa Fe on
Luke's arm, with Carmelita darting back and forth in
front of and behind them. The narrow streets of adobe
shops filled with fascinating sights and scents did not
seem so strange as walking with a man at her side, her
skirts trailing in the ever-present dust. The fact that
the man was supposedly one of her hired hands added
to the oddity, but no one would guess their relationship
this day. They had both disguised themselves with an
aura of respectability, and passersby did not stop to
stare as they would in San Pedro. Luke had even con-
descended to change from denims to a respectably cut
pair of tan trousers and a clean white linen shirt, although he declined to wear coat or tie and the unfastened collar lay open at his throat.

Maria's most immediate concern stemmed from the
discovery of a dressmaker's shop, and she stared at the
elegantly garbed dress form in the window with tears
in her eyes. The gown was a simple one of crisp lawn
in a lovely pale striped rose with fragile white lace
drapery adorning the slender bodice and pulled tight
in front to form a train in back. It was the style that
brought tears to Maria's eyes as she glanced down at
her own heavy, full-skirted gown. Not a garment in
her closet could possibly be converted to the simple
elegance of the one in the window, and not even Pieta's talented needle could construct something she had
never seen. Only a dressmaker could provide her with
a gown like that, and she could not afford a dressmaker in a million years.

Resolutely she turned away from the window and tried not to think of the dainty white kid shoes she had seen in the bootmaker's shop that would have peeked perfectly from beneath that gown. They would only laugh at her in San Pedro if she tried to dress like that. She might as well accept what she was and go on.

"The piece-goods shop should be nearby," she murmured, turning away from the window and heading rapidly for the next store. She would find some lovely material that would make Pieta weep with joy.

Luke resisted, glancing with puzzlement from Maria's strained expression back to the dressmaker's window. "I thought you came to shop for your trousseau. That gown back there was made for you. There are bound to be even better ones she could make up later."

Refusing to let the tears fall, Maria turned on Luke angrily. "You might know it all, Luke Walker, but you know nothing of women or fashion. I didn't ask you to come with me. Go find a saloon somewhere and let me take care of my business."

Luke's jaw snapped shut with a grim look of forbearance. "Fine. Go find yourself some black crepe to be wed in. That ought to be suitable. I'll wait out here."

Carmelita watched in distress as Maria hurried away with tears wetting her lashes. Glancing back at Luke's set expression with bewilderment and a faint look of reproof, the maid hurried in Maria's footsteps.

Maria swallowed her distress as she roamed through the dusty clutter of ginghams and calicos in the small dark shop. Pieta could cut lovely dresses for all of them out of materials like these, and they would be much more practical than the fashionable gown in the window. If she could find a suitable silk, she could be wed in it and use it later for formal occasions. A bridal gown would be a sinful waste.

Thinking of the lovely ruby necklace and earrings in her purse, Maria decided she must get the most for whatever little money they would bring. They were the best of her mother's jewels, her favorites. Even though she had only been nine when her mother died, Maria could still remember her mother's pride in the flash of red at her throat and ears. Her mother had played with the jewels in the sunlight, not saving them for just the evening and candlelight. They had set off her exotic coloring magnificently. The memory of her mother's youth and beauty lingered strong when Maria held those gems in her hands. She would have to get their worth, somehow, to make the sacrifice worthwhile.

Setting her chin with renewed determination, Maria sailed from the shop with Carmelita in tow. Luke glanced at her empty hands with impatience.

"Did nothing suit your royal highness in there, either?"

Maria ignored the sarcasm as she glanced up and down the road for some sign of a jeweler. "I told you to leave me alone, Luke. I have my business, you have yours. Why don't you attend to it?"

"Because I can't leave two greenhorn women prey to every conman and scoundrel in the territory, not to mention a trigger-happy outlaw or two. We're stuck with each other until we leave Santa Fe, so get used to it."

Maria turned her gaze up to Luke's chiseled features. "That is ridiculous. I've been taking care of myself for years. I don't need a nanny."

"You need a good whipping is what you need. Now let's get on with this so we can get back in time for supper."

Maria had no grand desire to let Luke see her last remaining asset, but she recognized the look in his eyes and knew the impossibility of losing him in streets he knew better than she. She shrugged carelessly. "Then find me an honest jeweler. I can buy nothing without money."

It took a few moments for her words to sink in, and then Luke cursed himself for three sorts of a fool. He stared at her with awakening incredulity. "You meant what you told that bastard when you said you would sell your jewels to buy a trousseau!"

This time it was Maria's turn to regard him with impatience. "Of course. How else would I pay for it?

I shouldn't think the merchants here would allow me credit. And I won't go to Manuel's family wearing nothing. I do not need jewels, but I must have clothes on my back. And Pieta and Carmelita should have some, too.''

Luke didn't want to hear the story behind the jewels. Just looking into the proud pain in those slanted green eyes told him more than he wished to know. He didn't want to get involved in her problems any more than he already was, and that was too damned much for anybody's good. He bit back other offers that quickly leapt to mind and made a gesture of impatience.

"Fine. If you wish to waste your time and money on a man who has more of it than he knows what to do with, then I will find a reputable jeweler. That's not my usual line, so I'll have to make a few inquiries first. Let's get back to the hotel. I'm starved.''

Maria sensed his withdrawal and, though puzzled, she did not question it. He had promised to help her and that was all she required of him. Just because she had enjoyed a few minutes of parading as his wife didn't mean she had to think of him as a husband. A man like Cheyenne Walker would make a perfectly horrible husband. Occasionally, though, he did make a good hired hand, better than most. If they could just limit themselves to business, the arrangement should work well enough.

Luke appeared to be in perfect accord with her thoughts as he left them at the hotel with a warning to bar the door until he returned. He spoke curtly, without a bit of warmth or even sarcasm to reveal his thoughts. His gaze did not stray to improper places, and his hands did not linger where they did not belong. He left without a backward look, and Maria let out a small sigh of relief, refusing to acknowledge the tingling of disappointment somewhere deep inside her. She did not need the grief a man like that could bring.

When Luke returned shortly before the evening meal, he had acquired a haircut and a square-cut coat of light brown wool that hung well on his broad shoulders. A printed silk scarf with a bright red, brown and gold pattern took the place of a tie, however, and though he did not wear his heavy gunbelt, Maria caught sight of a smaller pistol tucked in his trousers. The fashionable haircut did not disguise the bronzed leanness of his face any more than the clothes hid his menace. He had just changed his colors to fit his surroundings.

His amber gaze took in Maria's gray moire and the black ringlets neatly arranged at the back of her head, and he nodded approvingly. "Good. I would not want people to think I keep my wife in rags."

Maria bristled but replied in her sweetest voice, "I shall have some difficulty in accepting a husband who cannot keep his collar closed, but I'm certain the townfolk will accept that small defect. Shall we go?"

A dangerous glint lit Luke's eyes as he met her gaze, but he only offered his arm politely. "I am ready." He gestured to Carmelita, who hung back nervously. "Come along. I have found some friends for you in the kitchen who will be delighted to bend your ear for the evening."

Carmelita continued to look nervous, but grabbed up her best shawl at Luke's command. Maria, however, stopped dead in her tracks and glared at him with ferocity. "The kitchen? Why does Carmelita not eat with us?"

"Because this is not the ranch and Carmelita will be more comfortable with the people in the kitchen. They are good people, and there are even one or two of the men who might catch Carmelita's eye." Luke sent the young girl a roguish look that made her blush and bury her face in her shawl.

"You mean they are Mexicans and that is where they belong. Well, then, that is where I belong, too. Their company is probably infinitely preferable to yours."

Haughtily Maria headed for the door until Luke grabbed her elbow and swung her back to meet his furious gaze. "One more ignorant remark like that and I will turn you over my knee and pound some sense into that small mind of yours. Ask Carmelita where she would prefer to eat, and I will abide by her answer.''

His powerful hand gripped her arm painfully, but Maria was not so aware of that as she was of the anger in Luke's eyes. He was frequently abrupt and impatient, but she had seldom seen him truly angry. She shivered slightly, but daringly turned to confront her friend with the question.

''Tell him you would prefer to eat with people you know instead of strangers.''

Naturally shy, Carmelita could not meet either of their eyes, but her gaze fell down over her simple loose blouse and full skirts of brilliant red and blue, then back to Maria's elegant gown. She shook her head slowly.

''I would not be able to eat in that place with the big swinging lights and fancy cloths on the table.'' She peeped at Maria to see how she was taking this reply. Since Maria did not immediately scream in rage, she continued with a quick glance to Luke. ''I would like to meet some new people and make new friends.''

Feeling betrayed but not willing to admit it, Maria nodded acceptance and frostily headed for the door once again. Again Luke caught her arm and held it.

''If you're going to behave like a spoiled child, you may go to the kitchen with Carmelita. I have a reputation to uphold around here, and it does not include beautiful children.''

Maria's heart took a wild lunge at the implication of Luke's words. He was accustomed to wining and dining beautiful women, and he expected her to live up to that reputation or better since he had named her as wife in this place. She didn't know whether she was more furious at being another ornament on his arm or at knowing that he had a reputation with women. That he might think her beautiful gave cause for thought, but Maria had no desire to consider it.

Her expression remained frozen as she turned to meet Luke's gaze, but there was nothing cold about her eyes as they flared with emerald flames. ''Act the part of gentleman, and I will behave as lady. But beware that it works both ways. Revert to your usual crude self, and I will carve you into little bits and stomp on the pieces."

Amusement flickered along the lines around Luke's mouth. He could very well imagine this one turning a man into sawdust. Not with a knife perhaps, but with her words, carving out his heart and having it for breakfast and never knowing the difference. She talked boldly, but she had no idea as yet of her strength. It had never been tested.

"Very well, we will eat in peace and harmony, just as long as we eat. I'm too hungry to argue."

The evening began to roll more smoothly after that. Maria sat beneath the hotel's one gilded chandelier as if accustomed to such elegance and tried not to stare at the other guests with too much obviousness. Although the majority were male, here and there a fashionably garbed lady sat with her husband and sometimes a stiffly dressed child or two. Maria surreptitiously studied their plumed and beribboned hats, neatly gloved hands, and puffed bosoms, and felt her coarseness in comparison, but then, Luke didn't wear a top hat or cravat like the fancy gentlemen, either.

Luke watched her watching the others with amusement until Maria suddenly quit looking around and hid her lovely, long-fingered hands beneath the table. He frowned when she barely touched her food after that, keeping her hands hidden as much as possible.

"Is there someone here you know?" That was the first question that came to mind. If word of this little escapade got back to San Pedro it would jeopardize her marriage plans, although Luke doubted if Manuel would seriously give up all thought of the Connolly ranch if Maria talked fast enough and batted her eyelashes a few times.

Maria looked surprised and shook her head. "I should hope not. Why?"

"You don't like the food, then?"

Maria looked down at the lovely omelet and tender pieces of fresh asparagus and shook her head again.

"It is the most delicious thing I can remember eating."

"Then why in hell aren't you eating it?" Luke finally gave into exasperation.

His tone of exasperation caught Maria's ear faster since she was quite used to his impatience. Candlelight flickered across Luke's bronzed features, softening the look in his odd-colored eyes as he waited for explanations. He was the most impatient man she had ever known, but he did take the time to listen to her. That ought to be worth something. She wasn't even certain her father would have noticed such a small thing as her lack of appetite, but Luke noticed everything.

"I can't show my hands in here." Maria clutched her callused dark hands beneath the lacy tablecloth.

Luke stared at her as if she were crazed. "Why not?"

It was Maria's turn to express exasperation. "Because they're rough and ugly and I don't even own any gloves to hide them." Her glance went to the next table, were a short, plump, blond-haired woman waved a soft, white, carefully manicured hand in emphatic gesticulation as she berated her husband.

Luke gave the woman a brief, unimpressed glance. "If you looked like her, I would hide all of you under the table, after cutting your tongue out." He reached across the small table and pulled her left hand free, examining it thoughtfully. "Actually, the only thing wrong with this one is that it doesn't have a ring on it. I guess I haven't practiced this man-and-wife thing enough. Don't you have a ring on the other hand you can switch to this one?"

He knew very well she had a small, beaten silver band on the other hand, and Maria hastily made the switch under the table, flashing the result for his inspection. "This is madness. What on earth possessed you to sign us up as man and wife?"

Luke caught her hand and held it against the table as he sat back in his chair. "How else could I have brought you in here without every head turning to stare and whisper? Unless you prefer being thought a fallen woman, my only other choice was to sleep in the barn and let you eat alone, and I sure as hell wasn't going to do that. Now, do you have any more foolish questions?''

"My questions are not foolish.'' Maria jerked her hand away and began to attack her omelette, forgetting to be embarrassed by her hands in her annoyance with Luke. ''And if you're answering questions, why would someone shoot at me to get even with you?''

"Because he's a coward. He wants to scare you and make me nervous. He's hoping that will make it easier to get at me. But all it does is make me sorry I didn't shoot him instead of his brother.''

"You shot his brother?'' Maria stared at him, wide-eyed, trying to picture Luke gunning a man down. She knew that was his profession, but somehow she couldn't summon the image. Except for the mustache, he looked like any clean-shaven, well-to-do rancher, which was rather strange if she considered it. She knew the deadliness of his draw and had seen the menace in his eyes in times of danger, but mostly he seemed imperturbable, not at all her idea of a hot-tempered, bloodthirsty gunfighter.

"He gave me no choice. He made the mistake of trying to rob a Wells Fargo stage while I was on guard. His second mistake was in shooting me and leaving me alive. I didn't give him a second chance. Only when we picked him up out of the dust did I realize he wasn't more than a kid. His brother's been after my hide ever since and I can't say that I blame him, but it's too late to take the bullet back now.''

Maria could scarcely keep from staring at this unusual loquaciousness from the taciturn gunman. That Luke had once been one of the elite Wells Fargo guards also kept her off balance, leaving her to wonder how much more about him she did not know. She felt little sympathy for the outlaw and his brother, however, for it must have been a man like that who shot her father. It seemed odd that Luke seemed to sympathize with the brother.

"Why did you leave Wells Fargo?" she finally asked, hoping to encourage his talkativeness.

"Because I got tired of working for those who have against those who have not." He softened these curt words with a smile and a wicked gleam in his eye as he bent forward again. "Besides, the grass is always greener on the other side of the fence."

Maria shook off his encroaching hand and glared at him, but before she could formulate a suitable rejoinder, they were interrupted by a stranger garbed in ruffled shirt and dark suit.

"It seems your distaste for women leads you to better and better ones every time I see you, Cheyenne."

Several inches shorter than Luke and with a face more square than handsome, the stranger still managed to exude an irresistible charm that kept Maria from being angry at his comparison to Luke's whores. Dancing dark eyes watched her with amusement from beneath a crop of burnished dark curls, and Maria found herself returning the smile.

"I figured I could draw you out of hiding if the bait was tempting enough." Luke leaned back and watched the exchange of glances between Maria and the newcomer, but he felt only a bitterness on his tongue instead of amusement as she succumbed to the other man's charm. "Maria, this is an old *compadre* of mine, Sean O'Laughlin. Sean, meet my wife, Maria Francesca."

Dark eyes widened with shock at this introduction, and the stranger made a hasty bow over Maria's hand to cover his confusion. Then he grabbed a chair and sat down without invitation, his gaze flying back and forth between Maria's exotic and incredibly innocent features to Luke's impassive expression.

"Wife? You mean after all these years of cursing women as the scourges of hell"—he turned to Maria apologetically, "Pardon my language, ma'am," then continued as if uninterrupted—"you have actually found one to suit your exacting and totally impossible wishes?"

Maria sensed he substituted "wishes" for "desires'' at the last minute, and she could not keep the mirth from welling up in her at Luke's flummoxed expression. Caught in his own trap, it served him right.

"Yes, darling, tell Mr. O'Laughlin all about the pedestal you found me on.''

The laughter in her green eyes snapped Luke from his trance, and he met her gaze with amusement. "Don't let her fool you, Sean. She's a witch straight from hell with a temper like Medusa, but she sure knows how to heat a man's nights.'' He sent Maria a lascivious wink.

Sean roared with laughter at Maria's expression. "Ahh, my sweet colleen, sure and you cannot be believing I'd take this *spalpeen*'s words for truth? And you with the sweetest Irish eyes this side of heaven? I always knew Irish eyes could bring the devil himself to his knees.''

Maria's laughter joined the others at this outrageous brogue, and she returned it in kind with a piece of her father's repertoire. "And the saints be praised for your sweet-talking blarney, Sean O'Laughlin. 'Tis like the sweet winds of Eire after listening to yon heathen.''

Sean's incredulity started another wave of laughter until Luke took pity on his friend and explained Maria's half-Irish origins. A meal was ordered for the newcomer, and as the evening advanced, the feeling of camaraderie grew.

Later, when a burly man in a thick gray beard and expensive silk hat entered, Sean turned to Luke and gave a broad wink. "Here's my mark for the evening, boyo. Watch a professional at work.''

With a clatter of his chair as he stood up, Sean attracted the man's attention. A beaming grin crossed his boyish features as he pretended to just recognize the man, and with a genial gesture he indicated the newcomer should join them.

Obviously alone, the man hurried forward to join what appeared to be respectable company. His weathered face lit happily at sight of Maria, and he eagerly accepted introductions and an invitation to join them.

"What a happy happenstance, Mr. O'Laughlin. I

had resigned myself to a lonely evening. To spend it in the company of such youth and beauty is a treat beyond measure. Are you certain this is not an intrusion, Mrs. Walker? It looks very much as if this may be your wedding journey.''

Uncertain what game Sean and Luke played with this man, Maria smiled pleasantly and kept her voice neutral. ''It is, Mr. Dallas, but I've become quite accustomed to running into Luke's friends wherever we go. You are not intruding.''

Luke had moved his chair next to Maria's with the addition of the newcomer. Now he squeezed Maria's hand under the table and flicked her a look that had more mischief in it than Maria dared acknowledge. Primly she slid her hand from his.

Sean skillfully led the subject around to his objective for the evening. Maria listened in amazement as the two men discussed the sorry dearth of good card players in this town as compared to a place like San Francisco, but it came as no surprise when the ranchman suggested Sean and he might put together a little game for the next night. The surprise came when Sean casually suggested Luke as a third member of the party.

''He's no professional gambler, now, you realize, Dallas. He's a happily married man, and I wouldn't intrude upon his love life for the world, but he's a more than adequate player and should offer something of a challenge if he'll accept our request.''

Sean turned his charm toward Luke, who did not seem in the least surprised at learning of his prowess at cards. In fact, Maria suspected he had been waiting for the invitation and had his answer well prepared.

''Any other time I would be happy to oblige, gentlemen, but as a newly wedded man, my first duty must be to my lovely wife. I have taught her the rudiments of the game, but she can in no way be considered of a caliber to meet your talents.''

His southern drawl had increased noticeably through the evening, Maria noted wryly. Even his indolent movements gave the impression of a bored and wealthy planter with time on his hands. But fully aware of the deadly pistol in Luke's belt and the swiftness with which he could reach it, Maria knew better than to judge by Luke's actions. He was neither drunk nor indolent, but as taut as a mountain lion prepared to strike.

"Why, Mr. Walker, you have provided the perfect answer for another amusing evening. None of us need to play for great stakes, we seek only to sharpen our skills. What better way than to teach an ingenue? Will tomorrow be suitable?"

Through the evening, Maria had come to distrust the smooth vocabulary of this voluble rancher as much as she did Luke's deceptive indolence or Sean's charm. None of these men were what they seemed, but she could not prevent curiosity from engaging her interest in the outcome of these proceedings.

Luke managed to look skeptical of the older man's suggestion, but he obediently turned to Maria for her answer. "Would you be interested in improving your skills at cards, my dear?"

Maria could not read his expression. He kept it deliberately blank, neither encouraging nor discouraging her acceptance. The thought came that he did not even know if she could play, and that realization turned her eyes bright with mischief.

"Why, sir, I would not deny you your little game or myself your company. If you will have me, I will be happy to oblige."

Sean and Dallas roared their approval, but it was the sudden fiery light in Luke's eyes that took her breath away. She read unrestrained approval there, and something else that turned her insides to quivering jelly.

She didn't know what she had done, but she knew the meaning of that light. Luke was using all his considerable restraint to keep from taking her in his arms and kissing her.

11

Later, Luke merely escorted Carmelita and Maria back to the room and warned them to bar the door behind him before he returned downstairs to his friends.

The room contained only the one large bed, and with Carmelita as a bedmate Maria did not fear Luke's intentions. He and his friends would most likely drink themselves to insensibility and then find some genial brothel to welcome them. No, tonight did not worry her, but their plans for tomorrow night did.

Maria was still awake when the knob turned on the door and Luke let himself in. She had lifted the bar when she went to bed, but she had not expected him so early. She lay warily beside Carmelita, who slept like one of the dead, listening to the clatter of his gun against the dresser, the thump as he shook his bedroll out upon the floor, the rustle as he discarded his clothing. Not willing to imagine what he looked like without the respectability of a shirt to cover the width of those muscular shoulders, Maria held her eyes tightly closed.

At last Luke settled down to sleep, but it was a long time before Maria found that haven. The day had been a long one, and the variety of emotions she had experienced left her drained and on edge. She knew she had done a stupid thing, that her father would have been furious with her, but not for a moment did she consider turning back. She had escaped the valley and all its depressing restraints and had her first taste of freedom. She would not turn her back on it easily.

She woke to full daylight and the sound of Carmelita filling the water basin. Hastily Maria surveyed the room to find no trace of Luke there. Perhaps she had dreamed he returned. The bedroll lay neatly tied as before and the only trace of him lay in the coat hung on the back of the door. Her father had never been so tidy.

With dismay she contemplated donning the black bombazine once more and could not do it. With Carmelita's help she pinned and tucked and donned one of the maid's loose white blouses and colorful full skirts. If she were to be unfashionable, she might as well do it with style.

Luke scarcely raised an eyebrow when he returned to take them to breakfast and found Maria looking more like a Mexican than a fashionable young lady. She had even wrapped her hair in a coronet of braids that emphasized her aquiline features and flashing eyes.

"We'll go back to the dressmaker's after we eat," he announced laconically, taking Maria's hand on his arm as he led them from the room. Once out in the hallway, he unbent enough to add, "You need some big gold earrings to go with that outfit."

"I left my gold behind," she replied airily.

"We shall see about that." With that particularly enigmatic remark, Luke led them downstairs.

With a smoothness Maria had not expected, Luke detached Carmelita from her side shortly after breakfast with the simple ploy of introducing her to one of her numerous relatives. Astounded by his ability to locate this aunt she had never met, Maria could not refuse Carmelita's pleas, but threw Luke a suspicious look as she reassured the girl she would be fine.

Once Carmelita and her aunt happily wandered off, she arched an eyebrow in Luke's direction. "You do nothing for nothing, I suspect. So what was that about?"

Luke's admiring gaze rested on the place where the scooped neckline of her white blouse met with smooth, tanned skin before lifting to meet her eyes. "Well, if I can't talk you into returning to our room, I thought

I might talk you into a little plan Sean and I have in mind.''

Ignoring his first remark, Maria answered his second. "I'm no card shark, Luke Walker. I'll not be party to your thievery if that is what you want." Maria shook her hand loose of his hold as they stepped out into the sunlit plaza.

"And I'm no thief, Miss Connolly, so put that out of your mind. The thief is your Mr. Dallas, and what he steals is water from smaller ranchers. Sean is being paid a goodly sum by those ranchers to get the water back. If we can help him, we can share in some of his earnings, and then he will be free to return to San Pedro to help us.''

Maria's eyes narrowed as she contemplated the ramifications of this easy explanation. "I can't afford to pay him.''

"I know that, but he owes me one. He'll come just to impress a pretty face. That's not a problem." Luke steered her in the direction of the dressmaker's, paving the way carefully.

"And what can I do to help? I don't imagine you have in mind carrying the water back in jugs." Maria's mind worked overtime trying to ferret out all the facets he did not tell her. She knew how large ranchers used dams and ditches to irrigate their own fields and divert the precious water supply from the land beyond theirs. She could not see how she would be of any use in any scheme to redivert an entire river.

"You will be our bait. Dallas has an eye for the ladies. He'll not suspect Sean and me of anything but a little loose gambling while you're around. The pay is good. We can even buy you a few fancy gowns out of expenses so you can play the part properly. You'll get your gowns, keep your jewels, and maybe come out a little ahead." Luke stopped strategically in front of the dressmaker's window, where she could see the gown she had coveted so much the day before.

"What would I have to do?" Maria could not help but be suspicious of any plan of Luke's, but the temptation he offered was great. She could almost see herself in that gown now, her mother's necklace winking among the folds of lace, and her fingers ached to stroke the soft material.

"Nothing more than act the part of my lady wife, no strings attached. Of course, we'll have to follow Dallas out to his ranch when the time comes. Unless Carmelita can ride, she may pose a problem. I can always make arrangements for her to stay with her relatives."

No strings attached. He lied, of course, Maria could sense that from the casual ease with which Luke discarded her only protection. She wasn't a fool. He had more at stake than some pocket money, and she could guess what he had in mind. She had no mind to be a gunman's mistress, but she certainly would like to have that gown and a little money to buy something for Pieta. There ought to be some way to get what she wanted without giving Luke what he sought.

"Will you buy me a gun out of those expenses?" she inquired innocently, her gaze not swerving from the window.

"A gun?" Luke bent her a cautious glance. "We're not asking you to do anything that will require a gun."

Maria sent him a shrewd look. "No, Sean is counting on you for that. What I want is something to protect me from you."

Luke didn't insult her by inquiring if she knew how to use one. He knew she could, and in all likelihood, given the right circumstances, she would use it. That just added to the challenge. With a shrug he agreed.

"Will a derringer suffice? You might have difficulty carrying anything bigger while wearing that getup." He indicated the rose and white gown.

"Two barrels?"

"Bloodthirsty witch. Do you have any idea what one bullet close up does to a man's innards?"

"No, but I'm willing to find out." Leaving him to think that over, Maria proceeded into the dressmaker's. She would earn this dress and every other, but not the way Cheyenne Walker anticipated.

The seamstress was more than delighted to remove

the fashionable gown from the window and make the alterations necessary to suit Maria's petite figure. A larger woman could not have worn it, but it fit Maria as if it were made for her, as she had known it would.

Luke lazed in a ladder-back chair, his long legs spread out before him as Maria swirled around in her new finery for his benefit. He had seen her too often in trousers and shirts to be suitably impressed; a gown like this one hid what he most preferred to see. Still, he had to admit no other woman he knew would look quite as good in that piece of fluff.

"Well? Will it do? Will it impress your Mr. Dallas?" Maria finally demanded when he offered no comment.

"It will do fine as a day dress, but what you need is some of that slippery stuff over there for a dinner gown, and something a little sturdier to make one of those split skirts for riding in."

Maria's eyes widened. "Will that leave me enough money to buy material for Pieta and Carmelita and my wedding gown?"

"I reckon so." Luke hid his grin as she spun around in a little dance of ecstasy—before practicality reared its ugly head.

"I've got boots to go with the riding habit, and I guess I could wear these black things with a daydress if the skirt is long enough, but I really can't wear them with a dinner gown, Luke. If what I really need is the dinner gown and habit, I'd better not get this. Then there will be enough for new shoes and a proper petticoat and maybe even a pair of gloves and a hat." A spasm of regret crossed Maria's mobile features as she stroked the lovely lace. She had never seen anything prettier. It was even more feminine than Consuela's outrageous satin gowns. The town would have to recognize her as a lady if she wore this.

She didn't pout or cry or make any of those awful noises women could make when they really wanted something. She simply enumerated the facts and came to a logical conclusion, but Luke felt as if she had climbed into his lap, thrown her arms around his neck, and wept a bucket of tears. He felt her disappointment as keenly as she, and was stunned by his reaction to the sad downturn of her lovely lips. He wanted her to be as happy as she was a moment ago, and he would stand the world on edge to have it so.

"Don't be foolish, Maria. You may have that gown and the fancy slippers to go with it and all the other things, too. And the gun," he added as afterthought, trying to remember where he stood in her plan of things.

Maria hesitated, not quite able to believe she had found a pot at the end of the rainbow. She stared at Luke's lanky figure dubiously. "Where will all the money come from? Surely Sean didn't get paid in advance."

Annoyed with himself, Luke only shrugged. "Sean never lacks for cash. Didn't your father ever teach you not to look a gift horse in the mouth?"

Luke's apparent lack of interest took some of the fun out of the day, but Maria was determined to take advantage of every opening offered. If men didn't know the cost of these things, who was she to tell them? With a sunny smile she traipsed back to the sewing room to tell the seamstress she would take this one and needed two others.

By the time they had bought out the dressmaker's, the bootmaker's, and the milliner's, Maria was walking on air, and Luke had a hard time keeping a grin off of his own face. She was just as ambitious and greedy as any other woman he had ever known, but she carried it off with such an innocent charm he couldn't help but admire it. Few other women showed their delight and appreciation in quite the same way as Maria. She had a style all her own, right down to purchasing only the two bullets to go in the derringer.

"You're mighty sure of yourself, aren't you?" he asked wryly as Maria expertly loaded the tiny gun and tucked it away in her reticule.

"Well, if I can't hit anything as wide as you at close range, then I deserve whatever happens." Green eyes smiled with mischief as they turned up to him.

"Did anyone ever tell you that you're a spoiled brat?" Luke stood his ground in front of her, fully aware that this proximity made her nervous. He wanted to touch her, but there was a time and place for everything.

"Quite frequently," Maria assured him. "And I'm not the least bit arrogant, either, which is more than can be said for some people." Saucily, as if she had just been reading his mind, she turned around and swayed off in a different direction.

Luke watched the swing of narrow hips in the full skirt and knew he'd met his match. The challenge she offered was more than a test of wits or skill, and the prize much more interesting.

They returned to the house of Carmelita's aunt before their evening dinner. At the sight of Maria, Carmelita immediately burst into tears and fell into her arms.

"Oh, please, Maria! Let me stay here. There is to be a *baile* at the church tonight and Miguel has asked me to go, and *Tia* Anna has said I may stay with her. Miguel is to go with my cousins to San Pedro in a few days, and we could go with them and not in that horrible stagecoach. Please, Maria, say yes. I will help you buy all Mama's list tomorrow. I promise."

Maria felt the first sinking feeling of dismay as she realized she had reached that first point from which there is no turning back much sooner than expected. She had made the decision to go with Luke when she ordered the gowns this morning, but the consequences had not come home to her until now. She would be all alone with Luke. The lovely rose and white gown had been finished and packed in the box she carried along with all the other purchases she had made with Luke's money. She was mired in their plans up to her ears and there was no escaping. She sent Luke a look so full of dismay he nearly regretted his plan.

"She will be safer here," Luke reminded her. "If we had not introduced you to Dallas, I would recommend you stay here, too, but it's a little too late for that.'' His hard gaze reminded her of their arrangement.

Maria gulped and looked back to Carmelita's plain brown features. She was seventeen and had never had a suitor before. With Luke's enemies on the prowl, the girl would be safer here. Maria had no right to ask Carmelita to risk her safety or give up her happiness to prevent Maria from her own foolishness. She would have to face what she had done sooner or later. It just came much sooner than she had anticipated.

"If your aunt does not mind, it will be fine with me, Carmelita. Tomorrow we will buy the yard goods for you and Pieta, and you may carry them back to the ranch so Pieta can begin sewing on them. I must wait until the dressmaker is done with mine, so Luke will have to take me back.''

The stars in Carmelita's eyes kept her from seeing Maria's dismay or much of anything else. Maria had always done as she pleased, behaved much as the men on the ranch. She never gave another thought to the consequences of leaving Maria with Luke. She hugged her friend, blissfully introduced her to a cadre of cousins, and let her leave, alone, with the gunman.

As they climbed the stairs to the room they would share, Maria nervously fingered her reticule. She had been very brave when she told Luke the gun would keep her safe, but she felt only foolish now. Any other man perhaps, she could put a bullet in without a qualm, but any other man did not do to her what Luke did. Just his broad hand at her back right now sent shivers down her spine, and her heart beat faster than she could breathe. What in heaven's name would she do when they were in the room alone?

Luke momentarily solved the problem by leaving her by herself to dress for dinner, after first checking the room to be certain no one had entered in their absence. Maria sighed in relief as he closed the door behind him. He was a strange man and she did not often understand his thoughts, but sometimes he could be quite considerate.

Admiring the wealth she had accumulated because

of him, Maria felt some of her confidence return. Luke wanted her to play the part of his wife so he could help his friend and earn some money. If she refused to go along with his plans, he would be out of a lot of cash. He needed her. He would not dare offend her until he had carried out these other plans. Afterward she might have something to worry about. Not now.

With that happy thought in mind, Maria stripped off her old clothes and washed thoroughly with the warm water on the washstand. Then she brushed out her long hair until it gleamed and carefully pinned it in a loose coiffure as she had seen the ladies in town do. She twisted a curl at each ear and a graceful strand or two escaped naturally of their own accord about her throat. Not until she was completely ready did she contemplate the box containing the new gown.

Perhaps it was not a dinner gown, but she certainly wasn't going to wear the gray moire one more time if she could avoid it. With her new gloves and lovely white kid slippers, she would look every bit as elegant as any lady in the hotel. With anticipation she lifted the soft lawn and lace from the box.

A moment later Maria nearly cried in dismay as she realized she could not reach the endless row of tiny hooks down the back. Fashionable ladies had maids to dress them and need not worry about rows of tiny hooks. She had just sent away the closest person she had to act as maid. What would she do now and all the days to come when she tried to wear these ridiculous new clothes?

The answer came in the form of a warning knock on the door. At her call Luke strode in, his hair slicked back from washing and his shirt not yet completely buttoned. He had obviously availed himself of the gentlemen's bath, but Maria's gaze did not linger on his newly washed hair. Her glance fell uncontrollably on the muscular chest revealed by Luke's half-buttoned placket, and she gave a gulp of dismay. She had lived around men all of her life. Why was it only this one who affected her like this?

Since she stood with her hand desperately clutching

the back of her bodice, her slanted eyes dark with terror or tears, Luke did not have to puzzle out her problem for long. In a few strides he crossed the room and spun her around, his agile fingers swiftly fastening all the merciless hooks. If he guessed Maria held her breath the whole time he stood near, Luke gave no sign of it.

He let her go and efficiently pawed through his saddlebags for a clean shirt and tie. When Maria guessed his intentions, she swung around and closed her eyes until the laughter in Luke's voice told her it was safe to look again.

"You needn't play the part of the innocent for my sake, *poquita*. Innocence has no appeal for me."

Maria sent a guarded look to be certain Luke had finished dressing before she turned around again. He now wore a snowy white shirt with a small frill down the front and a thin black tie at his throat. The effect against his bronzed skin was magnetic, and she could scarcely lift her eyes to meet his.

Gathering her defenses, she finally braved the sight of the amber eyes beneath the tawny crop of hair. As usual, she could not read his expression, but Luke could know little more of her thoughts than she did his, she assured herself.

"Fine. If innocence has no appeal, I should be of no interest to you whatsoever. This will be strictly a business arrangement. Shall we go to eat now?"

Amusement curled his lips, but Luke obligingly shrugged on a coat and held out his arm, and they strolled to the dining room like any properly wedded couple.

Sean appeared shortly after they were seated and dark eyes swept admiringly over Maria's new attire. Without invitation he appropriated a chair and laughed at Luke's scowl. "You have her to yourself all night, boyo. You can afford to share a little the rest of the time."

To his delight, a touch of pink suffused Maria's cheeks, and he instantly bent his considerable charm in her direction.

"A foyne and grand lady ye make, me colleen. And has this husband of yours persuaded you to join our small charade?"

Maria wondered if Luke had not told his friend there was no marriage binding them, or if Sean spoke this way out of simple gallantry. It would be preferable not to ask. She liked this charming Irishman, but she sensed he could be as dangerous to her well-being as Luke.

"I have no objection to helping other ranchers, but only if you two promise to be gentlemen. Luke has trouble remembering that upon occasion, so I will depend on you, Mr. O'Laughlin, to remind him."

"Sean, you must call me Sean, and sure I will hold tight to the lad's collar. He's a mite hasty, to be certain, but he need only hold your pretty hand this trip. Do you play at cards, Mrs. Walker?"

Luke sat back and watched this byplay without comment, but this question caused him to send Maria an inquiring look. It had never occurred to him to ask. He had just assumed she could do everything he could. He was beginning to lose his grip on reality, always a dangerous sign.

A dimple Luke had never noticed before appeared at the corner of Maria's mouth as she smiled back at Sean. "I play a little, Sean. What game do you prefer?"

"Any type of poker, Mrs. Walker. Or may I call you Maria?"

Luke itched to wrap his hand in Sean's fancy white collar and bodily heave him from the table, but he kept his irritation to himself. Women were no reason to destroy a good friendship. It might be better to warn Sean that this little heartbreaker was interested in only one thing, but that would reveal she was not his to do with as he wished. That might complicate things a little if Sean really took to the little witch, which it seemed he did. Luke played with the alternatives as he waited for Maria's answer. It did not surprise him when it came.

"Of course, Sean, to both questions. How else does one wile away a long winter night?"

This question was phrased with such ingenuousness that Sean spluttered and threw a look to Luke, who merely lifted a sardonic eyebrow.

"You've not been long married in truth, I take it?" Sean laughed.

"You'll learn, O'Laughlin. The lady is not what she seems. Consider that as fair a warning as you're going to get."

A look of curiosity leapt to Sean's eyes, but he obediently changed the subject. Their laughter continued throughout dinner with even Luke joining in, but Maria sensed an odd tension in him. Perhaps a gunfighter had to live like that. She noticed he always sat with his back against a wall and kept his gun hand unencumbered, but she had been unaware of this tension earlier in the day.

She did not allow Luke's oddities to deter her from enjoying the evening. Sean's admiration flattered her bruised and battered ego, and the looks she received from the other male diners told her she had passed inspection. It felt good to be treated like a lady and looked at as a woman. If she had her way, she would never go back to Levis and work shirts again. Or almost never. They did offer a certain freedom upon occasion. Perhaps if she could have trousers made of silk . . .

That reverie came to an end when Mr. Dallas joined their table. After greeting everyone, he said with a broad wink, "Everything's arranged, my friends. If you're done with your dinners, our companions await."

Maria sent Luke a questioning glance, but he wasn't paying attention to her. Sean, however, reacted jovially to this statement, leaping to his feet and pounding the older man on the back.

"They came, did they? Excellent. Now we won't have to feel left out while these lovebirds bill and coo. Come, let us get on with it. The sooner I clean all of you out, the sooner the evening can really begin."

Sean expertly led the rancher from the table, leaving
Luke to pay the tab and make explanations.

As Maria's questioning gaze finally registered, Luke
shrugged and assisted her from the chair. With her
hand firmly tucked in the crook of his elbow, he finally
replied.

"Whores. They found two whores last night who
play poker. You won't mind a little competition, will
you?"

12

The women waiting for them in the private parlor were a little older than Maria expected. Their gaudy gowns lacked the sophistication of Consuela's vivid silks and satins, and Maria quickly decided she had no competition at all.

"We thought it might be more amusing to have the sexes equally represented, Mrs. Walker. You do not object, I hope?" The rancher made a statement out of his question, not contemplating any reply but the affirmative. He had already assumed her status as a lady to be questionable.

Maria's dislike for the man grew, but since his attention had already wandered to the vast, exposed plateau of his companion's bosom, she did not deign to reply. She sent Luke a scornful look which he caught and interpreted with a fleeting grin, then settled herself complacently in the chair next to the one she knew Luke would take—the one next to the wall.

"You're quick, I'll give you that, *poquita*," Luke murmured as he settled where she had anticipated.

Maria chose to ignore that remark also. His earlier insinuation had placed him lower than Dallas in her books, and she wasted no time in encouraging his outrageous beliefs. Men saw everything in terms of money or sex. If he wished to think she was a loose woman, that was his problem. She had two bullets in her reticule to persuade him otherwise.

The game began innocently enough. Maria found herself sitting across the table from the plumpest, oldest prostitute, the one who had attached herself to the rancher. Cynically she observed that the woman even

wore powder between her massive breasts, and it began to cake and streak as the evening grew longer.

The other two women had dismissed Maria in her
high-necked dress upon introduction. When Luke
didn't respond with any degree of interest to their flir-
tation, they dismissed him also. To their consternation, however, as the evening wore on, all three men
showed more interest in the game and small pile of
chips accumulating in front of Maria than in anything
or anyone else. In boredom the women threw down
their cards and wandered about the room, refilling
whiskey glasses and whispering between themselves.

In a moment of jubilation the rancher noticed Maria
had no glass in front of her, and he sent for a bottle
of champagne. After the wine was poured with great
fanfare, he lost interest in it and never noticed that
Maria didn't touch her glass. Luke did, however, and
while waiting for his partner to make a play, he nudged
the glass closer to Maria's hand.

"It won't bite. Have a sip."

Green eyes contemplated him with hauteur. "I know
what it tastes like, and I don't like it. Don't play me
for a fool, Luke."

Since the tone of her words had attracted attention,
Luke did not press the point. He had been curious to
see what would happen with a little alcohol to loosen
her inhibitions, but he should have known she would
not make it easy for him. The other two women were
already half drunk and growing increasingly amorous.
He couldn't imagine the little witch at his side doing
what Sean's whore was doing now.

Maria had watched the younger woman's antics with
suspicion from the first. Unlike the older one, she had
not leaned all over Sean, smothering him with kisses
and hugs and suggestive whispers. Instead she had tantalized him more subtly, drifting her fingers across his
neck as she poured his drinks, bending too close as
she lit his cigar, touching him frequently but briefly.
Sean had accepted it all with a grin of appreciation
and kept on playing, until the cards began to go against
him. Then he had captured the woman's waist and

pulled her down on his lap. Maria didn't care to contemplate what the two of them were doing under the
table that produced such giggles from the woman.

Maria squirmed nervously as Luke's hand idly began to play with hers. The table was a small one, and
his hard thigh frequently came into contact with hers
as he pushed his chips to the center and settled back
again. If it were not for his fascination with the cards
and her growing suspicion of the way the game was
played, she would have smacked him.

Instead Luke noticed her growing discomfort with
the shocking behavior across the table. His sharp rep-
rimand caught Maria by surprise and she threw him a
furtive look. It brought a mocking light to Sean's eyes
as he glanced toward Maria and back to Luke, but the
giggling halted soon after.

Trying to relax, Maria followed the play more
closely. The pile of chips in front of the rancher had
suddenly begun to grow larger, which seemed odd
since she had already judged him to be an easily distracted and sporadic player. When the two of spades
showed up in his stack giving him two pair when she
knew she had already discarded that card, she threw
Luke an anxious look. She did not mind losing if he
did not, but cheats were not dealt with easily in these
parts. She did not wish to contemplate Luke's retribution.

Luke's taciturn expression did not change, but his
hand slipped beneath the table to squeeze her knee in
warning. Or she assumed it to be a warning. His hand
continued to linger there until the play closed, its heat
burning an indelible scar against her skin through the
layers of cloth. She kept her suspicions to herself.

Sean sent her a broad wink when two kings miraculously appeared in her hand with the next play, and
Maria finally realized her limited skills had nothing to
do with the few coins she had accumulated this night.
As if to confirm her discovery, Luke acquired the other
two kings, and his arm dropped idly over the back of
her chair, pressing her shoulder back to prevent her
from making a move that would give them away.

From that point on, luck began to gradually slide away from the rancher. Maria could not imagine how this would encourage Dallas to invite them to another game, but she kept silent, playing the game as if she had any control over it. Just as the rancher began to grow restless and a little irritable, setting aside his plump companion to concentrate on the game, Luke folded his hand of cards and yawned.

His broadcloth-covered arm had rested intimately behind Maria for some minutes, and now the fingers of that hand began to stroke her throat suggestively, his brooding gaze turning fully on her instead of the action at the table. Maria's first reaction was to smack him away and concentrate on her playing, but remembering the part she played, she interpreted Luke's hint with rapidity. She turned him a warm, secretive smile that the other players could not fail to notice and folded her hand even though she had a pair showing.

When the rancher triumphantly claimed the pot, partially reducing Luke and Maria's winnings for the evening, Luke made no effort to reach for the deck. Instead he sent the other two men a meaningful glance that would have turned Maria's insides to water had she not known he played a part.

"Well, gentlemen, it's been a pleasant evening and I hate to leave while I'm losing, but other pleasures beckon. You will excuse us if my wife and I take this opportunity to retire?"

Sean leaned back and boldly fondled the woman in his arms, laughing eyes catching Maria's as he spoke. "I cannot blame you there, Walker. Had I such temptation available, I would not concentrate long on the cards, either. Perhaps we ought to try again some night without the ladies as distraction."

The rancher shoved his chair back and began folding his winnings into his coat pocket. "It would be a pleasure to meet with you gentlemen again, but I'm returning home in the morning. The old spread stands still when I'm not about to guide it."

Determined to earn her share of the prize, Maria took the initiative. Leaning forward and propping her chin on her hand, she gazed at the rancher with the wide-eyed admiration she had seen Consuela turn on her mark for the evening.

"Why, Mr. Dallas, do you own a ranch near here? My husband has a place back in Kansas, but I've never seen it. Do you have many horses? I do so love horses."

The pressure of Luke's fingers against her shoulders conveyed the extent of his control at this inane chatter. Maria only prayed it was laughter he controlled. She had a difficult time keeping her own face straight.

At this unexpected attention from the prettiest woman in the room, the rancher visibly expanded. The combination of alcohol consumed and lust aroused had muddied his usually sharp wits. "Besides the remuda I've got a few good lines of quarterhorses, ma'am. Are you interested in racing?"

"No, just horses," she sighed, keeping her gaze focused on him. "I've been trying to talk Luke into buying a few good ones for his stable. Ponies are very well for herding cattle, but I love the feel of a handsome horse myself."

The provocative drawl of her voice had Sean spluttering in his glass of whiskey. The woman in his lap helpfully pounded him on the back, but the rancher took no notice of this byplay. He captured Maria's hand against the table and grinned expansively.

"Well, ma'am, why don't you and your husband stop by my place on your way home? Maybe I can find a few good horses to show him what he's been missing."

"I'd like that, Mr. Dallas." Maria turned a flirtatious look back to her unamused "husband." "Could we do that, dear? Then you can have another card game without me."

"We'll see about that." Luke's reply held a suggestive tone that neither confirmed nor denied her request. His hand wrapped around the back of her neck and drew her toward him.

It took Sean to wrap up the negotiations. Carelessly

stomping out his cigar, he rose, dragging his lady of
the evening with him.

"Don't believe your place is far off the road I'm
taking them back on, Dallas. If the little lady doesn't
mind the extra ride, we might just take you up on that
offer. The station at El Moro is a little too far for my
liking. Nights on the trail can get mighty cold when
you spend them alone."

With a few further jests along this line, the party
broke up. Luke steered Maria from the room before
any of the others. She still could not tell if he was
angry or pleased with her handling of the situation,
but she knew he stayed uncomfortably near all the way
up the stairs.

This time when he entered, he did not leave. After
inspecting the room Luke closed the door and leaned
against it while Maria nervously lit the oil lamp. She
didn't know what to do after she did that. Luke did
not move from his position, but she felt the intensity
of his gaze as he followed her motions. She couldn't
turn to look at him, fearful of the effect of those hard
amber eyes. Angry or not, she knew what he wanted,
and the liquor consumed this evening would not make
him any easier to deal with. What should she do now?
Nervousness made it difficult to think.

"Maria." Luke's voice demanded attention though
he did not raise it.

Reluctantly Maria turned to face him. The lamp
made shadows of the hollows of his cheeks and hid
the color of his eyes in the darkness. He had discarded
his coat earlier and rolled up the sleeves of his shirt.
She could see the golden hairs on his forearms as he
crossed them over his chest, and she shivered, sensing
the power he controlled.

Luke watched the flicker of lamplight over Maria's
haughty features. Tonight the accents of her noble
Spanish heritage held sway over the softer hints of her
Irish ancestry. Even the slant of those green eyes did
not diminish the arrogance of her high cheekbones and
patrician nose. Though she could scarcely weigh more
than a hundred pounds, she would make a formidable

opponent. He preferred to keep the little witch on his side.

"You're catching on too damn quick, *brujita*," he murmured softly, almost to himself.

Maria allowed herself a breath of air. "I'll take that as a compliment. Thank you, señor."

"I don't like working with women, but I could make an exception for you."

"Your generosity is overwhelming." Halfway between the bed and the door, Maria felt trapped, but she held her head high, refusing to reveal her fears. "However, I would appreciate it if you would show your gratitude by leaving."

"That's not exactly what I had in mind, as you well know. Did you mean to sleep in that gown?" Luke shifted his position from the door and stepped toward her.

"No, Luke." Responding to his intentions more than his words, Maria backed toward the table and her gun. She did not know how she would unfasten her gown, but she felt too vulnerable to allow him that familiarity again.

"Don't be foolish, Maria. I don't need to rape you any more than you mean to shoot me. Stand still and let me unfasten the gown."

She had no choice. His strong fingers were digging into her shoulders before she could reach for her reticule, and it seemed foolish to dive for it when she knew he only meant to help. She couldn't shoot him simply because his touch made her legs tremble. Obediently she turned around and felt the heat of his hands as they moved slowly from hook to hook.

He took more time than he had earlier, lingering over each one until Maria felt she would have to scream and run to preserve her senses. When she felt cool air against her skin, she tried to jerk free, but Luke's hand continued to hold her tight. Before she could escape, both hands slid the lace-bedecked bodice from her shoulders, and he was so close behind her she could feel his breath against her hair.

"Where's the harm, Maria? A little pleasure never hurt anyone."

Luke's hands slid down her bare arms, stroking them, pressing her close until she felt the imprint of his hard, lean body against hers. A kiss whispered above her temple, but he did no more than that, leaving her to respond to the wild sensations rocketing through her, through both of them. She felt Luke's desire as strongly as her own, ached for the touch of his hand against her breast, needed the heat of his lips against hers, but she could not acknowledge any of it.

Jerking from his grasp, Maria pulled the shoulders of her gown back in place. Keeping her back to him, she ordered shakily, "Get out."

Luke could see the hint of smooth ivory skin above the back of her undergarments and his fingers ached to touch, to uncover the velvety flesh hidden beneath layers of clothing, but years of experience had taught him patience, and he called upon that reserve now.

Biding his time, he replied softly, "You're young yet, Maria, you have much to learn. I'll go now, but when you're ready, let me know."

The door clicked behind her, and shivers of loneliness began to rock Maria's body as she swayed back and forth, tears streaming down her face. She didn't know what was happening to her. She only knew Luke's soft words were far, far worse than all the curses and blows he could have beaten her with. And her body ached with his absence.

13

When sunlight finally found its way through the heavy curtains over the room's single window, Maria stirred restlessly in her cocoon of covers. With consciousness came memory, and she jerked from sleep to wakefulness in an instant.

The bed beside her was empty, but the room was not. Without waiting to locate the source of the sound that woke her, she gripped the derringer beneath her pillow and flipped over with the gun in hand.

Luke caught her movement in the mirror, but didn't flinch as he bent to get a closer look at his soap covered jaw while he inched the razor over it. Maria's reflection in the mirror gave him a full view of tawny arms and shoulders emerging from a simple cotton nightshift. The gun between her long fingers was to be expected.

"What in hell are you doing?" Irritably Maria thrust the gun aside and brushed her long braid back. She was unaccustomed to waking to half-naked men in her room, but even she could sense a man with soap over half his face represented no danger. In the morning light the breadth of his muscular shoulders was not nearly so provocative as the night before. Admittedly, if she dared to follow the hollow line at his back to where it met his pants, she would reduce herself to the same nervous state as last night, but she refused to be distracted.

Luke grunted at the tone of her voice. "Testy in the mornings, are we? What do you think I'm doing?"

"Carving your face into a jack-o'-lantern from the looks of it." Maria threw aside the covers and swung

her legs from the bed. Waking up to a man in the room
caused an infinite number of problems. She didn't want
to use the chamber pot behind the screen while he was
here, but she couldn't dress to go to the privy until he
was gone, either. She would have to get rid of him
some way.

"The barber down the street is a sadistic butcher. I
figured I could do better with a dull blade and a rake."
Luke winced as he nearly sliced his lip with the straight
edge.

Sighing at this example of masculine incompetence
in a man who could do everything else so efficiently
and so well, Maria strode across the room and picked
up the razor strop. She held out her hand for the razor.

"Give it to me. I learned to do it for my father when
he was ill and his hands shook. You'll be here the rest
of the morning elsewise."

Luke straightened and stared at her with suspicion.
"I'd be safer trusting the butcher."

Barefoot, she scarcely reached his shoulder, but
Maria was more than accustomed to dealing with men
twice her size. She shoved a chair toward him and
pointed at it. "Sit. You have not yet given me reason
to cut your throat, so you need not worry. The time
to worry is when you have done something for which
you know I will carve out your wooden heart."

Luke had to grin at this reasoning. She seemed not
in the least concerned that she wore less now than she
had the night before when she had thrown him out. If
she could trust him while she wore naught but a shift,
he ought to be able to trust her with a dull blade. He
handed over the razor and sat down as ordered.

Deliberately ignoring the furious beat of her heart
at the sight of that rugged torso within reach of her
hands, Maria carefully stropped the razor to a fine
edge, then took a deep breath. Telling herself this was
no different than shaving her father, she touched his
cheek and gently began to wield the razor.

As the job progressed more smoothly than she had
anticipated, a malicious idea took root and grew clam-
orously insistent while Maria's hands neatly shaped

Luke's sideburns. Perhaps he had not harmed her enough to cut his throat, but his lustful thoughts deserved some retribution, and she had always hated that mustache.

She had neatly hacked off half of one side of the hair over his lip before Luke realized her intention. With a yelp he grabbed her hand and turned toward the mirror. He hadn't had a better shave since he'd left home, with the exception of the missing half of his mustache.

He slanted Maria a wary glance. "Why?"

"Because it's ugly," she replied cheerfully, admiring her handiwork. He had a broad, square jaw and rather sensuous lips. Neither needed the distraction of that ridiculous hank of hair.

Luke sent his reflection one last look and shrugged. "It sure as hell is ugly now. Finish the job."

Humming happily, Maria obliged. Within minutes Luke's face was smooth to the touch, and she even trimmed his hair to keep it off his collar. The back of his neck had reached such a deep bronze that he had little need to concern himself about burning it.

When she had washed off the last of the soap, Luke leaned forward to admire the job in the mirror. He hadn't seen the face staring back at him since before he'd left for the war. It was no longer a young face, but time had not yet ravaged it. Amber eyes turned tauntingly back to the artist wielding her weapons.

"If it was the mustache you objected to, you should have told me sooner. I will assume now there is no longer any reason to avoid kissing me."

Caught off guard, Maria had no time to escape. With one hard tug Luke pulled her across his lap, and she could taste the lingering remnants of his shaving soap as his lips closed over hers. It didn't even occur to her to struggle. His powerful arms held her gently, protectively, while his mouth moved teasingly across hers, and it seemed more natural to slide her fingers behind the neck she had just been admiring than to fight. The warmth of his kiss stirred slumbering needs, gradually waking her to the wonders that could be had for the asking.

When his hands began to caress her hip through the thin gown, however, Maria regretfully pushed away, severing the sweet connection of their mouths. Her hand daringly rested on the bare expanse of his chest as she gazed into the golden lights of his eyes, but she found no anger in the oddly relaxed line of his jaw. She ran her finger along his freshly shaved cheek and wished Luke would limit himself to kisses, but she understood with this man she could not play games. The heat of his hand along the curve of her hip had already become possessive.

"Yes, I like that much better, but the answer is still no." Maria struggled to remove herself from this awkward position, and Luke reluctantly returned her to the floor, though his hands lingered about her waist.

Standing, he traced the dusky rose of her cheek and studied the deep wells of her eyes. "One of these days, *mi cariña,* you will realize what you are wasting by saving yourself for some foolish notion of love. Tell me when you are ready to grow up."

Then Luke released her as if he had never touched her at all. In a few precise movements he had gathered his clean clothes and moved toward the door. Over his shoulder he threw back, "I will send up the maids with warm water. Have one of them fasten your gown."

Maria wanted to throw something at him, but she had not the strength. He had taken everything out of her, drained her of the will to fight. If he should ever guess the state his kisses left her in, she could say farewell to her innocence.

They picked up Carmelita at her aunt's and listened to her excited chatter all the way to the mercantile store. Luke seemed less talkative than ever, and Maria felt relief when he left them to finish their shopping while he set out to do a little of his own. It would be much easier buying the necessities for her wedding without Luke around.

They found a bolt of lovely beige satin for Maria

and decided on a blue taffeta for Pieta and a sunny yellow for Carmelita. She also bought several yards of ivory lace and seed pearls for her wedding dress. With the supply of money Luke had given them exhausted, they emerged triumphantly into the bright sunlight.

Only as they began to discuss Carmelita's return to the ranch did the girl begin to develop some reservation about their plans.

Grasping her bundles anxiously, she stared at Maria's complacent expression. "Perhaps it would be better if I stay with you instead of go with my cousins. What will Mama say when I return without you?"

"She will scold, but it makes no difference. Tell her I wish these gowns made up as soon as possible so I sent you on ahead. It will not take long for the others to be done, and I am with Luke, so what can happen?"

"Maybe you should come with me, and Luke can bring the gowns with him?" Carmelita remained dubious, more of her mother's wrath than Luke's abilities.

"I must stay for fittings." Impatiently Maria started down the street to where they had promised to meet Luke. "I am a grown woman now and must do these things for myself. You will see. When I come home, I will be such a grand lady you will not recognize me."

Giggling at the thought of Maria turning into any such creature, Carmelita stayed content with their plans. It was true, in her new gown and dainty shoes Maria looked much as the elegant ladies in their shiny carriages riding by, but such gowns would be useless on the ranch. In the past the lovely gowns hanging in her closet had seldom been worn twice before she outgrew them. Maria had always preferred to ride with the men.

They found Luke waiting for them in front of the haberdashery. He had returned to denims and his placketed black work shirt this day, and he smelled like the stables he had obviously been visiting. Even in this familiar garb he made Maria's heart beat quicker as he watched her approach. To distract the path of her thoughts, she focused on the disreputable Stetson and wrinkled her nose in distaste.

"Is that what you're planning to wear when we ride out of here?" She gave the offending head gear a derisive look.

Luke made a mocking bow at this greeting, lifting his sweat-stained, bullet-ridden hat and continuing to hold it as he took some of the parcels from Carmelita's arms. "You have taken some aversion to my hat?"

"I doubt even a good scrubbing would remove the grease. Besides that, it has a hole in it. If I'm to ride out wearing ribbons and lace, the least you could do is invest in a new hat."

Luke looked startled and amused at this suggestion, and he slanted Maria a wry look. "Ashamed to be seen with me already?"

Maria stared at him as if he had taken complete leave of his senses. "I want you to have a new *hat*, not take up a new profession, although there are times . . ." She let that thought trail off suggestively. Luke's grin told her he got the point.

He fingered the bullet hole while holding her gaze. "Well, now, I'm rather fond of this old hat. It's been with me for many a year, and a new one just never fits quite the same. I attach fond memories to this hat. I wouldn't want to part with it just like that."

Ignoring the gleam in his eye, Maria caught his arm and turned him to face the haberdasher's window. After studying the interior for a moment, she pointed to a low-crowned brown Stetson with a band of black. "That one. Try on that one. I'll put a new bullet hole in it soon enough, I wager."

With a laugh Luke conceded to giving it a try. Catching Maria by the waist, he swung her into the shop with a familiarity he shouldn't have shown, but she offered no protest. When they came out again, Luke was wearing the new Stetson tilted at a jaunty angle over one eye, and he behaved in a friendlier manner than Maria had ever seen in him.

Not willing to question the reason for this change in

attitude, Maria held her tongue and accepted it happily. They took Carmelita back to her aunt's, stayed for the noon meal, assured themselves she was in good hands, then returned to the dressmaker's for a final fitting.

The dinner gown Maria had decided upon was a simple but sophisticated one. The emerald green watered silk of the bodice and overskirt pulled back over a bustle to form a short train and reveal a ruffled underskirt of white satin and lace to match the insert of the bodice. The fine lace of the insert had the effect of a respectably high-necked gown while still revealing glimpses of the hills and valley it ostensibly concealed.

Luke admired the effect with approval, his gaze following the full curve of Maria's breasts to a tiny waistline and the provocative sway of her slender hips as she turned around for his inspection. There was no doubt about it: the little tomboy made a fascinating woman, and she all too obviously knew it. Even now those green eyes peeped at him from behind a fringe of thick, sooty lashes, and the small smile flirting about her lips told him he had revealed entirely too much of his thoughts. Given encouragement, she would become an incorrigible tease, but Luke couldn't prevent the grin spreading across his face. That she merely practiced her wiles on him, he knew, but no law said he couldn't enjoy every minute of it.

That mood didn't last any longer than it took for Sean to join them again at dinner.

Luke watched with a scowl as a properly dressed Sean poured effusive praises of the new gown from his golden tongue, and Maria apparently lapped it all up as a cat would cream. The evasive dimple appeared in her cheek as she mimicked his Irish blarney with vividly embroidered compliments of her own. She had never turned on that charm for him, and Luke silently sipped his drink while watching the two court each other with words and gestures.

Finally noticing Luke's withdrawal from the conversation, Sean turned a merry glance toward his taciturn friend. "I don't know how a morose fellow like yourself deserves an Irish jewel like Maria for wife, but I congratulate you on your taste. She thinks faster than a professional at this game. If you could promise her services all the time, we could line up any number of jobs."

Luke sent Maria a speculative glance, noting her unease with this deception. He shrugged and poured himself another drink. "What Maria does is her own choice. I have no claim on her."

Maria refrained from kicking him under the table, but an angry blush began to stain her cheeks as she met Luke's gaze accusingly. She supposed Sean had to be told sometime that they were not man and wife, but it could have been done with a little more finesse and a good deal more explanation. The man managed to make a shambles of every bit of happiness she managed to glean from her position.

Sean's laughing gaze momentarily shifted to one of puzzlement and concern, then catching Maria's reaction, he began to comprehend, and he smiled easily, pouring oil on troubled waters. "If he means what I think he means, may all the saints be praised. That means there is yet a chance for me."

"Not unless you have a stash of gold hidden away somewhere, boyo," Luke mimicked his friend's accent. "She's engaged to a rich Spaniard who owns half the valley and wants to multiply his assets."

Maria could not hold her tongue a moment longer. Luke had ruined the meal, her evening, her happiness, and she lashed out in retaliation. "At least Manuel treats me like a lady and makes an honest living, which is more than I can say for a man with a price on his head and bullet holes in his hat!"

She rose hurriedly and raced from the room, leaving Luke to hurl a stream of invectives and leap from the table to run after her.

The bedroom door slammed in his face, and Luke had half a mind to throw it open again, but he had nothing to say to the little witch. Since no screams or gunshots emanated from behind the door, he could assume his old foe had not yet found the room, and he spun on his heel to return downstairs. A tall bottle of whiskey would suit his needs about now. He had no stomach for another woman, and the memory of the two whores Sean had produced did not encourage him to think differently.

Maria picked up her hairbrush and flung it across the room as Luke's footsteps turned away. She hated the man, hated every arrogant inch of that embodiment of masculine bigotry. From there her thoughts lapsed into the furious Spanish phrases her mother had sometimes hurled at her father's head. Men were all the same. Pigheaded fools. What difference did it make which pigheaded fool she spent her life with?

Deciding what she needed now was a good, relaxing bath, Maria grabbed her reticule and started out the door. She would ask the desk clerk to send up a maid. It would never occur to Luke to do so.

A single lantern flickered in the dismal corridor, but Maria knew the way. The stairway led directly into the lobby. The room might have a terrible view, but it was an excellent location just a few doors from the stairs. She did not have to go far to request a maid, ask for food, or seek the privy.

As she proceeded down the corridor, a shadow darted from one of those doorways, and Maria's step hesitated. Luke had always been with her before, and she never had to deal with fellow guests. Her fingers wrapped around the derringer handle in her bag, distrusting the furtive manner in which the man approached. There had been no sign of trouble since that first day here, but Luke had scarcely left her alone in all that time. She had not realized what a coward she really was when he wasn't around.

"Mrs. Walker, at last we meet." A small, wiry man with crooked teeth and greasy black hair came to a halt in front of her.

Maria felt no immediate fear. He was not much taller than herself, and she had learned to fight dirty at an early age. Before she could acknowledge his greeting, however, he slid a knife from his belt and grinned wickedly.

''We will see how brave your husband is when it is one of his own family who must die.''

Without stopping to think, Maria began to scream. Her new corset cut into her ribs as she gasped for more air, but half the town surely must hear her. The man's startled reaction gave the time she needed to pull the derringer from her bag, and before he could run, she pulled the trigger.

He yelped with pain and began to hobble toward the stairway, but his escape had already been blocked by people pouring into the lobby and corridor. He turned to grab for Maria, but she shoved against him, sending him off balance as she scampered for the stairs and the safety of Luke's company.

He and Sean came bounding up the stairway before anyone else had the presence of mind to act. Luke's gun was already in his hand, and his face was a study in fury as he raised it to the shadowy figure behind her. Maria didn't care if he looked like Attila the Hun. With a gasp she raced to meet him. As she approached the top of the stairs, her breath came in painful spurts, and her senses started reeling. Before she could grasp for the banister, her vision blurred, the world whirled, and she fell into a dizzying pit with no top or bottom.

14

Luke caught Maria as she fell, his arm grabbing her tiny waist as his cold gaze sought the cause of the turmoil. The gun in his hand jerked reflexively toward the little man trapped in the semidarkness of the dead-end corridor, but Sean knocked his arm upward.

"Don't. Take care of Maria. I've got him covered."

Without needing to be told twice, Luke swung Maria's lifeless form into his arms and carried her past her assailant. Someone else wrenched the knife from the terrified man's hand and a third man grasped his arms behind his back. With Sean holding a gun over him, the would-be murderer would not go far. He sent a venomous look after Luke, but Luke's attention was elsewhere.

Maria woke with a jerk as something sharp slid up her back, and she took a deep gulp of air before preparing to scream again. Only Luke's furious curses returned her to her senses. With a gasp of surprise she realized she lay on her stomach on her bed, and that she felt a definite freedom of movement that should not have been there were her garments properly in place.

With a small cry she grabbed for the back of her new bodice to find it gaping wide. Turning sideways, she caught Luke sliding a knife back into his boot, and she ignored the thunderous expression on his face.

"You cut my new corset! Who in hell do you think you are?"

"You wanted me to let you lie there and suffocate? I should have. Any woman damn fool enough to wear one of those things deserves what she gets. What in hell possessed you? My God, you're as skinny as a wet cat as it is, but it won't do till you look as pinched in the middle as a yellow jacket.''

Maria struggled to sit up and keep her decency at the same time. "You were the one who said I needed a dinner gown!" Her green eyes spit fire. "A lady can't wear gowns like that without proper undergarments, unless you want me to look like Consuela, of course."

"You might as well look like Consuela if you're going to act like her. What in hell were you doing wandering around the hotel alone? Haven't you got a lick of sense?"

Maria grabbed the nearest thing to hand and flung it at his head. The pillow hit Luke squarely in the face, but he scarcely acknowledged it. With murderous intent he advanced on her until an abrupt knock at the door intruded.

With a curse Luke reached for the door, throwing a look over his shoulder to be certain Maria was decent. She jerked the bodice closed with her hand and sent him a baleful look that warned he ought to be glad that hand was occupied. He had already removed the smoking pistol from her other hand.

A broad man in a leather vest and wearing a badge entered the room, giving Luke a wary look before his glance slid to the lady sitting at the edge of the bed. Her elaborate coiffure had slid loose on one side and long strands of black hair cascaded to her tawny shoulders, but she held herself with as much pride and decorum as could be summoned under the circumstances. The sheriff lifted his hat and nodded his head.

"Sorry to disturb you like this, ma'am. We've got the criminal in custody, but we'll be needing a statement from you to put him behind bars." At Maria's stony silence he turned to Luke. "The doc is just outside dressing Smith's toe. Should I send for him?"

"My wife simply fainted. She will be fine as soon as she has time to recover from the shock."

"His toe? Damn, the aim must be off on this thing. I aimed for his instep." Maria picked the pistol up with her free hand and lined the sight up with Luke's ear as target.

The sheriff looked startled but relaxed as Luke confiscated the weapon and unloaded it. "Ma'am, if you could just tell me what happened, I'll be on my way. I know something like this is upsetting to a lady's disposition . . ." He hesitated, not at all certain whether the lady's mood was directed at the criminal or something else.

Wearily Maria returned her attention to the sheriff. "He pulled a knife and threatened me. I screamed and shot him. He didn't seem dangerous enough to rate killing, but I figured I could get away easier if he couldn't run. I don't remember what happened after that."

"You fainted because you were wearing that corset too damned tight," Luke interrupted rudely. Turning to the sheriff, he added, "The man's name isn't Smith, it's Clemons. He's from down around El Paso, and it's me he's after. His brother had the misfortune to hold up a Wells Fargo shipment while I was on guard. If you have any further questions, I'll come by your office later. Right now I think my wife needs a little rest. If you'll excuse us . . ."

Expertly Luke shuffled the sheriff out, then slammed the door, and returned his glare to his rebellious "wife." "I'm not even going to ask again why you were out wandering the halls. If that sheriff has even half a brain in his head, he will be asking for our address in case he needs to reach us. That means he will know who you are, and if your boyfriend comes looking for you, he will be hot on our trail before our dust has time to settle. We're going to have to leave first thing in the morning so he doesn't have time to catch up with us."

Giving her that thought to contemplate, Luke stamped out.

Maria stared at the door in dismay, but no tears came to her eyes. She couldn't imagine Manuel bothering to trace her to Santa Fe. Why should he? It was only Luke's guilty conscience that made him think her *no-*

vio was after him. No, it wasn't Manuel who worried her, it was Luke.

She knew he could be cold and hard and ruthless, but she had never thought he would turn that side toward her. Yet he had just walked out that door with the only protection she possessed. The derringer was gone.

Maria could smell the liquor fumes and cheap perfume when Luke returned late that night. Without the gun for protection, she was nervous, but he made no move in the direction of the bed. He kicked open his bedroll and sat down abruptly. She could hear him cursing as he pulled off his boots.

When he had apparently completed that task to his satisfaction, there was silence. Before Maria had time to relax, Luke's baritone murmured across the space between them.

"From now on, I'll lace your corsets and don't you dare wear one tomorrow. The heat will kill you."

Maria did not dare express her outrage. She refused to even let him know she heard. Lace her corset! That man must think he was her husband in truth. She would put a swift end to that notion in the morning.

The day did not begin under happy auspices. Luke slept late and got up grumpy. Maria ignored him as he jerked on a shirt and stumbled out, but a few minutes later a maid appeared at the door. Apparently under strict instructions, she laid out a frilled camisole, Maria's new riding skirt, and a lightweight linen blouse. While Maria washed, the maid began packing her few remaining garments in the old valise. It seemed the plan was in progress whether she willed or not. She had the feeling that if she balked at this point, Luke would come after her with a gun.

At breakfast the sheriff appeared. Luke gave him a disgruntled look and continued drinking his coffee, but the man had turned his attention to Maria. Wearing traveling clothes and with her hair pinned up in a coronet of braids, she appeared much younger and more respectable than she had the night before. He made a polite bow before speaking.

"The judge won't be able to get to the Clemons' case for a few days. The desk clerk says you're checking out. If there should be some need to get in touch with you, where should we write?"

Maria primly set her napkin aside and ignoring Luke, answered, "You may write to the Connolly ranch in San Pedro, Sheriff. We will be returning there."

"Connolly? Irish Connolly? You wouldn't be some relation?"

"His daughter."

Sean had come up behind the sheriff by this time, and he lifted a surprised eyebrow behind the man's back, but Maria paid him little heed. She had come to the conclusion it might be preferable if the whole world knew where she was before she rode off into the mountains with these two.

"Connolly's daughter?" The sheriff began to grin as he eyed her with new respect. "Why, I remember you when you was just a tadpole hanging onto your mother's skirts. Never saw two prettier women, and your daddy was mighty proud of you both. Don't reckon he came to town much after your mama died, did he? And now you're all grown up and married. How's your daddy doing?"

"He's dead, Sheriff, shot in the back by some sidewinder last winter. But I thank you for your kind words." Maria couldn't say more. Tears already threatened to fall at this mention of her father and mother. She missed them both desperately. Should she ever marry, there would be no one to be happy or sad about the occasion. The loneliness was more frightening than anything else she had experienced.

The sheriff made a few hasty remarks, shook Luke's hand, and hurried away. Sean sat down in the chair across from her and studied Maria's tear-filled eyes. Without questioning, he produced an ivory-handled derringer from his coat pocket and lay it upon the table in front of her.

"I've tested it. This one has a better aim." He shot a quick look to Luke, who made no comment. Their argument of the night before had been a drunken one, but Sean had gleaned enough substance from it to know what needed to be done. He hadn't quite defined the relationship between these two, but if the lady felt the need for her own gun, he saw no reason why she shouldn't have one.

"Thank you, Sean." In a more subdued mood than the prior night, Maria checked the chamber for bullets, set the safety, and tucked the small gun away in her skirt pocket. "I'll remember next time not to trust the aim."

"You're sure you want to go through with this? Everyone in town is going to know who you are by the time the sheriff gets finished flapping his gums." Sean lifted his cup of coffee to his lips and watched her carefully.

"I don't go back on my word, Mr. O'Laughlin. I want to know who killed my father, and I will do whatever is necessary to find out." Maria retreated into silence, leaving the two men to discuss their plans alone.

By the time they had finished breakfast and Luke had carried down their belongings and strapped them to the pack mule he had purchased, the morning was well advanced. Wearing her twill riding skirt and a wide-brimmed hat to keep the sun from her eyes, Maria inspected the horse that had been purchased for her use. A bay mare not much over three years old, the mount had every appearance of quality breeding for speed and endurance. Someone was willing to pay quite a bit for this project if they could buy her a horse like this. Neither man gave the horse a second look, and she shrugged away their indifference. If they didn't care about expenses, who was she to question?

"Does the horse have a name?" Maria asked as Luke came to help her mount.

"Not that I know of. Call her whatever you wish." He formed a stirrup with his hand and swung her upward, then holding her ankle between his fingers, he stared up to where green eyes watched him warily.

"The owner should name her," she insisted. "She's too lovely to go without a name."

"Well, name her, then. Sean and I aren't going to need her when this is over."

"All right, I'll call her Erinmeade. When you sell her, you'll have to tell the new owner her name." Contentedly Maria leaned over to give the mare an affectionate pat. It had been a long time since she had ridden anything but the remuda ponies.

Luke gave her a quizzical look, but Maria seemed quite content with this arrangement, and he moved on. He had meant for her to keep the horse. Any other woman would have interpreted it that way. Perhaps she was too young to understand what could be hers for the asking. She would learn quickly enough. They all did.

They rode south out of town, and Maria frowned slightly at the direction. She had understood the path they were to take was toward the train station in Colorado Territory. Surely that would be to the north?

Before long, Sean expressed this same objection, and Luke halted long enough to allow his companions to catch up with him.

"Where in hell are you headed, Walker? I don't know any shortcuts by this road."

"We've got time. We don't want to be showing up at Dallas's place the day after he does. Besides, if any of Maria's pals start to track us, this will slow them down. We'll cross over by the river and go out that way. Any more questions?" Luke slanted them a cynical look.

Maria said nothing, and Sean shrugged it away. He didn't care what games they played as long as he accomplished his mission. The ride would only be the more interesting with a woman along.

By the time they corrected their direction and rode to a suitable place to camp for the night, Maria was too weary to provide entertainment for anyone. A trickle of water in the shelter of some cottonwoods

offered little refreshment. She would have much preferred to soak her aching muscles in a good long bath.
This mud puddle scarcely offered the opportunity.

''Do you cook?'' Sean began unpacking the cooking
gear while Maria gathered kindling in the center of the
clearing. Luke had taken the horses to the stream to
drink.

''Probably on the same level as you and Luke.''
Maria set a match to the dry wood and watched until
the flame took hold. ''Tell me what you need done
and I'll do it.''

Sean dumped his gear beside the fire and helped
Maria to stand. With her collar turned up to protect
her neck and the hat tilted to shade her face, she had
appeared cool and serene all day. Now that he stood
close, however, he could see the beads of sweat upon
her forehead and the dark circles under her eyes. Long
lashes turned up to him questioningly, and he couldn't
resist touching the rose-petal softness of her cheek.

''Why don't you sit beneath that tree over there and
cool off? I've got a specialty I can whip up in minutes.'' Holding her chin up with his finger, he smiled
into the cool waters of her eyes.

Luke returned to the clearing and caught the end of
this tender tableau. Grinding his teeth together, he kept
silent and watched with cynicism as Maria pulled away
from Sean at Luke's appearance. Without a word to
either of them, she disappeared into the trees. They
could follow the sway of her dark skirt for a while,
then she went down the embankment and out of sight.

Maria rejoined them in time for supper. Drops of
water still lingered in the valley exposed by her open
collar, and she had washed the dust and weariness from
her face. With delight she dug into Sean's concoction
of beans and rice flavored with spicy peppers, and she
drank deeply of the rich black coffee he had brewed.
Her reaction satisfied Sean, and they flirted lightly
throughout the meal, happy with their own wit and at
peace with the world.

It was Luke who could not find contentment in this
innocent scene. As night fell and the fire flickered

shadows over Maria's high cheekbones, concealing her eyes and accentuating her lips, he remembered all too clearly those times when he had held her in his arms and felt her desire. He had been a fool to let her go. He had only himself to blame if she turned to another man for what she wanted. Why did he persist in treating her as if she were some rare and valuable jewel that he did not deserve? She was a woman, just like any other woman. He must be mad to waste his time thinking of her. He should either act on his desires or give her up to Sean.

It would not do to dissect his reaction to the thought of Maria in another man's arms. He had found her first, and he would take whatever favors she had to give. It was pointless arguing with her when he had no influence over her behavior. Instead of arguing, he needed to be courting her if he wanted to be the one to share her bed. Not a man to resist a challenge, Luke returned to the fray.

Maria looked up in surprise when Luke refilled her cup and settled down beside her, but she had grown so accustomed to his presence that she welcomed his return rather than feared it. She gave him a warm smile and sipped gratefully at the hot liquid. Now that the sun had set, the air had lost its warmth.

"All we need now is a little music," she said without thinking, remembering the moon-filled nights at the ranch when Luke had played his magic serenades.

"I should have taken you dancing while we were in Santa Fe. You never got a chance at the fiesta, did you?" Luke rested his hand behind her, remembering the way her face had lit up with excitement at the sound of the musicians.

"It was too soon perhaps, and not really proper. But I do love to hear them play."

Luke chuckled at her idea of propriety. "You will ride about the countryside with me, but you will not dance while you are in mourning? I think someone needs to teach you about priorities."

"I'm all in favor of her choices, myself," Sean laughed from the other side of the fire. "It seems perfectly reasonable to me that she should be with us and not dancing with strangers.''

Maria laughed at this foolishness. Whatever they might be, she liked these two men, and she enjoyed their company. Thoughts of propriety were far from her mind while she was enjoying herself.

''If we cannot have music, tell me stories. How did you two meet?''

She felt them exchange glances over her head, but she did not concern herself with that when Luke took up the tale.

''You'll think us old men if we tell you the truth. What lie would you prefer to hear?''

Maria threw him a haughty look. ''No lies, sir. And what matters it if I think you're old? I already know you are dirty.''

Sean smothered his laughter, and Luke grinned at this riposte. ''One of these days I'll turn you over my knee for one of those cracks, so watch yourself. I'm not so old that I can't whale the tar out of you.''

''The truth, I am waiting.'' Maria propped her chin on her fist and met his gaze defiantly.

''We met at Appomatox. Sean was wearing blue and I was wearing gray, and we were neither in any shape to fight. Our rifles were empty, our bayonets were lost, and we'd both been wounded. I'd taken a minié ball through the leg, so when he kicked me, I crumpled, but not before grabbing his broken arm on my way down. The roar he made could have been heard over the cannons.''

''Had there been any cannon,'' Sean added. ''As it was, his side had already surrendered and all we did was attract the attention of my colonel.''

Luke grimaced. ''He rode over to find two bare-cheeked boys grappling in the dust, so filthy our colors must have been nearly indistinguishable, not that mine had been proper army issue anyway. He ordered us to attention, but we could neither of us stand. In disgust he demanded to know what was going on. Do you have any idea what that lying Irishman said?''

''Would you have me let you go to prison with the

other poor bastards? How was I to know they were going to send the lot of you home?''

Luke ignored this interruption. ''He claimed I was his little brother and I had disobeyed his orders and left our dying mother home alone. It's a wonder the colonel didn't fall from the saddle laughing.''

Instead of laughing as both men were, Maria stared from one to the other with concern. A decade ago these two could only have been boys. What were they doing far from their homes in a war that nobody could win? And wounded! She gave Luke's leg an involuntary glance.

He caught the look and squeezed her hand. ''We both survived, *querida*. We were luckier than a lot of others. We only got in on thc tail end of the war, and the colonel sent us both home that day.''

''Except that Luke was the one who took me home, since I didn't have any.'' Sean spoke quietly, watching the byplay between the couple across from him.

Luke made a rude noise. ''I wouldn't have made it home if he hadn't been my crutch. You don't know how damn big Kansas can be. To this day I don't know how we did it.''

''If I remember correctly, on horseback. Luke had one of the biggest, meanest roans I'd ever seen in my life. Or ever want to see. I swear, there were times when I would have killed and eaten that nag if there had been any other way of transporting that great clodhopper. Whatever became of that nag?''

''You stole it when my sister told you that you would never amount to anything, and you decided to go off and make your fortune. I remember something about lost gold mines and California in there, but you were pretty drunk at the time.''

''I had to have been if that's what I stole. Why didn't you stop me?'' Sean shook his head at this memory of his youthful foolishness.

''You were old enough to know what you wanted by then and I had my mind on other things. But that's a tale for another day.'' Luke caught Maria's hand and tugged on it. ''Time to turn in for the day if we want to make a start while it's still cool. If we time it right, I have a place in mind to stop where we can find a good watering hole.''

''Bigger than a mud puddle?'' Maria turned a mock suspicious gaze on him. The firelight gave Luke's lean features a more rugged look, and she fought the urge to caress his cheek as she had done just a day ago.

''Bigger than a mud puddle,'' he promised.

It would be so simple to lean over and kiss his cheek, but then she would need to go over and kiss Sean's, too. At this minute she loved them both, but there was no point in giving them ideas. Yawning, Maria rose to find her bedroll.

Over the fire, amber eyes met Irish ones in a challenge both men understood. They had shared women together before, but this would not be one of them.

Luke rose to gather up his rifle and take the first shift of guard duty. Indians, wolves, and thieves might roam the night, but it was an internal predator he feared the most.

Recognizing the dual purpose of Luke's position, Sean picked up his bedroll and carefully carried it to the opposite side of the clearing from Maria. He could bide his time as well or better than Luke.

15

The next day the heat soared by mid-afternoon to unusual proportions for early May. Mesquite offered little respite from the sun, and any hint of a tree provided excuse to rest the animals. Both men's shirts were soaked with perspiration, and even Maria's crisp linen wilted long before they found their camping spot for the evening.

When they rode down into the arroyo and found a green valley shaded in cottonwood, a trickling stream that wound through thickets of trees and broadened into a pond behind a beaver dam, Maria felt as if they had discovered heaven. Caught between the eroded bluffs towering above them, the heat still lingered here, but the shade and the water made it bearable.

Luke swung her down from the horse, and her hat slid back, the strap catching on her chin and preventing it from falling off. Through her damp shirt Luke could feel the firm slimness of her back, and he did not release her willingly. He grinned at the dust smudged across her sun-burnt nose.

Maria frowned at his unwarranted perusal. "And what do you find so amusing?"

"The first time I saw you, you were wearing britches and your father's hat, and I thought you were little more than a lad of fourteen. How could I have been so wrong?"

"That wasn't the first time," Maria reminded him haughtily, pulling away from the hard hands sending forbidden shivers up and down her spine. "And I haven't noticed that you make a habit of being right."

"Heat getting to you?" Luke goaded with a wry quirk of his lips.

Maria didn't mistake the look in Luke's eyes. His gaze burned through to her soul, telling her he felt the tremor she tried to ignore, and that he had no intention of pretending otherwise. She had been a fool to make this journey with a man as dangerous as Luke, but oddly, she trusted him. Unable to cope with these contradictory emotions, Maria backed away.

"No more so than you, Cheyenne Walker." Not noticing the ambiguity of this statement, Maria swung on her heel and headed for Sean and the pack mule he was unloading.

He grinned at the sight of the fire in Maria's eyes and the angry red flush of her cheeks. For as long as Sean had known him, Luke had never made any attempt to charm women, but his effect on the fairer sex had always been the same. The more Luke ignored them, the more determined they became to have him. It did appear, though, as if Luke may have met his match in this one. Maria seemed as determined to avoid Luke as Luke was to demand her attention. The situation was so unusual, Sean couldn't help but watch it develop with great delight.

As Maria angrily began jerking at the ropes carrying their baggage, Sean stayed her hand. "I'll do it. You go test the water first. We could all use a good soaking."

Maria glanced at the perspiration running down Sean's broad cheek and nodded agreement. Without a word she turned to her own mount and unfastened her bedroll. Gathering up one of Carmelita's loose blouses and her boy's denims and carrying her blanket with towel and soap rolled inside, she headed for the beckoning stream. If she could find a place private enough, she meant to wash the garments she wore. It would not do to arrive at a wealthy ranch garbed in sweat-drenched linen.

The hot, sweet scent of cottonwood filled the air as Maria shook out her blanket on a sandy inlet protected by the outcropping of the arroyo walls. The trees leaned well out over the water, providing the privacy of their foliage in a lacy curtain.

Maria stripped off her riding boots and stockings and, holding up her skirts, wandered out into the cold, running stream with a grateful sigh. Looking up at the clear brilliance of the blue sky through the lace of leaves and feeling a soft breeze lift the loose hair at the back of her neck, Maria felt contentment seep through her for the first time in months.

Making no attempt to discover the reason for this elusive happiness after so many months of bitter sorrow, Maria waded deeper into the water. She wanted to dive in and soak herself all over, float upon the pond's rippling surface, and forget the world outside existed. The thought was more tempting than the embarrassment of being discovered, and with a mischievous smile Maria waded back to shore to take off her clothes and grab the bar of soap.

Kneeling beside the stream and attempting to shave in the water's rippling reflection, Luke heard the sound of Maria's splash in the pond downstream. He had no doubt that it was Maria; he knew exactly where she had disappeared into the trees, and could well imagine what she was doing. Were he in the deep end of the stream, he would be doing the same thing right now.

Doing his best not to contemplate the thought of Maria's long black hair floating around her ivory bare shoulders and arms, Luke scraped the straight edge over two days' growth of beard. Knowing Maria, she had probably even discarded her camisole and whatever else she wore under her skirts. The picture of what she would look like rising completely naked from the water caused Luke to nick his jaw, and he cursed fluently to himself.

Had he been a religious man, he would swear women were the work of the devil. A woman had driven him from his home to follow this wandering life, and it was a woman who had put the price on his head that prevented him from returning. Why in hell did he think he'd find satisfaction in a little temptress who was no better nor worse than the first two?

Luke finished shaving and lathered himself thoroughly in the stream's cool water before lying back against an outcropping of rock to dry out. With the ease of many long years of practice, his mind drifted back to another such sultry day, but the grass had been greener, the air sweeter with the scent of roses. Summer had not yet come and his mother's gardens had been ripe with intoxicating blooms, or so it had seemed at the time.

He had been mindlessly, thoroughly smitten by love as only a young man of one and twenty can be. He had come back from the war no longer a youth, but a man starved for the peace and comfort of his own home. As luck would have it, the first person he had met as he and Sean staggered across the ranch boundaries was a girl he had known all his life. Never had she seemed more beautiful than that day when she appeared from the orchard, her golden hair streaming carelessly down a back as slender and graceful as any willow. She had rushed to bring them water and hugged Luke with tears in her eyes, and he hadn't known a minute's peace since that day.

Oh, for the few years after he had been happy making plans; he had to grant her that. He had been young and their courting had gone slowly. He was content thinking she was his alone, that as soon as he established himself they would be wed and live happily ever after, just like in the penny novels. But that was before he had learned the true nature of women.

The evening he had come upon her in the garden, her gown down about her waist while she lay in the arms of another man, all illusion had flown. It did not take much imagination to know what had just taken place, what had been done a hundred times before in this place, what had probably been done that very first day he had come upon her after the war. Disgust and revulsion and a furious bitterness had risen up in Luke like a sickness for which there was no cure, and no amount of explanation healed the pain.

Time had taken away the sharp edges, but the memory still turned Luke's stomach, and his lean face tightened into hard planes as he listened to the sound of Maria's splashing only a few short feet away. From the way she behaved with Manuel, she probably had already given her virtue to another man. What mattered it if he sampled some of what she had to offer before he left her to her ambitious fiancé?

The knowledge that she responded to his touch as hungrily as he did to hers cemented Luke's decision. Stripping off his denims, he slid from the rock into the water.

Rinsing the soap from her hair, Maria had no warning of his approach until Luke's muscular arm seized her bare waist, raising her partially from the water. She only had time to register the shock of his hard torso pressed against her nakedness before his mouth swept down to plunder hers.

The shock of this sudden attack worked in Luke's favor. The treachery of her own body worked against Maria. Before she had recovered enough sense to fight him off, her body was on fire with the heat of his hands, the friction of his rough skin against hers, and she had no strength to put up more than a token resistance. As Luke's lips moved persuasively over hers, even that resistance died, and Maria's arms slid over his muscular shoulders to cling desperately to his back and neck. Clothed only in water, their bodies molded and adhered to one another.

Maria shivered as her lips parted and his tongue seared a path to her soul. With growing awareness she felt his hand slide across her slippery skin to caress the fullness of her breast, and it wasn't just terror that found a place to spread in the center of her belly. An aching need opened within her, a need that could destroy her world, as she knew it.

Still she didn't fight. As Luke's fingers found the straining tip of her breast and caressed it into a ring of fire to join the conflagration rapidly spreading throughout her body, Maria's hands fled desperately up and down Luke's broad back, grasping for some hold, for something to cling on. He gave her nothing, forcing her to dig her fingers into his flesh as the water lapped around them. Her feet didn't touch the ground, and she felt helplessly adrift in a whirlpool of sensation.

"Maria, *mi cariña, querida.*" These and other words whispered through her senses, as if no tongue had uttered them, yet they lingered there, caressing her in the same manner as Luke's hands.

His kisses traced the drops of water along her cheek, nibbled at her ear, bit into the flesh of her throat, making her tremble so violently Luke had to hold her closer. One strong hand cupped her buttocks, and Maria nearly cried out her panic as she felt the heat of him branding her thigh.

With this first forewarning of what would come, Maria finally recovered enough sense to struggle for freedom from the lethargy Luke's kisses induced in her. Her whole body yearned for the closeness he offered, melted at the rough texture of his skin against hers, but the invasion to come gave the courage to rebel.

Her fists knotted against the damp mat of hair on Luke's chest, shoving frantically to be free of the strong embrace imprisoning her. Luke gave scant notice to the pressure. Lifting her higher in his arms, he bent his head to sample the sweetness of her breasts, and this time Maria did cry out. The sensation sweeping through her was like a fire out of control, and she had no more power to turn him away than flames did to the wind.

When the moment came, the pressure of Luke's hand guided her, and Maria's legs parted of their own accord, wrapping around his hips as the water lapped against them. She felt the sensation of water first, caressing this intimate place that now burned for something she did not understand. Then a hardness moved between her thighs, rubbing against her vulnerability until she could no longer bear the flames leaping inside her.

Sensing her surrender, Luke pressed his advantage, and Maria cried out in surprise at the pain of his thrust into this narrow passage. Luke stopped immediately, but the damage was done.

He stared down at the dark head bent against his shoulder, courageously gulping back sobs, and something within him shattered. Never before had he been given so precious and fragile a burden to hold and to care for, and he scarcely knew how to behave. That he had already damaged her trust, he knew, and it was this that destroyed all his earlier confidence. Not stopping to examine his reaction to her innocence, Luke strode purposefully out of the water, carrying her slight weight carefully within his embrace.

Laying Maria on the blanket, Luke stretched beside her, giving her time to readjust to the feel of his body against hers. His kisses began again, more gently this time, not roughly hungry but caressing, reawakening the passion she harbored just below the surface of her brittle composure.

Too far gone now to protest, Maria drank in the drug of Luke's caresses as if starved. Her body responded instantly, turning to his for the closeness of earlier. The sun dried the water on their skins, but the flames leaping within her had a different effect. As Luke's hand claimed the dark triangle between her legs, she grew moist with desire and groaned with a mixture of desperation and impatience as his fingers captured and invaded this most intimate stronghold, her hips rising eagerly to his touch.

Unable to restrain himself any longer, Luke gently pushed Maria back against the blanket. His long body moved over her, and before she could fight him again, he entered her.

The pain seemed less this time, and Maria arched urgently for the fullness he offered, wanting an end to the aching emptiness he had created. Luke's gentle thrusts caused another kind of ache, but not so great as the one consuming her, and she fell eagerly into his rhythm, giving herself up to his possession, surrendering to the flames.

The conflagration leapt to a ball of fire as Luke's body suddenly jerked and erupted within hers. The explosion triggered multiple tremors through her middle, and Maria wept and clung to Luke as her body became a part of his, one flesh with no control beyond his. She had never felt so helpless as the flames of desire consumed her, making ashes of the innocent she once had been.

Wishing he had done everything differently, Luke gathered her in his arms and rolled over to release her trembling body from his heavy weight. Maria buried her head against his shoulder, refusing to look at him. Staring up into the cloudless sky, Luke stroked her tender flesh, refusing to think in the same manner as Maria refused to acknowledge him. His body was momentarily at peace, but his mind was in turmoil.

Finally Maria lifted herself up, steadying herself with one hand against Luke's shoulder as she glared down at him, oblivious to her nakedness.

"Why?" she demanded.

Luke's gaze swept assessingly over the soft, ivory curves exposed to his view. Her skin was not the milky white of a Southern belle, but a creamy hue that blended well with the deeper tan of her arms and throat. Her breasts were much fuller than expected for so slender a frame, and when his hand rose to caress the rich pink of her nipple, the tip grew erect instantly beneath his touch.

He smiled lazily, feeling his own body respond in a similar fashion. "Why? Why does the sun rise in the East? Why do the stars shine in the sky? Because that is the way it is between us, *querida.*"

Her emerald eyes flashed furiously. That hadn't been what she wanted to hear, and Maria shoved away from him, reaching for the old clothes she had laid out before bathing. "You have taken the one thing of value I had left to give, and you give me poetry in return." She jerked on the boy's britches and reached for the blouse.

Luke made no attempt to stop her. "I could not know you were a virgin, Maria, not after what I watched with you and Manuel."

One arm in and the other out, Maria stared at him

incredulously. "And would you have believed me if I had told you, providing such a topic ever came up in conversation?"

Luke pushed up on one elbow and openly admired the full curve of her exposed breast before she hurriedly covered it. Lifting his gaze to meet hers he replied as honestly as he was able. "I am not accustomed to women who speak the truth."

"You are not accustomed to *hearing* women who speak the truth." So furious she could not bear the pain of his gaze upon her, Maria leapt up without her boots and left him lying there.

She walked away, but the image of Luke's broad-shouldered, sun-browned body lying against her blanket did not fade, nor did the ache of his possession. Maria could still feel the imprint of his skin, the rawness of her newly opened body, and tears rimmed her eyes at the disaster she had made of her life.

No one had told her that one did not choose to commit the sins of the flesh. They simply happened.

16

When Luke returned to the camp, Maria was bravely chatting with Sean, smiling as if nothing had happened. Sean appeared totally enraptured with her charms, particularly the molded fit of her tight denims, and Luke growled under his breath.

Deliberately he came up behind Maria and wrapped his hand possessively in the luxuriant fall of silken hair she had not had time to braid. When she looked up, startled, he bent to place a less-than-brotherly kiss upon her lips. Before she could react, he released her and turned to place her forgotten bedroll on the ground beside his.

Sean immediately got the message. Although his gaze rested speculatively on the angry flush of Maria's cheeks, he no longer teased her with his eyes, and his hand slid away from hers.

Maria was too angry to notice his withdrawal. If Luke thought he could repeat this afternoon's performance, he would find a bullet between his eyes. He had ruined her innocence, but he would not make a whore of her. She understood now where his kisses led, and she would never give him that chance again.

Apparently blithely unaware of her plans for his demise, Luke tended to their horses. As she stirred the biscuit dough and dropped the balls of moistened flour into the hot grease of the frying pan, Maria could not keep her gaze from wandering in Luke's direction. He had not bothered to fasten his shirt, and it lay open nearly to the waist, exposing curls spreading over the muscular planes of his chest her fingers ached to touch.

Despising herself for the drift of her thoughts, Maria

jerked her attention back to the fire, but as the biscuits cooked, her gaze continued to wander. Luke moved with the fluid grace of a mountain lion, and she had difficulty avoiding picturing those narrow hips and muscular thighs without the civilization of clothes. She knew now what he concealed beneath the decency of trousers and work shirt, and somehow the clothing seemed superfluous.

A knot tightened in her stomach as she remembered what it had felt like when he held her like that. How could she have allowed him to do what he had done? Embarrassment flooded her cheeks with this clearer realization of what had happened in the unreasoning heat of passion. Luke had done nothing she had not wanted him to do. The horror of that thought worried her, gnawing at her self-confidence. She had never thought of herself as promiscuous or a wanton sinner. Words like that were reserved for women like Consuela. Maria had always fought off any attempts on her virtue. Even Manuel had never gone further than touching her breast, and she had not even wanted him to do that. So why, then, had she allowed this stranger, this man she did not really know, to possess her as a husband would a wife?

There was no logic in it. Unaccustomed to examining her feelings so intently, Maria lacked the ability to reach any conclusion in the matter. Perhaps the sun had affected her brain. That was as good an answer as any.

But it did not explain why she did not rise up in protest later that night when Luke unrolled his bedroll next to hers and lay down upon it without a word. The camp fire provided a small glow in the heavy darkness, but Maria had sought the shadows outside the fire's light when she settled down to sleep. She heard Sean pick up his rifle and retreat to the perimeter of the clearing. And she knew when Luke moved to throw himself down beside her. She could have escaped had she moved faster, but she had not.

Now, when it was too late, Maria threw back her blankets to leave, but anticipating this action, Luke rolled over and wrapped his arm around her waist, pulling her into the curve of his body.

"Don't, Luke." Maria uttered the protest weakly, despising her lack of conviction. She struggled to remove herself from his imprisoning embrace, but she already knew the futility of that fight.

"It's too late now, Maria." Luke pulled the blankets over both of them, absorbing the welcome sensation of her heat against him. His palm captured the slender curve of her waist, and he heartily wished the harsh fabric of her Levis to Hades.

"Now I am a fallen woman, I have no right to deny you?" Maria whispered bitterly, holding herself stiff against the temptation of his strong embrace.

"No, *querida.*" Luke knew the qualms of guilt even as his body longed to possess the gentle softness enclosed in his arms. "You may deny me if you wish. It is too late to pretend you do not want this as I do, though. Lie still, Maria. I will only hold you."

Conscious of Sean only a few short yards away, Maria could not relax. Luke's words offered no comfort; they came too close to the truth. The heat of his hand through her thin shirt stirred unwanted hungers, and she moved restlessly in his hold.

"Leave me be, Luke," she pleaded. "Do not do this to me." She did not try to explain what he should not do. The tension between them held them bound.

Luke's hand moved longingly from her waist to caress her hip. He had never denied himself before, but conscious of the injury he had already done her, he could not demand more. Not now. Not yet.

Silently he lifted his hand to cup her cheek, turning her face so he could discern the pale outlines through the tangle of midnight tresses. Maria leaned back slightly to gaze up at him with questioning eyes.

"I'm not sorry it happened, Maria, but I'll apologize for not making it better for you. I promise, the next time I will do nothing without your consent."

The next time! The conceited arrogance of the man! Maria turned to scratch his eyes out, but Luke caught her in this more convenient position, pinning her shoulders against the blanket. Before she could resist, he leaned over and kissed her lips gently, without any of the hungry demand of earlier.

It took only that single tender kiss to extinguish her ire. She tasted the warm hardness of his mouth against hers, and all was lost. With tears in her eyes Maria met his kiss with one of her own, and when the fire of desire rekindled, she reluctantly accepted his decision to move away. Damn his murdering, thieving heart, but he was right. She wanted him more than she had ever wanted anything or anyone in her life. He had made a fool of her, but she could not break away. When he lay down beside her and covered her with his arm, she turned closer to his warmth and closed her eyes, secure in the circle of his embrace.

Maria woke when Luke rose to take his turn at standing guard, and she hastily pulled the blankets to cover the places where he had warmed her. Not willing to think about the import of her behavior, she quickly returned to sleep, refusing to acknowledge the empty place beside her.

Maria woke to the aroma of hot coffee. Turning on her side, she pried one eye open to observe Luke squatting by the camp fire, sipping from a mug of the steaming brew. He had slicked back his unruly hair, but already one strand had fallen down across his wide brow. Sunlight glinted along the golden-brown sideburns framing his square jaw, and the sensuous line of his lips softened as he spied her wakefulness. With wonder she read the welcome in his previously cold eyes, and her heart did funny flip-flops at his penetrating stare.

Heavy hair streaming in black tangles down her arms and back, her gathered blouse sliding off one golden shoulder, Maria appeared more than ever a gypsy, and Luke smiled. Perhaps her patrician nose and high cheekbones betrayed her noble ancestry, but her passion was as wanton as any man could desire.

Seeing the path of his thoughts, Maria flushed and hastily rose, striding away from the fire and into the woods. By the time she returned, Sean had joined Luke

at the fire, and she quickly rummaged through her belongings for a brush. She must look a fright.

Watching her struggling to pull the bristles through
the thick length of tousled hair, Luke gestured for Maria to join them. Puzzled, Maria shook her head in
refusal, but when he started to rise and come after her,
she hastily advanced into the clearing.

Sean watched in amazement as Luke took the brush
from Maria's hand and began to ply it through the
tangled silkiness of her hair. Patiently he loosened the
knots, then separated the strands, and began to braid
it.

Maria sat docilely beneath his ministrations, basking in the gentleness of his touch. She had not expected gentleness from a man like Luke, and she was
still nervous of his proximity, but she relaxed as he
skillfully bound her braid into its usual long rope.

They rode out of the arroyo in harmony. Maria knew
she had no right to feel this sense of contentment, but
it had been so long since she had enjoyed the kind of
protective security Luke offered that she did not have
the courage to examine her feelings. She should be
angry, but she was not. She knew she should not allow
Luke to use her as he had, but she also knew she did
not have it in her to resist. She did not know where
this heedless idiocy would lead, but for now she was
content.

The contentment lasted until late that afternoon,
when they reached the evergreen-studded mountainside that marked the boundary of the Dallas ranch.
Maria grew increasingly uneasy as the two men led
the horses deeper into the wilderness far from the
public path, obviously skirting any sign of human hab-
itation.

''Where are we going?'' she demanded as they by-
passed a road that must certainly lead to the main ranch
house.

Luke merely caught her reins and steered her mount
up a steep incline leading away from the fertile valley
below.

When they finally reached a secluded depression between the thrust of rocky walls high above the ranch itself, Luke drew the team to a halt. With a gesture and a few curt words he sent Sean off in the direction to his right. Left with Maria and the pack mule, he gestured toward the protection of the trees surrounding the lip of this clearing.

"Hide the horses in there. Give them some grain to keep them quiet until we can find some water. If it gets late, you can build a small fire between these rocks, but put a blanket over the vent to keep the smoke from rising. We'll be back before nightfall."

Realizing they meant to leave her alone in unknown wilderness, Maria's nervousness increased. "Where are you going?"

"Looking for the dam," Luke responded curtly, with none of his earlier warmth. He rode off, leaving her to fend for herself.

Maria knew how to take care of herself, that part did not bother her. She even understood that Luke gave her credit for being sensible enough to do as told. She knew he was a man who did not willingly work with others and particularly not with women, but still she would prefer to know what was going on. What could they possibly do when they found a dam?

Gazing at the various satchels strapped to the back of the mule, Maria had a chilling premonition of what they had in mind. Sean had assigned himself the task of packing and unpacking their supplies. She had no idea what was in half of those bundles, and she suddenly had no desire to know. She would do as told.

Once the horses were situated and firewood gathered, Maria began to explore. It seemed amazing how some of these trees could grow out of sheer rock, but they held firm when she used them to pull herself up to the next ledge.

The sun was going down by the time she found the cave. It opened up into a fairly level room with a sandy floor not far above the place where she had hitched the horses. The opening itself was negligible, but bending low, Maria could squeeze through it with ease. Once inside, she decided there would easily be room for three people.

With diligence she climbed up and down the rocky ledge carrying firewood and bedrolls. If they were to hide their presence from the ranch inhabitants, it would be much easier done inside a cave. The horses provided a problem, but Luke and Sean could solve that. She felt much safer hidden behind a wall of rock.

Worn out by her exertions, Maria spread her blanket in the coolness of the cave's interior and lay down to catch a brief nap. She was asleep within minutes.

When Luke returned a short while later to the place they had left Maria, he admired the expertise with which she had hobbled the horses well out of sight. He found the camp fire she had laid in the rocky crevasse, but he found no trace of Maria. Not panicking at first, he began to explore the lower ledges for signs of the path she might have taken. He did not expect Sean back until dark, which meant he had a few hours to enjoy the pleasures of Maria's company.

Thinking of how he would remove her clothing and take the little witch more slowly this time, introducing her to the pleasures he had yet to show her, Luke did not realize the direction of the path he took for some time. When he finally understood he was walking in circles with no sign of Maria anywhere, Luke's heart came to a skidding halt before returning to a furious beat. Where in hell was she?

He stood back and surveyed the rocky ledge climbing above him. If she had fallen from that, surely he would see her crumpled body lying in the rocky debris below. That thought caused irrational panic, and Luke began searching for other such dangerous ridges where he might not see her if she had fallen.

It was some minutes before he recognized the hollowness growing with leaps and bounds inside him. He knew that emptiness from another time, another place. He had had his heart ripped from his chest before, and the loss had made him just a shell with nothing left inside. Why did the disappearance of the little witch give him this same feeling, as if someone twisted a knife in his gut prior to disemboweling him? He had thought there was nothing left to lose, yet the pain was every bit as real as the first time. More so perhaps, because he was older and the emotions were buried deeper.

It made no sense. He had a responsibility to bring Maria home intact, or almost intact, but if she had been damn fool enough to fall off a mountainside, he could not be responsible. Yet the thought of finding her broken body at the bottom of one of these precipices filled him with irrational terror. He could not lose her like that. It would be too damn unfair.

Trying to reason logically, Luke methodically retraced every step he had taken. He had heard no screams; she had to be safe. The bitch had probably followed Sean, and they were off in the bushes laughing somewhere. Or she had decided to set off on her own to look for the dam. Or to look for Dallas. Anything but the grim possibility looming before his mind's eye. She could not be dead.

By the time he located the cave, Luke was in a fury. Logic had fled with his normal calm, and he acted out of pure mindless emotion. Maria was his and he would find her. What he would do when he found her did not enter into his thought processes. The cave opening sent a sharp ray of hope piercing through him.

Pulling his gun, he entered cautiously. The light had slid deeper into the valley, and he could see little once past the narrow aperture.

The sound of Luke's curse as he bumped his shoulder against the rocky wall brought Maria instantly into wakefulness. At the sight of a towering male figure blocking the daylight of the opening, she started to scream.

Luke fell down beside her and covered her mouth with his hand. Unbalanced by his sudden move, they fell backward against Maria's bedding. By this time Maria had recognized him, and she relaxed, shaking away his hand.

"What is wrong with you? You leap on me like a crazed panther and expect me to keep quiet?" Indignantly Maria attempted to pull away from his hold, but Luke's arm held her like a steel trap.

"Me? You ask what is wrong with me? You disappear in this godforsaken wilderness and you wonder why I grab you? I'd like to throttle you, among other things."

She did not need to imagine what those other things might be. Luke made that all too plainly clear as he rolled her back against the bedroll, and his lips quickly located hers in the gloom of this secluded cavern. The knowledge that he had actually been worried about her did not keep her from fighting him, though it did no good. Even as she tried to push him away, joy rose rapidly inside her with the excitement of his touch. In mindless seconds her hands were no longer pushing but circling his shoulders.

The intoxicating sensation of his mouth hot and hungry across hers did not rob her of all sanity, however. When Luke's hand rose to claim her breast, she moved uneasily beneath his touch, resisting her need for this caress by turning from his kiss.

Instantly he loosened his grip, and Maria could feel his worried gaze upon her. "I am sorry, *mi cariña*. I did not mean to hurt you. Shall I stop?"

Perversely, tears leapt to Maria's eyes at this return of his concern. She didn't want him to stop. She wanted it to go on forever and ever, but she knew it wouldn't, and therein lay the rub. This wasn't love. This was madness. Somehow, against her will, against her desire, she must extricate herself.

"We cannot go on, Luke. Let me go. I am betrothed to another. This cannot be right. I beg of you, Luke, do not do this anymore."

Luke heard the tears in her voice and knew that she meant it. He doubted that Manuel would have her now, but he had left her no alternative but to hope Manuel would marry her in exchange for the land. He had brought her to this, and there was enough of the gentleman left in Luke to know what he must do.

Propping himself on one elbow, wishing there were more light to see the flashing brilliance of her eyes,

Luke offered, "If Manuel will not take you back, I will marry you, *querida*. You do not need to worry on that account, Maria."

Luke was unprepared for the violence of her reaction. She knocked him backward in her haste to get away. The fury and bitterness in her voice struck him in the same manner as a physical blow.

"Marry you! How very generous." The words dripped sarcasm as Maria pulled her shirt back in place. "My land must be more valuable than I thought. Manuel will beat me black and blue, but he will marry me, have no doubt of that. The land is more precious than I am, it seems. At least with Manuel I will be able to hold my head up when I go to town. To be the wife of a gunfighter with a price on his head offers no great temptation."

Every word cut like a knife, but she spoke the truth as she knew it. Luke wanted to smack her and tell her not to be a fool, but what was the point? Instead his thoughts centered on the only hook she dangled before him.

"Manuel beats you?" His words were harsh and angry, hiding his inner turmoil as he sat up.

"He does not dare beat me now, but he will when he learns I am no longer a virgin, and rightly so. I am promised to him, and I have broken our pledge. What would you have him do? You had best be gone before he finds out, for you he will kill."

"You sound like Consuela. No man has the right to beat you, not when he possesses the greater strength."

Maria stared at Luke's shadowy form through the gloom with amazement. "You would not beat me if you discovered I had been with another man?"

"I might leave you. I might kill the other man. I might be tempted to paddle the hell out of you, but no, I would not beat you. There is no challenge in kicking dogs or stealing candy from babes. You are a fool to marry a man who would beat you."

"Where is the difference between beating and paddling?" Maria asked scornfully. "Manuel's father beats *Doña* Vasquero regularly. The whole town knows of it.''

She stalked out, leaving Luke to contemplate the perversity of the female mind. He would like nothing more than to turn her over his knee and paddle some sense into her.

The question remained, did he want to take up the challenge and accept the results?

17

The angry tension simmering between Luke and Maria
caught Sean's notice the moment he walked back into
camp. Maria's disheveled hair and hastily buttoned
shirt gave evidence of how they had spent their time,
so he could not fathom the reason for the coldness that
greeted him. Whatever the reason, it would have to
end or foil all their plans.

"Did you find it?" Sean demanded as soon as Luke
stopped hacking a rabbit he obviously meant for their
supper.

"Yes." The one-word reply was forced out between
clenched teeth.

"There's daylight left. Is it far? Can we go over it
now?"

Not bothering to look at Maria, Luke dumped the
rabbit carcass in a pot of boiling water and headed for
his horse. "Let's go."

Maria hid her angry tears as they rode away without
a word to her. She had no right to expect anything
else. She had behaved like a whore. She would be
treated as one. He had even compared her to Consuela. She ought to kill him, but in all conscience she
could not. The fault was hers. No lady would have
done what she had done.

The manner in which Luke had offhandedly offered
to marry her if no one else would had revealed her
shame. Even a hired gun did not have respect enough
for her to offer marriage in atonement for taking her
virginity, except as an afterthought. She had almost
convinced herself that Luke cared, that what they
shared was in some way special, but she was only

fooling herself. What Luke wanted from her was the same as what he wanted from Consuela. The only difference appeared to be the land that went with her. For that he would offer marriage.

Cursing violently to herself, Maria threw the rest of the ingredients into the pot. If anyone smelled the rabbit cooking, they would be discovered, but that apparently didn't seem to matter anymore now that they had found the dam. Let them blow it up, and Luke with it. She just wanted her money and out of here. She would set the wedding date with Manuel as soon as they were home. If he would not have her, she would sell the ranch and go to California. To hell with men.

Maria's anger had not cooled by the time the men returned. When they continued arguing quietly between themselves as if she were not there, her temper rose another degree. And when they sat down before the fire with their empty bowls and waited for her to serve them, she exploded.

"Is that why you brought me along? To keep you company in bed and wait on you at meals? If I am not to know what is going on, why don't you send me to warm Sean's bed while you eat? That only seems fair."

She dumped a ladle full of stew over first one bowl and then the other, spilling the steaming broth more on the men than in the bowls.

Sean jerked his hand away as much in surprise at her words as in pain from the hot stew. He threw a worried glance to Luke, whose impassive expression revealed no hint of his thoughts. Luke set aside his bowl and caught Maria's wrist, jerking her to her knees beside him.

"If you're asking to be beat, I'll beat you, but if you risk this operation in a childish tantrum, I'll hand you over to the men whose lives you will destroy by allowing this dam to continue. They will not be particularly pleased and their wrath will not be amusing. Do you understand me?"

Pain exploded through her wrist as Luke twisted and tightened his grip to hold her in place, but the pain caused by the icy look in his eyes caused Maria to squirm more. How could she have thought him a gentle man? She must have been mad.

"You're hurting me." Refusing to acknowledge his threats or give him the satisfaction of hearing her beg, Maria haughtily stated the obvious.

"Luke, let her go." Sean did not move from his seat, but the concern in his voice had the same effect as if he had physically intervened.

Luke released Maria's arm and stood up, wiping his soaked pants in disgust. "There's no point in hanging around here. Let's ride down tonight. The sooner we get this over, the better it will be for all of us."

A knot tightened in Maria's stomach as she realized what that meant. Once they reached the ranch she would have to behave as a demure wife and share his bed as expected, without Sean's protection. Luke's revenge would be swift and sure, and every muscle in her body contracted with fear. This afternoon had taught her how easily he could inflict his violence on her. It would be much worse should she give him cause.

But they were already saddling up the horses and preparing to leave. She had no choice except to carry out the plan as agreed. It was too late to run. Slowly Maria rose and began unpacking her wrinkled but clean linen blouse and riding skirt. She could not arrive wearing denims.

She held her chin high as she stepped from the protection of the bushes in her ladylike riding outfit, aware that both men watched her with impatience. She prayed her embarrassment did not show as Sean's speculative gaze swept over her and Luke mounted his horse without a word. She would rip his heart out one of these days, but for now she located a large rock and climbed up on her own horse without assistance.

They rode into the valley in silence. Shadows lengthened and made the path more treacherous, but as they reached the main road, the going was easier. They entered the ranch gates as the western sky turned a dull red and the first star appeared far above the setting sun.

Dallas greeted them with effusive warmth, shaking

hands all around and extending his generous hospitality. Maria found it hard to believe that this gray-bearded gentleman could allow the entire valley to dry out to feed his own greed, but the evidence of his massive wealth was everywhere.

Cool flagstone floors led through cavernous rooms lit by brilliant chandeliers at night and banks of windows during the day. Enormous paintings covered the walls, and glass cabinets tempted the eye with treasures too many to behold in passing. Maria had never seen a museum, but she very much felt as if she had entered one as they strolled through the corridors to the rooms Dallas assigned them.

With a broad wink to Luke, he opened the door on a chamber dominated by the curtain-draped tester bed in the center. "These accommodations might be a little more to the lady's liking than the trail you've just come up, don't you agree?"

With her elbow firmly caught in Luke's grip, Maria could only gulp and hide her dismay at the thought of sharing that single bed for untold nights with the notorious Cheyenne Walker. She felt the tension in his arm and knew he shared the same thought. Maybe he would hurry and blow up the dam so they could get out of here. She didn't dare meet his gaze as she exclaimed politely over the room's beauties.

Beneath the benign gaze of his host, Luke hugged his "wife's" shoulders at her evident pleasure in these accommodations. "You ought to be comfortable here, honey," he drawled without a hint of irony. "You won't even miss me if I bunk down elsewhere."

Before Maria could follow her startled look with a question, Luke turned to his surprised host in explanation. "My wife has just informed me that she's in the family way already. She's plumb wore out and needs her rest, and you know how it is . . ." He shrugged laconically, then sent Maria's petite form an admiring look. "It's kind of hard to keep away when temptation is right at hand."

Maria blushed to the tips of her ears, and Sean's chuckle behind them made her cheeks burn even hotter. When she got Luke alone, she would kick him where it hurts. In a family way, indeed! Conceited, pompous jackass of a male, she would make him pay for this.

The men laughed, making barely disguised lewd comments to each other as they left her alone to rest while they sought other rooms and the card table. Maria fought back tears of rage as she closed the door after them, a rage against herself as much as the men.

She should not have to endure it much longer. Soon they would be back in San Pedro, and then everyone could go their own way. If Luke insisted on helping her find her father's murderer, he could do it from town. She would ask Manuel to help her, as she should have from the first. Pride was something she had precious little of anymore. She would learn to ask for help.

Using Luke's excuse, Maria claimed herself too exhausted to go in for dinner and dined from a tray in her room. Let them tell dirty jokes and play poker into the night. She kept her bargain by playing the dutiful wife. No proper lady would have joined the men in her "condition."

She slept restlessly between the linen sheets that night. The bed offered more comforts than home, but she could not help feeling lonelier than she had ever been in her life. It would not do to ponder that thought for long, and eventually Maria slept, only to dream restless dreams.

She felt fear, a fear so overpowering as to paralyze her with indecision. She did not know whether to run forward or back, while all around an orange glow hypnotized her, filling her with a terror she could not understand. She whimpered into her pillow, striving to escape this paralysis, uncertain where safety lay, wanting to scream but unable to utter a sound.

Unable to stay away, Luke hesitated with his hand on the latch. He would just be certain she needed nothing. Opening the door, he heard her whimpers, and an icy breeze brushed his heart. Not knowing the cause of these terrified sounds, he crept across the room and sat down on the bed beside the huddled form beneath the covers. She seemed sound asleep, but her panicky movements spoke of unknown terrors. Praying he was not the cause of her nightmares, Luke pulled back the sheets and lifted her slender body into his arms, trying to offer what comfort he could.

Maria's eyelids fluttered and opened briefly at this contact with his strong hold. Discovering the dark concern of amber eyes peering through the clouds of sleep and recognizing the protective strength of Luke's arms, the nightmare subsided, and murmuring his name, she smiled sleepily and closed her eyes again. Luke brushed a kiss across her forehead, and within minutes she returned to peaceful sleep. Luke propped himself against the headboard and gathered her nearly weightless form closer against his chest. Her dark head resting against his shoulder and her breasts pressed against his chest, she made a soft, rose-scented bundle in his arms, and the feelings that stirred in him were not entirely lust. Closing his eyes to shut out such thoughts, Luke leaned his head back, and soon he, too, was fast asleep.

Maria woke abruptly to the bright light of day and glanced around her empty bed in momentary bewilderment. Remembering where she was, she fought to recover an elusive memory from her sleep. She had thought Luke was here, but that was foolish. He had a room of his own and had probably not even gone to it until dawn. She must have been dreaming.

Dressing with the aid of a maid in the new rose-striped gown, Maria allowed her hair to be carefully wrapped and pinned into a graceful chignon. Prepared for whatever would happen, she wandered into the corridor leading to the main rooms of the house.

She had no difficulty in finding the dining room. The echoing sound of deep male voices drew her forward, and the men glanced up with pleasure as she drifted into the room.

"Ahhh, the little mother! I hope you are feeling better this morning?" Dallas inquired enthusiastically, pulling out a chair beside his own at the table.

In truth, she was starved, and she stared at the heaping platters of eggs and biscuits and ham with pleasure until her eyes lifted to Luke's hooded ones. Vaguely she remembered expectant mothers weren't supposed to be inclined toward food in the morning, but defiantly she accepted the platter Dallas passed to her.

"I am quite fine, thank you. Did the cards go well for you last night?"

"Excellent, excellent," Dallas chuckled, setting his chubby body back in the chair and observing his domain with satisfaction. "Particularly after your husband started worrying about you and couldn't concentrate for looking at his watch." He gave a broad wink to Luke's impassive expression. "Since he didn't come back after going to check on you, I assumed you were feeling better."

Sean chuckled and sipped his coffee, enjoying this chafing at Luke's expense. Few people dared to antagonize Luke anymore, but Dallas thought him just another young pup with a new bride. It did his heart good to see the arrogant gunfighter in him reduced to the level of other mere mortals.

Maria glanced quickly at Luke, then looked away with a puzzled frown. So she had not dreamed his presence. Why had he come to her in the middle of the night instead of playing cards with his friends? She did not understand, but remembering the fear of her nightmare, she was grateful.

Unable to express her thanks out loud, she attempted a more subtle method by drawing Dallas out. "You have such a lovely place here, sir. Will there be time to show us around a little? I know Luke is in a hurry to get me home, but you promised to show us your horses."

She felt rather than saw the slight relaxation in Luke's stance as she turned her full attention to the older man. She was doing her job as required, even better, because there would be less suspicion attached to her questioning than to Luke's or Sean's. They listened closely to Dallas's replies to her chattering questions and occasionally directed the conversation with an idle remark of their own.

Since they had not deigned to tell her their plans, Maria had to infer them from the direction their remarks took and her little knowledge of their intention. When she hit upon the topic of water, she knew she had found the mark. Luke reached over to hand her a plate of strawberries.

Accepting the tribute, Maria continued the idle chatter. "Do you like fishing, Mr. Dallas? Do you know, I met my husband while fishing. He promised to show me how to catch big ones, but once he got me out in the boat, he seemed to lose interest in catching fish. I would love to try again someday."

"Well, I haven't been fishing in a coon's age, Mrs. Walker, but I'd be delighted to take you, if you'd like. We've got a good trout stream out there. Have you ever fished for trout?"

The only fishing Maria had ever done was with a bamboo pole over a half-dry creek bed when she was a child, and she sent Luke a quick glance. He used a knife to casually core a strawberry, seemingly only half paying attention.

"Don't rightly believe she ought to be trout fishing. The current could knock her down. What Maria really wants to do is dabble her toes in a little pond and play at fishing while we do the real work." Luke tossed the core and leaves on his plate and, biting deep into the fruit, looked up to meet Maria's gaze with a glint in his eye.

She felt that look in the pit of her stomach. It was a proprietary look, one that made her feel as if she had been purchased and found admirably useful. She wanted to fling her coffee at him, and at the same time she wanted him to kiss her and tell her she was every bit as good as his gaze said she was.

Dallas took Maria's bowl of strawberries and began to core them for her, giving her a smug look that sent a shiver down her spine. "Well, I guess I can arrange for that, too. I'll have the kitchen prepare a basket for our lunch, and Sean and Luke here can test their luck on the trout while we paddle around the pond, my dear. How does that sound?"

It sounded perfectly dreadful, but in this country the pond could only be behind the dam. Maria gave her host a beatific smile. "An excellent idea, sir. It sounds delightful."

With that matter settled and breakfast ended, they set about touring the stables and the ranch yard before returning to the house to prepare for lunch. Nervously Maria accepted Luke's accompaniment back to her room. As he closed the door behind them, she blithely drifted toward the dressing table, where she had left her hat. She wished she had the one with ribbons. That would look much smarter for a picnic.

"You'll have to change out of that gown and into your riding clothes." Luke stayed near the door, not daring to go closer. He had vowed to leave her alone, to not get involved any further after that fiasco yesterday, but she made it damnably difficult.

Maria wheeled and stared at him in surprise. "Why? My skirt needs cleaning and pressing. This looks much more ladylike."

"You can't ride in that, and we're going to ride like hell in a little while." Luke watched as her eyes grew darker behind their slanted fringe of lashes.

"What are we going to do, Luke? Don't you think you ought to tell me?" Maria's fingernails bit into her palms as she willed him to answer.

"Should anything go wrong, you're better off not knowing. You know too much as it is. That was an excellent performance this morning, my love."

He had murmured Spanish endearments often enough, but this was the first time Luke had ever called her anything resembling "love." Maria searched his face for some clue to his thoughts, but as usual she found none. She would have to accept his words as a compliment and not look for anything more.

"You think we will be going to the dam, then?" She sought for some hint as to how to act.

"Almost certainly. We found no other water holes yesterday. The dam is guarded, but with Dallas beside us, there should be no suspicion when we begin to roam. Just be prepared to move when I tell you, and don't you dare stop to argue."

They meant to do it this afternoon, then, in broad daylight. They must be mad. Maria stared at him in horror, then glanced down at her lovely new gown and the ruby necklace she had brought out.

"I will have to leave my new clothes and everything behind!"

Luke didn't know whether to laugh or wring her neck. They could all be blown to kingdom come in a few hours, and she worried about her dress. If he had his way, he would strip the damned thing away and keep her naked so he could touch her whenever he wanted. Just the thought of that caused a heat to spread through his loins, and Luke cursed his foolishness. He meant to keep his vow; she meant nothing but trouble elsewise.

"I'll get them away somehow. Just get them off and get into your riding clothes. We don't want to keep the man waiting."

"How can I wear that dusty skirt again? He will think I own nothing!" Maria protested this rejection of her lovely day dress. She wanted to go picnicking as ladies do, not as if she were on the trail.

"I'll tell him due to your interesting 'condition,' that none of your other clothes fit," Luke replied dryly.

"You damnable—" His sardonic look set the fuse of her rage, and Maria reached for the contents of the dressing table. With one swoop she took aim with a hairbrush.

Swiftly Luke fled out the door before she could let the brush fly. It slammed against the door as he closed it, and Luke chuckled smugly to himself as he wandered down the hallway. He would have to ask her someday how many children she planned to have, or if she had given that any consideration.

Considering she meant Manuel to be the father of those children, Luke did not linger long over that thought. Smile gone, he set out to check the dangerous contents of the "fishing gear" he meant to take along.

18

Not daring to take her boots off in case Luke suddenly appeared demanding that she ride, Maria tucked her legs beneath her and leaned back against the slender trunk of a tree. Her companion had just filled his mouth with an uncouth amount of tortillas, and she did not have to listen to his veiled suggestions for the moment. She was vaguely aware that his hot gaze fell frequently on the open vee of her collar, but she did not fear the fat rancher. She had her gun in her pocket and figured Luke to be within screaming distance. No, she feared what she could not see.

Luke and Sean had wandered upstream with fishing poles and gear some while ago, and Maria tried not to think about what they were doing. Dallas had made certain they picnicked at a spot well out of sight of the dam, but nothing else could have caused this extraordinary broadening of a mountain stream. Since Sean and Luke had gone in the opposite direction of the dam, Dallas must be feeling pretty secure, but she didn't dare give him time to wonder what her ''husband'' was doing. She reached for a finger sandwich, enticing her companion's gaze with a deeper glimpse beneath her collar as she bent forward.

The first small explosions sounded like little more than shotgun blasts. Dallas jumped nervously and began looking for the armed guard he had sent away earlier. The next sound, however, brought him to his feet without a second look back to Maria. The mighty strain of a dam giving away under tons of pressure echoed through the canyon.

As Dallas rushed downstream without explanations,

Maria wondered if she ought to run after him. There would be no danger on this end of the river. The flood below the dam would be horrendous, though, and her imagination provided vivid pictures of Sean and Luke being swept into torrents of water and carried away.

Uneasily she moved back toward the carriage horses that had brought her here. Luke had packed his fishing gear on Erinmeade, so presumably her mare was with him. If she had to go find him, it would be easier on horseback.

The pungent smell of smoke drifted from somewhere, and Maria glanced back to see if they had left the camp fire burning. Wildfire in this country was disastrous to everyone within miles. But the camp fire was cold; they had never taken time to light it. Her nervousness mounting, she began to unharness the carriage horses, prepared to ride in search of Luke. She couldn't just wait here and do nothing.

The decision was taken from her as Luke and Sean came racing up the mountainside with her horse in tow. Maria ran to meet them and grabbed the reins of her mare, finding a fallen tree to use for a mounting block. The horses swung their heads in wild-eyed terror, and as she mounted, Maria gave another nervous glance over her shoulder in the direction from which they had come. A ribbon of gray smoke appeared above the trees, and a flicker of orange sent a tendril through the dry debris on the riverbank.

''Fire!'' Maria screamed the word as Luke jerked on her reins to persuade her to hurry.

''A fuse got out of hand,'' he shouted as he smacked Erinmeade's rump, sending Maria up the path after Sean.

Maria glanced frantically at the carriage horses prancing nervously in their harness, and she started to turn her mount around and go back. ''The horses!'' she cried in explanation to Luke's bewildered reaction.

''I'll get them! Get out of here!'' He gave Erinmeade another hard smack, and this time the horse leapt eagerly to do his bidding. The air began to fill with the stench of smoke.

Maria galloped after Sean up the rugged mountainside, praying her horse wouldn't stumble at the mad pace he set. From the shouts farther down the hill, she gathered there was pursuit, and whenever she dared, she cast an anxious look backward in search of Luke.

She saw him once, as the carriage horses burst from the trees ahead of the flames, but Sean pursued a treacherous path, and she lost sight of him around a boulder. The terror of the prior night's dream came back to her, but she did not have time to dwell on it. With the fire and Dallas's guards on their heels, she could only keep going forward.

The horses grew lathered at this exhausting pace, but the smell of wildfire filled their nostrils, and their own fear drove them on. As they came around a bend and raced over an open ridge, Maria caught sight of Luke below them. Flames roared across the desert dry landscape, but it was the sight of three men in hot pursuit farther down the trail that sent fear snaking through her veins. They were almost upon Luke, and she had no way of warning him.

She screamed, but only Sean heard her. He swung his mount to grab her reins and force her forward. "He can take care of himself. Come on, I've got to get you out of here."

Maria knew if she had not been along, Sean would have gone back to help Luke. She didn't even need to think about it. There was a rifle tied along with her saddlebags on Erinmeade's saddle. There was a rock slide providing a barrier of boulders down the hillside ahead. If she could hide her horse in the crevasse . . .

Sean gave a shout of fear as Maria swung down from Erinmeade and reached for the rifle. When she didn't respond, he had no choice but to leap down and run after her. Luke would kill him if anything happened to Maria. Tethering the animals and grabbing his own weapon, Sean ran down the rock slide after Maria's fleeting figure.

She ran like a mountain goat, leaping from one treacherous perch to another in an attempt to reach the overhang before Luke's followers. Gunshots came echoing up the mountainside, and Sean ran faster, his heart in his mouth. If anything happened to Luke, the little firebrand would most likely charge into battle. How in hell would he get her out of here alive?

At last she dodged behind a rock and lowered herself to the ground before someone coming up the path could see her. Sean breathed easier until he realized she was now moving like a snake to the edge of the ridge to get a better view of the path. He cursed and ducked behind a boulder to do the same.

The smoke was thicker at this level, the acrid stench filling the nostrils and choking the lungs. The heat of the flames scorched the skin and sent perspiration rolling down the back. Over the loud crackle of snapping limbs came the ominous popping sounds of gunfire. A horse whinnied, and the pounding hoofbeats of a mad race for time beat along the rocky trail below.

Maria held her breath until she found the glint of golden brown hair in a rocky crevasse across the path directly below her. She didn't know how Luke had managed to get his huge stallion into that tiny cranny, but the spot made an excellent ambush. Only, too many pursued them for Luke to do any more than slow them down.

Realizing that Luke's intention was to keep their pursuers from reaching Sean and herself, Maria cursed his arrogance and vowed violently never to let him drag her into one of these escapades again. If they made it out of this alive, she would never go anywhere with these two madmen. Why in hell did they think her so helpless she couldn't protect herself?

Within seconds the horsemen came around the bend in a pack. The dust blended with the smoke to form an effective screen, obscuring their targets, but Maria heard shots ring out and a man's cry, then watched as a horse jerked upward and one man went sprawling.

The rest happened too quickly and with such confusion she only had time to react. Luke's first shots had disabled one of the gunmen but given the other two time to locate his hiding place. To Maria's dismay, a fourth man had come up from behind and now crawled over the rock above Luke's head while Luke tried to get a sight on the others below.

More shots rang out, but Maria could no longer see Luke or the two gunmen on the ground; the rocks and the smoke hid them too well. She could, however, see the man on the rock, and carefully—just as her father had taught her—she lined up the sights of the rifle.

When the man aimed his revolver at a target only he could see, Maria pulled the trigger.

Coming up beside her, Sean whistled as her mark grabbed his arm and he writhed in agony. Luke had been right. The lady could shoot, and better than most men. What she couldn't do, however, was keep her pretty head down while she searched for Luke. Two shots whistled over their heads now that their location had been discovered, and Sean grabbed Maria's lovely hair and shoved her face down in the rocky soil just as a third shot ricocheted off the rock in front of them.

The flames had grown so close that sparks and flying ash fell all around them, burning tiny holes in their clothes and glowing dangerously on their bed of rocks. The heat withered the mesquite below the ridge to tinder which quickly leapt into flames when the sparks fell upon it.

Another flurry of gunshots broke out below, but there was no hope of seeing anything through the wall of flames and heat waves. They could only hope Luke would ride out before the entire road blazed into an inferno. Grabbing the seat of Maria's skirt, Sean tugged a command to leave.

Just as she turned to yell a protest, the sound of hoofbeats broke through the crash and crackle of fire and falling timber, and two horsemen broke out on the path below, racing for the safety of the mountaintop. One leaned crazily in his saddle, but the other paid him little heed. Neither man was Luke.

Sean and Maria exchanged glances, then turned to watch anxiously for a third man to ride out. None did.

Maria was first on her feet, scrambling down the ledge on foot rather than returning for the horses. Besides Luke, two other men should be down there, but

Sean suspected neither would ride again. Luke did not aim for the wrist like Maria. Neither would his opponents.

Knowing they had no chance of getting out of that ravine alive without the horses, Sean ran in the opposite direction from Maria. He could only pray the rocks would not provide sufficient fuel for the fire to follow until he could get down there.

Not until she reached the bottom and began to gasp for air did Maria realize the full extent of their danger. She could stamp out falling sparks and avoid flaming mesquite, but the clouds of smoke smothered the lungs and made haste impossible.

Groping over the rocks to where she had last seen Luke, Maria tried to conserve her breath to prevent inhaling more of the fumes than necessary. Clouds of smoke kept her from seeing more than a few feet ahead, but she could see well enough to pull back against the wall of rocks when a shadowy form emerged in front of her.

It took only an instant to recognize Luke's broad shoulders and belted hips, and Maria gave a ragged cry of relief. Luke swung around at the sound, then staggered at the sudden movement. He caught himself on the wall as Maria's cry of alarm echoed up the canyon; then he waited until she came to him.

Luke cursed her in Spanish and English and in a few words she didn't recognize, but when she wrapped her arms around him and held him tight, she felt his kiss upon her hair. Slowly they began to make their way up the path out of the ravine.

Sean met them with the horses, and Maria watched anxiously as Luke pulled himself into the saddle. The blood caking his shirtsleeve warned he had not escaped without injury, but there was no time to tend to it. They had to get out of this inferno before they burned alive.

Sean set a steady pace and Maria rode in the rear, her gaze worriedly following Luke's progress. Occasionally he swayed in the saddle, but then he would jerk himself upright and ride like a soldier for a few more miles. She felt the pain of every bump and hole they hit, but Luke never flinched.

By nightfall they had crossed the river and come about and headed away from the fiery mountain. Maria glanced over her shoulder, wondering if the ranch house with its magnificent treasures had survived, but she never intended to return to find out. Her gaze returned to Luke's proud back drenched in sweat and swaying dangerously once again, and her stomach tightened nervously. What had seemed like a quixotic adventure had become a nightmare. Yet neither man ahead of her heaped recriminations on each other or anyone else. They seemed to take it all in stride, without a second look back.

She was the one who worried, but she had no desire to let the others know. Still, if Luke didn't call for a halt soon, she would. That wound of his had to be bound.

Sean decided the question for them. Bringing his horse to a halt, he waited for the others to catch up. Then he indicated a narrow crevasse in the wall of rock they had been riding beside.

"There's a valley back through there, good grazing and a little water. Why don't you two camp there for the night while I ride in to meet the men who pay our way? There's no sense in them knowing any more about you than necessary."

He carefully avoided mentioning the fact that Luke needed rest. In the darkness Maria could not read Sean's expression, but it did not matter. He could ride off and collect the money and disappear for all she cared right now. Her main concern was Luke. She did not wish to think why that should be.

Luke gave a nod of agreement and silently turned his mount in the direction indicated, more for Maria's sake than his own. For once Maria felt no irritation at this assumption of her weakness. She knew without her, he would have ridden on with Sean.

Once off the hill of flames, the air was considerably cooler, and with the onset of darkness the wind turned chilly. Maria shivered in her light linen shirt as they

walked the horses slowly through the narrow aperture.
She doubted if the men had been able to bring away
any bedding or other supplies. The plan had obviously
called for a hasty escape to the safety of some outlying
ranch. They would have to do without until Sean's return. If he returned.

The crevasse widened into a narrow valley as Sean
had promised. High walls towered overhead, cutting
off the wind and giving a distant view of the night sky.
Maria quickly found a stepping-stone for dismounting
and slid off her horse, then turned to be certain Luke
negotiated his safely.

She could tell the effort it cost him to stand by the
way he clung to the horse's mane. He said nothing,
though, and she walked beside him as they led the
exhausted horses to water. She had no idea what they
had managed to take away with them, but as soon as
the horses began to drink, she began rummaging
through the saddlebags and other assorted accoutre-
ments tied to the straps.

She found a small bag of dried beans and beef jerky
and a few other rudiments of a trail meal, so they
wouldn't starve. That wasn't what she was looking for,
however. She reached for the valise tied awkwardly to
Luke's saddle. She didn't know how he had ridden
with that thing banging at his knee, but she opened it
eagerly now. With a cry of satisfaction, her clothes
spilled out of the opening. He had brought her striped
dress and the new dinner gown and the new shoes and
all the lacy pantalets and chemises and petticoats to
go with them.

The chemises would work best, she decided: clean,
soft cotton with a minimum of frill which could be
torn off easily. She grabbed the first one she came
upon and turned to find Luke.

He sat on the creek bank gingerly attempting to remove the blood-soaked shirt from his arm. Maria slid
down beside him and took the knife from his hand,
neatly slicing off the sleeve on either side of the wound,
then dipping the soiled sleeve in the creek to clean it
out and use it for a washrag. She worked the wet cloth

over the clotted blood, gently cleaning away the rest of the ragged shirt, then sponging at the flesh until she could find the extent of the injury.

Blood began to flow heavily again, but Maria gave a sigh of relief that it was no worse than it was. She began ripping the lace off the chemise with the knife.

"It went all the way through, may the heavens be praised. I never had to dig out a bullet. *Mi padre* always did that. I wish we had something to clean it with."

"There's a flask in my right-hand saddlebag." Luke wrapped his good hand around a rock and squeezed to hide the pain. "What is that you're cutting up?"

Maria looked at the frilly piece of cotton in surprise. "A chemise, of course. Do you object to wearing a woman's garment for a bandage? I doubt if anyone will recognize it when I'm through." She got up to find the flask.

Luke followed her with his eyes. "Not one of your new ones, I hope. My shirt would have worked just as well."

Maria carried the flask back and felt his forehead. It did seem a little too warm. "You must be delirious. Here, hold still while I pour this through. It's going to hurt, so don't knock me down. There's not a lot left in here and you might want a sip in a minute."

Luke growled at the pain searing through his arm as the whiskey penetrated the open wound, but he held still. "You shouldn't be wasting your trousseau on a scratch like this. Next time, use my shirt."

"Your shirt is filthy. I will wash it and use it to hold the bandages in place in the morning. And I certainly hope there will be no next time."

Maria began carefully packing the wound with the expensive lingerie. With a flair for mischief, she used the long strips of lace to knot the bandage in place. Let him live that down when Sean returned with help.

Luke gulped the dregs of the whiskey she gave him and eyed the lacy bows on his arm with misgiving, but he made no further comment. Her sacrifice of one of the few good pieces in her limited wardrobe for his benefit left him with nothing to say. He knew how precious every feminine garment in that satchel was to her, yet she had not thought twice about making it into bandages. He would never understand women.

"What happens now?" Maria asked matter-of-factly as she set about making their skimpy supper. "Will Dallas come looking for us?"

closing his eyes and resting his back against a rock, Luke fought the clouds of whiskey and weariness surrounding him. "He can't prove we're responsible. The dam could have given away beneath the strain. If he comes looking for us, I'll threaten him with a lawsuit for causing the loss of our child."

Maria heard the hint of dry humor behind his words and refrained from throwing the frying pan at his head. The man could be irritating, but he had turned and freed the horses for her and then had tried to give her a chance to escape when their pursuers had closed in. She would save the frying pan until he was well.

"We would have to be man and wife for that to work. You would be better off taking your chances with Dallas."

"Then I'll send him to Manuel for explanations if he shows up." Luke's words contained none of his earlier humor, and Maria had the sense to shut up.

By the time they made their bed by covering themselves with saddle blankets, Luke's forehead burned with fever, and Maria had no need of additional covering. Just the heat of the man beside her scorched her flesh.

When his hand finally relaxed and loosed hers, Maria knew he had lost consciousness. Staring at the patch of stars above her, she began to pray as she had never prayed before.

19

By morning, Luke raved in delirium. Biting her lip and trying desperately to stay calm, Maria soaked rags in the creek to cool his brow. She made a shelter of their blankets to keep him cool when the shade of the few cottonwoods on the bank was insufficient. She washed and cleaned his torn arm again, watching in trepidation for the first signs of infection. She had no medicine and little knowledge to prevent infection from spreading. If he did not recover soon, she had no means of getting him to a doctor if Sean did not return.

For the first time in her life Maria was forced to confront a life-and-death situation on her own. The temptation was great not to think about it but to pray a solution would appear. Instead she considered all her alternatives one by one as she rinsed Luke's forehead in cool water and listened to his ravings.

She could stay here and pray Luke recovered or Sean returned. Or she could ride out and seek help. Fear and impatience urged her to ride, but the thought of leaving Luke alone was repugnant. With conscious decision she chose to stay until certain signs of infection developed. The decision did not sit easily with her, but she had made it and she would stand by it.

Unaware that Maria had made a large step forward in maturity, Luke continued to alternately sleep and cry indecipherable phrases. After a while Maria could recognize the name "Caroline" because he said it with such anguish that it wrung her heart. Gently she wiped his face with the cool water, trying to imagine how a man as cold and imperturbable as Luke could love a woman with such desperation. Ignoring the flare of jealousy in her breast, she tried to imagine what kind of woman this Caroline would be.

She would have to be tall and willowy to fit Luke's rangy height. Maria could see them standing shoulder to shoulder, Luke's lion-maned head bent to admire the dimples beside her pink lips. The rest of the image came easily. Caroline would have long, golden curls and baby blue eyes and a sultry smile. She would murmur flattering phrases in a soft Southern voice, and Luke's tanned features would crack into that lopsided smile he used so seldom. When it came to the part where Luke placed those chiseled lips of his across that pouting pink mouth, Maria cursed and stalked off to the creek to rinse out the rag again.

When she returned, his cracked lips were muttering "Maria" and he was restlessly plucking at the bandanna she had used to tie his arm against his chest. All Luke wanted from her was his freedom, she thought irritably as she loosened the sling. Well, he could have it, should he live long enough.

After a while he grew silent again. Ascertaining that no sign of infection had appeared and that he felt a little bit cooler, Maria took a break from her nursing duty. The hot sun had baked the dirty shirt to her skin, and she felt a dire need for a bath.

Not daring to linger too long in case Sean returned, Maria stripped off her dust-caked clothing and waded out into the cold stream in only her camisole and pantalettes. Pebbles cut into her feet, but the rippling water felt good after hot boots. After a moment's hesitation she sat upon a flat shelf of rock and let the current flow around her, soaking her all over. Throwing back her hair and letting the sun beat upon her face and neck, Maria luxuriated in the sensual combination of warm sun upon her skin and cool water below.

The spray of water as the stream crashed over the rocks soon had the delicate linen soaked, and she shivered as a breeze played across her skin. Rising abruptly, she washed herself and her clothes and climbed from the water to find her old Levis.

Not until she had removed her old clothes from the valise did Maria feel that she was being watched. Glancing in Luke's direction to reassure herself he still slept, she was shocked to discover him sitting, amber eyes wide and aware and following her every movement.

Luke admired the flush of red rising above Maria's breasts, spreading up her slender throat to her sun-bronzed cheeks. The soaked undergarments revealed every curve of her young body, and his gaze lingered on the upthrust breasts beneath ribbons and lace. His loins ached at the memory of how she felt in his arms, but he was in no condition to fight her to the ground again. Instead he watched with regret as Maria disappeared behind the horse to make a hasty change.

His lips twitched at the sight of long, bare legs kicking off the damp, clinging cloth and hurriedly struggling into the navy blue denims. If she had any idea how provocative that one tiny glimpse was, she would have arranged for the other horse to lie down beside the first to block both top and bottom views.

Drained by just the simple exertion of propping himself up, Luke lay back against the blankets and waited for Maria to come to him. He detested weakness, but the coolness of Maria's fingers against his brow almost made it worthwhile.

"How do you feel?" Her fingers smoothed his forehead and Luke caught the faint scent of roses. How could she smell like roses out here in the wilderness?

"Like the devil." Catching her hand, Luke pulled her down beside him. He'd much rather have her at his side than hovering over him.

"How unusual," Maria responded dryly, settling herself in the seat indicated. "I will admit, you have been hot as hell with fever for a while, though I should think that would be an atmosphere with which you would be well acquainted."

"I can see my plight has softened your heart. Will you give me a drink or should I fetch it myself?"

Maria had to smile at his irascible tone, and she handed him the canteen of cold water with alacrity. "I have been trying to pour this down your throat all day. I should have known you would prefer to do it yourself.''

A small grin lifted the corner of Luke's mouth as he gave Maria an appreciative look. ''We may be beginning to understand each other too well. You'd better watch out.'' With that, he tilted his head back and drank thirstily.

Maria chose not to understand the warmth spreading through her at his look and words. She did not need the admiration of the gunman. He did not belong in her life and she did not belong in his. His admiration meant only one thing, and she could take no further chances on that foolishness again. She rose from his side and set about preparing their meager meal.

Luke dozed off and on again as Maria boiled coffee and beans and baked a hard bread of flour and water. Heavy loss of blood had taken his strength, but he was wide awake enough to concentrate by the time Maria brought the meal to him.

He ate the less than tasty food without complaint, then sipped the strong coffee while Maria scraped and cleaned the tin plates in the creek. In britches and work shirt once again, she still seemed slender as any boy, but Luke's hands ached to touch the full curves beneath the old clothes. He had learned to control his physical needs long ago, but he seemed unable to rid himself of his obsession for a woman who had already made it clear she had no wish to further their relationship.

''Sit by me, it will be turning chilly soon,'' Luke said, making room for her on the blanket.

The rock he leaned against still held the heat of the day, and Maria relaxed against it. She had no fear of a man who could scarcely stand on his own two feet, and she enjoyed the intimacy of just being together without the strain of tension between them.

''Could we just be friends?'' she asked quietly after a few minutes of silence in which Luke drank his coffee. She looked up at the angular planes of his face: the hard, thin nose and square jaw, the deep-set eyes with the dark curve of brow above. She recognized the tightening of the muscle along his cheek, but his reply did not come in anger.

His amber eyes gazed down at her inquiringly, searching her face in the last few rays before the sun set. The golden glow of sunlight seemed captured in her complexion, but the green of her eyes hid beneath the shadows of her lashes like cool waters beneath overhanging foliage.

"I don't think so." Luke's answer came slowly as he searched to give her the honest truth.

Maria glanced away, unwilling to reveal the spasm of pain his words engendered. "I suppose you're right. We're too different. Tell me about Caroline."

Luke gave a startled jerk and turned a suspicious gaze to Maria's bent head. "What about Caroline?"

His voice was harsh, and Maria glanced up at him in surprise. "You kept calling her name while you were feverish. Is she the reason you don't go back to Kansas?"

"You're too damned smart to be human, *bruja*. Why don't you tell me?"

He hadn't called her witch in quite a while, Maria realized, and she watched his expression speculatively. "Does the price on your head have anything to do with her?"

Luke snorted in relief and pulled her closer with his good arm. He liked to feel the softness of her breasts pressed against his side. "Your sorcery fails you on that one. How did you know about the price on my head?"

"Sorcery," Maria replied promptly, "and the sheriff. He warned me about you."

"And you ignored him. Do you always ignore what you don't like to hear?"

"When I can. Half the men out here have pasts that don't bear scrutiny. I'd never have help at all if I insisted on lily-white reputations. In your case, the only question would be how many rewards are being offered for you. A man as quick with his guns as you are could not escape trouble indefinitely."

"Wise little witch, aren't you?" Luke stared up at the pattern of stars above them, perplexed by the mixture of innocence and cynicism he held in his arms. How could she lie trustingly beside him knowing the

kind of man he was? She had given him what was only
hers to give, yet refused him the chance to make it
right. He had thought it just a matter of money, but he
was beginning to understand Maria was more complex
than that.

"Did you love her?" Maria returned to the subject
that interested her most. Luke was deft at avoiding
answers, but she sensed he had begun to soften.

"Love?" Luke frowned, trying to remember the
frantic passion and ecstasy of those years ago. "I
thought so, but I was pretty green back then, not much
older than you. I don't know if I loved her, but I sure
as hell wanted her. That was enough then."

"And now?" Maria whispered, not wishing to disturb his thoughts or cause him to clam up again, but
hoping to encourage him to continue.

Luke rewarded her with a sardonic leer. "And now
I know any woman can satisfy a man if he is hungry
enough."

Maria punched him in the ribs and tried to scramble
away before he could retaliate, but Luke merely slid
his arm around her waist and held her still. "Don't,
Maria. I didn't mean that. I'm not used to saying what
I mean. Tell me something. If I were as wealthy as
Manuel, would you marry me?"

"Of course, in secret. Then I'd murder you in your
sleep, take your gold, and hie myself to California
where the living is easy." Maria relaxed at this line
of questioning. She never knew when he was serious,
but she was beginning to learn he hid a very odd sense
of humor behind that stern expression. She felt him
chuckle, and she grinned. One of these days she would
teach him to laugh.

"Is that what you intend to do to Manuel?"

"Oh, no!" she replied in mock horror. "He will
not inherit his wealth until his father dies. What do
you take me for, a fool?"

"A murderous wench perhaps, but never a fool. So
why did you choose Manuel?"

Maria sighed as she realized he was once more serious. How would she explain? "For his family, for

his place in society, I guess. Do you know what it is like to never feel at home anywhere? My mother's people do not claim me. The people of the town don't know what to make of me. I have no friends, no relatives, no one but Pieta and Carmelita to talk to, and they just don't understand. When we still had money and I had a wardrobe full of fancy gowns, they meant nothing to me and I went around just as I am now. The only way I could fit in anywhere was to be one of the boys. So now everyone thinks that's what I am, but I'm not. I've grown up since then, and I want people to see me as I am, but they can't. They just see Connolly's tomboy kid, and now that there is no more money, they don't even think it's funny anymore. Does any of that make sense to you?''

Luke pulled the long river of ebony hair over her shoulder, smoothing it silently while he listened. He wasn't sure he understood at all, but he had never been in the same position as she. He had grown up knowing who he was and where he stood in the eyes of family and friends. He had possessed all the security anyone could possibly ask, and he had thrown it all away. Perhaps his decision to return home had some of the same elements of what Maria sought in Manuel. If so, security was the last thing he could offer. There was no security in facing a gallows pole.

"A little, *querida*. But it still sounds as if this position in society he offers you means you are marrying him for his money."

Maria gave him a look of exasperation and reached to take his empty cup. "Manuel's family could be poor, but they would still be looked upon with respect because the Vasqueros have always been the *patrons*. You may speak a little Spanish, but you do not understand the Spanish mind."

Luke watched as she neatly cleaned up and stowed away the rest of their cooking gear. He found it hard to believe that a woman would settle for pride when there was money to be had, but that was what she would have him believe, it seemed. He could see no good reason for her to lie, and he toyed with the idea as she disappeared into the bushes. If Manuel had no wealth of his own and his father controlled the reins of power, then pride was all she could hope to gain. She already owned a comfortable home, and if she lost that, she always had distant relatives to turn to, but pride prevented that. Damned if he could see anything else but pride in her choice of the arrogant Spanish whelp. Unless it was lust, but Luke already knew better than that.

When Maria returned, she made a pillow of her saddle and lay down on the small piece of blanket beside Luke. Although emotionally exhausted, she didn't feel sleepy, and Luke's wakefulness beside her didn't help.

"I've been thinking." Maria finally broached the subject that had been worrying her. "It might be better if we don't return together. Manuel will be furious with me for going off with you, but if he thinks I have turned you away, he will be much more reasonable. I will understand if you no longer wish to search for my father's killer."

Maria held her breath, fearing his response. She had to do it, make the break clean while he was in no position to argue. A better opportunity might never come.

Luke's reply was disappointingly calm. "You've helped us, now Sean and I will help you. I wasn't making any progress from your end. Maybe it would work better if I stayed in town."

He had agreed with her. For the first time she had known him, he had actually agreed with her. She wanted to weep, but they would not be tears of joy.

Turning her back on him, Maria sought the solitude of sleep. She could not allow this wave of disappointment engulfing her to affect the future. Luke had gotten what he wanted of her. She had no right to expect more. But two tears trickled down her cheeks as she felt him settle down for the night without reaching for her again.

20

Sean arrived shortly after daybreak. He blended in with the landscape, materializing as a moving gray haze along the streambank. Luke's hand propped a Colt across his knee as the shadow rode into view, but Maria slept at his side without disturbance.

Sean sent a glance to Maria's trustingly composed features, noting the way her shirt gaped at the throat and her hip rested next to Luke's, and he sent his comrade an expectant look. "I take it you are alive and that the two of you have kissed and made up. Is it too early to offer my congratulations?"

Luke lowered the revolver as Maria stirred at his side. "We are taking her home to her fiancé. Got any food in those bags?"

Shaking his head in disbelief, Sean slid from his horse and began unpacking his saddlebags, but his gaze continued to follow the scene beneath the tree. Luke's voice had awakened Maria, and she turned instantly to touch her long fingers to his brow. With amazement Sean noted Luke accepted this gesture without irritation. In fact, his usually impassive expression softened remarkably as he gazed down upon Maria's sleep-flushed features and tousled hair. Sean felt a tug at his own heart at the sight of Maria's slow smile. The man had to be mad to give that away.

Maria stretched lazily before finally realizing Sean had arrived. As he threw the contents of his bag beside the remains of the prior night's fire, she leapt to her feet.

"Thank goodness! I thought you'd left us to starve.

I didn't relish the idea of learning how to dress a deer.''

"You could have tried for smaller game, my foolish colleen." Sean grinned as she began sorting through the assortment of food. "Even our wounded hero over there could have managed a rabbit."

Gingerly holding his arm as he staggered to his feet, Luke sent his friend a sardonic look, but didn't deign to reply as he strode off into the bushes. Sean sent him a beaming grin.

"You don't want a man who gets up like a black bear in the morning, anyway," he announced. "What you need is a man like me—always cheerful, always helpful."

"And always in someone else's bed." Maria completed the list for him as she pounced upon the bacon hidden in the folds of a gunny sack. "Light the fire and let me get this cooking, presuming it is safe to light a fire?" She sent him an anxious look.

Sean gazed into the green depths of her eyes and grimaced. "You are a hard woman, Maria Connolly." He bent to strike a match to the kindling neatly laid between the circle of stones. "Rumor has it that we nearly perished in the fire while chasing the culprits who set it. Dallas had some kind of stroke and is in no condition to refute the claim. His henchmen would like to have our heads, but they're not the kind to bother coming after us without orders. Meanwhile, we have become minor local heroes and if we only brag as long and loud as Wild Bill, we can become celebrities, too."

"Do you know him?" Maria stopped stirring the cornmeal mush to glance up at the Irishman.

"Know who?" Luke strode back into the clearing, his face paler than usual but his jaw set with determination.

"Wild Bill Hickok. I've read about him in *Harper's*. Is he really as good as they say?"

Luke hunkered down beside the fire and shook the pan of bacon. "There's better. He just makes a bigger show of it."

"But he's good, you've got to admit that." Sean tore off a piece of a fresh loaf of bread and began chomping on it. Between chews he finished, "Bill's showy, but I think I'd place my bets on Wes Hardin, if anybody knew where the hell he is." He sent Maria an apologetic look. "Beg your pardon, Maria."

Not accustomed to anyone apologizing for their language in front of her, Maria shrugged it off and continued her questioning. "John Wesley Hardin? You know him, too? But he's an outlaw!"

Luke appropriated the pot of mush from her hands and set it over the fire. "We're all outlaws, *chiquita*. When the law doesn't work, someone has to act outside of it to get things done. I'm not excusing the bad tempers and the drinking that get so many men in trouble; Hickok and Cody and the rest of them are just as guilty of that as Wes and some of the others. They talked faster and managed to stay just this side of the law often enough to get away with it. When you're wearing the badge, people don't mind the killing."

Maria grew silent, turning this information over in her mind. She'd read all the wild tales of the gunfighters as avidly as anyone else. She knew the men behind the tales were nowhere near as glamorous as the papers made them seem, but she had always thought the ones wearing a badge were heroes. Luke's words cast doubts on that notion, and she began to examine the facts more closely.

"Are you saying Hardin isn't a criminal or that Hickok is?"

"I'm saying they both killed men they didn't have to. We've all killed men we didn't have to, just because we wear guns."

"But if you didn't wear guns, you could have been killed," Maria pointed out.

"There's that chance, yes. Once you develop a reputation, the danger is worse. Hardin could have really retired his guns and the sheriff still would have come after him. I'm betting he's finally got smart and changed his name so his reputation can't follow him, but if he's still wearing guns, the past will eventually catch up with him. It's no kind of life for a family man."

Sean glanced up sharply, but as usual Luke's expression gave nothing away. "If a man doesn't wear guns to protect himself and his family and friends, some of these bigger bastards like that ring in Santa Fe will take everything they own. There's going to be a war out here one of these days, and the law isn't going to be the deciding factor."

Maria listened intently, waiting for further explanations. She had often heard her father and the other ranchers discuss the powerful men in Santa Fe and the wealthy landowners in other counties who controlled the government and the economy, but she had never understood how they affected her. She waited in vain, however. Luke shrugged this threat of war away.

"In Lincoln County maybe, that's where the money is. Not in San Pedro. The land around there is poor. Most of the ranches are so small a chicken couldn't scratch a living from them. Only a few of the older families have anything worth keeping. Maria's father bought wisely. There's enough good land and water there to get through the lean years. But it's the others that are being bought out. Who would be fool enough to buy up all the worthless land in a worthless county?"

They had turned from the general to the particular, and Sean frowned at the problem Luke posed. "Who's buying the land?"

Luke shrugged and began dishing the mush onto his tin plate. "They're using different names. I haven't been able to trace the owners."

"Well, it looks to me like they would want the big ranches, too, whatever they're doing. It just takes a little longer to put the big ones under. You're saying that's why Maria's father was killed?"

"I don't know that. He could have known too much. It could have been some wandering thief, Maria's not had any offers to buy her out." Luke didn't look at her, but he felt her go stiff beside him.

Unaware of the tension building between them, Sean

pondered his thoughts aloud. "It doesn't make sense to go after the small fish and leave the big ones alone, unless the big ones are doing the buying, and why would they want worthless land? Not simply out of sympathy for a man down on his luck, I'm certain."

"That's what we've got you for, *compadre.*" Luke sipped his coffee and eyed his garrulous friend with approval. "You can find a place on one of the bigger spreads and see if they're in the same kind of trouble as Connolly's. If so, then it could be someone outside of the territory."

Maria couldn't stand it any longer. Throwing down her dish, she confronted Luke angrily. "You're talking about Manuel and his father, aren't you? They have the biggest ranch in the valley and now they want mine and you think that makes them murderers! You're wrong, Luke Walker! For once in your life you will have to admit you are wrong."

"I've been wrong before, Maria," Luke replied quietly. "I sincerely hope I'm wrong again. But if you think I'm going to send you back to him without finding out one way or another, then you're the one who is mistaken."

His amber eyes bored deep and hard into hers, and Maria felt her heart lodge in her throat and a shiver go down her spine. Luke had taken her and made her a part of him, and now he was letting her know he would not let her go so easily. She had been a fool in so many ways, but this was the worst. She felt him as if he were a physical part of her, felt his possession all over again, and she could not look away.

Sean coughed to remind them of his presence. His thoughtful gaze followed their expressions as they turned back to him, and he sought to reassure Maria's troubled one. "I will be the one to decide if everything is on the level, Maria. I have no ax to grind with your Manuel. If you have chosen him, I'm sure he is an honest man."

Honest wasn't the word she would have used to describe Manuel, but in the sense Sean meant, it would do. Maria nodded her head. "They are not easy people to know. I have known them all my life, but only recently have they let me close to them. That is their way. It has been for centuries. Do not expect to discover anything at all, Sean.''

''And what will you be doing, boyo?'' Sean cast an amused glance to Luke's carefully controlled features.

''Searching out the new owners of those ranches, I guess. There's got to be a reason somebody wants land a thousand miles from nowhere.''

''If the railroads hadn't gone bankrupt, San Pedro would have had the first line to Santa Fe.'' Maria defended her village gallantly. ''The last I heard, they're stalled up around La Junta in Colorado Territory, but that was awhile back. The Santa Fe trail goes right through San Pedro and that's what they're following. That's why we have a stagecoach. So we're not in the middle of nowhere.''

''They'll kill themselves trying to get through Raton Pass. You'll be in the middle of nowhere for a while yet, and be thankful for it. You could wind up like Abilene, meanest cow town this side of the Mississippi.'' Sean stood with his empty plate to wash it in the river. ''They finally had to move the pens elsewhere to keep the cattle drivers from destroying the place. It's not worth it.''

He strode off, leaving Luke looking pensive and Maria trying to ignore him. That was nigh on to impossible, but she managed to avoid speaking while cleaning up the pots, and he made no effort to end the silence. She might as well not have been there at all for all he noticed, she decided, miffed at his lack of attention. Somehow she would have to learn to cultivate that same attitude.

They rode out a short while later, Luke insisting his arm was well enough to manage. Knowing the extent of the injury and the amount of blood he had lost, Maria doubted such superhuman abilities, but she did not argue in front of Sean. Men like Luke might occasionally surrender an argument to a woman when they were alone, but seldom in front of another man. She had learned that right along with her ABC's.

By mid-afternoon Maria decided she couldn't bear to watch the suppressed pain in Luke's face any longer. She feared the wound would open again if he used that arm, and the road was difficult to negotiate with just one hand. She let her horse drop farther and farther behind until the men were forced to wait for her to catch up.

Sean greeted her impatiently, but Luke's gaze was speculative as she wiped at her brow with a bandanna and smiled wearily. "Is there some hurry? Couldn't we take this trip a little more easily?" she asked Sean, avoiding Luke's eyes.

"If you're in no hurry, I'm not." Sean shrugged and turned to his partner. "Shall we let the lady rest for the night?"

"The lady doesn't need any more rest than you do, but I'm ready to call it a day. There's some shelter down at the bottom of that hill." Appropriating the reins to Maria's mount, Luke let Sean move ahead while he pointedly ignored her look of surprise.

Once Sean was out of sight, Luke reached over and caught Maria's silken braid, turning her head up to meet his gaze. She regarded him questioningly, without fear, and a hint of a smile played about his lips. "You don't have to coddle me, Miss Connolly. I know my limits better than you."

"Do you?" The challenge lit her emerald eyes from within. "Somehow I doubt that very much, Mr. Walker."

What he wanted to do was take her in his arms and teach her the lesson she begged to learn each time she looked at him like that, but that was not his place to do. Still, Luke's gaze lingered long on the full, pouting lips before traveling to the generous curve revealed by the open collar of her shirt. He wanted her more than any other woman he had ever known, even more now that he knew what she offered, but he had no desire to share her with another man. He grimaced at the path of his thoughts and released his hold on her.

"I know my limits, Maria. That doesn't mean I

abide by them. Just don't tempt me too far.'' He rode off, leaving Maria to stare after him with widened eyes.

The next days they rode slowly, giving Luke time to recover his strength. At night, Maria was more physically aware of him than before, though he made no attempt to join her when Sean left them alone at night.

She caught herself gazing at the V of the springy mat of curly hair across his broad chest when Luke emerged, dripping wet, from washing in a stream. She wanted to stroke the rippling muscles revealed by this casual state of undress, tantalized by the way both muscles and the mat of hair narrowed at the slim hips disguised in heavy denim. Except for that first time, he had come to her in darkness, and she knew little of the secrets of his masculine physique. That first time didn't count. She had been quite out of her mind and had registered nothing beyond the assault on her senses. Now she wanted to know more, but it was too late. Luke treated her as if she were no different from Sean.

Concealing her disappointment that he no longer even attempted to steal a kiss, Maria tended his wound with a brusqueness not usual to her nature. It was easier to avoid Luke's company than suffer the pangs of longing generated by just his presence. Soon she would be home, and Manuel could assuage these feelings of loneliness. Now that she knew where his kisses led, perhaps she wouldn't find them so irritating.

By the time they reached the ridge overlooking the Connolly ranch just after dusk some ten days after their departure, Maria was eager to be home and rid of this obsession with Luke. Sean had gone on down the trail toward town to arrive as a stranger, but Luke had insisted on accompanying Maria back to the ranch. They watched as the lamps were lit in the windows below, and Maria had the sudden urge to turn and flee. She didn't know what she wanted, but it was no longer down there with the ghosts of her past.

Instead she tilted a stubborn chin as she turned to Luke. "I'll be safe now. I better ride in alone."

"I don't like it, Maria. Let me go down with you

and make certain it's safe." Luke sought the shadowy outlines of her face, unwilling to put the distance between them that his mission required.

"Don't be ridiculous. The kitchen lamp is on. That means Pieta is sitting there with her head in a book. There's a light in the back of the bunkhouse, so Charlie and the men are inside playing poker. No wild Indians are going to leap out at me from behind the rose bushes."

She was right, of course, and Luke didn't press the argument. "You know where to reach me if you need me. And if I'm not there, don't hesitate to call on Sean. You're not to take any risks, you understand?"

"Aye, aye, sir," Maria answered mockingly. "I'll wear my silks and satins and sit on the front porch and knit until you tell me all is well."

Luke gave a short laugh. "Like hell, you will. Just don't go rushing off to Manuel, that's all I ask."

Maria sent him an enigmatic look; then without a word she spurred her horse down the trail, the valise with her trousseau bouncing alongside.

Luke remained on the ridge, waiting to see her safely inside. When she disappeared through the golden light of the kitchen door, he swung his horse back down the trail toward town.

Somehow he was not surprised by the soft whicker of horses on either side of the road ahead. Casually drawing his injured arm from its sling so he could reach his gun, he approached the narrow gate cautiously. With his stronger arm needed to guide the horse, he had little hope of outgunning more than one or two.

The shadows did not wait for him to reach the safety of the open field. A line of horsemen began to filter from the cover of the tree-lined ridge. Luke counted three ahead of him and at least two behind, and he swore silently to himself.

Raising his hands so they could see they were empty, Luke inquired sardonically, "Anything I can do for you, gents?"

He didn't recognize the voice that replied. "Turn

around and head right back down the hill. I reckon you got some fancy explainin' to do.''

Since that route would take him back to Maria, Luke raised no immediate objection. Silently he trotted his horse in the direction indicated, any chance of escape cut off by the armed men around him.

BOOK II
Summer, 1876

1

Not finding anyone in the barn, Maria tended to Erinmeade herself before hurrying in the kitchen door to find Pieta. She was starved for a piece of fresh pie or even some lean beef that had not hung in the sun and dried to the consistency of a hickory stick.

Disappointed that there was no one in the kitchen to greet her, Maria wandered into the main house, wondering where everybody had gone. Perhaps there was a fiesta somewhere tonight.

The light streaming from her father's study turned her feet in that direction. She used to come in at night and find her father bent over the ledgers or week-old newspapers, and he would always look up with a warm grin when she entered. No matter what he was doing, he always found time for her, and even seemed to enjoy taking a break from his work to listen to her chatter. It had been months since she had seen that lamp lit. She had not been able to bring herself to use that desk and the worn leather chair that was her father's. Just the sight of it was capable of bringing tears to her eyes, as they were dangerously close to doing now. If she could only throw open that door and find it had all just been a nightmare . . .

The planked door opened with just a touch, but the nightmare did not end. Maria stared in disbelief at the man behind the desk, who looked up at her appearance. The features were so much like her father's, but not as leathered and brown as her father's weather-beaten complexion. The eyes, too, were lighter, without the deep laugh lines carved beside them. This face was softer, plumper, not so harsh as Irish's, nor so

generous with its display of emotion. Irish had possessed an explosive temper, but he never hid it. This
man betrayed little of his thoughts as he came to his
feet.

"Maria! Thank God." Before he could say more,
confusion erupted on the porch outside, and he swung
his head to look behind her.

Luke stumbled into the room, shoved by the overzealous cowboys behind him. Hands tied behind his
back and gunbelt empty, he offered no protest, simply
righting himself and sweeping in his surroundings with
one quick glance. His gaze noted Maria's astonishment and traveled on to the man behind the desk.

The man's face grew taut and cold as he met Luke's
enigmatic gaze. Without looking at Maria, he demanded, "Is this the man you were with in Santa Fe?"

Confused, not at all certain what was going on, Maria gave the only reply she could, the truth. "Yes, of
course. Why? What is wrong?"

Her uncle gave a curt nod to the men behind Luke.
"Take him out and hang him."

Maria screamed in outrage as the men grabbed
Luke's arms, but they paid no heed to her cries until
she ran to the wall and jerked one of her father's rifles
from the rack. Pumping a bullet into the breech, she
aimed it at the man nearest the door.

In the confusion Luke jerked himself free of the imprisoning grasp on his injured arm, and before Maria's
hasty temper could result in disaster, he stepped between the pointed rifle and his adversary. "Put the gun
down, Maria. Your uncle is only trying to protect
you."

Silence filled the room while the man behind the
desk gaped at Luke in astonishment, and Maria lowered the gun with ill grace. Resentment flashed in her
eyes as she turned to her father's brother.

"Is that what you think you're doing? Who gave you
the right to come in here and interfere in my life? Just
what do you think I am? One of those fluffy-brained
fools who have to be coddled behind a man's coattails
all her life?"

Without waiting for a reply to this tirade, Maria reached down and jerked the knife from Luke's boot so she might cut his bonds. This apparent familiarity with the gunfighter's wardrobe set her uncle's temper to flaring.

"Get that knife and gun away from her, for God's sake! Where are your brains? Maria, put those weapons down and go to your room. I'll deal with you later."

Unfamiliar with the handling of a knife, Maria found it easily snatched from her grasp, but the rifle was another story. Backing away from Luke and his jailers, she swung the barrel dangerously upright and glared at the ranch hands approaching her. The humiliation of being treated as a child did not gentle her temper.

"It might be wiser to talk first, Mr. Connolly. Maria has a bad habit of getting her own way, and I'd rather not see her kill a man over the likes of me."

Maria sent Luke a killing glare over this speech, but the ranch hands halted their advance with relief at this excuse. They were more accustomed to taking orders from a man, but Maria's temper was legendary, and no one doubted her skill with the rifle. They had no desire to die for nothing.

Connolly struggled for control over his temper as he regarded the gunfighter who had taken his niece from her home and ruined her, then calmly returned her before riding off again. "You're right about that, you bastard. I don't know how you know my name, but you're not worth the hemp for hanging. Why don't you try to run for it? That will be quicker."

Maria slammed the butt of the old rifle against the floor in fury. The explosion that followed burned a hole through the lathe and adobe ceiling and covered the occupants in a thin film of dust. All attention immediately swung to her and the hole over her head.

"This is my house. Those are my men. I want you all the hell out of here before I bring the whole damned place down around your ears!" She breeched the rifle, replaced the shell, and aimed it at the man holding Luke's knife. "Cut him free. Now."

The ranch hand glanced around to the other men for guidance. Since Maria had adopted Luke's ploy of standing with her back to the wall, there didn't seem to be any immediate likelihood of disarming her without getting shot to pieces. He started sawing the rope around Luke's wrists.

"Maria Francesca, you're not too old to be turned over my knee and whipped. Now put that gun down before somebody gets hurt. Johnson, leave those damned ropes alone!"

The battle had reached an impasse. The man sawing the ropes hesitated, but since no one made a move to disarm Maria, he returned to hacking the ropes.

"If you would give us a chance to explain, we might succeed in coming to a better conclusion." Luke supplied this suggestion dryly while waiting for the freedom to use his hands. His arm ached abominably, but it should have sufficient strength to wring a certain slender neck. "If Maria's reputation has been harmed, I've offered to marry her. I might not be as ideal a husband as her Spaniard, but it is one solution, you must admit."

This suggestion met with looks of scorn from both Maria and her uncle. Her uncle responded fastest. "We've kept her whereabouts from the Vasqueros. They still think she's in Santa Fe buying a trousseau, and you'll not be around long enough to tell them otherwise." He came out from behind the desk and stepped toward Maria. "Give me the gun, Maria. Whatever romantic notion you harbor about the bastard will be easily dispelled when you learn the kind of man he is."

"I already know what kind of man he is. He offered to find my father's killer when no one else even cared enough to visit his grave. He saved Pedro's life, paid cash for my grain when no one would give me credit"—she caught Luke's startled expression at this piece of knowledge but she didn't halt—"and took me to Santa Fe when I asked him, against his better judgment. He is also a gunfighter, a card shark, probably a confidence man, and wanted heaven's know where or for what, but I know of no reason why he should hang. If nothing else, he's the best damn foreman this ranch has ever had, and I haven't even paid him.''

"I daresay he's exacted his price in other ways," Connolly replied angrily, shooting Luke a venomous glare. "We haven't been waiting idly for you to return, Maria. We've been tearing the territory apart looking for you, and we may know a little more about the bastard than you. He's got a reputation with women, and it's not a good one.''

As Connolly approached her, Maria lifted the rifle and took aim at his throat. "Not one step closer, Uncle Patrick. You're not listening to me. I don't care about his reputation with women.'' That was a lie. She wanted to know all about it and rip his heart out and shove it down his throat, but she refused to allow anyone else to have her revenge. "He is going to help me find the man who killed my father. If it's a hanging you want, that's the man you should go after.''

"Maria, be reasonable! A thief like that will be gone from the territory by now. There isn't a chance—''

Maria clicked the bullet in place and Connolly stopped in his tracks.

With an exclamation of impatience Luke jerked apart the frayed ropes at his wrists and strode briskly across the room. In one swift movement he pulled the rifle from Maria's hands and caught her by the waist before she could swing around and grab another. Holding her kicking, twisting figure firmly with his good arm, Luke gestured toward the far shadows of the room.

"You, señor, step out where I can see you. I would like to know all my enemies before I release her.''

Maria's head snapped up and she stopped struggling to see who Luke could possibly be addressing now. She went pale as a tall, lithe man with graying black hair stepped into the lamp light. "*Tío* Juan!'' she moaned. The fates were stacked against her this night.

A look of admiration glinted in his dark eyes as the aristocratic stranger reached out his hand to his sister's child. Her linen shirt and riding skirt bore the traces of hours of hard riding, but Maria still carried herself with grace, her shoulders stiffening proudly as she stepped from Luke's grasp, her chin lifting defiantly. She did not accept his hand but watched him warily.

"I would have recognized you anywhere. You look just like Camille at that age. And your behavior is not much better," he added with a wry twist to his thin lips.

Since Luke now possessed the rifle, the ranch hands reached nervously for their own weapons, uncertain how the gunfighter would take his captivity. He held the rifle almost carelessly, but no one made the mistake of thinking he was not paying attention. That he had spotted the man hidden across the room was evidence enough of that.

Smoothly Luke paved a path to ease the tension. "Perhaps a few introductions are in order. You seem to know who I am. I've met Mr. Connolly before, although it's been some years and I'm certain he doesn't remember. You must be Maria's other uncle, the one from California? Correct?"

"Juan Degas Valencía, at your service, Mr. Walker. You will be so kind as to put up the weapon, and I will listen to what my niece has to say, but do not think I will look lightly on what you have done. You have acted with great dishonor, and you must pay the price. Only for the sake of my niece and my late sister will I listen at all."

His tone had gradually hardened into shards of ice, and Maria shivered. This was the haughty man who had not acknowledged her mother's marriage to a man he thought beneath her. She would find little sympathy here. She heard Luke hang the rifle back on the wall, but noticed he did not move far away from it.

"Johnson, Wilcox, give Luke back his guns." Maria jerked her head in the direction of the nervous ranch hands, giving them an excuse to leave the room to fetch the guns if they would only listen to her.

They hesitated, but now that Luke stood free and offered no struggle, Maria's uncles had relaxed and paid them no heed. All three left at Maria's command.

"Maria, we are waiting." Connolly leaned against

the edge of the desk, his arms across his chest. His piercing gaze never strayed far from the sinewy form at Maria's shoulder. Luke never touched her, but the way he stood at her side conveyed a message of protection. For all that mattered, they seemed to protect each other.

"You may wait as long as you like. I need explain nothing. I am a grown woman. I have been running this ranch quite well on my own. I appreciate your concern, but I did not invite you here. I would have welcomed you had you arrived as guests, but I will not welcome dictators." Maria deliberately slipped around Luke and reached for the rifle she had used earlier. Since she also picked up the cleaning case on a shelf nearby, no one interfered, but her intent made itself known. She sat down and began swabbing the long barrel of the gun, deliberately ignoring the men.

Connolly gave a ragged sigh and turned his gaze back to Luke. "I can see why you brought her back. Where have we met? Talk fast, I'm rapidly losing what little patience I possess."

"You know my father, Joshua Walker, from Kansas. I was just a youngster when you moved back to St. Louis; I don't expect you to remember me."

"How in hell did you remember me, then?"

Luke shrugged. "Family resemblance. Irish stayed at our place whenever he was in town. He was a good man."

Valencía settled in a high-backed leather chair across from Maria and watched as she surreptitiously swept away a tear. Although he appeared indifferent to the conversation, he followed each word, but his gaze never wavered from the young girl with the long braid hanging over her shoulder.

"He was a damn good man, and he would have blown your head off before you set a foot on his property after what you've done. Or are you going to deny doing anything wrong?"

"What I have or have not done is between Maria and myself and not the point. If I have harmed her reputation, I will marry her. You know my family. I cannot offer her an unblemished past, but I can offer her some measure of respectability. As my wife, she will be taken care of.''

"Oh, shut up, Luke. We have been over this before.'' Maria made a gesture of disgust with the hand holding the polishing rag. "You don't have to marry me out of some perverted sense of decency. Just get your guns from Johnson when you go out.''

"Maria.'' The voice from the corner was deathly quiet. "We are your guardians. However much you dislike it, we will be the ones to make the decisions. This man has dishonored the name of your family. There are only two choices to be made. Before you arrived, we had already decided he must hang. If you still mean to marry your *novio*, then it is imperative that he hang. There is no other solution. However, if your Uncle Patrick is acquainted with his family and approves, we will talk to the Vasqueros and have your betrothal broken so you may marry this man. I suggest if you have any feeling at all for this one you have taken as lover that you speak very politely and respectfully to your father's brother and plead your case.''

Maria lifted her head and a muscle tightened along her jaw, setting her lips in the formidable thin line that she inherited from her mother. "You mistake me, *Tío* Juan. I have no intention of marrying any man. I once thought marrying Manuel would be the respectable thing to do, but you and Uncle Patrick have taught me tonight that to submit to the malicious whims of men would mean a lifetime of hell. You cannot force me to repeat marriage vows, and if you threaten Luke, you will force me into doing what I would prefer not to do. You must remember, I know him better than I do either of you.''

Connolly came to his feet in rage and Valencía restrained himself by clasping his long fingers over the arms of the chair. Their exclamations of annoyance went ignored by the man most threatened by this family warfare. Luke spun around and, removing the rifle from Maria once again, he caught her hands and half jerked, half lifted her to her feet.

She barely came to his chin, but her slanted green eyes met his with the fury of an injured wildcat. To stroke her would be deadly. Luke had not forgotten the pistol in her pocket and was not fool enough to think she would not use it if cornered. Cornering her was the worst possible thing to do. Too bad those inept uncles of hers did not realize that.

"Maria, I will not hide behind your skirts, so stop threatening the only blood family you will ever have. They mean well and in their place, I would do the same. Had I known they would arrive, I would never have taken you with me. The deed is done and there is no looking back. Face facts for once in your life, Maria."

He was wanting her to do something; she could tell that from the way he gripped her arm and stared into her eyes with that odd look of yearning in them that she had caught once before. With his back to the others, Luke concealed the message in his eyes from all but her. He counted on her for something, but she could not believe what her heart wished to believe.

"Let me go, Luke," she answered softly, not meeting his gaze as she spoke. She had too much to think of in too little time, and she did not need the distraction of his eyes.

He released her and stepped back so she might stand before her uncles. Keeping his expression as impassive as the arrogant Spaniard across the room, Luke crossed his arms and waited.

Maria's voice was soft, but her words were so forceful no man dared to interrupt. "My mother and father loved each other. They fought and they cried when they lost the little ones, but through it all, they loved each other. They would not have survived otherwise.

"I do not know you or your families. I barely remember yours, Uncle Patrick, and I have never met yours, *Tío* Juan, so I do not know if you love them. I can only tell you that if you remember my mother and father with the same love in your hearts as there is in mine, you will listen to me now."

Connolly stood abruptly and turned his back on the

room. Valencía rose and offered Maria his clean handkerchief to wipe the tears streaming down her cheeks.

"We are listening, Maria." He spoke gently this
time, remembering a time when he had not listened
and had lost his beloved sister forever.

Maria waited until Patrick sat down in her father's
chair. He did not look at her, but played with the letter
opener on the blotting pad. "Go on."

Maria nodded and summoned all her inner strength,
very aware that Luke's life and her own were at stake.
"I am my father's daughter and my mother's daughter.
What you disapproved of in them, you will disapprove
of in me, but I cannot be otherwise. I cannot obey
rules simply because I am told they are rules. I must
understand why the rules are there. I will not obey
your commands simply because you tell me I must.
Neither would I obey a husband who would demand
the same subservience. I was not brought up that way.
I see that now where I did not before.

"Out of love and trust, I listened to my father and
mother. I would offer you the same if you give me half
a chance. I cannot, however, be commanded to love
and trust no more than I can be commanded to marry
where there is no love.

"If you have any love for me or my father, you will
ask Luke to stay and help find my father's murderers.
Had you listened, Luke would have told you my father's death was only one incident among many. When
you are ready to open your hearts instead of closing
your minds, then we may talk. For now, I am very
tired and wish to go to bed."

With casual dignity Maria turned and walked out,
her heart pounding with fear. She had poured out her
soul to them, and she did not know if they even heard.
She wished desperately to look at Luke, but she could
not. Instinctively she knew that would draw attention
back to the fact of what they had done together. This
way there would still be doubt in their minds.

Her fingers clenched the ivory handle of the derringer hidden in the depths of her pocket as she turned
down the corridor. Luke might be needing his guns.

2

All three men remained silent until Maria's steps died down the hallway. Luke remained standing, unarmed, in the room's center, but he had not been fooled by Maria's performance with the cleaning rags. He had only to step backward to grab a newly oiled and loaded rifle ready for use instead of the rusty, unused piece that had exploded earlier. It was an old single-shot Springfield, but it would suffice for making his escape if necessary. He had no wish to harm these men, but he didn't intend to hang, even for Maria.

Warily he waited for his elders to return to the subject that most concerned him. Would they listen to Maria or ignore the pleas of a nineteen-year-old girl? He had told her he did not wish to hide behind her skirts and miraculously, except for the rifle, she had obeyed. Luke wished he had the time to think about the significance of that after her words of tonight, but he couldn't allow his thoughts to drift. He had a battle yet to fight.

"All right, Walker, we'll give you a chance to convince us. Maria's letter said only that you had arrived with a letter from Mike and that Mike's death might have been part of a bigger plan. She is a terrible letter writer, reserving only one sentence per topic, but it scared me enough to come all the way out here. The only problem I found when I arrived is that you had absconded with my niece."

"It's a long story. Do I have your permission to sit?" At Connolly's nod Luke pulled up Maria's chair and carefully set the rifle down beside it. Luke sensed Valencía eyeing the weapon with misgiving, but he launched into his tale before any objection could be made.

The two men listened without comment to the contents of the letter that had brought Luke here and the small discoveries he had made since. His unfounded suspicions he kept to himself, but Maria's uncles were not fools. They pounced upon the same questions that had eluded Luke.

"Why would anyone drive out those dirt farmers? Times being what they are, they're likely to go broke before the year's out anyway. Are the same things happening on the bigger ranches? Or is it only on this one? Have you any proof that they're not just accidents? Have you any motives for killing Mike?"

Luke hadn't even known Irish's real name, but then, few people out here did. It would be interesting to learn more about the man who had reared a daughter like Maria, if they let him live so long. He crossed his legs in front of him and shook his head.

"I've got plenty of suspicions, but they're based on instinct and not proof. I need time to talk to the other ranchers; I've got a man I want to plant on one of the larger spreads; and I need to go back to Santa Fe and maybe even Albuquerque to trace the owners of those companies buying up the deeds. There's a rotten odor here somewhere, and I suspect Irish knew more about it than he let me know. That is one motive. There may be others."

"Have you called on the Vasqueros?" the man in the corner asked quietly.

Not in the direct light of the lamp, Juan Valencía's features were obscured by shadow, but Luke figured there was more than one reason behind his question. "I'm not here in any official capacity. I can't question men I do not know, and the Vasqueros avoid being known." He couldn't put it any more politely than that.

Valencía nodded his head in agreement. "Have you an official capacity? What makes you think you can solve this problem? Why did Irish write to you?"

Luke shrugged. "I've been with the Rangers, and

then I worked awhile with Mr. Hume of Wells Fargo. Are you familiar with him?''

Valencía nodded again. "A gentleman, rather eccentric, but extremely intelligent. You are one of his men?''

"No longer. By the time men reach the desperation of robbing a Wells Fargo stage, they're only begging for a bullet to end their misery. I still lend a hand occasionally if Mr. Hume asks, but the lawlessness out here isn't confined to men with guns. My partner and I have developed a reputation among some of the smaller ranchers back in Texas. Word travels slowly, but Irish knew me. He knew it was the kind of job that would interest me.''

Valencía looked at him oddly. "Are you certain that is the only reason he invited you out here? I do not remember my brother-in-law as being a man who asks for help. Did he mention Maria? Or her *novio*, the Vasquero boy?''

Connolly looked up sharply. "What in hell are you saying, Valencía? My brother wouldn't invite this outlaw out here to seduce his own daughter away from her fiancé. Where's the sense in that when she's betrothed to a perfectly respectable family?''

Luke's gaze met that of the Spaniard's. The flicker of anger was so brief, he couldn't be certain he read it right, but the animosity of the other man's reply confirmed one suspicion.

"The Vasqueros stole my father's land. They stole it legally, within the courts of law, but it was theft just the same. I do not think Irish had any fondness for them. He tried to warn my father of them when we moved out here to claim the land that my grandfather and his father had owned for decades. The American courts upheld only the Spanish deeds that brought them the most money. We had the land. Vasquero had the money. He is a wily, cruel old man. I do not know the son, but if he has grown up as his father, I would not want my niece to marry him.''

Connolly looked stunned. "Why didn't you tell me this earlier? I let the man think I approved of the mar-

riage. But I'll be damned if I'll marry a girl like Maria
off to a gunfighter. By God, I have daughters her age
and I wouldn't let them in the same room with a man
like this.''

Luke's lips twisted into a grimace of a smile. ''I beg
your pardon, Mr. Connolly, but I doubt that your
daughters could shoot a man's hat from his head at a
hundred yards. Maria has a way of keeping a man in
his place. You've been too long from this land if you
don't remember how it is out here. You're not likely
to find many men suitable for sitting in the parlor with
your daughters.''

''Then damn it, I will take Maria home with me!
We'll sell the confounded ranch, and she can come
live among civilized folk. Why in hell Mike insisted
on remaining in this hellhole is beyond my comprehension.''

Before the conversation could drift too far from the
subject, Luke interrupted. ''A word of warning, if you
mean to end Maria's betrothal, I would keep the news
quiet until—''

A small figure in a simple cotton wrapper appeared
in the doorway. With her long silky hair spilling over
the pale yellow material, she didn't appear old enough
to be out of the nursery. Only the angry slant of her
eyes gave her away.

''Excuse me, Luke, but it sounds as if it may be
time to defend myself. May I come in, gentlemen?''
The sarcasm wasn't meant to be concealed.

''Maria, you should be in bed.'' Valencía spoke
softly and without reproof.

''Thank you, *Tío* Juan, but it is somewhat difficult
to sleep while worrying over a friend who might be
hanged for no crime of his own. But since the subject
seems to have changed, perhaps I might add my
thoughts to the discussion of what is, after all, my
future.'' Maria did not move entirely into the circle of
light, but lingered at its outskirts while she studied the
three men before her. Though the tension had not left
them, their tempers had cooled to a reasonable degree.
She gave Luke credit for that.

"I cannot see where you have any choice, Maria. I have gone over the books. You don't have money even to buy feed when winter comes. You will have to start selling the herd to keep them from starving. At today's prices, you won't get enough to cover half of your debts. You will have to sell or marry a rich man who can feed the herd until times get better." Patrick added this last with an air of satisfaction, using her own argument against her.

Maria tilted her head and considered this. At least they had stopped talking about hanging Luke, but she sensed the subject had only been temporarily diverted. To salve their pride, they had to have sacrificial blood, figuratively if not literally. That was why her fate had surfaced.

"I don't believe I would be comfortable in St. Louis, Uncle Patrick, and I can't believe your wife and daughters would be comfortable having me around. Wouldn't it be easier if you helped me obtain a loan to keep the ranch operating until beef prices go up?"

Luke smiled to himself and sat back in his chair. He didn't fool himself into thinking Maria would win this battle, but the compromise point between her position and her uncles would buy time. He just hoped Maria understood when she had pushed them as far as they would go.

The argument went on for some minutes with offers to take her to the Valencía ranch in California, promises that she would have all the proceeds from the ranch to do with as she wished, under her uncles' protection, and barely concealed threats to send her to a convent if she must remain unreasonable.

Maria remained implacable throughout. "The ranch belonged to my father. It is all I have of him and my mother. I would not mind visiting St. Louis or California and meeting my cousins. The life out here is lonely and, as you say, if I do not marry, my reputation will suffer. I can agree with you on that. But I cannot leave until I know who killed my father, and I certainly won't sell the ranch until I can be certain it is not his killer who buys it. I would prefer not to sell the ranch at all, but as you give me no choice in the matter, you must at least give me satisfaction in the others.''

She had them there. She would not sell unless they found her father's killer, and the best hope they had of that was Luke. Both men turned speculative gazes toward the silent gunfighter.

''Leave us alone, Maria. We will take up the matter together and discuss it with you in the morning.''

Maria grimaced at her Uncle Patrick's order, but turned to do as told. On her way out, she gave Luke an audacious wink. He had to swallow his laughter with a cough. A female might not possess all the powers of a male, but there was more than one way to wield what power they possessed. Perhaps Irish might not have accomplished it in as devious a manner as his daughter, but Luke felt certain he was sitting back smiling proudly somewhere.

''Well, Mr. Walker, it looks as if the only way we can control Maria is through you.'' Patrick Connolly hadn't missed the exchange, though he didn't follow its meaning. ''Unless we wish to sell the ranch over Maria's wishes and alienate her forever, we must find my brother's killer.''

He turned to Valencía. ''Do you feel free to write this Mr. Hume for a reference on this scoundrel? I would feel better if we knew at once whether we dealt with a crook or a con man.''

''I will write.'' His piercing dark eyes turned to Luke. ''If you try to leave this area, we will come after you. Between us we can command a fairly large army of pursuers. I do not believe you are the kind of man who enjoys living on the run.''

Luke met his gaze evenly. ''I seek trouble in my own way, señor, and running is not one of them. I will use everything within my power to find the man you want. I would have without your interference.''

''Then let us understand one thing more. If you come within a hundred yards of Maria, it is more than your hat that will be blown off.'' Connolly rose to confront the arrogant gunfighter.

Luke pulled himself from the chair. It had been a long day and his patience had worn thin. "That is a risk I will have to take. Good night, gentlemen."

Without asking their permission, Luke strode out.

When Maria went in search of breakfast next morning, she discovered her uncles waiting for her in the massive dining room that she never used. She could hear Pieta banging pots and cursing one of the dogs in the kitchen, but she did not dare antagonize her uncles by passing them by while she went to greet the cook. Wearing her usual work shirt and boy's britches, she hesitated in the doorway.

"Good morning, Uncle Patrick, *Tío* Juan. I did not expect you up so early. Let me speak to Pieta and I will join you."

The disapproval of her attire was frank in both pairs of eyes, but the command that followed did not mention her clothing.

"Sit down, Maria. The maid can serve you when she serves us. We need to talk."

Pieta was family, not a servant, but Maria was aware her proper uncle with his aristocratic ways would not understand this. After her mother had died, Pieta had been the only woman remaining on the ranch. It was not to be expected that she would remain in the kitchen with a man and a child to look after in the rest of the house. Maria sat but not without a measure of impatience.

"I trust after last night that you have come to some sober, sensible solution of how to deal with me." Not disguising her irritation, Maria poured herself a cup of coffee from the pot left on the table.

"Other than suggesting my brother could have used the rod on you with a little more frequency, yes, we have, but we expect your cooperation in the agreement."

Pieta entered wearing a new gingham gown from the material Maria had sent back. Her gaze immediately fell upon Maria with a frown, but instead of the tongue-lashing and hugs she usually would have administered, she set the platter of *huevos rancheros* on the table and departed with only a warning look to Maria.

"To what am I to agree?" Maria waited politely for her uncles to serve themselves, though her stomach roared a protest as the air filled with the welcome scents of Pieta's cooking.

"We have hired your gunfighter to discover what he can of your father's death. Once he has made his final report, we will begin accepting bids for the ranch. Much as we regret having to do it, neither of us can remain to oversee the operations of a spread this size, and we cannot possibly allow you to continue to do so under present circumstances. We had thought you safely betrothed to a neighbor who would look after you. Since it seems both your father and now Juan object to this marriage, it appears imperative that we remove you from the vicinity. Both our homes are open to you. With railroads crossing the country, it will not be so difficult for you to visit with both of us until you decide what you wish to do."

Breaking open a roll and spreading it with butter, Maria listened carefully to Patrick's ultimatum. As they had told her, she really did have little choice, but it went against the grain to knuckle under. Perhaps she would be better off with Manuel.

Keeping her thoughts to herself, she kept to the topic under discussion. "Luke will be free to do as he pleases? You do not hold any more threats over his head?"

This time her Spanish uncle spoke. "He will go free for so long as he stays away from you. Stay away from him, Maria. You will do him no favor by disobeying us in this."

Maria's gaze grew mutinous, but she made no reply as she bit into the roll. It was one thing for her to tell Luke to get out of her life, quite another for them to do so. Surrounded by men and everyone of them dictating to her—Lord, how did other women endure it?

Without any definite plan in mind, Maria wandered into the kitchen after breakfast. Pedro threw himself into her arms and she hugged him ecstatically, the first warm greeting she had received since returning. Sitting with the little boy in her lap, she talked to Pieta awhile, slowly getting information on what had been happening these past weeks.

After discussing at length the dresses to be made for her from the various lengths of material she had sent—she did not inform Pieta that there was no longer a need for a trousseau—Maria finally steered the conversation to other subjects. Carmelita had arrived safely, *sí.* Her Miguel had been hired on by the uncles, *sí.* Mr. Connolly had arrived several days after Maria's departure and had sent for Señor Valencía when Carmelita arrived without her. No, Manuel had only been by once. He was gone on business for his father somewhere, they said. No, there had been no more accidents here. The barn had burnt at the O'Brien's, but he drank too much and it could have been a spilt lantern. No, she knew nothing about how the sheep were. Charlie would have to tell her that.

Worn out after prying this much from the usually loquacious Pieta, Maria consented to follow Pedro out to see how the puppies had grown.

Passing the horse barn, she spied Charlie shoveling out straw, and she stopped to speak to him. He grinned a greeting, then almost immediately went stiff. Behind him Luke stepped from the barn into the sunlight, leading his stallion. He had on his new Stetson and gunbelt and he nodded curtly to Maria. Without a word he mounted his horse and rode off.

Maria stared after him, her heart skipping an erratic beat. He had looked through her as if she weren't there. He hadn't even spoken. She had not even been given time to inquire how his arm was healing. A hollow pit began to form in her stomach.

She was not going to like this, not one single bit.

3

He couldn't keep the hundred-yard limit. That would be an impossibility. She was always there.

Luke tried to keep his distance. Now that her uncles were there to look after things, it wasn't necessary that he be at the ranch all day. He stayed as far away as he was able, traipsing across the countryside in a pretense of busyness, asking questions while buying grain, gathering information while discussing a horse for sale, learning what he could while arranging a cattle drive for the first part of the herd to be sold. Night was the problem.

He felt obligated to report his findings to Maria's uncles. He'd eat in the bunkhouse with the other men, meet Connolly and Valencía in the study after dark, but she always knew when he was there. And Luke always knew when Maria entered. Without even turning his head, he knew when she stood in the doorway. The air would suddenly get warmer, more sultry, and the scent of roses would wrap around him. It got so Luke almost knew what she was wearing before he politely stood up at her greeting and turned to meet the fathomless depths of those green eyes. She had a new calico gown that was laced in ribbons and wrapped around her waist to fall in simple folds. To his mind, it was the most beautiful gown she owned because it hid none of her natural charm. The soft curve of her bosom and hips were revealed in every movement, more tantalizing that the sway of petticoats or the artificial pull of bustle and train. Luke was hard-pressed to keep his gaze on her face.

He slept in the bunkhouse at night because no one

told him he could not. He preferred the rough clean-
liness of the cots and the familiarity of Charlie's snores
to the rowdy noise of the saloon's few rooms. Besides,
the temptation of the liquor near at hand in town was
dangerous to life and limb. He had a job to do and he
would do it. Then he would get the hell out of here.

But some nights Luke couldn't sleep, and the solace
of the guitar strings beneath his fingers eased the pain.
Maria was with him then, hovering in the garden behind him while his fingers plucked every tune he knew
just to please her ears. He relaxed knowing she was
listening, and when a song came to him, he sang with
all the emotion the words deserved. There could be no
harm in singing.

Maria lingered on the terrace, drinking in the sound
of Luke's voice as if it were mellow wine and she were
parched for thirst. She heard the words and the emotions, memorizing the lines of the love songs, pretending they were meant for her and not the mysterious
Caroline. Sometimes, when the tears came too easily,
she fled back to her room. Or if she heard her uncles'
voices, she would pick a rose and nod politely, then
leave them to talk as if she had come only for the
flower. Other times she stayed until Luke was through
and wondered if he knew she was there, or if he even
cared.

One night her Uncle Juan came upon her silently
while she perched on the garden wall, listening to the
song of a lonesome cowboy on the trail. She gave
thanks to heaven that it had not been one of the love
songs that made tears streak down her cheeks when
her uncle stopped in front of her.

To her surprise, he did not mention the serenade,
but gestured toward the flower in her hand. "Camille
loved roses. This was her garden?"

Maria sat beneath an arched bower filled to overflowing with the miniature blooms of climbing roses.
She reached to pluck one of the fragrant blossoms and
lifted it to her uncle to smell. "My mother loved it
out here. My father brought her roses from wherever

he traveled. If he could not buy one that particularly caught his eye, he was quite capable of stealing it.''

She did not need to say more. Her father would have given her mother the moon if she had requested it. To grow roses like these out here required tireless energy, but even after her mother had died, he had kept the garden as she loved it. With all the other work that had to be done, between the two of them they had still managed to keep the roses thriving.

''A love like that is very rare.'' Juan roamed restlessly about the bower. The serenade had drifted into an unemotional display of guitar technique, as if the player sensed another performance in progress.

''Yes, I suppose it is.'' Maria sadly began pulling the petals from the flower in her hand, letting them float to the yard beyond the terrace. ''I suppose that is why he never married again.''

Her thoughts had been on that much of late. Her father had been a vigorous man in the prime of life when her mother had died. He had wanted sons and a large family. Now that she understood a little more of the needs of men, she had cause to wonder how he satisfied them. Irish Connolly was not a man to mourn publicly or become a monk. These were not fitting topics to think on, but events of late kept them always on the edge of her mind.

''He had you. That made him a very lucky man.'' Juan held out his hand and helped Maria to her feet. Even after the heat of the day he managed to appear cool and detached. His dark hair with the wings of silver at his temples lay neatly in place, and he appeared every inch the gentleman she had pictured in her mind. But his hand was warm and his voice was gentle, and Maria found no coldness in him.

''Thank you, *Tío* Juan, but I proved a disappointment to him many times over. Love has its flaws.''

''So it does, Maria. One must have the experience and wisdom to overlook the imperfections or recognize dangerous defects, but love does not let even experience and wisdom think clearly.''

"it is a wonder people find it at all. Good night, *Tío.*"

Maria drifted into the house, leaving Juan to stare out over the barren yard, where the music no longer played.

Relieved of many of her duties by the presence of her uncles, Maria had more time to spend with Pedro and Pieta in the house and kitchen. The chunky little boy responded with enthusiasm to this extra attention, but Pieta continued to watch her with a certain degree of suspicion. For the first time in many years, Maria was not telling her everything, and the channel of communications seemed to be narrowing.

Maria could not blame her, but she had too many problems of her own to know how to solve this one. Since Manuel was out of town, she could not inform him of her guardians' refusal to accept their betrothal, and she was not at all certain that it would be wise to mention that fact to his family as yet. So she continued to stand for the fittings of her bridal gown as if nothing had changed. Yet everything had.

Relieved of the worry soon after she returned that she might carry Luke's child, Maria still found her thoughts wandering in that direction. What would it be like to carry a man's child? She wanted children very much, but to have to submit to a man's will for the rest of her life did not sit well with her. She did not like being ordered to avoid Luke, and she resented Luke's willingness to abide by the order. And a man like Manuel would be even worse than her uncles. So where was the solution?

The other problem lay in her sudden concern over Pedro's parentage. If the ranch were to be sold, Pieta would have no home. Charlie and the other cowboys would wander on to other bunks, as they were inclined to do anyway. Jose, Pieta's eldest, had already left home seeking adventure. Carmelita would soon marry her Miguel if all went well. The father of these two had left and never returned soon after Carmelita's birth, which was why Pieta had joined the Connolly household in the first place. She had extended family all over New Mexico, but no home of her own. Where would she go? To the father of Pedro would be the simplest solution, but that was where Maria's thinking had wandered astray.

She had only been fourteen when Pedro was born. She had been enchanted with the baby and had not questioned where it came from. Only now, with her own worries over what she had done with Luke, did the question enter her head. Pieta was not a loose woman. She did not attend church, that was true, but she had taught Maria the differences between wrong and right as well as the church had. And she never strayed from that path, except for Pedro.

Not daring to question Pieta on such a sensitive subject, unwilling to give her a chance to question herself about Luke, Maria continued to hide her uncles' plans for her and the ranch from the woman who had acted in her mother's place. It was no wonder Pieta treated her with suspicion, but Maria did not know how to close the gap widening between them.

With no one to talk to, Maria began to grow restless under her uncles' restrictions. They tried to be kind, but they could not help but act as they would to their own daughters, and Maria in no way resembled those gently nurtured children. She was unaccustomed to walking when she could run, and horseback riding was done in work clothes as part of the daily chores, not a pleasure jaunt on sidesaddle with long skirts. She sighed as Uncle Patrick reprimanded her for unsaddling her own horse and then getting into a jousting match with pitchforks with one of the stable hands. If she couldn't make a little fun out of the work and couldn't even work, her hours would drag on eternally empty.

After two weeks of these minor skirmishes, Maria decided they certainly couldn't object to her attending church. Garbing herself in the lovely rose-striped gown and the hat Manuel had returned while she was gone—now neatly adorned with rose ribbons instead of yellow—Maria greeted her uncles, who lingered over Sunday breakfast.

"Charlie is taking me into church and I'm going to stay a little while in town to visit. Would either of you care to accompany me?" With her hair stacked in soft waves, long skirts trailing the ground, and pulling on her new kid gloves, she appeared every bit the lady they wished her to be. Both men smiled approvingly and sent her on her way without a qualm.

Triumphantly Maria climbed into the buckboard while Charlie tied Erinmeade on behind. In a small satchel at her feet she had packed a change of clothes. It would be simple enough to slip into her riding skirts at the back of Jesse's store after church. She would stop in and visit Consuela, then ride out to see how the O'Briens were doing after that fire. She would be home by dark and no one would be the wiser.

She threw the clouds gathering on the horizon an anxious look, but it did not seem likely that they would cross the distance quickly, if at all. A shower would be pleasant and give her an excuse for being late. The day would be perfect.

Giving Maria's smug expression a sideways look, Charlie rattled the reins and set the buckboard rolling. He knew when the little devil was up to mischief, but she looked so prim and proper in that getup, he could not imagine what it could be.

Luke leaned against the door in the second-floor room, where the air had already reached stifling proportions. The roof slanted away from him toward the woman on the window seat on the opposite wall. She turned her face toward the street below, and a curtain of black hair hid her profile. Her hair did not have the silky consistency of Maria's, but billowed out in a thick cloud that might have been curly had it been properly brushed. As it was, she twisted nervously at small strands, making it worse.

"You cannot know anything, Cheyenne Walker. It is not your business, I have told you before. Why didn't you keep Maria away while you had her? Then there would be no problem."

"You can't harbor any idea that he will marry you? You are too smart for that, Consuela."

"I wouldn't marry the *cochino* if they handed him to me on a platter with an apple between his teeth. I want his money. In a little while I will almost have enough to get away from here forever. No, it is Maria I worry about. She is a child. She does not understand these things."

"She is a child no longer, Consuela. You should have told her before. You may need to tell her yet. She is headstrong and her uncles may drive her into doing something she should not. She understands Manuel might beat her, but she does not understand the nature of the beating. Like you, I would rather not tell her of these things, but there may come a time when she must be told."

"He will kill both of us. It cannot be done. Take her away. I have seen one man die for knowing the truth. I will not accept such responsibility again. You do not understand the power of his family. I may run away and they will find some replacement for me. I mean nothing to them. But Maria is important. They will not let her go so easily. If you try to interfere, they will kill you." Consuela's voice shook and she continued to refuse to look at him.

Luke crossed the room and grasped her by the shoulders, turning her around so she could meet his eyes. "Everyone knows Manuel is the man who beats you, who pays your rent, who buys your clothes. It did not take me long to find out. Sooner or later, Maria is going to hear about it. What then? What is it he wants from Maria? Do you know?"

Consuela shrugged and avoided his eyes. "We do not talk. I know nothing. What purpose is there in coming to me?"

Luke threw his hands up in the air in disgust, releasing her to the window seat again. "I want information. If you have none, then I want you somewhere safe in case I need to keep Maria from doing something foolish. Besides that, I can't tolerate a coward who beats women."

Consuela sneered. "I am a whore. Who cares what happens to a whore? I will tell Maria nothing. She thinks I am her friend, and so I will be. Telling her that Manuel comes here would only drive her away from him and into your arms, and then you will both be dead. Go away. Take Maria with you before he returns."

Luke ran his fingers through his hair. "It is not that easy. I wish it were. If we do this with care, Maria will return to St. Louis or California with her uncles, and she will be safe. Until then I want you out of here. She has not told Manuel of her plans yet, and it will be safer if she does not. Should she find out about you, she is likely to go after him with a gun. I'll give you the money to take the next stage out of here, Consuela. Just leave me an address where I can reach you."

Consuela studied the gunman through narrowed eyes. She didn't trust men, and she didn't know what this one really wanted. Her gaze roamed over Luke's muscular shoulders and lean hips and traveled back to the chiseled lines of his sun-bronzed face. Even an innocent like Maria could not miss this one's virility. She had seen the kiss the two had exchanged upon first meeting. He would not have missed any opportunity to repeat that chance since then. He would not be here now if Maria hadn't succumbed to his seduction to some degree. The only reason she could think that he had not carried the girl off by now was the gunman's natural inclination to avoid the entanglements of marriage. Maria would never accept anything less.

With a sudden movement Consuela glided from the window seat to stand in front of Luke, so close that her heavy breasts brushed against his partially opened shirt. She lifted one hand to his unruly hair and stroked it lightly while the other rested tauntingly on his chest.

"I will be your woman, señor. You do not need a silly girl. Take me with you, and you will never need another woman. Hold me. Let me show you what I can do."

Luke couldn't control the response of his hungry

loins as Consuela pressed against him, and his arms instinctively wrapped around her. One hand circled her breast, and for a moment he seriously considered the temptation. Barred from Maria, he needed some release, but this was not it.

He pressed a rough kiss of appreciation against Consuela's mouth, then firmly set her at arm's length from him. "Relatives, Consuela. Have you relatives to go to?"

From beneath heavy black brows she gave him an appraising glance, then swung away with a fling of her long skirt. "In Albuquerque. Buy my ticket and leave it there for me to pick up so he won't hear of my leaving until I am gone. I will get word to you when I arrive."

"If you need money, Consuela . . ."

She tossed her hair and glared proudly at him. "If I need money, I will blackmail Manuel. You will need yours for Maria. You will have to marry her to have her, but that should not be difficult for a man like you. Go, before I change my mind."

Realizing he had just passed some sort of test, Luke's mouth twisted ruefully, but he took her at her word. "I will see that Maria is taken care of. The ticket will be at the office."

In the midst of his argument with Consuela, Luke had not heard the mission bells ringing, nor would he have associated the sound with trouble if he had. Instead he strode from Consuela's room feeling as if he had accomplished one small thing this day, and he started down the stairs with the intention of meeting Sean at the stable.

After changing from her Sunday clothes to her riding skirt, Maria had hurried to see Consuela before the saloon opened. Entering by the back door, she had almost reached the foot of the stairs, the same place where she had first met Luke, when she grew conscious of someone coming down.

Her gaze lifted to encounter Luke's, and in that instant she felt all the blood rush from her face. She felt as if she had been dealt a blow to the stomach. Unable to deal with her violent physical reaction to the thought of Luke availing himself of Consuela's services, she could not utter a word. Before Luke could stop her, she wheeled around and fled out the door she had entered so merrily just a minute before.

Luke cursed and ran after her.

4

Maria had already disappeared down some side alley by the time Luke hit the street. Townspeople in their Sunday clothes still milled about in the mission yard and up and down the dirt road, but none seemed to be staring after the wide-eyed, horrified creature who had fled the back door of the saloon. Luke surmised she had taken the first turn to avoid being seen.

Blood thundering in his head, Luke ran down the nearest alley in pursuit. He didn't need to stop and consider why he chased after her or why he felt the need to explain. He only knew the pain in Maria's eyes and could not bear the gut-wrenching anguish he felt at knowing he had caused it. He had to explain, he *would* explain, before the little brat did something explosive.

He lost more time when he staggered into the main street and still could find no sign of Maria. Where could she have gone? The stores were closed. Even the saloon wouldn't open until later. All the good people of San Pedro worshiped the Lord's day in their home. So where was Maria?

Cursing his own stupidity, he realized she had been wearing riding skirts. She had crippled his mind with that wounded look—where else would she have gone but to the stables? Cursing himself for a fool, cursing Maria for her fleetness of foot, Luke ran for the livery.

As soon as he dashed through the open doorway Luke knew he was too late. Sean stood there, dazed and gazing after the cloud of dust billowing against the dark clouds on the horizon. Since he had seldom seen the Irishman left speechless, Luke could only guess the cause, and his hand knotted into a wrathful fist.

"What did she say to you?" The words came out harshly, shaking Sean from his stupor.

The Irishman saw the cold, hard fury in Luke's eyes and knew what it must feel like to face him with his guns drawn. He gulped and tried to answer coherently, knowing only a facile tongue would get him out of this one.

"I don't think it's in your best interest to know, Walker. She wasn't precisely happy with your behavior."

"O'Laughlin, if you touched one hair on that woman's head, I'll have your scalp," Luke threatened without raising his voice. He could tell by the guilt in Sean's eyes that he had hit the mark. "She's mine, Sean. I don't intend to share her. *Comprende?*"

"I swear, Luke, it was none of my doing! She came in here in a tearing rage. I tried to calm her down, that's all." Remembering how Maria had felt when she flung herself into his arms and kissed him, Sean felt a surge of irritation at the man who had driven her here. "If you can't learn to handle her any better than that, then I sure the hell will! She's too damned good to be treated like one of your whores."

Weeks of pent-up frustration found an outlet. Clenching his fist, Luke swung it at Sean's jaw, sending him flying into the straw. Not bothering to wait for Sean to get up, he stepped over his friend's prostrate form and went after his horse.

Sean scrambled out of the way as Luke mounted. With a twist of his wrist, Luke flung a few dollars at his feet. "Buy Consuela a ticket out of here and leave it at the office. And keep your mouth *shut*."

With that command Luke spurred his horse from the stable and down the road Maria had taken. The first clap of thunder rocked across the cloud-laden sky.

She rode like a demon, but Luke easily kept pace with her smaller mount. Figuring it safer if she did not know he was in pursuit, he let her keep her lead until her trail led up into the rock-strewn regions of the ridge overlooking the valley. Biting his cheek to keep from crying out at her foolishness, Luke urged his stallion up the treacherous path.

Huge boulders lined the rocky roadway fit for neither man nor beast. The sheep used the trail to find water on the lower range. The young sheepherders occasionally used it for a short cut down to the ranch, but no one in their right mind would ride this gravel-strewn creek bed on a horse with a thunderstorm threatening. Luke's curses grew more explicit the higher he climbed.

The path trailed out of sight as it emerged from the scrubby shrubbery onto the high, flat ridge. In the distance Luke could see Maria sitting astride her horse, staring out over the valley that spread below her. The Connolly ranch made up most of that valley. Far off, near the horizon, the fences of the Vasquero ranch could be seen. The road through the hills to town couldn't be seen from here. Even the ranch house appeared as a small blot on the landscape. The drop down to the valley was littered with yawning crevasses, loose gravel, and precariously lodged boulders. Luke shuddered and spurred his horse after Maria.

Maria heard him coming and reared Erinmeade around to race down the hill in the other direction, but Luke had anticipated that move. Cutting across the plateau at an angle, he intercepted her path and reached for the reins.

Maria jerked them out of his hand and tried to swing away. Refusing to let her escape, Luke grabbed her waist. She squirmed to avoid his grasp, but lost her hold on the stirrup in so doing. That was all the leverage Luke needed. With one quick jerk upward, he lifted her kicking, screaming figure from the saddle and threw her down across his lap.

The saddle horn bruised her ribs and Maria struggled to land on her feet. Luke assisted ungallantly, letting her fall to the ground while keeping a grip on her hair. Throwing his foot over the saddle, he joined her.

Maria kicked at his shins as he landed beside her, but Luke dodged the blow. Loosing her hair, he caught her in both arms and crushed her against him so she could do no more than squirm helplessly in his hold. Ignoring her curses, he bent his head to find her mouth.

Maria bit his lip and pummeled his shoulders with her fists and lashed out desperately with her booted feet, but Luke took it all in stride. She had no strength against him. His muscular arms closed like bands of steel around her waist, and the rock-hard planes of his chest resisted her futile punishment. Only his lips offered any softness, and they were more devastating than his greater strength. She could not tear away as they parted her lips and plundered her soul. She drowned in the urgent hunger of his demand, and her fingers soon found a hold in his hair and clung there as her feet disappeared from under her.

His callused hands ran down her back, pressing her closer, making her aware of where their bodies touched, warning her of what would happen when the heat between them burst into flames. As his tongue touched her throat, Maria moaned a protest, but her arms clinging to Luke's shoulders had already signaled surrender.

When his hand circled her buttock and the other slid deeper between her legs, Maria knew he had no intention of stopping with just a kiss. Against her will, her hips arched achingly against his until she felt the bulge of his maleness pressing into her. It was wrong. She knew it was wrong, but she could not seem to find the strength to pull away.

The first drops of rain began to patter against their skin as Luke's mouth moved downward, searing her cheek and throat and finding the hollow where her shirt fell open. Maria buried her fingers in his hair as he bent her backward to follow the full curve of her breasts with his lips. The aroused tip brushed achingly against the soft linen of her camisole, begging for his touch. A crash of thunder broke overhead as Luke's hand came up to search for the treasure hidden beneath the layers of cloth.

"Do you think this is what I was doing with Consuela, *mi cariña?* Do you really think I could go from her arms into yours, taste her lips when I've known these?" Luke returned his lips to Maria's, plying her mouth with kisses as his fingers tore at the buttons of her shirt. The rain came harder, but he was possessed with a need to make her understand what he felt.

"I am not a fool, let me go, Luke," Maria cried, twisting away from the spell he tried to weave. "Men have only one reason to visit Consuela. I cannot stop you from seeing her, but do not insult me like this, Luke. I beg of you."

Luke released her half-opened shirt, took her by the shoulders, and shook her until she looked up into his eyes.

"You told me Consuela was your friend. If I am to help you, I must know your friends. I cannot see her as anything else. The only woman I can see in my arms is you, Maria, may God forgive me. Tell me to stop if you want me no longer, but do not seek excuses. I will not believe them."

The rain poured down her face, turning her loosened hair into dripping streams that ran over her cheeks, soaking her shirt to transparency. Water droplets framed the lashes of her tilted green eyes as they searched his face, and Luke brushed his fingers across her brows to wipe away the moisture.

His expression was as hard as ever to read, but the gentleness of his touch broke Maria's resistance. She did not know if she believed him and did not care. All she wanted was the tenderness they conveyed. She buried her face against his chest and felt his arms wrap around her, and then he was lifting her from her feet, carrying her to the shelter beneath an overhanging rock.

The sheepherders had made a crude hut of the jutting rock, using the natural formation for ceiling and walls and building a fourth side and door with purloined slabs of wood and adobe clay. The inside was miraculously dry, and Luke gently lowered his shivering burden upon the blankets near the wall before returning outside to find shelter for the horses.

When he returned, Maria had removed her soaked clothing and hung it on outcroppings of rock. Luke's gaze went from the woman's garments dripping from the wall to the small bundle of blankets in the corner. Green eyes shone defiantly from the gloom, and his heart gave a lurch of joy.

Within minutes he had a small fire warming the damp. The thunder rolled continuously overhead, but the horses were protected and he had nothing else to worry about for the rest of the afternoon. His amber eyes sought the corner again as Luke sat down and began to remove his boots.

Maria watched anxiously as Luke took off his shirt next, hanging it on the stones with hers. Water ran in rivulets across the muscular hills and valleys of his shoulders, and when he turned, she could see the droplets glistening in the dark curls spreading across his chest and down his belly. A warmth took root in her center as his hands went to the fastenings of his pants, and she could not free her gaze of its fascination as she followed the path of curls downward.

She held her breath as Luke stepped out of this last layer of sodden clothing. Firelight flickered and gleamed along the golden tautness of his masculine torso. She had to clench her teeth to keep them from chattering as she fully absorbed the impact of his lean hips and muscular legs. She did not need to be told of his desire. Even after the drenching of the cold rain he was aroused and ready for her, and fear slid along her veins. She had never looked at him like this before. How could she have done what she had done? It seemed impossible.

As Maria's eyes raised to Luke's, he saw her fear and uncertainty. She still knew so little of men; he longed to teach her everything in long nights of love-making while lying by the fire, just the two of them, with no one to interfere. But he could not even take her in a proper bed, and their time together would be forever limited to brief snatches of stolen time. Curbing his impatience, he lifted the blanket from her fingers and settled down beside her.

His skin whispered along her own, and the conflagration of heat between them was instantaneous. Maria kept her eyes fastened on Luke's as he lifted his hand to caress her bare breast, and she gave a shudder of longing at the sensation invoked.

"You are so beautiful, Maria." His gaze touched upon the kiss-swollen pout of her lips, then slid lower to the full, upthrust curves of her breasts. He brushed the blanket back from her shoulders and let his eyes drink their fill of the loveliness revealed. The aureoles of her nipples tightened insistently against his palm, and he bent his head.

Maria gasped at the hot sensation flooding through her as he drew her into his mouth. Luke's arm wrapped around her back to support her as he suckled greedily, sending quake after quake shivering through her until her hands tangled in his hair and she begged for mercy.

There was no stopping after that. His lips were everywhere, exploring her mouth, snaking down the column of her throat, scorching her breasts into fountains of sensation. His hands roamed at will, laying her back against the blankets so they could travel silken curves, gently stroking intimate places that made Maria writhe with an agony of longing, until she learned to touch him and repeat the caress.

At the innocence of her touch, Luke groaned and buried his face in the sweet scents of her drying hair. As Luke covered her, Maria eagerly wrapped her arms about his shoulders and arched urgently against him, all fear flown. She wanted him with a desire so deep she could envision no other means of calming it. When she felt his entrance, she gave a cry of joy and thrust upward, taking all of him into her.

Lightning struck nearby, sending a quivering haze across the rocks and causing the horses to whinny restlessly. Thunder broke in a splintering crescendo over their heads, and the rain poured in torrents, leaking beneath the crude door. None of it mattered. They were one with the elements, part of nature, and what they did was as natural as the rain.

Afterward, Luke pulled the blanket over them to keep out the dampness, but Maria felt as warm as if the sun shone inside of her. She spread her hand over the soft fur of Luke's chest and gloried in the steady beat of his heart beneath her palm. She felt the strong length of his leg beneath hers, and excitement danced between them as she rubbed her toes along his calf.

"You are a wanton tease, *brujita*," Luke whispered against her ear, his breath setting the fine, dry wisps of her hair in motion. His hand cupped her breast possessively, as if registering his claim to this right.

"I know nothing of teasing but what you teach me, *señor*." Maria reached up to nibble his ear and felt a shiver of delight at his reaction.

"I know, my love. That makes you even more enchantingly dangerous." Luke groaned as her hands roamed exploringly down his ribs while her lips played havoc with his ear. She was his, entirely his, for the moment. The feeling that gave to him was more overpowering than any other he had known. He wanted to hold her and protect her and let the world know she was his. Not wishing to contemplate the implications of such thoughts, Luke rolled over and pulled her close. "It is still raining, little witch. There is time to teach you more."

Maria's hands flew to his chest and her gaze lifted to his in wonderment. His amber eyes blazed with a hot desire that scorched a path to her soul, and she could no more resist his hunger than the tides can resist the moon. She succumbed, and he carried her away with him once more.

When the rain finally stopped and they were forced to return to their clothes, the tension between them grew again. Luke's fingers lingered on the buttons of her shirt while he gazed upon her bent head. She did not move from his touch, but he could feel the distance she was creating between them by not meeting his eyes.

"Why did you kiss Sean?" He had not meant the

words to come out so harshly, but she had stirred old fears, and he knew of no other way to resolve them.

Maria looked up at Luke in surprise. His fingers still rested gently at the collar of her shirt, but the warmth had fled his eyes. "Because he was there and I was angry. I thought if you could kiss Consuela, then there was no reason I couldn't kiss anybody I wanted."

Her answer was so simple Luke had no trouble believing it. Other women would have denied the kiss or placed the blame on Sean or any of a thousand little lies he'd heard before. Not Maria. A small grin turned up the corner of his lips.

"Don't give him any more ideas, *querida*. His jaw won't take it."

Maria looked indignant, but the gleam had returned to Luke's eyes and she relaxed to a small degree. She couldn't relax entirely, however. Too many problems loomed on the horizon.

"I'd better ride down first, Luke. They will be looking for me, and it won't look good if we come in together."

Luke's jaw tightened. "I'm not letting you ride down through that mud alone. It's dangerous."

His arms slid around her and Maria leaned gratefully against his chest, not wanting this parting, not wanting all the partings to come. She had much to think about after this afternoon, but she could scarcely think at all when he held her this way. She only knew that she had to protect him from her uncles; she did not dare to be seen with him.

"I will take the long way down. I've ridden these roads ever since I was old enough to sit on a horse, Luke. Don't worry about me."

Luke's hands bit into her shoulders. He knew what she was saying and why, but it burned at his gut just the same. He had not seen the consequences of his reputation in this way before. He knew he had courted death as well as the fear and revulsion of other men when he had chosen the path of gunfighter, or it had chosen him, but he had never thought of it affecting his future. He had never anticipated a future, but he desperately craved one now. But now the past stood in his way.

"Maria." Luke willed her to look up at him. The smudged darkness around her eyes made him cringe with shame. "I can't stay away from you. We might as well let them know that now."

Maria's heart leapt at these words, but he offered no other explanations, and she shook her head in despair. "Don't be foolish. I have no desire to see you hung, and I have no wish to be exiled to St. Louis immediately. Go back to town and apologize to Sean, and I will find some excuse for my tardiness."

He had said more than he meant to say already. He had no right to ask anything or expect anything of her when he could offer nothing in return. With a grim set to his mouth, Luke agreed, for the moment.

"I'll follow you out to make sure you get down safely."

With these gruff words he threw open the door and let her go.

5

Maria rode home to find her uncles and half the ranch saddling up to go looking for her. Her arrival brought instant relief, and her explanation of her usual Sunday visiting fended off a scolding. Pieta ordered her into a hot tub of water and carried off her soaked clothing, and the household returned to its usual routine.

All except Maria. Just this morning she had gone to confession and accepted her penance and prayed for some resolution to these feeling for Luke, only to fall victim to the devil just hours later. She lay in her bed and stared out into the moonlit garden pensively. Why did it have to be a gunfighter like Luke who made her feel that it was right to be in his arms? Why did his kisses have the power to melt her resistance and bend her will until she no longer knew right from wrong? If she didn't come up with some answers soon, she would ruin her life as well as her reputation.

Restlessly she rose to stand by the French door to the terrace, listening for the sounds of the guitar to tell if he had returned yet. The night was silent, but she continued to stare over the neatly laid garden. Her body felt strange, as if it no longer belonged to her. She felt peculiarly empty, and her hand went unconsciously to the hollow between her hip bones. Luke had made his claim as certainly as if she had sold her soul to the devil. She had no other thoughts but of him.

She returned to her bed but not to sleep. What did Luke intend to do now? What had he meant when he said he could not keep away from her? All the sweet words he had poured in her ears this afternoon came

back to haunt her, and Maria dissected them mercilessly, searching for some crumb of hope. He couldn't
love her. He had never said the words or given her any
reason to think them. He loved the mysterious Caroline. Her father had never found another woman after
her mother. She doubted if Luke would ever love
twice. He wanted her. She knew that much now, and
she might even think that enough if everything else
wasn't stacked against them.

Her uncles would never approve of Luke. He was a
gunfighter, a roaming adventurer with a price on his
head. He would never settle down to a home and family. For a while perhaps she could live like him and
Sean, but not forever. She wanted children, and the
wandering life was wrong for children.

If she could only keep the ranch, it might work. She
could stay here, and he could come and go as he
pleased. Maybe someday he would get tired of wandering or admit he preferred her to a restless life. That
was a pleasant daydream, but no more. Without cash
she would be driven off the ranch like all the others.
And the shame of living as a gunfighter's mistress or
even his off-again, on-again wife would not make it
easy to endure the hard life out here. She would like
to have friends and the respect of the community. Luke
could not give her that.

Burying her tears in the pillow, Maria finally succumbed to her body's exhaustion and slept.

As the moon disappeared over the horizon, leaving
the night to darkness, Luke located the latch to the
French door and opened it gently. He slid in without
waking her and quietly removed his boots before approaching the bed.

The scent of his shaving soap and the fresh-scrubbed
smell of his skin wafted into Maria's dreams and she
smiled, stirring restlessly. Luke gazed down at the ebony hair tumbling across the pillow and touched it
worshipfully, smoothing it over her shoulder. She wore
a skimpy, lace-edged chemise with tiny trimmed buttons down the front and a blue ribbon tied at the neck.
He held his breath as he slid in beside her and his hand

reached to caress the smooth curve rising from her bodice.

Long lashes flickered languorously as Maria drifted from her dreams. Emerald eyes finally peered upward to discover Luke's square jaw hovering above her, but the look in his eyes made her sigh with contentment and close her lids again.

Luke lay down and drew her into the curve of his body, and she snuggled there, completely at home. They needed no words, only closeness.

Maria woke more fully before dawn when Luke stirred and began to pull away. She panicked at the presence of someone else in her bed, but Luke covered her lips with a gentle finger and warned her of the need for quiet. Her long lashes flew wide as she stared up into his broad-cut face, and gradually the dream of the prior night came to her and she blushed.

"Are you mad?" she whispered, aware now of the hard length of his body pressed close to hers, fully clothed.

"Probably." Luke caught her chin with his hand and turned it up to face him. He brushed a light kiss across her lips and smiled at the molten look in her sleepy eyes. "I am just leaving, don't worry. I thought it would be nice, just for once, to share a real bed with you."

"Fool," she murmured, touching a warm finger to the hollow of his throat. His words finally registered, and she glared at him suspiciously. "Leaving? Where?"

"Shhh." He touched her lips again, then stroked her cheek, not daring to do more. Not here. Not now. "Just your bed, for now. I've got a plan, and I will have to go to Santa Fe for a while, but not yet. Kiss me, Maria, and I will go."

She didn't understand, but she obeyed his command willingly. Pushing herself up on one elbow, she pressed a kiss to his lips, and her pulse throbbed with delight at his answering pressure. Tracing the curve of her breast with his finger, Luke reluctantly ended this tender farewell.

"If you can get away this afternoon . . ." His eyes searched hers as he leaned over her, hoping to find his answer without asking the impossible.

"I'll be there." With a murmur of insane happiness, Maria gave her promise and let him go. He was out the window and gone without a trace that he had not been a dream, after all.

She drifted back to sleep again, her hand covering the place where Luke's fingers had touched her breast.

With all the men busy rounding up animals and making certain they were all branded before the cattle drive, Maria found it easy to slip away from the chaos of the ranch. Once she would have been in their midst, but without her father there, they made her feel no longer a part of it. If the truth were told, she no longer cared to be a part of it. She had no need to prove herself as a man any longer. She wanted to be a woman.

She approached the sheepherder's hut with trepidation. Suppose she had misunderstood what he asked? What if he were waiting for her somewhere else, or worse yet, had not meant her to come at all? She was making a fool of herself. She shouldn't be here. She ought to turn around and go home before he saw her.

But she rode up to the hut anyway, and her heart exploded with joy as Luke stepped out and reached to help her down. She went to him gladly, and fell into his embrace with cries of happiness. His arms were her world, and she could not be happy without them.

After tending to the horses and tieing them out of sight, Luke lifted Maria into his arms and carried her inside the hut. The interior had undergone dramatic changes since the day before, and Maria looked around her in wonder.

A small fireplace had been constructed of stones and vented out the front wall. A braided straw rug adorned the dirt floor and wooden pegs jutted from the back of the door. Tin cups and plates waited on a tabletop precariously perched on the stumpy branches of a dried tree carcass, and coffee boiled in a kettle over the fire.

Her gaze wandered to the corner where they had made their bed before, and she bit her lip to hide her gasp of surprise and fear.

Luke had constructed a small bed of green wood and leather thongs and covered it with a mattress made of blankets and some filling she suspected to be dried grass and evergreen. Over that he had thrown a colorful quilt acquired from somewhere. The care he had taken told her much, and she feared to meet his eyes. He had not built that bed for an afternoon's dalliance. He meant to share it with her for much longer than that.

A small frisson of alarm swept through Maria as Luke lowered her to the ground, but at the same time a surge of desire prevented her from turning from his embrace. Luke held her gently, stroking her hair, and she laid her head against his shoulder, clinging tightly to his shirt.

"The sheepherders will think they've been visited by fairies," she managed to murmur weakly. Luke's strong arms tightened around her, and she surrendered gladly to his hold.

"There's no grass left on this side of the range. They won't be using it for a while. It's not much, but it's better than the hard ground. Once I get this job done and a few things straightened out, I'll do better."

Maria glanced up at him, but she could not determine his meaning. His hands were already moving to the buttons of her shirt, and it didn't matter what he meant. She wanted his touch against her skin, and her fingers eagerly slid to help him.

Aroused by her sudden willingness, Luke slid her shirt off and let it fall to the ground. A camisole similar to the one she had worn the night before still prevented him from seeing the full glory of the ripe curves beneath, and Luke cursed under his breath as his fumbling fingers sought the fastenings of her skirt. Maria quickly stepped out of it when he slid it from her hips. With a casualness she did not feel, she perched on the edge of the bed to remove her boots while Luke did the same.

They did not even have time to remove the remainder of their clothes before they fell backward on the bed, tangled in each other's arms. Luke's searching kiss drove all thought from her mind, and Maria responded with ecstasy. His heavy weight pressed her down against the covers, but she reveled in the muscular strength surrounding her.

They had no thunder to urge them on now, but they needed none. With more care than their previous passionate couplings, Luke guided Maria to the brink of bliss time and again before joining her there. He would have her know all that could be between them before he left. She learned so eagerly, he had no doubt that her need was as great as his. It would take time, but he would teach her where such desire could lead.

In the hours and days that followed, Luke accomplished his objective most thoroughly. A day didn't pass that they couldn't find some time to steal away and meet in this shelter from the world's eyes. Only here could they truly be together. In the company of her uncles they barely dared speak to each other. To look and touch were out of the question. Here, they could speak their minds and hearts and learn those secrets lovers need to know. Although Luke never talked fully of his past, Maria learned of the long hours he had spent on cattle drives and stagecoaches, hours when he had accumulated the wealth of songs he used to shorten lonely nights. She spoke of her mother and father and the love she had known when she was young.

When the words died beneath the need to touch and learn the secrets of their bodies as well as their hearts, they turned to each other's arms without doubt or hesitation. No longer did Maria question Luke's right to touch her like this. It could not be any other way between them.

As Luke drove her one more time to that world beyond this one, where they could come together as one whole being, Maria longed to linger there. His strength filled her to overflowing, and she could feel the warmth of his seed spreading through her womb as their bodies cleaved to one another. There could be no separating them now, and feverishly her mind began to search for ways of convincing her uncles that this would be right.

Luke kissed her closed eyelids and eased his weight to one side, carrying her with him. He sensed he had won, and though ashamed of his methods, his heart rejoiced. Maria had a soul as pure as gold, and he knew she would wait through whatever it would take until he came back to her.

"Mi cariña, mi novia, I wish you were going with me," he murmured as much to himself as to her. Her full breasts pressed temptingly against the mat of curls on his chest, and the firm roundness of her buttocks fit nicely into the curve of his hand. He would miss her in more ways than one, but this one captured all the others in his mind. She was made for him, and he was reluctant to let her go.

He had not called her his *novia* before, but the words rolled so effortlessly from his tongue that Maria did not trust them. She trusted the tales his hands taught her and nothing more, so it took a minute before she registered the full import of Luke's words. With his body still inside of her, she could not believe she heard right.

"Where you go, I'll follow," she whispered in his ear, choosing to believe her heart and not her head.

Luke sank his fingers deep in her hair and pulled her head back so he could study the deep green of her eyes. The pupils were wide and dark as she looked back at him, and he found gold flecks on the edge of the green. He memorized their beauty as he spoke.

"You will stay here and act as if everything is normal," he informed her carefully. "To do otherwise would only bring danger to yourself and to others. Are you listening, Maria?"

Anger flared and the gold disappeared as her pupils narrowed. "I am listening and I do not like what I hear. You really mean to leave me here to dance attendance on my uncles and Manuel while you ride off to

heaven knows where to do heaven knows what? I see
no reason why I should stay behind.''

"You will stay behind because I tell you to.'' Luke
slid from beneath the covers and reached for his pants.
He saw no need to explain himself before hand. If all
went well, she would know in good time. If all did
not, she was better off thinking him a wretch best forgotten.

"Luke!'' Alarmed by his sudden indifference, Maria threw back the covers and caught his shoulder. Her
hand looked small and defenseless against the bronzed
width of his back.

She would not beg or plead—pride stood in the way
of that—but her touch had the same effect. Luke understood and turned to press a gentle kiss against her
brow. "I will be back, *poquita*. Just do as I say and
be patient. Sean will be nearby if you need him.''

"You are going to do something dangerous and get
yourself killed.'' Frightened and hiding it with anger,
Maria sprang from the bed and grabbed up her clothing. "Then I will have to marry Manuel because no
one will want me.''

Luke stood and grabbed her by the shoulders, jerking her around until his amber eyes gleamed into hers.
"You will go back with your uncles to the city in that
case. Under no circumstances are you to marry that
bastard, do you hear me?''

"Don't be ridiculous.'' Maria pulled away from his
grasp and gave him a scathing look. "I am betrothed
to Manuel. He will come home expecting to declare a
wedding date. What do you want me to say? 'Oh, certainly, Manuel,' '' she mimicked a sweet, lilting voice,
" 'just let me wait to see if my lover returns'?''

"You will not tell him anything. You will string him
along just as you have been doing, but if I ever catch
you alone with him, I'll blister your hide.'' Luke sat
down and began to jerk on his boots.

"String him along! Is that what I've been doing? Or
is that what you've been doing? Just stringing me along
until the next town or the next woman?''

With only her chemise and her hair falling in thick

ebony waves over the full curve of tawny breasts, Maria presented a picture Luke could not face without throwing her back to the bed again. Stonily he continued pulling on his boots.

"If it will make you happy to think that, fine. Just remember I'll be back, so think twice before you do anything foolish."

"I'm thinking twice now. I'm thinking I've already been a fool. I knew it all along, but I kept telling myself you were different, that I couldn't be so stupid as to be one of those poor, lonely women who fall for exciting, dangerous gunfighters. But I'm just like all the rest, and you're no better." Maria jerked on her shirt and reached for her pants, her wrath growing with his silence. "You'll be back, all right, if they don't hang you or shoot you first. You'll be back long enough to have me believing you're going to stay, and then you'll be gone again. I'm telling you right now, Luke, I won't have that kind of life. I want children and I want them to have a father, and you're damn well not the kind of man to do that."

Boots and trousers on, Luke stood up and caught Maria by the waist, pulling her against his bare chest while his mouth expertly found hers. She fought like a tigress, but he had taught her too well the pleasures to be had when she gave him his way. Her body responded long before her will, and her nipples had sharpened into sharp points against his palm even while her eyes flashed dangerously when Luke lifted his head to study her.

"Maybe I'm not. I never said I would be. I make no promises I can't keep, Maria. I'll be back, of that you can be certain. What you wish to do with the knowledge is your choice." He wanted to warn her again of Manuel, but in this mood she was just as likely to do the opposite of what he said. She didn't know Consuela had left town yet, but she was quite capable of putting two and two together if he told her of Manuel's habits. She would go after the Spaniard with a knife if she learned what he had done, and Luke had no mind to come back and find her in pieces. He would have to rely on her survival instincts and Sean's proximity until he got back.

"Good. I'm glad we understand each other." Maria flung herself from his arms, despising her weakness, despising him for playing upon it. Furiously she turned her back on him and began to button her shirt, shoving it into her boy's britches and fastening them, too.

"Too well," Luke replied sarcastically. Why in hell he'd got mixed up with a firebrand like this one, he'd never know, but he wasn't turning back now. The challenge was still there. She wasn't his yet. But someday . . . He let that thought go and strode outside to saddle the horses.

6

Maria listened in frustrated silence as her uncles argued over her future as if she were not there. Luke had been gone nearly a month, and they seemed convinced he would not return. Now that the cattle had been sold off, they were eager to return to their families. Maria could not blame them, but she wished they would leave her out of their plans.

Treading a path well worn over these past few weeks, Maria's mind returned to a more personal threat to her peace of mind: the neat stack of unused linen in her drawer upstairs. Pieta was already giving her odd looks, and she was only two weeks late. She had never been two weeks late since her monthly flux had begun. Perhaps Luke's lovemaking had done something to her insides. Perhaps if she went riding it would jog the blood into flowing again. She would try again in the morning.

She tried to concentrate on the conversation around her, but her uncles' arguments missed the one salient point that made them all moot. It was bad enough that they meant to pass her off as a respectable maiden to the unsuspecting gentlemen of their towns, but they could never explain away her swollen belly if she carried Luke's child. She would have to tell them before it got to that point. It was too early yet. She had to be certain before facing the condemnation that awaited her.

Worse yet, she knew Manuel had returned, and he had yet to visit her. She didn't know whether to be relieved or frightened. He could just be making her suffer for her temper tantrum before she left for Santa

Fe. She would even that score quickly enough should she tell him there was a possibility she carried another man's child. The thought of telling him frightened her, but she could not offend his pride by allowing him to court her under the circumstances. If he continued to court her. Perhaps he had grown tired of waiting and had found a more willing woman in Santa Fe or Albuquerque or wherever he had been. That would be much simpler to deal with, but it would deny the child the one tiny possibility she possessed to give it a father and a home. She didn't know how badly Manuel wanted the land, but he did offer that one small ray of hope.

She didn't dare let her thoughts dwell on Luke for long. To do so invited visions of his body hanging from a gallows, his neck bent and buzzards circling overhead. She wondered if the symptoms of pregnancy included an overactive imagination and morbid thoughts. It was better to remember her anger. He would return, the foul, rotten beast, expecting her to fall back in his bed again. She would announce her pregnancy and he would run like a scared rabbit and hide in Wyoming Territory. Perhaps he was even married. Maybe Caroline was his wife, and he had done something dreadful and could never return to her. That sounded likely.

Maria gave up on the conversation and asked to be excused from the table. Her uncles almost appeared surprised that she was still there, and they dismissed her to return to their argument. Maria wandered out to the kitchen, where Pieta was mixing bread dough. She didn't even dare venture to this haven with any frequency unless Carmelita or Pedro were nearby. Pieta's questions were too sharp by far, and she could not relax for a minute.

Too late she realized the hour and that Pedro would be in bed. Instead of helping her mother, Carmelita was out mooning over her *novio*. A date had already been set for their wedding, and guiltily Maria realized the gowns that had been made up for her own wedding would most likely be worn at Carmelita's instead. Perhaps with a little altering she and Carmelita could trade gowns. Before Maria could make some excuse and escape, Pieta handed her a towel and a pot to be dried.

"You do nothing else anymore. Make yourself useful. Or do you still plan on wedding Manuel and not having to work at all?"

Maria bit back a sigh and began to rub the heavy iron pot. "If you want to plot my future, go talk with my uncles. My opinion has not been asked."

"Bahhh, men!" Pieta threw up her soapy hands in a gesture of disgust. "They never see what's right before their faces. You will have to tell them what you want and act on it, if you know what it is you want." This last part she added with a shrewd look to Maria.

"Right now I'd like to see all men banished to hell, except Pedro. I'll keep him." Maria set the dry pot aside and reached for another. If she went with her uncles, she might never see Pedro again. That thought generated her earlier uneasiness, before this latest addition to her problems. With an abruptness she would not have dared a month ago she asked, "Who is Pedro's father?"

Pieta accepted the rude question with amazing calm. "You do not know?" She looked up from the dishes and read the surprise on Maria's face as her answer. "You were too young to understand. It does not matter. Pedro is my own. I will care for him."

Doggedly Maria persisted. "When my father was ill, he talked of calling his lawyer. When he started getting a little better, he mentioned going to Santa Fe, but he never got there. Is there a reason he might have wanted to change his will? That is the only reason I know of that he would want his lawyer."

Pieta shoved another pot in her hands. "You ask too many questions. It does not matter now. What matters is what will become of you. When is this gunfighter of yours returning?"

"For all I know, they're stringing him up somewhere. And if you won't answer my questions, I'll ask Charlie. He's not too young to understand." Maria set the pot down and swung around to head for the door.

"Maria." Pieta's sharp command brought Maria to a halt. "The lawyer and the will does not matter. *Comprende?* The land was as much your mother's as your father's and now it is yours. Do not let them steal it from you."

Maria rested her hands against the table top and stared at the plump, black-haired woman who had been like a mother to her for half her life. "I don't care about the damned land. May the lightning come down from the clouds and strike me dead, but the land is nothing to me. I love my home and my flowers, but without the people in it, it is just another empty house. I want a *home,* Pieta. Not just any home, but *mine.* My mother and father are gone and I was never blessed with brothers and sisters, and those two men in there are strangers to me. Perhaps someday I will learn to love them but not now. If I had a home to fight for, Pieta, I would fight."

Pieta's dark eyes softened and a tear glistened in the corner of her eye as she smiled at her unruly, headstrong charge. "Sometimes I forget you are not a man. The land was everything to your father. He loved you and your mother equally with the land. Perhaps he loved Pedro in the same way, because he had always wanted a son, but he had too much else to occupy his mind by then. You have a home, Maria, anytime you want it. Do not go away thinking there is nothing left for you here."

Maria burst into tears. She could not help herself. All the torment and confusion of these last weeks and months came to the surface. Her misery and loneliness sought an outlet, one that even Luke could not provide. She fell into Pieta's comforting arms and sobbed as she had never done in her life. She had lost so much, she had so little left, and the future loomed large and terrifying before her. The love Pieta offered filled a gaping need.

She had a brother. The miracle of this discovery soon swept aside her tears. They should have told her before. She had missed so many years of this joy. She had dozens of questions to ask, but she could not voice them. She understood now what she might not have understood before Luke came along. Her father had been a lonely man with a passion for life. Pieta was a loving, understanding woman. She could not ask for details, but she could see her father now with whiskey in him, turning to a woman whose arms would welcome him without question or expectation. And Pedro was the result.

Maria looked up to her foster mother with a gleam of mischief in her eye. "Do we look alike? Can you tell we are brother and sister?"

Pieta snorted indelicately and wiped her hands on a towel. "You come of two different mothers. You both have your father's temper, but Pedro has my control and you have your mother's lack of it. Beyond that, who's to say? Your coloring is alike except you have your father's eyes. You both favor your father about the mouth. Your smiles are his. But there will always be a difference. Keep that in mind, Maria. You are a wealthy young lady. Pedro is an unnamed—"

"Don't you say it!" Maria clenched her fists fiercely. "He is my father's only son. He has an uncle he ought to know in that other room. What do fancy words said in a church or a piece of legal paper mean? It is blood that ties us together."

Pieta gave her a curious look. "That may be, but it is the piece of paper that people believe. Without that your child is nobody with no claim to anyone or anything. Pedro at least has a name, even if it is not the right one. I am the only one who can name him bastard. Think about that carefully, Maria."

Maria blushed and looked away. "If it is the name that matters and not the blood, then perhaps no name at all would be preferable in some instances. I will think about it."

She left the kitchen and wandered through the yard to the patio on the other side of the house. She had much to think about. Learning Pedro's parentage complicated things even more. Taking Pieta's word for it would not sit in a court of law, but Maria knew she did not lie. She had no reason to lie. There was no

money left. Pedro could not benefit even if there were.
Her uncles would see to that. No, the only one who
benefited from the knowledge was herself. She was
not completely alone now. She had someone to love,
someone to take care of. If she carried a child, she
would see that he knew his uncle better than she knew
hers. They would grow up together.

That was a lovely thought, but not a very practical
one. Her uncles would sell the ranch and Pedro would
be without a home. She didn't know where she would
be. If only there were some way of keeping the ranch.
Would Manuel let her keep Pieta and Pedro here?

By the next morning, Maria had dark rings under
eyes, but she had come to no conclusions. She rode
out on Erinmeade alone, despite Charlie's warnings.
She had always rode alone. She saw no reason to stop
now that she wore skirts more frequently than pants.
Men had odd ideas of propriety.

The day would be a scorcher. Already the hot sun
beat down upon her hat and shoulders. She could not
ride Erinmeade too hard in this weather, and she was
no longer certain that she wanted to jar her insides
until the blood flowed again. She felt strangely content
with the idea that she might be carrying a new life
inside of her, as improbable as it seemed.

The heat began to make her dizzy and she stopped
in the shadow of an overhanging rock to fan herself
with the sombrero Luke had bought for her in Santa
Fe. She had contemplated going up on the ridge as she
had nearly every day for weeks to the shelter Luke had
prepared, but it no longer seemed worth the effort. If
Luke were going to return, he would not go there
first—if he returned at all, which seemed highly unlikely at this point. It did not take a month to ride to
Santa Fe or even Albuquerque and back. Something
had happened, but she refused to think of what it might
be.

A cloud of dust on the horizon from the direction of
the Vasquero ranch caught her eye. Idly she patted
Erinmeade's mane and waited for the riders to ap-

proach. She had not seen Sean since that fateful day
in the stable a month ago. Luke had said he'd found a
job at the Vasqueros, but she had never had an excuse
to ride over and see. It occurred to her that she owed
Sean and Luke for Erinmeade, but neither man would
mention it. Perhaps she ought to sell the horse of her
own accord.

Not liking that thought, she concentrated on picking
out the riders coming up the road. Manuel was among
them, and her hands tightened nervously on the reins.
It had been two months since his father's fiesta. Would
he be very angry with her? Or indifferent?

Manuel signaled for a halt as they came abreast of
Maria. His dark gaze swept sharply over her crisp linen
blouse and long skirt, then returned approvingly to the
loops of hair she had tied loosely behind her ears. For
once she apparently pleased him, and his teeth flashed
in a welcome smile.

"You have changed, Maria, and I think I'm going
to like it. Do I have your uncles to thank for this?"

He was handsome, there was no denying that. His
black hair gleamed in the hot sun, and the piercing
intensity of his deep-set eyes set off the tanned
smoothness of his aquiline features. In comparison,
Luke's face was swarthy and rough, and the expression
in his eyes harder and more cynical, but she trusted
Luke's cynicism more than Manuel's sudden affability.

"They try," she answered curtly. She had known
Manuel all her life and Luke for only a few months.
Why did she find herself listening to Luke's warning
and doubting the man she was engaged to?

"Not hard enough, I see. You should not be riding
alone. Come, we will escort you back to the ranch and
you will introduce me to them."

A statement, not a request. Maria threw him an angry look, but bit her tongue. "They are not there today. If you are interested in meeting them, I will send
you an invitation for dinner some evening. I'm certain
they would like to know you." Remembering her Uncle Juan's opinion of the Vasqueros, she felt equally
certain it would be an interesting evening.

Something in her voice must have given away a hint of her thoughts, and Manuel gazed at her with curiosity. His words, however, revealed nothing. "My father says they will honor our bethrothal. Perhaps we should meet to discuss plans for our wedding. They must be eager to return to their homes now that the cattle are sold."

She ought to say something now, warn him that everything was not as it should be, but she could not. He would have questions, and there were too many of his men around to hear. Besides, she did not know yet what to say.

"I will talk to my uncles when they return. It is hot out here. Do not let me keep you. I can return to the house without an escort."

"Nonsense. I have not seen you in months. We will ride back together." So saying, Manuel swung his mount in the direction of the Connolly ranch.

Maria found herself riding at Manuel's side with an escort of half a dozen of his *vaqueros* around them. He seldom rode anywhere alone, though she never learned the purpose of this accompaniment. Surely if she could ride the range freely, Manuel would not need bodyguards, but it wasn't her place to question him.

Instead, to her shock Maria discovered the rider nearest her was Sean. He gave no indication that he knew her, not even one of his familiar winks, and the grim look on his face looked strangely out of place. A sudden joy shot through her at his welcome presence. Perhaps he had word of Luke. She had to find out some way.

Pacing Erinmeade so that she stayed abreast of Sean, she forced Manuel to keep beside her. With a casualness she did not feel, she opened a conversation guaranteed to bore Manuel to irritation.

"My uncles do not often have time to attend Mass with me on Sundays. Would you come to join me when I go into town this week?" She gazed up at Manuel through a long fringe of lashes, hiding her anticipation. She knew Sean could hear every word, but she did not glance at him.

Manuel gave her the expected look of annoyance. "We attend chapel at the hacienda. I will send someone with the carriage so you may join us if you wish."

Maria smiled agreeably. "That is kind, but I have friends I like to see in town. If I cannot persuade one of my uncles, Charlie will take me. It will be good for his soul."

If Sean didn't take the hint, she would come after him with a knife and skin him alive. Even the Vasqueros gave their men Sundays off. He could find time to attend Mass. All she had to do was arrange to be "introduced."

By Sunday Maria was nearly ready to walk to town if necessary. Surely Sean had some word of Luke. If she could only know what to expect, it would be easier to make some decision. He had said he would return, but he had given no indication that he meant to return for her. She was not even certain that she would go with him if he did. She just needed to know. If she carried his child, he had the right to know. Beyond that she could not think.

She did not even venture to invite her uncles to accompany her. It would be easier if she could get Sean alone. Charlie made no complaint about dragging out the wagon. He didn't admit it, but she suspected there was a lady in town he paid court to upon occasion. Whatever the cause, she was grateful for his agreeableness.

By dallying, she managed to arrive late. The service was just about to begin when she walked in. With glee she noted Sean had done just what she expected him to do and sat in the back pew. She slipped in beside him, keeping a proper distance since there were no others with them.

It took all the patience she could muster to sit serenely through the service without even throwing him a glance. Tongues would wag all over town before day's end if she were seen to talk to a stranger during Mass. No, she had to make this look proper or Sean might end up in trouble with Manuel.

After church Maria waited respectfully for her elders to leave first, giving Father Díaz time to join the congregation in the mission yard. She sensed Sean waiting patiently behind her, but he made no gesture to give them away. Several people threw them sly glances as they passed by, but Maria simply smiled and greeted those she knew without acknowledging the man behind her.

At last they were outside, and as Maria had known he would, Father Díaz rapidly approached the stranger in their midst. He loved to greet new faces in hope that his congregation would grow. Sean cordially shook the old man's hand and lingered to speak, while Maria stopped nearby to greet one of Pieta's cousins.

As she had hoped and prayed he would do, Father Díaz called her name, and she excused herself to join him. The priest was grinning broadly at Sean and slapping him on the back, and Maria cast him a furtive glance. What in heavens name had the idiot said to cause this reaction?

"Maria! Come meet a young man from your father's home. He knows of some of your people from the old country." Father Díaz grasped her hand and introduced her proudly to Sean. "You two will have much to talk about. Perhaps you should take him to speak with your Uncle Patrick. Persuade them both to stay in San Pedro and attend mass regularly." He gave Maria a wink and wandered off.

Sean gazed down at her surprise with amusement. "The good father would not be matchmaking, would he?"

"It would never occur to him, although he would be thrilled to death if you would find yourself a nice Catholic wife and settle down and have a dozen children in San Pedro."

Maria's face glowed with pleasure, and Sean drank in the loveliness of those exotic eyes and fragile features in a kind of trance. Not daring to touch, he kept his answer light. "I'm ready. Will you marry me?"

To his surprise, her face suddenly clouded, and her answer did not come with humor.

"Don't ask or I may take you up on that offer. Have you heard from Luke?"

"Why? Is there trouble? I can get you away from here anytime you tell me."

Maria tried to force her expression to appear as if they were only exchanging pleasantries. "I am fine, for the moment. I am worried about Luke. It has been over a month."

Sean shrugged. "Luke is not inclined to put anything on paper that can be said in person. You will not hear from him until he rides back in here with all the evidence needed to hang whomever he is chasing. It could be months, Maria."

Maria's lips thinned to a grim line. "It had better not be or I will be long gone before he returns." She started to move away, but Sean's voice stopped her.

"Tell me where I can meet you. We need to talk."

Maria glanced around. They were attracting attention, but no one came close enough to hear. She nodded her head and spoke in a low tone. "The ridge above the valley. There is a sheepherder's hut under the ledge at the top. When will you be free?"

"I cannot get away this afternoon. It will have to be next Sunday. Will that be too late?"

"I will be there."

This time Maria did walk away. She hoped her panic did not show in her eyes as she joined the conversation of other women. Months! She could not wait months. She would have to come to some decision alone.

7

By the following Sunday, Maria was almost certain she was pregnant. It had been nearly six weeks since Luke had left, two months since her last flow of blood. And the past three mornings she had woken in misery, spewing up everything she had eaten the night before. She was thoroughly frightened now, but she tried to be calm as she approached the hut where she had told Sean to meet her.

She came here only every other day now, keeping the blankets aired and the worst of the dust out. She no longer expected Luke to return here, but she needed the closeness she felt in this place that had been theirs together. If she closed her eyes, she could almost see him standing there, his hair down in his eyes, his bronzed chest hard and warm to her touch, amber eyes glowing with pleasure as he looked on her.

Too late now she realized where the sins of the flesh led. They were not something that could be turned off and on at will, and they did not involve only the flesh. If it were just her body that longed for him, it would be simpler, but it was not. He had found the way to her heart, and she would never be free again.

Maria had coffee boiling by the time Sean arrived. She stepped to the doorway so he could find her, and welcomed him in as if this were her home. His gaze swiftly took in the simple comforts and narrowed with suspicion at the well-built bed in the corner. That alone gave evidence this was no ordinary shelter from the cold.

"Very nice," he commented dryly, accepting the cup Maria handed him and sitting on the stump they used for a chair. His glance took in Maria's unnatural pallor and the dark circles under her eyes, and he limited his comment to that.

"Sometimes I think Luke must be looking for some substitute for a home." Maria perched on the edge of the bed with her cup, suddenly shy of this man she could honestly say she did not know, except that he was Luke's friend.

Sean didn't need any explanation. He could see Luke's handiwork throughout the hut, and he gave a silent nod of agreement to Maria's wisdom.

"Do you love him?" he asked abruptly, shattering the strangeness that had come between them. Looking at Maria's pale face, he felt his own heart twist in agony, and he had no desire to play games.

Maria didn't answer immediately. It was a question she had avoided asking herself until recently. She found it difficult to believe she could love a man who had walked into her life without warning one day, seduced her, and walked out again. But what she felt in her heart for Luke was not anger. She lifted her eyes to meet Sean's.

"I wouldn't have done what I did if I did not. But that doesn't matter much, does it? I'm willing to accept the consequences of my folly, but there are so many others involved now, I don't know which way to turn. You still have heard nothing from him?"

Sean shook his head. "I can send for him, if you ask. Tell me what is wrong and let me see if I can help."

Maria smiled wryly. "Are you God? It is His help I need. If I could divide myself into quarters, I might be everywhere I am told I must be. If Luke could only tell me for certain who my father's killer was, I could feel free to make some decision. As it is now, I am being torn to pieces."

Sean stirred a cube of sugar into his coffee and stared across the small space to Maria. "Luke will be back. Wait for him before you make any decisions."

"That will be too late." Maria made a gesture of dismissal as she stood and wandered to the door. "If

I thought it would make a difference to him, I would wait, but I know as well as you that Luke is returning only because of my father. Once he has solved this problem, he will go on to the next. I told you I am prepared to accept that.''

Sean set his cup down gently and came up behind her, putting a hand on her shoulder and pushing her through the open doorway. "Come outside and admire the view. It is time we had a little talk.''

Maria obediently perched on a rock outside the door. Clasping a knee between her hands, she leaned back and stared out over the vast open spaces around her. She did not know what Sean had to say, but she felt happier than she had in weeks just being here with someone she could talk to about Luke.

"Luke never makes promises he cannot keep.'' Sean opened the conversation flatly, sitting next to Maria on the rock but not looking at her or touching her.

"So he tells me,'' Maria murmured with a slight grin.

Sean sent her a quick look at this hint of amusement. "Did he ever tell you he never returns to a place once he leaves?''

Maria tried to puzzle that out. "That doesn't make sense.''

"It does to Luke. He doesn't have a high opinion of the female sex. Gentleman that he is, he seldom turns down a lady's invitation, but he never pursues her, either, and he never makes promises. If she's content to let him share her bed while he's in town, he'll take advantage of the offer.'' Sean darted her another quick look to see how she was taking this. "Pardon my bluntness, Maria, but I think you're tough enough to handle it.''

Maria contemplated his words. She had known Luke was no innocent, but what Sean was telling her was strangely at odds with Luke's behavior toward her. She hadn't invited him to her bed. And he *had* pursued her. She couldn't imagine herself so bold as to throw herself into his arms. A puzzled frown appeared between her eyes.

"Why are you telling me this?"

Sean grinned and covered her hand with his. "Because I know damn well you didn't invite the scoundrel to your bed. Those other ladies he leaves without a word of parting. When he's finished with what he's doing, he gets up one day and rides off and never returns. If he told you he's coming back, he's coming back, and it isn't just to sip tea with your uncles."

"But his job here isn't finished," Maria protested, not daring to let hope build. "He's simply coming back to tell us what he's found."

"Maria, he wouldn't have stayed in the first place if that was his only concern. Open your eyes, woman! He could have found out what he needed on that first trip to Santa Fe, but his mind sure the hell wasn't on digging through court records. I've never seen the man so smitten. I thought he was going to call me out at gunpoint there for a while. It gave me immense pleasure to watch him suffer the way his ladies usually do."

She wanted to believe him. Desperately she wanted to believe him, but she could not. Luke had not acted like a man in love. He had cursed her, threatened to paddle her, seduced her, ignored her, then used her for his needs before walking out without farewell. He wanted her maybe, against his better judgment, but he did not love her.

"Well, I will be certain to give you a front row seat if there is a final performance, but I cannot plan on it. Perhaps you ought to find his Caroline if you want a truly shattering act."

Sean looked at her in surprise. "Caroline? What do you know about Caroline?"

Maria shrugged, hiding her excitement that Sean evidently knew the woman she cursed in her dreams. "When he was shot and feverish, he kept calling her name. As many women as you say he's known, it seems odd that he would call for only one."

Sean grimaced and his hand closed tight around hers. "That's not a pretty tale. He won't thank me for telling it."

"You do not need to. I have understood from the first that he's not the settling-down kind. He would make a perfectly terrible husband and a worse father. Perhaps once upon a time it was different."

"Once upon a time it was. Long ago in a faraway place," Sean intoned the words of a child's fairy tale, "there was a beautiful, golden-haired child named Caroline. She was spoiled and enjoyed being spoiled. Everyone doted on her, but none more than Luke. He promised her the world and near worked himself to death to accomplish it. My God, he was a boy of seventeen when he came back from the war and fell for her. For four years he worked at everything that came his way, plowing his money back into his share of his father's ranch, making it bigger and better for the Princess Caroline, so she would have him."

An angry scowl formed on Sean's brow as he remembered those days. He had played while Luke had worked, and neither of them had fared very well.

"When she finally gave her consent, Luke bought her the biggest engagement ring you've ever seen and then set about building her a house. I left before the house was built, so I wasn't there for the final act. Luke doesn't talk much about it except when he's drunk, and I had to get most of the story from mutual friends."

Maria took his hand. "I can guess the ending. You needn't give it away."

Sean shook his head. "It was even worse than that. She didn't just find a wealthier man. Luke had placed her on a pedestal and not touched one golden hair of her head; he worshiped the ground she walked on. Then one day he came home early and took the shortcut through his father's orchard. He found Caroline with his older brother, and what they were doing shattered any notion he had of her innocence."

Maria closed her eyes and sent a silent prayer to heaven for the soul of that long-ago Luke. She hugged her knees against her chest as a tear trickled from one eye. The smashing of a dream was cruel enough, but an ending like that would make it nigh impossible to

ever build another. His work, his home, his family, all
would end after that. She knew Luke well enough to
understand that.

"That's when he left home?" Maria asked softly.

"After he raised such a ruckus that his brother was
forced to marry the bitch, which was what she wanted
all along. He packed it all up and rode off and never
returned."

"I wish I'd known," Maria said sadly. "I just
thought it was me he despised."

"Despised? By all the saints, Maria, what do you
think I'm telling you? It's happening all over again.
Besides Caroline, there was only one other woman in
Luke's life that he's treated like you. A few years back
he got tired of hitting the road and he settled in at a
ranch along the Cimarron. The school there had a prim
and proper teacher, and since she was the best-looking
female in the area, Luke started walking out with her.
He didn't make the same mistake he did with Caroline. The lady had some experience and pretty soon
they were shacked up together. Don't look at me like
that, Maria!" Sean spoke sharply, forcing her to listen. "Luke isn't a saint. You said you knew that. I'm
trying to tell you he's not the devil people paint him
to be, either."

"I know he's not, Sean, but I hate being just another
one of the women fool enough to fall for him."

"Damn it all, Maria, you're the only decent one he
has found! The schoolteacher told Luke she was pregnant, so he agreed to marry her, and went right back
to the same old routine. He bought her gowns and a
ring and a cottage. Within weeks he came to town
early and found her above the saloon with a fancy
gambler who had bought the place a few months before. As Luke tells it, he simply turned around and
walked out, turned in his resignation at the ranch, and
rode away."

Something in Sean's voice told her that wasn't all
there was to the story. "And as everyone else tells
it?"

Sean gave her a piercing look. "The gambler was

found dead with a bullet hole through his chest. The teacher was beaten up pretty severely. She had a miscarriage and died a short time later. The sheriff put out a warrant for Luke's arrest and a posse went after him, but they never found a trace. He was pretty well liked around there and the gambler wasn't. I don't think they tried very hard, but the warrant's still there and it carries a reward.''

Maria rested her chin against her knees and stared out at the butte in the distance. The father of her child was an accused murderer. She had known the kind of man he was from the first, but the details hurt. She tried to think of Luke beating up a woman who had betrayed him, but she could not, no more than she could imagine his violence, although she knew it existed. Luke did not lose control of his temper the way she did. Even when he pulled his guns, it was with a cold, hard ruthlessness that meant he would use them if needed, but not in the way this story said. Luke's version sounded like the Luke she knew. He would say something particularly scathing and walk out, unless the woman was an unwilling victim. From Sean's tale, Maria gathered she was not.

''I am supposed to take heart from that?'' she asked wryly, hiding the sinking feeling of misery in her heart. After the treatment he had received at the hands of those women, Luke would never trust another. Love was out of the question.

''Maria, you are either the most innocent or the stupidest woman I have ever met.'' Sean shot her a look of curiosity, knowing there was nothing stupid about Maria. She simply didn't realize the powerful effect she had on men.

Maria arched a quizzical eyebrow and waited for the enlightenment he would bestow upon her.

''He's buying you things just like he bought those other women. This isn't much of a house in comparison, but it's the same idea. He's providing you a home. He'll be riding back in here with a ring any minute.''

Maria shook her head in bewilderment. ''What has he bought me? He found the derringer for me, but he said that came out of expenses just like the other things.''

Sean gave a whoop of laughter and slapped her on the back, his broad face alight with joy. "You are the most innocent, gullible female he has yet to meet up with! Expenses? What expenses? If you're talking about the Dallas job, we were lucky to walk away with maybe two-fifty apiece. That blasted horse probably cost him that much. Expenses! I like the way the man thinks.''

Maria's fists knotted with rage and she stood up angrily so she could meet Sean's eyes. "Erinmeade belongs to you and Luke. I've been using her, but she's yours to sell anytime you like. And he told me the gowns were needed for the job. I could have bought my own! Why did he lie to me?''

"Would you have accepted them if he hadn't?''

"Of course not!''

Sean looked upon her approvingly but still with a smile. "Well, there you have it. He wanted you to have them and that was the only way you would take them. If you'd refused him altogether, it would have put him in a real quandary. 'Fess up, Maria, you liked his buying those things for you.''

Maria sat back down with misery written across her face. "That makes me like all the others. I should have known better. I guess I'm stupid.''

Sean hugged her shoulders. "No, just naive. And it tickled him when you insisted he buy something for himself. I don't think that would ever have occurred to a woman like Caroline.''

"It would have tickled him more if I had bought the hat myself,'' Maria replied gloomily. "All I've done is take, just like the others. If he's smart, he'll stay away.''

"If he's got any brains at all, he will be back here with that ring to claim the best thing that has ever happened to him. Now quit pouting and just let time take care of the details.''

"I haven't got time, Sean,'' Maria murmured wearily, drained by the emotions of this last hour. "Manuel is to come to dinner this Wednesday, and he will press his suit. My uncles are equally determined to carry me off to St. Louis or California now that the cattle are sold. They won't let me stay here alone anymore, but I can't bear to sell the ranch. They're growing impatient, and soon I must decide what to do.''

She didn't tell him the most pressing reason for making a decision. After what Sean had told her, she wasn't at all certain telling Luke of the child would be a wise thing to do. He would feel obligated to marry her, just like the schoolteacher. She didn't want anybody to feel obligated, and she wasn't at all certain marriage was a solution.

''You'll stay away from Manuel, that's what you'll do.'' Sean's voice grew suddenly serious and his tone of warning was unmistakable. ''Go to California if you must. Luke can always track you down. Just stay away from Manuel. He's no good.''

''I have known him most of my life, Sean. Don't make it sound as if he is the evil villain in a penny dreadful. He's arrogant. Occasionally he is harsh, but he is not evil. If I marry him, I will be able to keep the ranch, and Pieta and Pedro will have a home.'' There were a number of ''ifs'' involved in that, but Maria felt she had only to explain things to Manuel to straighten them out. She wasn't sure about the child. He would never accept the child as his heir, but perhaps if it were a girl . . .

Sean put an end to her daydreams. ''He is a brute beast, and he and his family will make your life hell, Maria. Go to California. The ranch isn't worth what you would have to endure to keep it.''

Maria stared into Sean's worried eyes. ''Even if I tell you Pedro is my brother and the ranch is half his?''

8

Sean stared at her in disbelief, rose, walked back and forth and stopped back in front of her again. "Luke told me nothing about a brother. Where is he?"

"Luke knows nothing about him. I have only just discovered it myself." Maria hastily explained her predicament. It would not do to sell the ranch and go off with her uncles and leave Pedro with no home or family or inheritance. She couldn't do it. The little boy deserved his chance to make his way in the world as his father's son. Her father would have expected it of her.

When she was finished, Sean growled something irascible about "honest women" and "trouble" and began to pace again.

"It won't do. I don't know what is going on. I don't know what Luke is looking for. I just know what I've seen and heard and it isn't good. Stay away from Manuel and let me get a message to Luke. I think it's time he got you out of here."

"He can't," Maria replied simply. "If my uncles found out about us, they would hang him. They almost did once. They won't hesitate a second time. Unless you can tell me Manuel killed my father, he's the only chance I have of keeping the ranch. I have thought about it. If I can get a lawyer to draw up the deed, I will see that Pedro is given his fair share before I wed. Then we won't have to be separated."

"Maria, keep it up and you will convince me you are the biggest damned fool alive! Manuel won't let you give up half a ranch to a bastard half-breed anymore than your uncles will. Now shut up and let me think this out.''

Sean paced some more, but his only conclusion did not swerve from his earlier one. ''I can't help it, Maria. Cheyenne has a right to know. Don't do anything until he gets back.''

Maria shrugged as if accepting his decision. ''Why is he called Cheyenne? I thought Luke came from Kansas.''

Relieved that she didn't argue, Sean grinned. ''Because when he's riled, he fights with more viciousness than a Cheyenne Indian. He doesn't need those guns. He can tear a man to pieces with his teeth, if need be. He had that reputation long before he earned one with his guns.''

That piece of information didn't reassure Maria in the least. She only felt the distance between them grow larger. How could the man who had taught her love with such tenderness be the same one Sean told her about? Luke seemed a stranger to her now, a dream that had almost come true but that she could no longer believe in. She wanted him so badly it didn't seem real anymore. Nothing did, not even the child. She had too much growing up to do in too little time. Reality was a difficult concept under the circumstances.

Wednesday night, when Manuel arrived for dinner, did not seem any more real to Maria than anything else. They ate by candlelight, but even the flickering shadows did not disguise the wariness in Uncle Juan's eyes, or the tension in Uncle Patrick's face. Realizing all was not as it should be, Manuel went out of his way to be charming and ingratiating, and that was less real than Maria's memory of Luke.

Wearing the new dinner gown Luke had bought for her, Maria felt Manuel's gaze turn to her frequently, but she kept her head bent and did not meet his eyes. Covertly, through lowered lashes, she studied his arrogant features, the high cheekbones and flashing eyes, the strong jaw and white, even teeth gleaming against sun-darkened skin. She ought to be excited that such a man desired her. Once she had been, but it had been a childish excitement, like wishing for Christmas. She felt nothing now, no anticipation for his kisses, no pride that he had chosen her. She was not even sure she liked him anymore.

The underlying tension in the room made it difficult to discern her uncles' opinions. They were affable hosts, pouring wine and discussing the ever important topics of beef prices and the gold standard. The presidential election was mentioned, but it seemed so far removed from this country that it held no interest for Maria. Perhaps if she were to go to St. Louis she would learn to become more involved in important issues, as she knew some women were doing. She had heard women were even demanding the right to vote, but she wasn't certain what they would do with it. How did one tell one crooked politician from another? The ones she had heard discussed all sounded alike.

The topic of the coming railroad interested her, but Manuel dismissed it with a careless wave of his hand. Maria wanted to see one of these magnificent machines that could carry her to such far off and exotic places as New York. Manuel claimed they would never be successful in country like this. Maria thought her uncles might disagree, but they were too polite to do so openly.

The whole evening was too polite. Everyone performed like actors on a stage, and not a single honest emotion was allowed to intrude. She wanted to scream at them all, tell them this was her life they were drowning in silence, but she did not dare. She had to find some way of convincing them that half the ranch could not be sold or given away. Sean was right. They would never give it to Pedro, but she suspected her uncles might be willing to insist that half be left in her name, or theirs. They were honest men. She trusted them not to sell what was hers without her permission, but even she knew things could not go on as they were. Something had to be done, but no one said a word about the topic closest to her heart.

After dinner, Maria excused herself while the men lingered over brandy. Wearing her expensive dinner gown, she could not join Pieta in the kitchen, so she wandered to the patio for a breath of fresh air. She had not realized how terrified she had been until she gave a sob of relief at finding herself alone at last.

The pleasure didn't last long, however. She didn't need to look up to know when Manuel came around the house. He used some scent in his shaving soap that she would recognize anywhere. It had an almost sweet odor, and it turned her stomach nervously. Luke seldom used a scented soap, and she preferred the masculine, musky smell of his skin, even after he had been out in the sun all day. Just the thought of it stirred feelings deep within her, and she had to concentrate on driving them away. It would not do to be distracted with Manuel around.

"You are looking lovelier than ever tonight, *cara*." He came up behind her, resting a hand on her bare arm. "We have things to discuss, Maria. Shall we sit down?"

"I am fine here." In the clear moonlight, where anybody watching from the house could see her, but she did not tell him that. "What did you wish to discuss?"

"You. Me. Us. Why are your uncles so cool toward me? I thought you had explained everything to them."

Maria shivered as his hand ran up and down her arm. She forced herself to stand still beneath his touch. "I did, but there seems to be some old grudge between your family and *Tío* Juan's. I have told him it has nothing to do with you. I am not certain he is convinced."

"Have you now? That is good. I was beginning to doubt if you meant to honor your promise. I have heard tales I do not like, Maria." He swung her around until his gaze could bore into hers. "You do not behave as an eager bride, *cara*. Is there something you wish to tell me?"

His fingers bit deep into her shoulders, deep enough to leave painful bruises, and Maria flinched. "You are hurting me, Manuel. Let go."

His hands instantly returned to stroking her, drawing her closer to his tall, powerful frame. "Is that better? Now tell me, Maria, will you keep your promise?"

"I must do as my uncles say, Manuel, you know that. They are the ones you must talk to." Maria looked away, unable to bear the scrutiny of his piercing gaze. She ought to tell him of the child. She ought to tell him their wedding could not possibly be unless he were willing to accept her as she was, but she could not face the humiliation.

Manuel's mocking gaze noted the color rising to her cheeks. "I think not, Maria. You do not need their permission to marry. Once we are wed, they will not deny you what is rightfully yours. I think it is time we make an announcement. We will have a big wedding and your uncles will attend. Then they will go back to their homes, and you will be mine. I am tired of waiting, Maria."

"Manuel, it is not as you think. There is much I must tell you, but we cannot do it here. My uncles will be looking for us. Please, give me time."

"Not much more, *cara.*" His breath whispered across her ear as he bent her slightly backward, pressing his lips to her temple and along the line of her jaw. "You have had time to put together your trousseau. Your father has been gone well over six months now. Your family is here. The time is right, Maria. A few days, no longer."

His mouth closed hard and insistently over hers, but Maria could not bear the intimacy of his tongue where Luke's had been. She kept her teeth firmly clenched and almost fainted with relief at the sound of Uncle Patrick's voice.

Manuel released her and the evening broke up as formally as it had begun. Only Maria knew now that the period of grace had ended. Her punishment for sinning would soon begin.

For a few days she arranged never to leave the house alone. Manuel had never forced his attentions on her before, but she sensed something had changed. He was not a man to fool, and she had seen evidence of his temper before. She had no doubt that he would beat her, and for the child's sake, she was afraid.

But she had promised to meet Sean again, to see if he had any word from Luke, and Sunday was the only day he could get away. Surely Manuel could not follow her every minute of the day, and the hut on the ridge was well in the center of her property. He would have no excuse for riding there. The child made her over-anxious. She had to see Sean again.

The hut was as she had left it, only the dust was a little thicker. Maria shook out the bedding and washed out the cups with water she had brought. The sound of a horse coming up the trail was a signal to put water on to boil for coffee. Having done that, she went to the doorway to greet Sean.

Her face grew pale as she watched Manuel ride over the ridge.

His expression was not pleasant as he dismounted and tied the reins of his horse to a nearby mesquito. His gaze swept insultingly over Maria's slim figure garbed in her new riding clothes. She wore her hair in a single long braid and she had left her hat inside. The afternoon sun beat down upon her ebony hair with a glistening sheen that matched the fire springing to her eyes.

"What are you doing here?" she demanded, leaping to the offensive. This was her place, the place she came to be alone, and no one else was welcome without invitation. Manuel's intrusion was a violation of her privacy.

"Were you expecting someone else?" The mockery in his voice hid a hint of something else, and the gleam in his eye was dangerous. "Your lover perhaps? Or one of them?"

Maria checked a gasp of surprise and, biting her lip in a grim smile, she returned his glare. "Would you care? If it is only the land that interests you, I don't see that my affairs are any of your business."

His hand swung up so quickly Maria did not have time to avoid it. The cruel slap knocked her head side-

ways, and she staggered backward, feeling the blood
trickle into her mouth. Dizziness washed over her, but
she fought it, standing her ground and meeting his
fury with a dangerous calm.

"That mark will show, Manuel. You are not very
clever. Do you think my uncles will give me to a man
who would do that to me?"

The sight of Maria standing there challenging him
infuriated Manuel further, and the blood lust rose in
his eyes. "When I am through with you, they will have
no choice, Maria. I would have taken you as my wife.
Now I will have you as my whore."

She saw his blow coming this time and stepped back,
but he still caught the corner of her chin with his fist.
She cried out in pain and caught herself by grabbing
the rock ledge behind her. Her senses reeled, but the
danger gave her strength. Her hand dived into her
pocket—and came up empty. With a moan of dismay
she remember cleaning the gun last night and leaving
it beside her bed. This morning she had been too ill
to remember it. The pain and the heat rocked her
senses, but she had to concentrate. Manuel had become a beast she did not know.

He grabbed the front of her shirt and dragged her
against him, pulling off buttons with the force of his
grip. "Deny me again, Maria. Tell me I have no rights.
Tell me your lover will come to protect your virtue."

He was mad. He had to be. Maria struggled against
him, kicking his shins with her sharp boots, digging
her nails into his arm. "I don't know what you're talking about, Manuel," she gasped as his hand came up
to twist her breast painfully. Pregnancy made them
tender, and again she cried out.

"Scream all you like, *cara*, no one will hear. My
men have taken care of your spy. He will not come
running to your rescue. I will have you now, Maria,
and when I am done, I may or may not take you to
your uncles. There are other ways besides marriage to
have that land."

Sean! He had found out about Sean. That was the
only logic she could make of this attack, and for the

first time real fear began to twist in her stomach. He shoved her back against the rock wall, pinning her shoulder with one hand while his other invaded her torn shirt. His cold fingers against her flesh made her skin crawl, but her fear for Sean was more desperate.

"Manuel, stop it! You're hurting me! I don't know what you're talking about." If she could plead innocence, there might be some escape. She had to get back to the ranch and send men out to look for Sean.

"Fight me, Maria. I like it better that way. Consuela used to do it very well, but she was a whore. You should do it even better, *cara*. Outraged innocence is always amusing."

Manuel's mouth came down to smother hers, and Maria gagged as the pain of his onslaught forced her teeth apart. She tried to bite him, but his hand twisted again at her breast, and her cry of anguish invited further invasion. In the heat, she had worn no camisole, and his hand had full freedom to roam where it would.

With a wrench she brought her hand up between them to scratch his face. His hold loosened and she brought up her knee, fighting as her father had taught her. But Manuel had too much experience at these tactics, and he dodged her blow, smacking her head backward into the wall.

This time she did crumple. Pain exploded through her head and blackness claimed her as she slid down the rock to the ground.

Manuel's greedy hands jerking off her shirt raised a clamor of alarm in Maria's muddled brain, and she fought back without thinking, clawing and kicking as he tore her clothes. The child! She had to protect the child! That thought found clarity and she doubled her fist and smacked with all her strength at the man sitting astride her hips.

Manuel only laughed, a low, throaty laugh that raised Maria's hackles. Her eyes flew open to read the glazed lust in his, and terrified panic returned consciousness.

He had spoken of Consuela. Consuela had disappeared weeks ago. What did Consuela have to do with what was happening to her now? Maria screamed in rage as Manuel began ripping the fastenings of her skirt.

The riding skirt evidently caused him problems. He could not throw it up in her face and rip at her undergarments as he could a normal skirt. He ignored Maria's frantic pummels as he gave up on trying to rip the heavy twill. Swinging his leg off of her, he held her pinned with his hand as he tried to slide the heavy fabric from her hips.

Moving quickly, Maria rolled away, twisting from his grasp and trying to rise to her feet. Her head still spun crazily, and she felt her stomach rise to her throat. She was going to be sick.

Falling to her knees, she began to retch, and thus did not see the figure rising above the rock roof of the hut.

Manuel's next blow halted as Maria bent over, vomiting. His hesitation saved his life. As the shadow of a man fell over the sunny plateau where they knelt, Manuel glanced up, his hand going to the gun at his side.

Luke stood with legs braced against the rock, both guns aimed at Manuel's heart.

9

Manuel's hand grabbed for his gun.

"I'll give you time to pull it." Insolently Luke stood there waiting for Manuel to draw his weapon. The stone-cold color of his eyes set the lie to the calmness of his words.

Manuel's hand instantly fell to his side as he glanced at the man standing above him. "I'm no fool. Shoot me, and it will be murder."

"I might have taken you up on that a minute earlier, but there's a better way."

Luke's eyes gave no indication that he saw Maria crawl out of Manuel's reach, but the muscles of his jaw bunched as he leapt lightly to the ground between them. With a flick of his wrist he returned one gun to his holster, then removed Manuel's from his grasp.

"We won't be needing these."

Manuel stared in disbelief as Luke unbuckled his holster and flung all the weapons to the side. Luke didn't give him time to question. His left hand struck out, doubling the tall, aristocratic Spaniard in two. His right instantly snapped up to connect with Manuel's jaw.

Clutching at the front of her torn shirt, Maria tried to follow what was happening, but the pain in her head beat like a hollow drum, and wave after wave of dizziness prevented her rising. She heard the blows and grunts of the men as they tore into each other, but her concentration was on bringing her reeling senses back into focus.

Manuel flew backward, sliding through the dust at Maria's feet from the force of one of Luke's blows. He reached for her, but Luke was on him in an instant, smashing his fist into the side of Manuel's face as the other man had tried to do to Maria earlier. The sight of Maria's bruised jaw and tattered clothes incited renewed strength in him, and he used his fists as a battering ram against Manuel's handsome features.

With a roar of rage Manuel grabbed Luke's arm and tried to hold him off, but his opponent's wiry strength had a frenzy all of its own. In desperation Manuel flung himself to the side, attempting to throw Luke off, and his hand came in contact with one of the discarded guns.

The fight at her feet forced Maria to turn her attention to her surroundings and away from the pounding in her head. She started to move away, protecting the life within her, but Manuel's desperate lunge returned another reality. Luke had returned, and he was in danger. With more instinct than thought, she kicked the hand reaching for the gun, and Manuel howled in pain and fury.

With the renewed strength of anger, the Spaniard unseated Luke and dove for Maria, catching her by the knee and flinging her backward from her uncertain position. If he thought to shield himself, he made the wrong move.

The sight of Maria collapsing against the ground decimated what remained of Luke's control and he broke Manuel's hold with one well-placed kick. Manuel screamed and grabbed for his privates, but Luke was upon him again, ramming his fist into any soft part he could find. Only Maria's weakened stirring removed the haze of rage from his eyes, and he awakened to the knowledge that he battered an inert opponent.

In an instant Luke was on his feet, leaning over Maria to search for broken bones, finding the dried blood upon her lip and cursing in three tongues.

Maria forced a faint smile to her lips as she recognized the Spanish idiom among the rest. A man who knew those phrases knew the language well, almost better than she. Her mother had not taught her to curse in Spanish.

At this sign of consciousness Luke knelt beside her and gently lifted Maria to a sitting position. He offered the canteen that she had left sitting on the ledge outside the hut. "Drink slowly, *poquita,* or you will be ill again."

Maria cleansed her mouth with the warm water, spitting out the first swallow to rid her tongue of its foul taste. Luke's strong arm supporting her offered more comfort than made logical sense. She slowly sipped the water, recovering her equilibrium. The pain in her head remained, but it receded to a dull, aching throb. Gradually she grew aware of the sun beating upon her breasts, and she groped for the edges of her shirt to pull it around her.

Luke's hands gently found what she sought and tied the corners beneath her breasts to protect her modesty. Maria turned her gaze fearfully to his face, but she read only concern and a searching bewilderment in his eyes. He touched her jaw, running his fingers over the bruise, making certain no other damage had been done. Then he reached to restore his guns and their holster.

"We had better get you back to the ranch, little one. You may need a doctor."

She caught his hand fearfully, pulling it from the gun. "Sean? Manuel said he'd found the spy—"

"Manuel and his men followed him out here. He didn't have much of a chance against those three thugs, but Sean is good at playing possum. His message said he would be meeting you here today, so I came here first. I found him down below. He will survive. Sean always does."

Before she could protest, Luke lifted Maria in his arms and carried her to Erinmeade. When he climbed up behind her, leaving Manuel in a bloodied heap in the hot sun, Maria threw him a questioning look. Luke shrugged as he took up the reins, holding her against him with one arm.

"We will send a message to the Vasqueros when we

get back to the ranch. That is more than they did for Sean.''

Realizing that Luke must have left his horse for Sean and climbed the rest of the way up here on foot, Maria offered no argument. She leaned back against his hard chest gratefully, unwilling to think about anything. His arm tightened protectively around her waist as they swayed down the trail, and she closed her eyes and just let the feel and smell of him fill her senses.

Luke's eyes remained thoughtful as he guided the mare carefully over the rough terrain, avoiding the jostling of a faster gait. Maria's acquiescence to this familiarity and her unusual lack of resilience worried him. Sean had said she was not herself, and he began to see why he had called him back. Luke's mind carefully retraced the events of this past hour as they rode toward the ranch, and his jaw set in a hard line at the conclusions reached.

Pieta ran from the back door as they rode into the yard. Charlie came running in from the back field, yelling. The men standing at the front gate broke into a lope after them. Maria swayed silently in Luke's arms and opened her eyes to see what the commotion was about. Only then did she realize how it must look to the others to have Luke riding in like this with her in this condition. She tried to signal to Luke to let her down, but he ignored her and rode directly into the stable.

Before anyone could follow, he swung her onto a fresh stack of hay, jumped down, and slammed the stable door in the faces of the men running across the yard. With a pitchfork he pinned the doors closed.

Maria clambered down from the haystack, staring at him in amazement. Sun filtered through the cracks in the walls and from the loft windows above, filling the gloom with sparkling dust motes. Luke's expression was unreadable as he came forward, catching her by both arms before she could run.

''Before we leave here, I want a few questions answered. Why were you meeting Sean up there?''

Incredulity clouded the brilliance of her long-lashed

green eyes, but remembering who this was holding her, what he meant to her, prevented the flash of anger that would normally have followed. Maria met Luke's gaze easily.

"To find out if you were coming home."

Home. The word hit him like a blow, and Luke studied her face with care. "Why weren't you carrying your gun?"

If jealousy had made him ask the first question, she could not fathom the reason for this one. Maria shook her head in puzzlement. "I forgot it. What does it matter? My uncles will be coming in here with guns in a minute. Why do you ask me these foolish questions?"

"You answered the first and I believe you. You are evading the second, Maria. You are not well. There are dark circles under your eyes. You were ill up there, and I do not think it was just from Manuel's slap. Were you sick this morning, Maria? Is that why you forgot the gun?" It was a bluff that succeeded.

Panic leapt to Maria's eyes, and she tried to break away from Luke's grasp but could not. He was too quick, too perceptive, and she was not prepared for him. She shook her head furiously, making it spin again.

"You have no right to talk to me this way. Let me go. They are trying to batter down the doors."

"They will need more than fence posts to break down that door. Why won't you answer me, Maria? If the child is mine, shouldn't I know it?"

The shock of hearing it on his lips destroyed what remained of her defenses, and Maria collapsed in his arms, fighting back the sobs as she buried her face against his chest. Luke's arms closed about her, holding her gently while the sobs tore through her. His expression had become a grim mask of determination even as Maria's will broke under the weight of the tension of these past months.

When she began to quiet, Luke gently touched her tender breast, then slid his hand down to the flat place between her hip bones. The changes were slight, unnoticeable to anyone but one who had memorized every contour of her lovely body. Sadness lingered in the dark places behind his eyes as he tilted her head up to meet his gaze.

"I will speak to your uncles. However much they may object to me, I think they will agree the child must have a name."

With her secret out, Maria regained some portion of her spirit, and she pushed against his chest, escaping his hold. "Marriage is a sacred vow, not one to be taken just to give a child a name. I can make up a name, go to California, call myself a widow. I don't need your charity."

"Charity, is it?" Luke would have laughed had the situation not been so grave. As it was, they were running out of time, and the silly idiot argued over charity. "I am not a charitable man, Maria. The child is mine, and I will claim it. I am glad to hear you think marriage is a sacred vow, because once we're wed, I'll not have you look upon another man."

"Wed? I'd sooner wed a philanderer like Sean than a man who loves his guns more than me!"

Amber eyes appraised the spitting wildcat standing before him in the dust-filled gloom. Her long, thick hair lay in a rope across the open collar of her shirt, and her breasts heaved with anger and fear. He could surround the slenderness of her waist with his hands and kiss those pouting lips into submission, but instead his fingers went to the buckle of his gunbelt. She had issued a challenge, and he accepted it.

With a single flip of his wrist, the heavy guns landed in the haystack beside them. Slanted green eyes watched in disbelief as the belt arced in the air and disappeared into the stack. Then they turned warily back to the man whose lean, broad-shouldered frame filled her vision.

"It will have to be a hasty wedding. I'll explain why when we talk to your uncles. Are you ready?"

He left her no choice. Still dazed, Maria accepted his rough hand around hers and with one last glance to the haystack, she followed obediently as Luke tugged her in the direction of the door. Up above, she could hear the scrape of a ladder as someone attempted to climb in the loft. Outside, she could hear mounting curses and the splintering of wood as someone attacked the stable door with an ax. It all seemed unreal. The only reality was the solid man at her side, his large hand claiming hers. Had she really agreed to marry him? And why?

Maria still wasn't certain how it had come about when they finally made it to the safety of her father's study. With the door closed and both uncles staring at them with animosity, she felt propelled backward in time, but this time the circumstances were different. This time she was not denying men and marriage but agreeing to it. Luke gave her no time to think, no time to recognize the impossibility of it. He held her hand and announced his intentions as if the matter was already settled and he only uttered the inevitable.

The men stared at him in amazement and kept silent as Pieta ruthlessly barged through the door with ice from their dwindling supply. She gave all the men a wrathful glare as she applied the icy towel to Maria's jaw, then departed after seeing Maria seated among the pillows of the cracked leather couch.

Luke turned a concerned glance to Maria. "Perhaps you should go to your room and lie down while I make the explanations. I can tell you later, after you have rested."

"I am resting," she replied crossly. That Luke had brought news of some sort from Santa Fe, she had begun to realize. She wasn't about to be the last to know.

"Maria, it might be better if you left the room." Patrick Connolly kept his cold blue gaze on the arrogant gunfighter.

"Let her stay." Juan Valencía's voice was remote. He had stationed himself apart from the others as usual, but this time he sat in the space between Maria and Luke. One could not reach the other without his interference, and despite his slightness he was a physically strong man.

"Thank you, *Tío* Juan, but I had no intention of leaving. If Luke has found my father's killer, I want to know of it." Maria held the ice gingerly to her jaw. She ached all over, and she would like nothing better than to sleep for a week, but she wouldn't be parted from Luke until she heard it all.

Luke's gaze rested on her a moment, then turned to confront her uncles. "I cannot pin a name on the killer. There hasn't been time for that. My partner may be able to give me the likeliest names, but proving it will be difficult. Irish was almost certainly killed by the same people hired to create the 'accidents' that have made it easy to acquire the rights of way to the new Atchison, Topeka, and Santa Fe Railroad line coming down from Colorado Territory."

"Names," Valencía demanded softly.

"The Santa Fe deals with several lawyers in acquiring the land. Those names will mean nothing to you. They are on the charters of the companies buying up the deeds between Santa Fe and the Raton Pass. Also on those charters are several of the men known to be connected with the Santa Fe Ring. They are powerful men with both money and influence. They will be even more powerful when the railroad comes through and they own all the property on either side of it."

"You are saying these men are responsible for my father's death?" Maria watched Luke's face carefully.

He lifted his gaze to look directly at her. "The other name on those charters is Alfonso Vasquero, Manuel's father."

Patrick Connolly reached for the brandy decanter and Valencía reached for a cheroot in his pocket.

"This ranch is in the path of the railroad?" Connolly spoke first.

"This land is the best watering and fuel stop between Santa Fe and the Pass. The village of San Pedro will disappear if the railroad places a station here. It will be the ideal location for cattle chutes. It could very well end up being another Abilene."

"Then they will stop at nothing to get it." Valencía

lit up his cheroot and watched Luke intently. "That is what you are saying, is it not?"

"That is what I am saying. Vasquero has promised these men to deliver all the land needed to complete the line when construction begins again. The small ranchers and his own property were easily handled, although he still has to have expended a great deal of cash to obtain them. Until he gains this land, the connecting link, it is doubtful that the railroad will buy the deeds he has already acquired. The only thing standing between Vasquero and this ranch was Irish. And now you," Luke added. "If you had stayed away, Maria would have married Manuel and you would have given your blessings and released the ranch without question. Manuel would have had a new woman to beat into submission, and his father would have the land that would give them wealth enough to keep anyone from questioning."

Patrick Connolly looked sick, and Valencia lifted a thoughtful eyebrow in Maria's direction. "Maria?"

She met Luke's gaze with the pain of realization. "What happened to Consuela?"

"She is safe. We sent her back to her family. That was stupidity on my part. It just hastened Manuel's eagerness to set a date."

"No, not just that. He knew about us. He must have heard something when he was in Santa Fe. Can we not have them arrested?" Maria was aware of the tension springing up between her uncles while she talked directly to Luke, but she was beyond caring. If the Vasqueros had killed her father, she wanted them hung.

"No, *poquita*, there is no proof. You and Consuela might testify that Manuel beats women, but it will hurt your reputation more than his. Sean can testify against the men who beat him up. He might even give evidence of some of the raids he went on while riding with the Vasquero hands, but there is no proof to show Manuel and his father ordered the raids or that they had anything to do with your father's death."

Valencia spoke up with a cynical twist to his lips. "In all probability, even if we have them arrested, the

Ring will set them free to come back and destroy Maria and the ranch and anything connected with it. Am I right?''

Luke nodded. ''Actually, as soon as they find Manuel and discover Maria has escaped them, they will destroy everything within their reach before we could have them arrested.''

Maria understood his urgency now. Within days they would storm the ranch, burn the barns, the house, and everything and everyone within them. Perhaps Indian raiders would be blamed. They could even damage some of the Vasquero outbuildings to verify the story, kill an innocent Indian or two as proof. The Connolly ranch had no defense. They had never needed any. Until now.

She lifted her eyes to meet the pain and sympathy in Luke's. ''What do we do now?''

10

Luke gave her defiantly tilted chin a look of approval, then turned back to her uncles. "First, we get Maria out of here. Their hands are tied if she's not available to sign the deed. Next, we get everyone and everything of value to her out of here. That means both of you. With the ranch empty, they can do little more than vent their anger until they can find another scheme. There will be others, you can be certain, but we will have time to prepare for them."

Before her uncles could get in a word, Maria sat upright. "Pedro and Pieta! We cannot leave them here. They must go with us."

"They have family here. That shouldn't be a problem." Juan dismissed the matter and started to speak again but Maria interrupted.

"It *is* a problem. I cannot leave them. Pedro is the only brother I will ever have. I will not leave him homeless."

"Brother!" The glass of brandy slipped from Patrick's hand and crashed to the desk, soaking the blotter.

Maria turned her emerald eyes pleadingly to her father's brother. "Please understand. I know my father would have acknowledged him if he had lived. He intended to talk to his lawyers when he was well enough to ride to Santa Fe. I know he would have wanted the ranch divided between us. Please, we cannot leave him here."

The effort to explain strained already overwrought nerves, and Luke intervened. Stepping past Juan, he caught Maria's hand in his and pushed her gently back against the couch. "Maria, I would be happy to take

Pedro with us, but you cannot take him and Pieta away from their family. I know it hurts to leave him behind, but he will be safe. For now you must think of our child, and let Pieta take care of Pedro.''

"What child?'' Patrick roared, coming to his feet at this latest development. Juan simply closed his eyes and touched his fingers to his head as if in pain.

Luke smiled reassuringly at Maria's worried expression, winked, and turned back to the Irishman. "Our child. I regret that the wedding must be a hasty one, but I have to get Maria out of here. There is a stage leaving for El Moro Tuesday morning and we must be on it. If the priest comes tomorrow night, we will have the day to prepare.''

"You damned whoreson of a lying, lily-livered . . .'' The epithets trailed on for some minutes.

Luke's hand held Maria's tightly, but he made no attempt to interrupt. A grim line formed at the corner of his mouth as he accepted the curses he so justly deserved. The words no longer held a power to hurt him; he would fight only if they tried to take Maria from him.

"I told you we would hang you if you so much as came within a hundred yards of her! My God, I ought to throttle you with my bare hands.''

Juan held up a hand for silence, his penetrating stare falling on the couple in the corner as he sensed Luke's thoughts. "She is my niece. I will not see her hurt. Maria, you know you may come with me without shame. You do not have to marry this man.''

He waited for Maria to nod her understanding. When she said nothing more, Juan turned on Luke. "I am a wealthy man. How much will it take to persuade you to leave her here and never return?''

Maria gave a cry of outrage, but Luke pressed her hand in warning. "I have no need of your fortune, *señor*. Maria goes with me.'' Luke lifted his gaze to the man behind the desk. "You have every right to call me what you will, but do not place me in the position of having to fight you for Maria. I will win, whatever the odds, but she will hate me forever for harming you. I promise, she will be safe with me. I can do no more than that.''

Patrick glared furiously at Luke. He turned an appeal to her good sense to Maria, but she was gazing up at Luke as if he just donned a halo. He sat down heavily and reached for another brandy. ''Well, Juan, what do we do now?''

Juan swung his cheroot in a gesture of defeat and watched Maria's lovely face with affection. ''We give her what she wants, just like her father always did. I hope you appreciate Señor Walker, what a gift you have been given.''

Maria gave a sigh of relief and unclenched her fists. Luke lifted his hand to her shoulder and caressed the long braid there, but he continued to focus his attention on her uncles.

''I am a man who recognizes value and does not neglect it when he finds it. I will tell you anything you wish to know about me to reassure yourselves of Maria's safety, but I think right now we had better decide what to do with Pedro so she will go off and get some rest.''

A hint of amusement touched Juan's lips and Patrick gave a gesture of defeat.

''If there is no doubt that Pedro is Michael's son, I will make the arrangements for providing a home for him wherever his mother chooses until the ranch is safe again. Maria, can you tell me of a certainty that Pedro is your half brother?'' Like the businessman he was, Patrick Connolly negotiated a compromise. Losing a niece and gaining a nephew in the same day had worn the sharp edges from his temper.

''I can tell you of a certainty that Pieta does not lie, and that she has nothing to gain by lying now. She wished nothing for herself or Pedro, she simply wished to offer me a home and family when she told me. You have seen him. There is a physical resemblance.''

Patrick grunted skeptically. ''Black Irish and Mexican. Holy Mother of God, what would you have me see? I have known you all your life and you look more and more like your mother every day. But every time you look at me like that, I see Mike. At least the lad doesn't have those damned Irish eyes.''

There were too many things in her head to feel the proper joy at the knowledge that her uncle would recognize Pedro. She felt satisfaction that he would be protected, but weariness prevented her usual spontaneous response. These men were neatly wrapping up her future and did not require her presence to do so. At the moment she felt only relief that all the decisions had been taken from her.

With Luke's help Maria rose from the chair. "If that is decided, then, I think I will lie down for a while.''

Luke had the urge to pick her up and carry her out, but the result of that would not be conducive to resting. He had gone nearly two months wanting her, and the desire did not cease when she was this close to him. He clenched his teeth and watched her go, wondering what was in her thoughts as she sent him that last helpless, bewildered look before she went out. He would have to find out.

After watching the door close, Luke turned back to face his antagonists. "Well, gentlemen, where would you like to begin?''

"With your hide,'' Patrick snarled, but he gestured for Luke to take a seat for the first time since he had entered the room.

Maria had little time to grow accustomed to the idea of being a wife. By the time she had emptied her stomach into the chamber pot the next morning and exclaimed in horror at the sight of her face in the mirror, Pieta had already appeared with her wedding gown and Carmelita in tow.

There were not only the final alterations to be made and a coiffure invented to hide the worst of the bruise on her jaw, but everything she wished to take with her must be packed, and those things to follow in wagons sorted out. One day was not enough time for any of this, and certainly not all of it at once.

Pieta threw herself into the preparations with calm authority. Reassured that Luke intended to make an honest woman of her little girl, she had no further complaints in that direction. She did not need to be told what to do when it became apparent that the ranch would be abandoned. Trunks and boxes sprang up throughout the house, and all the valuables Maria would need in her new life found their way into an appropriate container.

Pieta took Patrick Connolly's acknowledgment of Pedro in stride. It was good for the boy to have rich relatives who would recognize him, but as long as she was around, he would not need them. She said as much to his bemused uncle, but did not deny the offer of a home until matters at the ranch could be settled. There might come a time when Maria would need her again. It would be better with a home of her own.

They saw nothing of Luke as the day progressed, and very little of the uncles. Events moved rapidly, everyone pitching in as the state of emergency became apparent. Rumor already carried the news of Manuel's beating at the hands of the gunfighter. Though everyone knew it was over Maria, speculation was rife on the retaliation that would follow. No one expected the powerful Vasqueros to take the matter lightly, and they were not a family known for going to the law. Several of the other ranchers began appearing at the gates, volunteering their support with just their presence.

Maria knew little of the events outside the house. She had her hands full just keeping up with Pieta. She hugged Pedro every time he came near until in little boy fashion he began avoiding her. She had no time to consider the consequences of her rash decision to marry Luke. Leaving the ranch had been inevitable from the first. That was the only problem she could deal with for the moment.

Pieta ordered her to take a nap, but every time Maria considered it wishfully, half a dozen other things that needed doing crowded into her mind. By evening she was too exhausted to be nervous. Even a warm bath could not revive her, and when Pieta carried in the wedding gown, Maria donned it without giving the significance a second thought. It was just one more thing that had to be done before the day could end.

The gown fit more tightly than intended, but Maria refused to tightly lace the corset that Luke had so maligned before. The gown's narrow bodice dropped low over her hips, emphasizing the curve of her waist, and rose to cup her breasts snugly. If Luke had any doubts about his bride's beauty, he had only to look upon her in this gown to be reassured.

Rolling Maria's hair to the bruised side of her face, Pieta pinned it into a loose swirl and three dangling curls. With the addition of the thick folds of lace as a mantilla, the discoloration could scarcely be discerned. She stood back proudly as Maria turned in front of her, showing off her handiwork.

"Such a beautiful bride! You will put all others to shame. Here, you must carry these, so your mother will be with you, too." From the table she removed a small bouquet of white roses, wrapping the plucked stems in remnants of lace.

Taking the flowers, Maria looked at Pieta proudly standing there in her new taffeta dress, her brown skin gleaming in the lamplight, and felt a sudden wave of tears brimming her eyes. Throwing herself into the older woman's arms, she fought back sobs for the life she would be leaving, the only life she had ever known. However would she get along without Pieta's scolding to remind her of what must be done?

With tears still in their eyes, the women separated at the sound of a knock on the door signaling the impatience of the men outside. Pieta hurriedly patted Maria's eyes with a clean handkerchief, made a final adjustment to the mantilla, and opened the door.

Both uncles awaited her, and Maria smiled timidly at their splendor on this occasion. In formal dark cutaway frock coats and trousers, their high collars gleaming whitely against their sun-darkened skins, they presented a symbolic image of the solemnity of the ceremony to follow. The first twinges of fear began to tug at Maria's nerves.

Each uncle took one of her hands on their arms, and

the pride in their eyes as they tried to express their emotions in useless words warmed Maria's heart. She stood on tiptoe to press a kiss against each rough cheek.

"I'm so glad you could be here for this. I wish I could thank you enough. I love you both." She said it without crying, although her eyes glistened with unshed tears.

They squeezed her hands and solemnly escorted her to the study, where the priest and the few guests waited. Pieta and Carmelita followed behind, settling in the chairs left for them as Maria and her uncles walked to the front of the room.

Maria's eyes found Luke with complete disregard for anyone else. He, too, had somehow managed to find a formal white cravat and a tailored frock coat. The strings of his tie were slightly askew, and he appeared as if he might suffocate in the confining clothes, but his eyes were warm and proud as they found her. Maria felt the blood rushing through her veins at the sight of him standing there, waiting for her. The hard, square jaw and taut muscles of his face that could look so cold and forbidding at times now appeared almost handsome, and she could not control a blinding smile of delight. He could have been angry for being forced into this, but he was not, and her love for him began to take root and grow.

Luke could not take his eyes from Maria as she drifted toward him, green eyes alight and glowing in a golden face of fragile loveliness. High cheekbones, wide slanted eyes, and ebony hair added an exotic touch promising more than the serenity of the smooth satin floating around her slender form. Momentary anxiety clouded his gaze. What kind of future could he offer a woman like this?

With her entire being centered on the man in front of her, Maria noticed his hesitation at once. Her smile faltered, but her feet inexorably led her toward him. So he had his doubts, too. That thought dampened Maria's brief pleasure, but she obediently took Luke's hand when her uncles presented it to him.

Father Díaz searched her face questioningly as she turned toward him. There had not been time for any of the prenuptial questioning or blessings he preferred, but Maria knew he would not be here at all if Luke had not passed inspection. She had not given thought to whether Luke was Catholic or not, another example of how witless she had become. He must have agreed to allow their children to be brought up in the church, and for that she was grateful. She would not have felt married if it had been anyone but Father Díaz standing there. She smiled, and the priest looked relieved.

The ceremony went so swiftly, it did not seem quite real. The heavy silence of the study muffled the priest's words, and Maria sought desperately for some sign of her father's presence here, in this room that had been his alone. She wanted his approval of this man she had chosen, but she could feel nothing beyond Luke's fingers pressing into hers. The presence of her uncles behind her would have to suffice.

The sound of Luke's warm voice intoning the vows that would bind them to eternity brought Maria back to startled attention. How much of what he said did he really mean? As he lifted her hand to place a small, plain band upon it, their eyes met, and Maria's lips parted with a small exhalation of wonder. The cold glints of amber in Luke's eyes had softened to a warm, gentle brown that brought a hint of rose to her cheeks.

She scarcely heard herself repeating the words of the ceremony, and before she was ready, Luke was brushing aside her mantilla and bringing her close to seal the words with a kiss. She trembled as his hands closed firmly around her, but the touch of his lips had the usual electrifying effect. She had to steady herself on the muscular solidity of his arm when their lips parted.

The familiar gleam was back in Luke's eyes as he took her hand formally in the crook of his elbow before turning to acknowledge their guests. Maria felt that look burn through her center like a piercing brand. It had been two months since they'd been together. Tonight they would have the whole night. Just the thought sent butterflies leaping through her stomach.

People crowded around them, shaking Luke's hand, pounding his back, demanding a kiss from the bride. Pieta and Carmelita came forward for hugs, and Maria trapped Pedro long enough to give his neatly combed hair a kiss. He gave her a masculine look of disgust, but refrained from wiping it off. Uncle Juan came forward and, noting Luke's possessive hold on his bride, smiled slightly and bent a light kiss to Maria's cheek. Uncle Patrick nervously wiped his brow, pumped Luke's hand, and looked at Maria with dismay.

"My God! I'll have to go through this with two more daughters. I'm going to call on the two of you to come hold me up for the next one. Did we carry up the whiskey?"

Luke grinned. "The last of the supply is in the parlor. Shall we lead the way?"

The crowd parted as the bride and groom strolled to the doorway. It was not the same kind of crowd as would have been there had she married Manuel, but Maria preferred this wedding with the ranch hands and the people she knew and loved around her. Her eyes widened with surprise as she caught a glimpse of Sean's battered face sporting a wry grin. One eye was swollen closed and his jaw had a distinctive color that had nothing to do with his need for a shave, but his smile was as charming as ever, and Maria sent him one back.

Luke caught this exchange and bent to study his bride's face before opening the door. The smile she gave him was more than answer to any question he had, and he let his doubts dispel. For better or worse, the capricious creature at his side was his to have and to hold, and he would let no man put them asunder. This time he was willing to fight for what he wanted.

As the door opened, the house exploded with sound, and Maria grabbed Luke's arm in panic. And then the noise leveled off and Maria could distinguish the rhythms and her smile of ecstasy nearly lifted everyone watching from their feet.

Luke had hired the mariachi band for the reception.

11

Luke swung his wife around the parlor floor one last time as the band strummed and beat out a spirited rendition of what should have been a waltz. Maria's cheeks glowed with the warmth and the exercise and the excitement, and when Luke ended the dance by clasping her in his embrace, she came willingly, to the claps and hoots of their well-wishers.

A slight cough behind them reminded them they were not alone, and Maria hastily stepped backward as the band struck up a livelier tune. Sean beamed as benevolently upon them as he was able through the swollen bruises on his face forcing Luke to grin despite his annoyance.

"Isn't it about time you learned to fight?" Luke ribbed him, giving Sean's disfigured features a sardonic look.

"I leave that to fellows like you. Your head's so hard it wouldn't be hurt by an avalanche, though it appears to me Manuel put a few holes in it." He gave the bruises and cuts of Luke's face a cursory glance. "Actually, this is probably the most colorful wedding party I have ever attended. I trust all weddings out here aren't preceded by that kind of bachelor party." His glance returned to the concealed bruise on Maria's face.

"We don't plan to make it a habit to attend any more. You haven't given me an answer yet. Are you going to drive that wagon?"

There was something in the tone of Luke's voice as he asked which brought Maria's head up sharply to watch the pair. Sean seemed to retreat to a distance, though he did not move from where he stood. Luke maintained his usual impassive demeanor.

"I'll see your wagon out of here since I didn't accomplish much else. Don't be expecting me to stay once I get it there." Before Maria could ask any questions, Sean held out his hand to her. "If I cannot kiss the bride, may I at least have a dance with her?"

"Dance her over to that hallway over there, and I'll meet you there. I'll be damned if they try to chivy us out of here."

Sean's eyes twinkled once more as he swung Maria into his arms. "Thought you might feel that way, boyo. Come, lovely señora, let me enjoy you one last time before I give you up to wedded life."

Sean danced with much enthusiasm and little grace, but Maria withstood the rigors knowing when the music stopped she would be in Luke's arms again. The room was filled to overflowing with men in various stages of drink. They stomped and clapped and, when no woman was available, swung each other around in time to the music. The few women daring enough to attend this impromptu party had their hands full and their feet worn off and were in no position to scale down the riotous activity. Luke was right, it was time to go.

They slipped from the room without notice, Luke waiting in the shadows of the hall until Sean led Maria to join him. Luke stood silently as Maria pressed a swift kiss to Sean's cheek. When she turned expectantly back to him, taking his hand without hesitation, Luke allowed himself a small smile of triumph.

In all else he had full confidence in himself, but not in his choice of women. He had been fooled before by pretty faces and innocent airs. He found it difficult to believe this woman was any different, but it was too late to turn back now. She carried his child. That alone compelled him to make his claim.

Ignorant of Luke's doubts, Maria led him to the bedchamber that had been hers since childhood. When he entered and looked around, she felt suddenly, inexplicably shy. Despite the packing that had taken place, the room revealed parts of her that she seldom shared. It was still a child's room, though, and she felt out of place in it with this man at her side.

"I should have sent for your shaving gear." Nervously Maria dropped his hand and drifted to the dresser, where her personal brushes and combs awaited the morning. He would want his own things before they left.

"I'm an early riser. I'll get it in the morning." Luke's gaze traveled over the almost Spartan interior of the room. The curtains and bed covers had no frills or flounces, but brightened the room with the brilliant colors of red and gold and some deeper hues between. The hardwood floor had only a woven rug near the bed to cover it, but the wood gleamed with polished wax. His hand gently touched the delicate ivory combs on the dresser. These were hers, and he must soon get used to seeing them combined with his own things.

With an embarrassed look over her shoulder, Maria disappeared behind the dressing screen, and Luke could hear the rustle of her heavy wedding dress being removed. He leaned against the door frame with his arms crossed against his chest, contemplating giving her a few moments alone, but he could not bear letting her out of his sight, or at least his hearing. He had this insane fear that she would disappear from his grasp like a wisp of fog if he did not hold onto her.

A single lamp burned at the bedside, throwing much of the room in shadow as Maria stepped out from behind the screen. Luke continued to study her as he had the contents of the room, his gaze absorbing the long, tangled mass of her hair released from its pins, the frail muslin nightgown that did nothing to hide her slender curves. When her green eyes turned up uncertainly to meet his, Luke hesitated. What had he done in marrying this child and planning to steal her from her home for the disillusionment of his future?

Luke's hesitation made her shiver, and Maria glanced away from the bronzed hardness of his features. Had it only been lust that had brought him to her? Did she question now the chains that bound them?

Why had she ever allowed herself to be persuaded that marriage to a gunfighter, a wanderer, was the only reasonable course?

Guessing the hurt behind her eyes, Luke pushed away from the wall and came to stand before her. Gently he pushed the thick strands of her hair from her shoulder, then slid his hand to cup her face and turn it toward him. The confusion he found in her gaze swept away his own doubts. It was done. She was his. He would have to find some way to keep her and protect her from the pain of his past.

The certainty of his kiss resolved Maria's momentary doubts. Her arms slid about his neck, and Luke drew her firmly into his world, out of the childish innocence of her own. Whatever the future held, they would share it together, as they shared the needs of this moment.

Luke carried Maria to the bed, gently laying her across the covers before falling down beside her. Propped on one elbow, he leaned over her, his other hand exploring the soft contours of her body while his mouth continued to greedily drink her kiss. Maria's hand tentatively slipped to the collar of his shirt, removing the studs inexpertly so she might at last touch the heat of the bare skin below.

Luke obligingly sat up and began ripping off the fastenings to throw the shirt aside. Broad, bronzed shoulders emerged from the white linen, and Maria watched in admiration the ripple of powerful muscles beneath the soft fur of his chest.

Luke raised his foot to remove his boot, and Maria sat up to help him. He looked down at her bent head as she struggled with the tight leather, and a slow smile began to form on his lips. Being married was going to have its good side. He caught her hair and tugged it backward until Maria looked up at him, and he bent to plunder her mouth once more.

Exhaustion made her weak, but Luke's passion made her weaker. He stole everything she possessed and demanded more. Pressed back against the bed again, Maria felt Luke's hand unfasten the buttons of the gown, and she arched against him as his fingers laid claim to her breast. It had been two months since he had touched her so. She had forgotten how it made her feel.

His hand continued to prowl, circling her breasts until the nipples grew hard and erect, sliding from there to her abdomen, setting off small explosions as his fingers carelessly rubbed lower. Desire flamed through Maria's blood as she felt her gown being drawn upward over her hips. The coolness of the night air caressing her moistened heat made her shiver, but not more so than the feel of Luke's stroking fingers entering her.

His kisses continued finding harbors of ecstasy behind her ears, at the base of her throat, and lower, lovingly suckling the sensitive peaks of her breasts. Maria emitted a cry of longing when Luke moved away to remove the remainder of his clothes, but she rejoiced when he returned to lay his hard body against hers.

The nightgown disappeared over the edge of the bed and then there was nothing between them. How much she had forgotten in his absence! Maria drank in the musky scent of him, pressing her lips eagerly over his newly shaven jaw. Luke's whispered endearments caressed her in the same manner as his hands, and her fingers wrapped gladly in the curls of his chest. Her legs became entangled with his, and their roughness made her feel more vulnerable than ever. His knee pushed against her thigh, and before she had time to catch her breath, he entered her.

Beyond doubts, beyond thinking, they came together with a need they could no longer deny. The rhythmic rise and fall of their bodies left no time for thought or regret, only the striving to reach that secret place that was their very own.

Luke moaned against her ear as his body exploded inside hers, and he felt the tightening quakes that drew him deeper, signaling Maria's release. Not wishing to be parted from this little piece of heaven, he held her

in place while rolling over to release her from his
greater weight.

"Don't let me hurt you," he murmured as Maria
wriggled into the nest of his arms, kissing those places
on his skin that her lips could reach.

"You can't hurt me like this. Just don't leave me."
Her voice was husky and low and her meaning ambiguous.

Luke's arms tightened about her as he pulled the
sheet up to keep the night air from cooling her. "I
can't, you're a part of me now."

Although his reply was equally ambiguous, Maria
accepted it with contentment. Within minutes she was
sound asleep in his arms.

Luke woke her before dawn, his kisses on her forehead producing a sleepy response. She reached to draw
his lips down to hers, but he lifted his head. His hand
slid appreciatively over the curve of her hips before
moving away.

"We need to leave before it grows light. I don't
know if the ranch is being watched, but that's the saf-
est thing to do." He gave her bare buttock an affectionate slap and removed himself from the bed.

Maria groaned and he grinned at her reluctance to
leave the comforts of their mutual bed. They had many
nights ahead of them to enjoy the delights of married
life. She would have to learn patience. He began jerking on the pants he had thrown on the floor the night
before. Not until Maria rolled over, rose hastily from
the bed, and stumbled to the chamber pot did Luke
realize the true cause of her protest.

He knelt beside her and held her as the remains of
the previous day's dinner came up. He cursed himself
for doing this to her, vowed to find some way to make
it up to her, and anxiously dipped a washrag in the
water pitcher to wipe Maria's face as the shudders
racked through her. He tried to make her comfortable
within the curve of his body until she gave a final
shudder and relaxed against his shoulder.

"Lie still a moment, *querida*. Don't move too quickly. I am sorry to make you get up like this."

Maria buried her face against Luke's bare shoulder, feeling a hot flush of embarrassment spreading through her. She had nothing on, but he held her in his lap as if she were fully clothed, and she blessed him for that. The sight she must have presented would have been enough to turn a strong man's stomach.

"I can see our son is going to be hard to get along with." A thread of amusement wound through Luke's voice as he settled her more comfortably in his lap.

"Like father, like son. Or perhaps it will be a daughter. Would you be disappointed?"

With curiosity Luke traced the flat place between her hipbones where his child grew. The swelling was so small as to be barely discernible, but he knew it was there. "Disappointed? Not unless you refuse to give me a chance to try again."

"Ugh, I don't know if I can go through this again. Why can't men have the babies some of the time?"

Luke chuckled and slowly rose to his feet, carrying Maria with him. "If we could get them the same way, I would gladly share your burden. The sickness should pass soon, though. You will be as fit as ever in a few weeks."

"But fat and ugly," Maria pouted, stepping from his arms to hunt for her clothes. "Then I suppose you will ride off and not return until it's all over with. I hope there is a good midwife wherever you're taking me."

Luke caught her by the waist and twisted her chin up until he could kiss her. Maria tried to turn away, but he wouldn't let her, and he proved his passion with the deepness of his kiss.

When he released her, Maria staggered slightly and tried to gain her equilibrium. The sickness had left her mouth sour and repulsive even to her, and she brought the back of her hand up to cover it, her eyes going wide to search Luke's expression in the dark. How could he kiss her with such enjoyment?

Luke steadied her with his hand and rubbed her

shoulder gently. "I have not had to plan for others for quite a few years, Maria, and I may not be very good at it. Be patient with me, and I will try my best to be the husband you want. The first thing I will do is make certain there is a good midwife available."

He did not tell her where they were going because he had not yet made up his mind. He had told her uncles of his home and family in Kansas and that had reassured them, but he had not told them why he hadn't returned in years. If there had been time, he'd meant to go back and settle the differences before they wed, but it was too late for that now. Maria wouldn't understand if he left her alone in a strange place while he returned to make peace with his brother and find out the status of the warrant for his arrest.

He could not take her back there and risk being thrown from the ranch or arrested or both. It left him in a considerable dilemma, but the important thing was to get her out of here now.

While Luke went out to make his preparations, Maria hastily donned the traveling clothes left out the day before. The wedding dress would be packed up and sent on the wagon later. For now one of the simple calicos Pieta had made would have to do. She did not cut an impressive figure in the simple, belted wrapper with just a touch of lace at the high neckline, but the stagecoach ride would be too dusty to risk her better gown.

They slipped away from the ranch silently, saying their tearful farewells in the darkness of the kitchen before going out to mount their horses. Luke rode in front, keeping his eyes and ears open for any sign of watchers. Maria glanced at the empty place on his hips where his guns used to rest, and she wondered if she had made a mistake in that impulsive challenge of two days before. He had a rifle across his saddle. She prayed it would be adequate. A man with Luke's reputation was a walking target for other gunmen when he wore those colts. She had to be confident that he would be safer without them.

They joined the stage as it prepared to leave from

San Pedro at dawn. They were not the only ones up and about, and it would not be long before word got out that Maria Connolly had left town with the gunfighter. She did not care to think what Manuel's reaction would be when he learned of their marriage. The ranch was safely out of his reach now, but sadly, out of hers, too. She lifted the window shade and took one last look back as the first hints of gold brightened the corners of adobe brick in the town behind her.

She was leaving all that was known and familiar to ride off into the unknown with a man who had come into her life only two months before. She had no idea where he was taking her or how they would live. Turning her gaze back into the stage's dim interior, she looked up at Luke's hard jaw, and for the first time she felt fear.

BOOK III
July, 1876

1

The stagecoach ride did nothing to alleviate Maria's growing anxiety. As soon as she realized she was locked inside that narrow space, shoulder to shoulder with the stiff, silent man beside her with no escape, no future, no family or friends to protect her, she began to panic.

She was married to a gunfighter, an outlaw with no home, no job, no discernible means of living beyond his wits and his guns. Violence was his way of life, but it had no place in hers. She had no idea of where he was taking her or what he would do with her. As the child lurched and nausea rose in her, Maria wondered desperately how she would survive, how she would protect the innocent being growing within her. Luke never once turned to her with any reassurances. His continued silence built a wall between them, and she came to see only the stranger in him.

By the afternoon of that first day, Maria's panic dissolved in a desperate effort to hold her head up. She rolled limply against Luke's shoulder, all strength drained away. The rocking, jolting motion of the stage was worse than she remembered, and more than once Luke was forced to shout for a halt so she could be sick alongside the road. By that point she had not even the strength to be embarrassed as the other passengers glared at her in irritation. She ached all over, and her head hurt abominably, making the torment in her stomach even worse.

When they stopped for the night, Maria did not even make it to the supper table. Luke carried her into the station and lifted her to the top bunk, and she lay there like one dead while the others ate. She groaned when Luke returned bearing a plate of food and turned away after only sipping the water he brought for her.

Stomach empty, she could only choke on bile by morning. Luke's brow puckered into a frown when she refused breakfast, and he forced a little coffee between her lips. It came up not much later.

The day turned cloudy and before long brisk winds added to the rocking of the low-slung vehicle. Maria turned pale as one gust tilted the stage while the wooden wheel hit a rut at the same time. She gagged, but by this time she had nothing left to heave up.

They arrived in El Moro in the evening. Maria's listless form inspired sympathy even from their irritated fellow passengers, but the fever beginning to burn red circles on her cheeks worried Luke more.

The hotel at least provided a clean bed, but when Luke tried to undress Maria and place her in it, she protested the movement and turned away. He left her lying fully dressed on the mattress and went in search of a doctor.

He returned in despair to find her sleeping fitfully, her forehead burning with fever. The town's lone physician was the barber, and the medicine he had prescribed was an opiate. Luke doubted the efficacy of drugging someone already asleep and shoved the bottle into his valise. Desperation made chaos of his mind.

He had warned her he had no experience in caring for another. He felt totally responsible and completely helpless as he watched Maria's frail features toss restlessly on the pillows. She had been nearly unconscious for hours now. He had not gotten more than a sip of liquid into her since the day before. It couldn't be good for her, and it couldn't be good for the child.

Thinking of the life growing within her, Luke broke out in a cold sweat. Two lives depended on him. He had thought it would be a simple matter to reach the train station and travel wherever the next train took them. He had never had difficulty finding a job, and he knew people in towns scattered across half the territory. He had sufficient cash to travel until Maria found a place she liked. The impossibility of roaming at will as he had before struck him full force now.

He finally managed to get Maria's clothes off so she would be cooler in the stuffy room. When he discarded his own and lay down beside her, she rolled into his embrace, and he could feel the chill of her skin against him. He did not fool himself into thinking the fever had broken; it had just reached another stage.

Maria woke when Luke tried to dress her in the morning, and she helped him guide the clothing into the appropriate places, but she scarcely had the strength to sit up. Leaving her again while he sought food and water and checked the train schedule, Luke felt the hands of fate close in on him as he read the destinations. The next train was heading east, and the names of the stops rang a familiar litany.

He had no choice. Maria needed care he could not provide and as quickly as possible. The small town along the Arkansas River he called his home was not the first stop, but it was the only one where he knew he could find help. He bought the tickets and hurried back to Maria.

Her first sight of a locomotive and Maria could scarcely focus on the immense, steaming beast puffing and throwing out clouds of black dust. It seemed a monster from her worst nightmare, and she clung to Luke's side as he lifted her gently to the first step. Inside the car the stench of unwashed bodies, full cuspidors, and cigar smoke turned her stomach painfully, and she had to stop until her head quit spinning. She hated being helpless, and feverish, she tried to stand alone and make her way down the aisle with the same confidence as the other passengers.

Luke caught her as the train gave a hiccup and lurched, and a woman nearby frowned haughtily and swept her skirts out of Maria's drunken path. Luke didn't try to explain. Catching Maria in his arms, he carried her hurriedly to the first open bench before the train could roll into motion.

Maria tried to watch the landscape as the train

rushed across dry plains and knee-high grasses, but the motion of the train was little better than that of the stage and soon her stomach rebelled against the sight. Closing her eyes, she leaned her head against Luke's shoulder, and before long she was conscious of nothing around her.

Gazing on pale features splashed with a fringe of long black lashes, Luke choked back a primal cry of despair. He had never been given such a fragile life to protect before, and he knew he was failing dismally at his first try. She had trusted him, and he had betrayed that trust. If her life were forfeit because of him, his own would not be worth a damn.

Not wishing to acknowledge the importance the woman had taken in his life, Luke did not try to contemplate a life without her. He had lived alone for years. He could do so again. He just could not live with the responsibility of harming his laughing, loving Maria.

The train traveled through the night. Luke paid some of the more sympathetic passengers to buy food and drink when they came to a town or bought what he could from the vendors on the train, but he never left Maria's side. When she woke sufficiently to see to her personal needs, he carried her into the privy of whatever station they happened to be in or behind the screen at the back of the car. Maria was too weak to protest, and the intimacy of married life now included the drawstrings of delicate pantalettes and the cumbersome folds of heavy petticoats.

By the time they reached their destination, Maria had been insensible for hours. The tall, grim man striding from the train platform carrying the unconscious lady in his arms drew stares as he crossed the station and entered the street. Passersby moved aside to give him room, and before Luke had reached the town's lone hotel, whispers were already rustling up and down the street. Cheyenne Walker had returned to town.

Luke paid no heed to the hotel clerk's startled reaction as he demanded a room and a doctor. He scarcely even missed the heavy weight of his guns on his hips as he carried Maria across the lobby, although he knew he had entered territory where he would need them more than ever. Silently he carried his unmoving burden up to the room assigned, not noticing the sympathy on the desk clerk's face as he gently laid Maria upon the bed covers.

Within minutes the man had gone about delivering the messages Luke dictated, leaving the hardened gunman sitting alone beside Maria's silent figure, waiting.

Maria grew conscious of strange voices nearby. Cool hands unbuttoned her bodice, and she struggled weakly, murmuring Luke's name though it came out as a rasping whisper. Luke must have heard because he came to stand beside her, holding her hand and murmuring those phrases she loved to hear. Reassured, she returned to sleep.

Before the doctor had time to leave, a buckboard barreled down the town's main street at a reckless rate. Hearing the commotion below, Luke turned to glance out the window. A faint smile touched his lips. His father hadn't changed.

The gruff, burly man who barged into the room stopped short at the sight of the physician bending over the petite, lifeless form on the bed. Eyes of the same gold and brown hues of Luke's lifted to gaze at the lanky stranger who was his son. Greedily they noted the hard jaw with the tired lines, the sunburnt brown of Luke's face and hands, the muscular leanness of his wiry frame. Then seeing the anguished uncertainty in his son's eyes, he held out a hand in greeting.

"Welcome home, son. I wish it could have been under happier circumstances."

Luke clasped his hand gratefully, assured that at least one person welcomed him. Had his father turned his back on his wayward son, he would be without a home for Maria. His glance quickly swept back to Maria's silent figure.

"Your wife?" At Luke's nod the older man studied the pale Spanish features of his new daughter-in-law and nodded approvingly. "She is lovely. Doc, how soon can we move her out to the ranch?"

The doctor frowned thoughtfully as he finished his examination. "I would not advise moving her except that she will need constant attendance. It might be more comfortable if she was out at the house."

"Lettie will see to her. She'll be in good hands," the burly man with the graying hair reassured them, his words as much for Luke as the physician.

"My house, Dad, not yours. If it's still there."

Joshua Walker sent his stubborn son a piercing look, but he nodded his understanding. Within minutes they were loading the wagon, preparing for the hot journey.

Soft hands stroked her brow, pushing back the hair that had fallen there. A cold compress took away some of the heat, and Maria moved restlessly, trying to waken.

"She is young, Luke," a soft voice said.

"Older than you when you married, Mother. You should see her when she's awake. She has eyes like green fire, and she can cut a person in two with her tongue. You'll like her."

The words came from a distance and Maria wasn't certain if she had heard them or dreamed them, but the affection in Luke's familiar voice made her smile, and she drifted off to sleep again.

The next words intruding on her consciousness were not so pleasant. She knew someone had removed her clothes and put her in a nightgown, and vaguely she remembered sipping something liquid. Her throat and lips were parched now, and she longed for a glass of cool water. Stirring restlessly, she could not quite get out the words, and the voices intruding on her dreams forced her to lie still.

"What in hell are you doing here, Caroline? Get out. I can take care of her myself."

Luke's voice was harsher and crueler than she had ever heard it, but it was the name that sent a vibrant warning deep inside her.

"I'm just trying to help, Luke. What kind of sister-in-law would I be if I did not come when she needed me?'' The voice was low and unconsciously seductive.

"Maria can decide that for herself when she wakes. For now, get out of here, Caroline. I don't want you around.''

Luke's voice sounded so weary Maria ached to call out to him, but the ache in her head prevented any word from escaping. She turned to tossing restlessly.

From that moment onward, Maria began to improve. She came to recognize the soft presence Luke called "Mother.'' Cold compresses and cooling broths appeared whenever she was about, and the sheets beneath her were straightened. Soothing words whispered over her head, and she felt better.

Until one day, she was able to force her eyes open and see this wonderful being for herself. Slowly her gaze took in the strange room, the high, old-fashioned poster bed, billowing blue curtains at the open window, and a rocking chair by the bed. In that chair sat a plump, maternal figure with golden hair fading to gray and a smile upon her lips as she noted Maria's open eyes.

"Welcome, Maria Francesca. Luke's told me all about you. Would you like some water?''

Her voice was soft and sweet, just like Maria's dreams, and she nodded. She tried to return the greeting, but her parched throat would not let the sound escape.

Letitia helped her to sit up against the pillows and held the glass so she could drink. When her thirst was quenched, Maria leaned her head back and closed her eyes. It was then that the terrible thought struck her.

"My baby!'' Horrified, she reached beneath the covers to touch the small curve of her stomach. Her mother had lost so many children. She could not bear it if she lost this one.

"The child is fine,'' Letitia reassured her. "You are the one who is weak. We need to make you strong again so you carry the child safely. Luke wasn't a big baby, but his brother was, so you must be prepared for anything.''

In relief Maria's restless fingers stroked the gown over her abdomen. She would get better again. She could not quite remember the details, but she knew she had a fight on her hands. She knew how to fight.

With each passing day she grew stronger, stayed awake longer. When Luke came in to find her sitting up in bed waiting for him, his tired face lit with joy.

"*Querida*, do you know how beautiful you look sitting there?"

Since her hair had not been washed or plaited and she had caught a glimpse of the pallor of her face in the mirror, Maria knew he lied, but she loved him more for the lie.

"Your tastes are becoming positively crude, if that's what you think," she teased. "Where are we?"

"In my home, my love." Luke settled on the bed's edge and watched her face with concern. After so many days of despair, he didn't dare hope again, but the green of her eyes seemed full of intelligence and curiosity. He breathed a small sigh of relief and touched the fading bruise on her cheek.

"In *our* home, I should say."

Maria's eyes widened in wonder as she looked around. She could tell from the view out the windows that they were on the second floor. The room was much bigger than the one she had at home, bigger than the one that had been her father's. Lovely wallpaper with white and blue flowers decorated the walls, and a huge hearth would serve as a wonderful source of warmth come winter.

"Ours? Why did you not tell me you had a home like this?"

Pleased that she approved of his handiwork but curious about her reaction, Luke answered cautiously. "Would it have mattered?"

Maria looked at him in surprise. "To whom? For all I knew, our first child would be born in a cave. You're not prone to talking much about your home."

"Idiot child. I wouldn't have married you if I couldn't keep you in the same manner to which you're accustomed. I would have sent you away with your uncles.''

A brief shadow passed across Maria's face as he said these words. She knew he had married her because of the child, but it had not occurred to her that he might have sent her away altogether. She tried not to let him see her pain and disappointment.

''Are we going to stay?'' she inquired softly, looking out the window to the tall trees edging the yard.

''I think it would be best, don't you? The child doesn't seem to like traveling.'' Luke felt the sudden distance between them, but he could only blame it on her health. Gently he touched her shoulder. ''You should lie down and rest some more. You have been very ill.''

Maria nodded and scooted down between the sheets. She watched intently as Luke rose from the bed and removed empty dishes from the table. Giving her a smile, he walked out the door. He had not even kissed her. Was that the wretched Caroline's doing? Had seeing her brought back the old feelings, making it impossible to look upon his plain, dark wife? For she knew Caroline to be one of the lovely golden girls with white and pink complexions and rosy smiles. How could she possibly compete with that?

But she would not give up without a fight. She was a Connolly. She had been born fighting. Caroline would have to watch her pretty blond curls.

2

With the freedom to roam the upstairs under dire threats should she tire herself, Maria leisurely made her way through this part of the house that was now her home.

There seemed more than enough room for everything they could possibly need. Maria smiled at the lone piece of furniture in the small room next to hers. Touching her finger to the well-worn, polished wood of the old cradle, she made it rock. Luke had appropriated it from his father's attic, she knew. She and Rosa, the new maid, had scrubbed and waxed it until it shone like new. She would have to remember the rudiments of sewing Pieta had taught her so she could provide it with linens and coverlets and maybe a ruffle or two. She felt certain Luke would not disapprove of that occupation for her.

Hearing voices from the garden below, she wandered to the window to see what visitors had arrived now. After that long confinement in bed it seemed heaven to be able to do something so simple as look out a window. She chafed at not being able to see the rest of the house, but Luke had promised he would carry her down tonight so she could eat at the table. That thought brought a rush of excitement. Perhaps afterward he would carry her up again, and she could persuade him to stay.

The branches of a white oak nearly obscured her vision of the ground, but the tree was young enough that she could catch glimpses through the leaves.

Throwing open the window, she heard the low, sultry voice of a woman and identified the speaker at once. Caroline!

Setting her teeth, Maria attempted to see who accompanied her. Her sister-in-law seldom bothered to visit after those first few times when Maria had taken the fun out of her little verbal torments. Only when she had nothing better to do did Caroline accompany Letitia or Luke's sister Sara.

Maria wanted to hear if it might be Sara with her this time. She wanted news of Sean as badly as she suspected Luke's sister did. All her household goods were in that wagon, and their new home sadly needed the bright colors and familiar surroundings of her old one. Luke had apparently followed his fiancée's instructions in decorating, but Caroline's cold taste had provided what few rooms were furnished with pale, light fabrics and delicate, wobbly pieces of furniture. That wasn't the kind of house a man like Luke would be comfortable in, nor would it be practical for a house with children.

Caroline's yellow skirts swept into view. For some reason the fool was wearing silk and heavy crinolines. The heat must be unbearable out there in the sun. Perhaps she changed clothes and took cool baths every hour. She did not seem much occupied elsewise. Letitia appeared to be the one running the big house on the Walker ranch.

Smirking at these spiteful thoughts, Maria missed the first few words of reply to Caroline's chatter, but the sound was definitely male. Sean perhaps? Her hopes soared, then grew sensible. Luke's brother had been out of town these last few weeks. He must be back and ready to look Luke's new wife over.

Maria's hand instantly flew to her hair, and she almost left her post to check her mirror when the male voice spoke again and her breathing stopped. Luke! Why was Luke here at this time of day? He was constantly busy buying supplies to put the ranch in full operation, hiring hands, inspecting long neglected buildings, planning buildings he had not finished when he had left last time. He came home exhausted but quietly proud every evening. He had said nothing of coming home early today.

Through the leaves of the tree Maria could just make out the lower part of Luke's legs clad in an old pair of twill trousers. Caroline was tall, and she knew they would be standing face to face, and her fingers bit into her palms. They were standing much too close for her comfort.

Stifling a cry of fury, Maria watched as the yellow skirt moved forward to encompass the blue trousers, bringing soft feminine hips against Luke's hard masculine ones. She was kissing him, and from the length of time they remained there, he was kissing her back!

My God, she was going to have to kill them both! She would find Luke's shotgun and blow them together into the next world reserved for adulterers like that.

Maria reached to slam the window closed, but a cold, calculating fury made her cautious. The two figures below separated, probably whispering sweet farewells. How long had they been meeting like this? All these nights Luke had stayed away, it had not been for her sake. He had been meeting with Caroline! But her fury did not center on Luke's betrayal. She had known Luke loved Caroline. She had hoped to convince him otherwise with time, but unless he shared her bed there would never be the opportunity to show him. No, her fury found its object in Caroline, the adulteress, the wanton who had ruined Luke's life and now meant to ruin hers. A woman like that deserved to be taught a lesson. Why give her advance warning of the retribution to come? Silently Maria lowered the window.

Down below, Luke cursed and rudely set Caroline away from him. Glaring into her heated face, he exclaimed in disgust, "Hell, Caroline, Matt's only been gone a few weeks. You can't be that desperate yet. Why don't you take a long hard horseback ride and then take a cold bath? They say abstinence is good for the soul."

He started to march away, but Caroline's strident voice carried after him.

"There was a time when you would have begged for one of my kisses!"

Slowly Luke turned to gaze sardonically upon Caroline's voluptuous golden beauty. There had been a time when those brilliant blue eyes had made his heart stop and his lungs collapse. The thought of being given permission to caress those full, sweet lips had made his loins ache for days. Now he had only to think of the honesty of Maria's smile, the natural eagerness of her caress, and Caroline's appeal faded to nothingness. Even the grim set of Maria's lips when she was angry was more seductive than the malleable pout of Caroline's spoiled mouth. The flash of those slanted Irish eyes excited him more than any number of Caroline's wanton kisses. At the moment he really could not remember why he had ever thought Caroline was an innocent.

"There was a time when I was loco enough to ask you to be my wife, too," Luke replied softly. "I only thank God that I was saved from such a fate. Good day, Caroline." He tipped his hat and walked away, oblivious to the shriek of outrage behind him.

Now that Caroline's message had brought him this far, Luke decided to drop in and surprise Maria. The little witch had been remarkably well behaved of late. Her illness must have scared her as much as it had him.

Entering the front door quietly, he slipped up the stairs, hoping to catch her alone. He needed the reassurance of her lively wit and smiling welcome after his encounter with the treacherous Caroline. He always knew where he stood with Maria, whether it was at gunpoint or in her arms. Anticipating the glow of happiness that lit her face whenever he entered the room, he hastened his pace.

Only, when he got to the room, she was not there. Frowning but remembering she had said something about planning the nursery, Luke walked down the hall to the next room. And the next. He searched the entire upstairs and came back to Maria's room to be certain he hadn't missed her there. She was not to be found.

Not knowing whether to be furious or afraid, Luke clattered back down the stairs to question the women in the kitchen. His pulse pounded with trepidation as he hurried down the hall and slammed open the door to the kitchen.

Three women looked up at his abrupt entrance. Standing over the massive black iron cook stove was the tall Irish woman he had hired just last week. In her mid-thirties, she looked older, her too-thin features drawn tight across the skeleton of her face. The effect was emphasized by thin black hair pulled severely into a tight bun at her nape. Had the years not worn her out, she might have been an attractive woman. As it was, only her eyes kept her appearance from total harshness. Wide and gray, they turned to Luke in surprise.

Rosa, the little half-Indian maid, dropped the kindling she had been about to add to the fire. Her startled gaze flew to Luke, then back to the third figure in this tableau.

Maria sat calmly on a high stool, a pencil and notebook in her hand. The pencil was poised high in expectation, but she lowered it as Luke entered, sending him a cool look he could not fathom.

"What in hell!" Her temerity at defying him, risking her health and the child's, ignited an uncharacteristic rage. "What are you doing out here?"

Maria hid her nervousness at the sight of the amber eyes gone cold with fury. His rendezvous with Caroline certainly hadn't improved his temper. "Planning a menu," she answered with as much coolness as she could muster.

"You'd risk your damn health to plan a menu?" Incredulous, Luke stalked across the room, not certain whether to heave her over his shoulder and haul her back to bed or beat the living tar out of her.

"Balderdash." Maria arched an eyebrow in cold rebuke. "I am perfectly healthy. It's past time that I was of some use around here."

The heat in the kitchen had returned color to her cheeks, and the little beads of perspiration along her brow shimmered against her lovely, tawny skin. Remembering his thoughts of earlier, Luke's lips tightened in an ironic smile. Even the frosty look from behind that fringe of black lashes had the power to stir desire, and his body responded hungrily. Their wedding night had been weeks ago, and his need for her was so great he dared not touch her unless she was strong again. Looking at her perched above him, her slim hips just within reach of his hands, her rounded bosom breathing in and out with healthy vigor, he could easily forget her illness.

"In that case," he wrapped his hands around her waist and lifted her from the stool, "I know the perfect use to put you to."

Maria shrieked as Luke caught her by the waist and knees and swung her into his arms. Her pencil and paper fell to the floor, and she caught a fleeting glimpse of the other women's grins as he carried her out. Cursing, she pounded his back and shoulders, but Luke merely proceeded out of the kitchen with furious strides.

Her heart quailed as he headed for the stairs. Surely he would not tie her to the bed as he had once threatened? She was well. He must know she would never risk the child if she were not. He had no right to do this! None at all.

She gave another cry as Luke threw her down upon the bed. When she tried to scramble up, he fell down beside her, throwing his leg over her thighs to keep her pinned while his hand sought the soft purchase of her breast.

"If you're well, then prove it," he murmured tauntingly, his hand circling her breast, then sliding to unfasten her bodice.

Maria's body responded all too well to his touch, but her fury prevented her from succumbing. How dare he! How could he go from the arms of that slut to hers? How could he pretend the same desire for her that he had already unleashed upon Caroline? She could not bear it. Caroline's smell still clung to him. Lips that had just touched Caroline would not touch hers.

She fought with all the strength and fervor of which she was capable. She kicked. She brought up her knee, seeking a painful target. She bit Luke's hand and shoulder and tried to scratch his face. He could not come close enough to kiss her, and she smiled triumphantly as she finally freed one trapped hand to smack it across his jaw. His look of surprise was sweet revenge.

"What in hell has got into you?" he roared, not at all pleased with this reception. Maria had fought him before, but not like this, and not without reason.

"Not you!" Maria shoved against his shoulders with all her might. He gave way, not from the force of her shove but in bewilderment. She ignored his pained expression as she tried to scramble out from under him. "Get off me, Luke, I'm warning you!"

Luke's fury ebbed, replaced by a tired puzzlement. The ache in his loins demanded attention, but even in his need for her he would never take Maria against her will. He had not meant to take her at all, but things seemed to have gotten a little out of hand.

Maria was wearing her hair tied in a bow at her nape, and the long silken tendrils splayed across the bed as she glared back at him. "Who in hell do you think you are, Luke Walker?" Without waiting for an answer, she leapt from the bed, brushing indignantly at her rumpled calico.

"Your husband, unfortunately." Luke's face tightened into a grim mask as she walked away from him. "Are you going to tell me what's got into you or do I just resort to the beating you once told me disobedient wives deserved?"

Maria sent him an alarmed look. "You wouldn't! It would hurt the babe." Even as she said it, she knew he wouldn't. The child meant too much to him.

"Why, Maria? I told you I would take you downstairs tonight. Why couldn't you wait for me?"

"Because I feel fine. Because I'm tired of being treated as a china ornament. Because I'm bored out of my mind. Do you want me to continue?'' Placing her hands on her hips, she met his glare defiantly. He would pay for his cheating ways.

"No, I want you to rest. I want you to stay out of that kitchen; the heat could kill you. If you want to plan menus, have Mrs. Donleavy come to you. When I come home, I want to find you sitting demurely in that chair reading a book or sewing a seam. Do you understand me?''

He made no mention of her rejection of his physical needs. Guilt must have kept him silent on that subject, the same guilt that had kept him from pressing her further. Maria answered haughtily to hide her pain.

"I understand, but I only obey when I choose to. My patience is at an end. You had best grow accustomed to having a wife about. You can't hide me away forever.''

That struck Luke as a strange comment, but he no longer had the patience to argue. "I've given you fair warning, Maria. Whatever happens is on your head.''

He turned around and walked out. Maria had to fight back tears at the sight of his broad shoulders disappearing from her view. Oh, Lord, how she wanted to have him hold her again, to whisper sweet words in her ears, to touch her in love and not just anger. She wanted him any way she could have him, but to see the warm look of love in his eyes would satisfy her greatest desires. The weary, strained look of contempt she had just seen broke her heart into little pieces. She hated herself for causing it. She hated Caroline more.

That evening when he came home, Luke did not bother to mount the stairs to see if his wife had obeyed orders. He went straight through the house in the direction of the kitchen.

A sound in the room to the right caused him to change course, and he slid back the door of the unused dining room.

Garbed in her rose and white gown, her hair neatly arranged in loose swirls that softened her aquiline features, Maria looked up from arranging the flowers in the center of the neatly set table. Even in his amazement Luke noticed there were four places set. Before he could launch another tired diatribe, Maria spoke.

"Rosa is heating your bath water now. I'll send her up. Your clothes are laid upon the bed. I hope you do not mind, but I wanted everything to be perfect for this first meal."

Maria glanced uncertainly at Luke's lanky frame leaning against the door. He had his arms crossed over his chest, always a bad sign, and the light in his eyes was not appreciative.

"Whom are we expecting?" he inquired sarcastically.

"Your mother and father, of course." She looked at him in surprise. Who else did she know around here?

"Oh, shit." Without another word he turned around and stalked out.

Maria held her breath until she heard the sound of his boots upon the stairs. She had feared he would walk into the night and not return. As his footsteps crossed the boards above, she expelled her breath in relief. Luke would not thank her for her disobedience, but she had to act or go mad. In this war she prepared to launch against Caroline, she meant to enlist Luke's parents as allies.

The luxury of coming home to a prepared bath sapped whatever anger Luke had left. The little witch was up to something. He had the intelligence to divine that much, but not enough experience to surmise what. The sight of her dressed to please, overseeing a gracious table he had never used, smote him with a longing he could not quite put a name to. He would like to come home every night to a sight like that.

Actually, he would like it even better if she were here to scrub his back, but a man couldn't have everything. He scrubbed it himself, then submerged his head in the water to wash it. He didn't know what Maria had planned for the night, but he could do a little planning of his own.

Maria looked up expectantly at the sound of Luke returning downstairs, and a feeling of pride swelled within her at the sight. Wearing his brown coat and a black silk scarf above his leather waistcoat and buckskin trousers, he appeared more handsome than any man she had ever seen in a ladies' magazine. Of course, he had chosen not to wear the cravat or trousers she had laid out for him, but she could not object if he consented to wear his coat. She felt his amber eyes focus on her warily, and she couldn't help but smile.

"Thank you, Luke. I feared you would be angry."

She came forward and arranged the scarf more neatly against his stiff collar. The scent of roses wafted to him, and her proximity proved a torment Luke couldn't resist. His hands closed around her waist, causing her chin to tilt upward to watch his expression suspiciously.

"I am angry, *cariña*, but we will discuss ways of rectifying that later. Now will you tell me what this is all about?"

Maria shied nervously from his grasp. He knew her too well, and she had no explanation ready to give him. "It is not about anything. I want to thank your parents for their kindness. I thought you would like it if I invited them."

Not in the least fooled by this explanation, Luke bided his time. Sooner or later it would come out. Maria had an explosive temper and an expressive face that made it impossible for her to keep a secret. He grinned at the thought and caught her chin between his fingers, tilting it back up so he could see her eyes again.

"Whatever you say, Maria. Just don't overtire yourself, *comprende?*"

Eyes fastened on his, she nodded reluctantly. The physical tension between them strained her nerves, and if he chose to kiss her then, she would most likely shatter into pieces. To her relief, a knock sounded at the door, and she was given a reprieve.

The evening progressed splendidly. Maria had had little opportunity to get to know the gruff but amiable Joshua Walker, and she was delighted to learn he and Luke had much the same humor and opinions. Luke

favored his mother in looks, but his father in person-
ality. It made her feel more secure to know these
things. Luke was becoming less a stranger and more
a husband with every passing day.

The subject eventually got around to children, and
Maria listened with concealed interest as Luke's father
bewailed the fact that Matthew and Caroline had not
seen fit to produce any sons. Letitia berated him
gently, complaining even a girl would be welcome.
They both clucked warmly over Maria, admonishing
her to be careful and giving lists of totally impossible
and improbable instructions of what she should do to
keep the baby healthy. Maria caught Luke's laughing
gleam and summoned a tactful smile under pressure.
She had no ear for more commandments, but the
knowledge of Caroline's childless state gave her a point
to ponder.

From what she had learned from Sean, Matthew and
Caroline must have been married six or seven years
ago. Luke was twenty-seven now. He had only been
twenty or so when he left home. It seemed odd that
Caroline had not conceived in all that time. No mention had been made of any miscarriage, so that could
not be the problem. If Matthew was anything like
Luke, the opportunity certainly had to be there. If she
understood rightly, the two of them had been lovers
even before they married, which set Maria's devious
mind to thinking.

She did not have much time to pursue this line of
thought. Before she knew it, Josh and Letitia were
making their farewells, and she was left alone with
Luke.

3

To Maria's surprise, Luke merely ordered her to bed, saying Rosa and Mrs. Donleavy could clean up. She gazed uncertainly at the chiseled lines forming his inscrutable face, but she could read nothing of his thoughts. She knew he was still angry with her for disobeying him, but was there more to it than that?

Slowly negotiating the stairs, she felt his gaze following her all the way up, and her blood raced a little faster through her veins. Perhaps he realized she truly was well. Would this be the night he came to her?

Closing the door behind her, Maria gazed blindly over the bedroom that they should be sharing. A lamp flickered on the table, illuminating the cotton nightdress Rosa had laid across the turned-down quilt. Where had Luke been sleeping all these nights he had stayed away from her?

Not wanting to think of it, terrified he had found some way to spend those nights with Caroline, Maria forced herself into the motions of preparing for bed. She had known Luke married her only for the sake of the child. She could not expect fidelity from a man like Luke, but the thought of sharing him sent furious flares of jealousy shooting through her.

Biting her lip, Maria stared at her reflection in the mirror. The long tangle of ebony hair about her face made her look pale, and her eyes seemed too big for the rest of her. These past weeks confined indoors had drained the color from her cheeks, and she felt as much like a ghost as she looked. How could she compete with Caroline looking like this?

Abruptly turning away, she took off her clothes and

reached for the long nightdress. The night was warm, and Rosa had chosen one with no sleeves and a lace yoke. The thin cotton skimmed over her skin like a caress, and Maria shuddered as it settled about her shoulders. How long had it been since Luke had touched her like that?

Half listening for the sound of the front door opening, fighting her racing heartbeat over the hope of a footstep on the stair, Maria sat down on the bed and began to brush her hair.

Below, Luke contemplated the long flight of stairs separating him from his wife, then turned away. The doctor had said she needed rest, and what he had in mind couldn't be called restful. If he could only teach himself to just hold her, he could lie beside her in that big bed he had meant for them to share, but he could not. His need for her was too strong, a tangible presence between them, and it took all he possessed just to turn away from the stairs. Once in her arms, he would not be able to stop himself.

Roaming idly about the unfinished parlor and study, he stumbled across his guitar and picked it up. There had been so many nights on the prairie when he had sworn all he needed was his horse and his guitar, but he knew the foolishness of that now. He needed to feel the fire of emerald eyes burning through his veins, the yielding softness of tawny curves. He needed her laughter, her intensity, even her anger, just to keep him alive.

Cursing his idiocy, Luke sat down and threw off his irritating shoes. He had no business coming back here, bringing Maria into this life. There hadn't been time to settle old scores, and any moment he could expect that knock upon the door that would tear him away from the life he tried to build for her. What would she do then? Where would she go? Would she wait to see if he came back to her? Or would she pack her bags and go?

With Maria, he couldn't tell. Any other woman he could figure on taking everything she could get her hands on and walking out. Knowing Maria, she'd probably stay, claim everything, and shoot him if he tried to walk back through that door. Grunting in cynical amusement at the likelihood of a shoot-out with Maria, Luke picked up his guitar and cradled it against his shoulder.

His fingers caressed the chords the way he would like to caress Maria's cheek. Gently stroking a tune from the strings, he settled against the hard wood chair, letting his thoughts stray into the music. Once he would have been able to lose himself in the sound, but now the chords only sharpened his focus on the woman lying in the bed above his head. He remembered the shadow of her lingering under the rose trellis on moon-filled nights. The scent of roses drifted through the air, and a warm, husky voice murmured love words in his ear as the passion of the music intensified.

His fingers flew across the strings, but they couldn't drive Maria out of his mind. Luke leaned his head back and closed his eyes, letting his fingers find the melody they knew so well. Once he had memorized every love song he had ever heard to serenade his wife-to-be. That treasure trove of knowledge had given him much amusement in the years that followed when his heart had shriveled and grown thorns like a prickly pear. Now the songs haunted his mind, played mockingly in his ears, and he carried them with him even when his hands weren't on the guitar.

Upstairs, Maria's fingers lingered over the task of brushing her hair. The long tresses gleamed in the lantern light like moonstruck raven's wings, and she needed to plait them, but mindlessly she kept stroking with the brush, listening to the sounds from below.

She had not heard Luke play since before they were married, when she could only hide in the darkness and listen. Did he play for Caroline still? The thought that those passionate and mournful sounds could be for the fickle, shallow Caroline crushed tears from Maria's eyes. She could not expect Luke to love her as passionately as he had the young woman of his dreams, but surely he was old enough now to see what kind of woman Caroline had become. That song could not possibly be for Caroline. She would not believe it of him.

The longing to watch Luke as he played, to be close to the music and a part of it, rendered her incapable of logic. She should be furious with him. She should be scheming ways of removing Caroline entirely from the picture. She ought to teach him a lesson or two about faithfulness. But the music only made her think of the way Luke's hands would move across the strings, and her body ached for that gentle touch.

He was here, in this house, and not out in the night with Caroline. She should be grateful for that. He had not complained of her disobedience. He had even acted the part of husband for the sake of his parents tonight. Perhaps she shouldn't be so hasty in her conclusions. Perhaps there was some chance he could find the boundaries of marriage less than hateful.

That did not sound very likely, but Maria's heart longed for it to be true. Perhaps if she watched him play she could discern who the music was for. It sounded so lonely right now it would be an act of cruelty to ignore it.

Without clearly thinking of anything more than the strains of music floating up the stairs, Maria lay aside her brush and drifted toward the door. It opened silently beneath her touch, and her bare feet whispered along the wood floors, noting each crack and hollow as she descended the stairs.

She lingered in the shadows of the doorway, her slight gown a ghostly column against the darkness of the hall, but Luke knew the instant she appeared, as he had known when she haunted the terrace. Perhaps he had known the music would call her as it had then, but whatever fateful wind had blown her his way, he would not quarrel with it. He relaxed and let the music play itself, let his fingers speak the words of joy welling up in him, words he could not say. The scent of roses whirled around him until he could sit still no longer.

When Luke unfolded his lanky frame to stand before her, Maria did not hesitate. She stepped forward and slid her arms around him and rested her head against his chest, reveling in the rapid rhythm of his heartbeat against her ear. His hands automatically closed around her, drawing her up in his embrace, and she could feel the brush of his kiss along her hair.

"Maria." The word murmured like the unspoken chorus of his song. "Maria, *mi cariña,* my heart, my love, you should be in bed, asleep. Did I wake you?"

She ignored his attempt to be sensible, preferring the sound of the love words. Sliding her hands upward and standing on her toes, she lifted her face for his kiss and was not disappointed. Luke's mouth closed over hers gently, almost hesitantly, not certain whether to believe or to accept what was being offered. Maria showed him, letting her kiss say what she wanted, what she needed, how she felt.

With a short cry almost of disbelief, Luke gathered her firmly in his arms and returned this kiss with all the eagerness of a lifetime of loneliness. His lips molded to hers, blended with her flesh, parted to take her in deeper, exchanging a fury of emotions with the heat of their breaths.

He didn't want to leave this spot. He wanted her here and now before she could change her mind, but he also wanted her willing. He wanted her to share his bed without question for a lifetime. He wanted so much he could not speak of it but only hold her and hope she would understand.

His kisses drifted across her cheek and nibbled her ear before slowing to a halt. Reluctantly Luke held her back from him, staring into the shadowed hollows of Maria's face as he questioned her. "Are you sure, little one? I would not hurt you."

"Don't stop. Don't stop now." Whether she spoke of the music or the kisses, Maria had not the mind left to know. She knew she was where she wanted to be and nothing else mattered.

Strong arms wrapped around her, imprisoning her in the security of his embrace. As Luke's kiss burned through her senses, she scarcely knew at what point her feet left the floor. Held tightly in his arms, her hands locked behind his neck, Maria felt the sensation of floating as part of the passion flowing from her. Only when Luke lifted his head to negotiate the stairs did she realize where he was heading, and excitement raced through her. She curled against his chest and poured her kisses wherever they would reach.

The feather mattress sagged beneath her as Luke lay Maria against it. When he did not immediately join her, she scrambled to a sitting position. With a quick wriggle she pulled off her nightdress and flung it to the floor while Luke was still pulling off his shirt.

At the sight of her tawny nakedness perched in the middle of the bed, ebony hair streaming to her waist, Luke felt his heart leap painfully in his chest. His gaze quickly took in the full swell of her breasts, the slight rounding of her abdomen, the changes his child had made in her, and his desire multiplied a thousandfold. Throwing off his shirt, he fell down upon the bed, pulling her into his arms and down with him.

"Cara mía, you will regret this. I am a starving man,'' he whispered in her ear as his hands ran lovingly over the curves he had longed so long to hold.

"And you think I do not feel the same?'' Indignantly Maria bit his ear and nibbled her way down his neck while his hands roused her to a passion she could not long endure without seeking satisfaction.

"Then show me,'' Luke demanded before moving his mouth to cover hers, drawing on her hunger until they both clung as one.

When he released her, Maria's hands flew to his trousers, unbuttoning them and pushing them from his hips. Luke obligingly shoved them off the rest of the way, and then he was beside her again, his flesh searing hers as he pressed into her.

Maria emitted a low, piercing cry as Luke sank deep within her, stretching her to the limit. The pleasure he brought was so intense that she could not think about what she was doing, she could only respond. They had been too long apart, and they came together now in a white-hot heat that flashed and burned and melded them into one with a quickness that left them breathless.

Afterward, Luke drew her against his chest and they slept, only to wake again in the night and repeat their lovemaking more slowly. By morning, Maria was satiated with pleasure and sore in very peculiar places.

She came awake slowly to the discovery that the bed beside her was empty. Her eyes flew open and she relaxed with a smile as she found Luke bending over the shaving mirror, razor in hand. She admired the graceful play of muscles across his back, and her gaze dropped lower to the loose towel at his hips. A blush rose to her cheeks as she remembered some of the things they had done during the night. In the bright light of day she could not imagine such wanton behavior.

Luke turned to catch the stain of color across Maria's cheeks and the direction of her gaze, and he chuckled. "Pleasant dreams, *querida?* How do you feel this morning?"

"Sinful," she admitted, hastily pulling the sheet up over her nakedness while she searched for her gown.

Luke laughed and returned to shaving. "I am happy to see our son or daughter has decided to behave in the mornings."

Maria turned a suspicious gaze to him at his abnormally cheerful tone. "Why?"

Luke wiped the remainder of the soap from his face and turned to admire the sight of the naked nymph in his bed, hair streaming in silken ribbons about her tawny shoulders. "Because I like mornings."

Maria gasped as he approached the bed and the awkward angle of the towel at his waist gave him away. She threw herself to the other side of the bed but not fast enough. Luke was upon her in seconds, smothering her with kisses and wicked words, and before she could offer so much as a protest, she had surrendered.

They did not get up again until nearly noon, when the sound of Letitia's voice drifted up from the front

hall. Maria clapped her hand over her mouth to hold
back a cry of embarrassment, and even Luke looked
a little shamefaced as he hastily grabbed for his pants.

He recovered his composure quickly, however,
bending over Maria and brushing a kiss across her
forehead as he fastened his trousers. "Let me take
care of her," he murmured.

He grabbed the shirt he had worn the night before
as he headed out the doorway, and Maria had to stifle
a laugh at the image he would make going down the
stairs, hair standing on end and wrinkled shirt half
buttoned. His mother would die. So much for proper
behavior.

They had their first argument of the day over breakfast—or lunch—when Luke insisted Maria could not
go out riding until the doctor had said it was safe. He
threatened, she ranted, and Rosa had to duck as a cup
went flying over her head and crashed against the wall.
She grinned and hurried out as Luke settled the argument by wrapping his cantankerous wife in his arms
and kissing the fight out of her.

Still wrapped in the warm glow of Luke's embrace,
Maria even managed to greet Caroline's visit cheerfully. Now that she was not confined to bed she could
escort her guest into the huge parlor as if they were
both proper ladies. The fact that the parlor contained
little more than a few straight-backed chairs and Luke's
desk did nothing to diminish her mood.

The other woman, on the other hand, appeared to
have been eating lemons for lunch, and Maria hid her
smile of delight. Whatever was eating at Caroline had
to be good for her. She gestured for her guest to take
a seat.

"How thoughtful of you to stop by. Luke won't let
me out of the house yet and it is most frustrating to
know there are people nearby and I cannot talk to
them."

"Yes, that is quite understandable," Caroline said
without a hint of sympathy. "Where is Luke? I need
a word with him."

Even this comment did not burst Maria's balloon of

happiness. She began to understand that Caroline was the hunter and Luke the prey, and her eyes took on a mischievous gleam.

"He went into town. I had a list of things I absolutely could not wait any longer for. Surely he cannot go wrong if he hands the clerk at the mercantile store a written list." She started to chatter on, but Caroline stood up with a gesture of exasperation.

"I told him I needed to go into town. How dare he go without even stopping and asking?"

Maria's green eyes danced with more than sunlight from the window as she turned back into the room to face her enraged caller. Touching a suggestive hand to the slight swell of her waistline, Maria smiled pleasantly.

"We were shamefully late in rising this morning, and I was most eager to have those yard goods. I'm outgrowing everything I own. Let me apologize for him."

Caroline's eyes narrowed as she interpreted Maria's words correctly. With a sniff of distaste she picked up her gloves and prepared to leave. "Trapping a man into marriage by getting pregnant seldom works in the long run. Before long you will be pear-shaped, and repulsive, and Luke will be looking elsewhere. You will never see me turn into a horrid turnip to please a man."

Maria remained smiling, though the green of her eyes gleamed dangerously. "I rather believe in our case that Luke trapped me, but that is beside the point. I wasn't aware there were alternatives to having children." That was a bare-faced lie, but Caroline didn't know her well enough to know that.

As Maria had expected, Caroline gave her a superior look as if she were no more than an ignorant toddler playing in the mud. "There are several alternatives, but prevention is the most acceptable. Someday when you have a dozen squalling brats at your feet, I may take pity on you and give you the name of the woman who has the cure. Until then, enjoy yourself. I'll see Luke when he returns."

Maria seethed at the catty smirk on Caroline's lips when she departed. She had taken off her disguise and bared her true self today, and she was going to regret it. Maria intended to see to that.

Prevention! *Madre de Dios,* but the woman was a fool, a wicked fool. Consuela had told her how children could be prevented with salves of certain herbs. She had also mentioned that a child could be destroyed before it was born, but she had warned against that method. Caroline was no better than Consuela. What she had been doing for years was ungodly and selfish and downright dangerous. Maria would be doing her a favor to put an end to it.

With that totally hypocritical and vengeful thought in mind, Maria threw herself into the business of making chaos into a home. She wasn't certain how she would get that salve away from Caroline or how she would prevent her obtaining more, but something would occur in time. Perhaps there would be some way of diluting or replacing it once she found where Caroline kept it. It gave her something to think about in idle moments. Nothing would please everybody more than to see Caroline swollen with child, everybody but Caroline. Just the thought of such revenge was sweet.

4

Whatever might occupy her days, Luke occupied Maria's nights. As soon as the sun lowered in the western sky she began listening for his footsteps. She could not get enough of the look on his face when she ran to greet him. The hard lines vanished from around his mouth, and his amber eyes glowed with pride as she threw herself into his arms. The eagerness of his embrace told her more than words of how he missed her, and Maria savored every gesture that spoke of his affection. Luke was not a man of words, but she knew she could make him love her.

The hunger of his kisses never lessened. He treated each night as if it were his last, but Maria did not have enough experience to read any meaning to this beyond satisfaction. Although Caroline continued to dangle after him, Maria refused to believe Luke could take her with such passion at night if he shared his days with another. Even though she was outgrowing the waists of all her gowns, Luke still desired her. Sometimes she thought he preferred her that way, so intense was the look in his eyes when he measured the child's growth by stretching his hand across her belly.

Their only source of disagreement was Luke's overprotectiveness. He would not let her rearrange furniture or climb up on ladders to clean windows or reach elusive cobwebs. He wouldn't even let her outside in the heat of the day, and he refused to take her out in the wagon to visit his family. The lack of exercise was taking its toll on Maria's nerves, and she longed for nothing more than a wild gallop on Erinmeade, but the mare had been left with Sean.

She did manage to escape her confinement long enough to discover Luke kept several ponies in the paddock behind the stable. Surely he couldn't object to a mild ride on a pony. She had been riding almost before she could walk. The fresh air would be healthy. She rehearsed all her arguments carefully before presenting her case to Luke one morning.

Luke heard her out while he dressed, but his answer was still a decisive no.

Maria stared at him in disbelief. "How can you say that? What reason can you possibly give for keeping me prisoner here? I won't get in your way. I won't get anywhere near you. I'll be careful. I promise not to get hurt or overheated or overtired or . . ." She stumbled over the excuses he could possibly give for his behavior. How many excuses could there possibly be for his unreasonableness?

"I know you won't, because you're staying inside." Luke shrugged on his vest, trying to forget the nakedness he felt each time he dressed without buckling on his holster. Maria was right. To wear them courted danger, but he had lived on the edge of danger so long he could not shake himself of the feeling of impending disaster. "Now give me a kiss. I'm running late."

Maria gave a cry of frustration and flung a pillow at him instead, but Luke ignored these tactics and took what he wanted.

She clung to him weakly after he kissed her lips until they were puffed and swollen, and Luke had to grin at the ease of this victory. Maria's passion betrayed her every time, and he could not get enough of it. Holding her slightness against him, he brushed a kiss across her brow.

"Go back to bed and rest, *querida,* and all day I will think of you there until I grow too hard to sit a horse. Then I will come back to you."

Maria screamed in outrage at this lewd remark and shoved violently from his arms. She reached for another pillow, but laughing, Luke dodged out before she could even swing to let it fly. The nerve of the man! Is that all he thought of her? Did he think her nothing more than a simple whore to warm his bed like all the others? She would kill him. She would cut his hard heart into little pieces and stomp on the remains. Better yet, since he had no heart, she would take that part of him that he mentioned and do the same. Crude, disgusting man.

In a fury she threw open the dresser and removed her riding skirt. No more the obedient wife. Even Consuela had the right to come and go as she pleased.

Unaware of the rebellion on his hands, Luke faced a more serious problem in the downstairs hall. Matthew had finally returned home.

Luke refrained from any sign of greeting as he eyed his brother warily. Matthew was the eldest. He had always been the biggest and the first in everything and had never doubted his right to be so. He had grown into a tall, burly man bigger than his father, and Luke judged the prospect of tangling with him with a proper measure of caution. Matthew was the reason he had learned to fight as he had. Though he had finally learned to lick his brother in one fight out of two, he wasn't eager to suffer the beating it would entail.

But it certainly seemed as if Matthew had come hankering for a fight. His eyes flashed with fury as Luke clattered down the stairs, and his hands curled into white knuckled fists as he strained to keep them at his side. The smile on Luke's lips disappeared at once, and a grim line took root at the corner of his mouth.

"It's been a long time, Matt." Luke stopped at the foot of the stairs. He had dreaded this meeting for years, but the welcome he had received from everyone else had made him complacent. Obviously he had weakened too soon.

"Not long enough to suit me. She's my wife now, dammit, Luke. Stay the hell away from her."

"My God, Matt! What do you think I am? I'm married now. I've got a wife of my own and a babe on the way. Why would—"

"Do you take me for a goddamn fool?" Matthew roared. "You've always been hot after her, and now you come back here when I'm not around and she's over here and with you more than she is at home and you expect me not to hear about it?"

"Now wait one cotton-picking minute, you lug-headed jackass! Whoever is filling your ears with those . . ."

Maria heard the roar of their voices over the sound of her own fury, and she hurried to finish dressing. She didn't know what kind of brawl Luke was heading for now, but she didn't intend for it to be in her front parlor.

Grabbing up the rifle Luke always kept beneath the bed, she raced into the upstairs hall. Their voices carried clearer here, and she was able to distinguish the words of the argument. Heaven help her, but that must be Matthew, and he was in a tearing rage. Setting her lips in a grim line, Maria instantly knew the source. Caroline! Well, it was high time that little tart got her comeuppance.

Her ebony hair plaited and trailing over her starched white shirt, emerald eyes flashing, the stiff material of her heavy riding skirt swishing furiously, Maria took the stairs at a run.

"I'm warning you, Luke, stay away from my wife—" Matthew halted in mid-threat at the sight of the virago flying down the stairs, rifle in hand.

Luke turned and swallowed his astonishment. In another minute he and Matthew would have been at each other's throats. Any distraction was welcome, and Maria in a tearing fury was quite a distraction. His gaze noted appreciatively the high color of her cheeks and sparkle in her eyes. He choked back his words as Maria flung her own into the deafening silence.

"You take care of your wife, Matthew," she commanded coldly, "and I will take care of Luke. A wise man wouldn't let his wife run around unoccupied all day. Why don't you go home right now and take her by surprise? Not just today. Every day. Make a habit of it. You might be astonished by the results."

With these furious but enigmatic remarks, Maria proceeded out the door, defiantly heading in the direction of the stable.

Knowing full well how Maria's devious mind worked, Luke could not keep a twitch of amusement from his lips as he turned back to see how his brother had taken this encounter. He ought to beat her, he really ought, but right now he had all he could do to keep from roaring with laughter at Matthew's stunned expression.

"My wife," Luke said in dry introduction.

"My God, is she real?" The vision of those brilliant eyes framed by golden features and flying black hair on a wisp so slender she scarcely seemed more than a child impressed an indelible image in Matthew's brain.

"Very," Luke intoned solemnly. "I've been trying to tell you. If there were any truth to the rumors you've heard, Caroline would be slashed into ribbons and the house burned to the ground by now. Maria has a rather quick temper."

"Temper? Is that what you call it? I thought I was a dead man." Matthew's distracted gaze returned to Luke. "I can't apologize. Caroline said you had—"

Luke interrupted before he could go any further. "Listen to yourself, Matt. *Caroline* said it. Did anyone else say it? Give me a fair trial before you condemn me."

Knowing Caroline better than anyone, Matthew sighed and relaxed his fists. Shaking his head in bewilderment, he ran his hand through his hair. "I don't know what to do with her anymore. Nothing makes her happy. I keep thinking if we just had kids—"

"You want to go talk with Maria again? I think you missed her point." Luke couldn't hide his amusement at his older brother's confusion. Matthew had never been much of a ladies' man. Caroline had been all he had needed for some years. There were one or two things Luke could teach him in this category. Since his brother only looked more confused at the mention of Maria, Luke tried to explain. "I don't mean to pry, brother, but do you only go to Caroline at night, when she's in bed?"

Matthew managed to look embarrassed and irate at the same time. "That's none of your damn business."

"It is if you're going to go accusing me of occupying the rest of her time," Luke pointed out. "But that's not what Maria is trying to tell you. I don't know how much the little witch knows or what she suspects, but she's warning you to take the time to bed Caroline by surprise, anytime, anywhere. If you want reasons, you'll have to talk to her."

Since he could hear the canter of horses' hoofs on the drive, Luke suspected it would be a little late to ask Maria anything, and he cursed as she escaped on the forbidden pony. Still, he had no choice but to hammer this out with Matthew and get it out of the way. Then he would go after the rebellious little brat.

Whether or not Matthew understood the reasons, he entertained the idea with growing pleasure. His face began to beam like a little boy's at the prospect. "Don't see where it could hurt, by golly! Caroline always was one for saying there was a proper time and place, but I'm thinking it's time I start doing the choosing. I've been without a woman for weeks now. She ought to be more than ready, if you haven't . . ." He halted at the sight of Luke's lips tightening. "I'll not say it. Let's start fresh and see if we can work together this time."

Matthew offered his hand and Luke shook it with relief. It was bad enough guarding his back against enemies. He hated to have to watch out for family, too.

After Matthew left, Luke rode out after Maria. She had made no attempt to hide her trail, and his stallion caught up with her easily. She was riding with caution, gazing across the wide-open landscape while the sure-footed pony found its way over the range grass. Their apparent goal seemed to be the line of cottonwoods ahead.

Maria glanced up at his approach. He saw no sign of repentance in the stubborn set of her jaw, but the fire of fury had left her eyes. She watched him with open curiosity.

"I trust you refrained from shooting your brother."

She spoke conversationally as Luke rode up beside her.

"I didn't need to. The shock you gave him was sufficient. It may be a long time before he dares look you in the face again."

Maria tried to determine if he was serious or not, but Luke's implacable gaze revealed nothing. "Well, I hope he heeds my advice. I've never shot anyone before, but if I ever do, Caroline is first on the list."

Luke sent his wife a curious glance, wondering if that could possibly be jealousy speaking. It seemed unlikely. Maria had married him because she had no other choice. She knew what he was and had never made any complaint of it. Still, her fury of earlier had seemed a touch out of line.

"What has Caroline ever done to you?" he could not resist asking, though he kept his countenance clear as he spoke.

If he were that damned blind, Maria had no intention of explaining. She sent him a frosty look and kicked the pony into a canter.

Luke couldn't hide a pinprick of delight at this reaction. Maria had led him a merry chase across half the country and through a gamut of men he had wanted to kill just for looking at her too closely. It had not once occurred to him that Maria might be jealous of his attentions to other women, particularly since he had never given another woman a serious thought since he had first laid eyes on her. But the little witch hadn't figured that out yet. With an air of triumph Luke spurred his horse to ride beside her again.

Maria gave a shriek of alarm as Luke bodily hauled her from her saddle and across his lap. With the expertise of a trail-drive cowhand, he wound the reins of her horse securely around the pommel of his saddle without missing a stride. One arm around Maria's waist, he rearranged her position to sit more comfortably between his thighs.

"Back to the house, *mamacita*. You know better than to ride a horse."

She ought to be furious with him, but Maria felt

oddly content leaning against Luke's hard chest, feeling his arm around her. She felt the tightening in his loins as the horse's canter sent her backward against him, and she smiled to herself. He was not angry but having as difficult a time as she to behave himself.

When they reached the house, Luke climbed down and lifted Maria from the massive stallion. His hands lingered beneath her breasts, his thumbs openly toying with the pointed crests of these soft mounds beneath her linen shirt. Boldly she pressed against him, urging to do more. The hunger in his eyes was undisguisable.

"Tonight, *querida*. We must wait for tonight. Don't tire yourself too much. I am a hungry man."

"You are an arrogant, stubborn man, Luke Walker, but you learn quickly." With a flashing smile Maria stood on her toes and wrapped her arms around his neck, bringing his lips down to where she could reach them.

She would make him love her if it took all the breath in her body.

5

The sound of wagon wheels on the rough ruts of the drive sent Maria running to the front window. The day had been long and sultry, and she was feeling bored and restless. Luke had finally given in and agreed she could ride for a while in the evenings in his company, but that still left the days. If Luke intended her to make her home here, she would have to see about starting a rose garden. At least that was something she could do outside.

Finally catching a glimpse of the wagon coming around the bend, Maria gave a shriek of joy. Sean! Screaming for Rosa to join her, she raced down the stairs. At last she would have the makings of a home.

Reaching the yard, she discovered Luke's sister, Sara, sitting on the wagon seat with Sean. That meant he had stopped at the big house before coming here, and Maria wondered if that was out of politeness or if Sara was the reason. She sent the other girl a teasing grin, but Sara's expression remained unnervingly solemn.

Maria's gaze swerved to Sean, and a hammering uneasiness began to throb through her veins. Instead of his usual laughing looks, Sean appeared nervous and uncertain as he drew the mules to a halt. He swept off his hat, but no charming words spilled from his tongue.

Maria kept a grip on herself as Sean leapt from the wagon and helped Sara down. Nothing could have happened to Luke. He wasn't anywhere near his father's ranch today, and Sean couldn't have seen him coming in from the south. It couldn't be her uncles. They had wired when they were safely at home, and there had even been long, lovely letters from their families. It must be the ranch. She wouldn't worry about the ranch. It was just wood and stone and dirt. Sean had the valuable pieces in the wagon. She recognized the magnificent carved headboard of her parents' bed from here.

At another time, she would have run and flung her arms around Sean's neck, but Sara was clinging to his hand now, and the weeks of separation put a gap between them. She couldn't let him just stand there looking worried. Instead she smiled and held out her hands in welcome.

"Thank goodness, Sean, I had begun to worry about you. Come in, let me get you some lemonade. Sara, make him come in where it's cool. I see he found you before he found me."

Sean's eyes lit briefly as he glanced down at the lovely young woman at his side, and he sent Maria a conspiratorial smile. "Didn't recognize her at first. She wasn't hanging from a tree or making rude faces at me."

Sara's cheeks pinkened as she climbed up the steps to join Maria. "I don't know who else he thought would be answering the door, unless he thought I looked like my mother."

"You do look like your mother, but I haven't grown so senile as to confuse the two of you yet," Sean retorted before turning to catch Maria by the waist and giving her a thorough looking over from head to foot. He grinned at what he saw. "Married life agrees with you, colleen. You look a little more rounded than when I saw you last."

Both women cried his name in indignation, but Sean didn't look in the least abashed. Taking them by the elbow, he steered them into the front hall.

Spying Rosa hovering in the shadows, Sean grew sober again and spoke in her direction. "Go fix Mrs. Walker something a little stronger than lemonade, quickly."

Maria jerked from his hold and turned to find Sean's

expression had gone solemn again as he gazed upon her.

"I've got someone out in the wagon you might like to see, but I thought I ought to warn you first. There's a reason I'm a mite late getting here."

Again pinpricks of alarm ran up and down her skin, but Maria ignored them. There could be nothing so seriously wrong as Sean pretended. He was being his usual over-dramatic self. "If there's someone out in the wagon, by all means invite them in. Then you can sit down and tell me all about it."

Sean and Sara exchanged uneasy glances. Sean had purposely stopped at the big house first to enlist the aid of Letitia and send word to locate Luke before he came over here. Letitia had been visiting a neighboring ranch, but upon being told the story, Sara had agreed a woman needed to be on hand and had volunteered. Both wished Luke would arrive before Maria heard the tale. With her fourth month of pregnancy, Maria's slight stature appeared frail, and they dreaded her reaction to this news.

"He's sleeping, and you need to know first, before I wake him . . ."

Maria turned pale and her glance inadvertently swept to the open doorway. Sean took her hands and forced her to look back to him.

"It's Pedro. Pieta's dead, Maria. I was too late to prevent it. Charlie got me word, and I went back and got Pedro. I know how you felt about him and I thought maybe he would be more attached to you than his other relations. I didn't know what else to do. Maria, I'm sorry . . ." Sean's voice broke on the words as Maria's eyes filled with tears and she choked on a sob of disbelief.

Sara put her arm around Maria's waist and tried to lead her to a chair, but Maria shook her head, forcing herself to listen to Sean. She couldn't quite make herself believe the words yet. Pieta was very real in her mind, more real than her mother. Pieta was her home, her world for so long. She had been there after her father died. Pieta was strong, indestructible. Nothing could happen to Pieta. She must have misunderstood, and she struggled to grasp what Sean was telling her.

"I-I don't understand. Pieta is fine. Uncle Patrick said he bought her a house in San Pedro so she could be near Carmelita. I know the house. It's a lovely place, next to the mission. Pedro has his very own room, and my uncle gave him one of the ponies, and he took his puppy with him. Uncle Patrick said they were quite happy. He promised half the ranch would go to Pedro when he comes of age, and he's sending Pieta an allowance each month so she needn't work elsewhere. I made him promise. So why are you bringing Pedro here? Where is Pieta?"

Sean sent Sara a worried look, then greeted the maid's appearance with a glass of brandy with relief. He forced the glass between Maria's protesting fingers, tilting it toward her lips. "Drink, Maria, slowly, then let me try to explain again."

Maria made a face at the taste of the liquor and pushed it away from her. Sean held the glass as he tried once more to explain.

"Pieta left Pedro with Carmelita, and she went back to the ranch. I don't know why she went back. Maybe she forgot something. Maybe she wanted to place flowers on your father's grave. I don't know, Maria. I just know what Charlie told me. We had all left, and when her mother didn't return, Carmelita sent for Charlie. He and some of the other men rode back out to the ranch. They're the ones who found her, Maria. Someone had tried to make it look like Indians, but Charlie says it wasn't Indians. I'm sorry, Maria, I never thought they would pick on Pieta. It doesn't make sense."

"It would if Manuel wanted to know how to find Maria and thought Pieta could tell him." Luke's voice echoed harshly from the doorway. His eyes glittered like cold stones as they met Sean's, and his boots sounded loud and hollow on the hall floor as he entered.

Maria gave a stricken cry and turned to him, her eyes huge and dark against her thin, pale face. Luke took one look at her and issued a crude curse that made his sister blanch. In a single stride he reached Maria and gathered her into his arms.

Dry sobs racked her small frame as she buried her face against Luke's wide chest. He held her close, his expression bleak as he looked over her head to Sean. She didn't need this blow added to the others, but it was too late to do anything about it now. Remembering the proud, intelligent woman who had welcomed him to her kitchen when no one else would, Luke felt a tug of sorrow at his heart. This should never have happened.

At Luke's nod, Sean and Sara slipped out to bring Pedro in from the wagon. Maria still shook like a leaf in his arms, but her soundless cries terrified him. He had no place to lie her down but the bed upstairs, and he didn't think she would want to greet Pedro like that. Not knowing what to say or do, he continued to hold her, stroking her hair and murmuring inane words of comfort.

When he heard the sound of Sean's boots upon the porch, Luke grasped Maria's shoulders and set her back from him. Her eyes were nearly black with grief, but she met his gaze with understanding. Biting her lip, she turned her head to watch Sean enter carrying his small burden.

Pedro looked up sleepily from Sean's shoulder, and a small smile appeared on his lips. "Maria?"

The tears fell then, pouring in rivers down her cheeks as Maria held out her arms for the little boy. He was too heavy for her to hold, and she kneeled upon the floor, taking him in her arms and hugging him. Terrified of the long journey and not understanding why his mother was not with him, Pedro submitted willingly to Maria's familiar embrace. Here was someone he knew and trusted, and little-boy tears crowded the corners of his eyes as he hugged her back.

"Maria, you were gone so long, and Mama didn't come back, and I had to leave my pony, and Maria, can we go home now? My puppy is awful lonely."

Maria wept and laughed and held him close, looking

up to Luke with pleading eyes. "It's all right, isn't it? He can stay? I'll fix up one of the rooms upstairs. He won't be any trouble, Luke, I promise."

"I'll start bringing in your things. Tell me which room you want for him and I'll see what I can fix up. I suppose the hound came along, too?" This last Luke directed at Sean. A suspicion of moisture shone in his eyes, and he could not look again at the tearful joy in Maria's eyes at his approval.

Letitia appeared as the men began emptying the wagon. Taking one look at the forlorn pair kneeling in the hallway, she exclaimed with distress and began issuing commands that sent son and daughter and maids scurrying. Before long, Maria was curled up in her bedroom chair with Pedro and the puppy at her feet and a glass of cold lemonade in her hand while the rest of the household went about unloading furniture and preparing a cold meal. Letitia breezed in and out, making certain her patient rested comfortably, keeping an eye on the color of her cheeks and the state of her distress, while keeping Maria's mind occupied with questions about the furniture to be distributed.

Her mother-in-law was so successful that Maria didn't have time to succumb to her grief until long after everyone had departed, Pedro had been tucked into her old bed, and she lay in the big poster bed beside Luke. Even then the grief had become an aching hollow instead of the ravaging pain of earlier. Logic prevailed over unreasoning tears, but it provided less comfort.

"Why, Luke?" she whispered to the man beside her. He lay with his hands behind his head, staring at the ceiling, and she knew he did not sleep.

Luke reached to pull her against him, tucking her head against his shoulder and feeling her breasts searing his side. His body responded to the touch, but he made no move to make love to her. He sensed that wasn't what she wanted, and he contented himself with holding her in his arms.

"Don't ask for reasons, Maria. There are some

things in this world that will never make sense. Isn't that why you have God to talk to?''

"Don't you believe in God?'' Luke's words distracted her, and Maria pushed up on her elbow to stare down at the outline of his face in the darkness.

Luke touched a gentle hand to her cheek. "When I look at you, I believe in God. There is no other explaining of how you came into my life.''

Maria lay against his chest and pressed a kiss to his jaw. "There are times when I love you so much, it hurts. I don't know what I will do if you should ever go away.''

Luke's grip tightened about her waist, and his amber eyes burned through the darkness as he tilted her chin so he could read her expression. "I'm not going away, Maria. You might as well get used to the fact of my hanging around.''

He hadn't said he loved her, but Maria had not expected him to. Words like that would not come easily to a man like Luke. She would have to accept what he offered and believe with her heart.

She covered his lips with her own, taunting him with the brush of her breasts against his chest. His response was explosive, and she soon found herself lying beneath him, her hair wrapped in his hand, and her lips sore and swollen from the fierceness of his kiss.

"Do you think Sean and Sara will ever kiss like this?'' she asked wickedly, remembering the undercurrents around the table earlier. The unlikely pair had sat as far from each other as they could, but their gazes had seldom strayed far from the other.

Luke lifted his weight on his hands and stared at his remarkable wife with incredulity. "I should certainly hope not. I'd hate to kill my best friend over that foolish sister of mine.''

Maria laughed softly, wriggling her hips until they came in contact with his. "Sara isn't foolish, only stubborn, like you. If you don't want to kill Sean, you had better inquire into his intentions and find him a job. Didn't you hear Sara accuse him of not having changed a bit?''

That wasn't all she had accused him of, and Luke sent Maria a suspicious glance. Sean had played the part of idle charmer as usual, and maddened by his insouciance, Sara had called him a lazy, no-account, conniving drifter before abruptly leaving the room. Sean had looked momentarily shell-shocked, but he had made no attempt to follow. So what in the devil was Maria getting at?

"Well, he hasn't, so don't you go getting any ideas of matchmaking. He's not the marrying kind." Figuring that settled the point, Luke returned to the more pleasant pastime of drowning his wife in kisses. He could never get enough, and his body ached for the release to come.

"Men never are," Maria murmured beneath his mouth, but then she lost track of thought as Luke captured her and drove her into a world governed only by the senses.

With Luke's loving kisses breathing in her ear and down her throat, Maria felt the oddest sensation in her middle, and her hand instinctively moved to cover her swelling abdomen. Luke stopped to look at her, his large hand reaching to cover hers.

"What is it, Maria? Are you all right? I haven't hurt you, have I?" An instant of panic cracked his voice at this thought.

The sensation came again, accompanied by a small ripple beneath her hand, and she smiled happily. Lying back against the pillows, she placed Luke's hand where her own had been. "I am fine, but I think you've awakened your son. Can you feel him?"

At this first stirring of life beneath his hand, Luke stared in wonderment at the delicate woman with the courage to carry his child. She didn't seem old enough or strong enough to grow a child within her womb, and fear found a place in his heart.

"Isn't it too soon? My God, Maria, you've got five more months to go. You'll need to rest more. I'll call on the doctor and—"

Soft laughter surrounded him, and gentle hands pulled him down to rest beside her. The fear gave way to joy as Luke filled his arms with the slender bundle of life and love that was his wife. Her whispered words of love were sweeter and headier than any liquor, and he willingly drowned in their liquid languor.

Tomorrow would be time enough to figure out why Manuel had killed Pieta, or what he would do when the Spaniard found Maria.

6

"I'm telling you, she's a damned unreasoning, unfeeling excuse for a woman, and I'm not going to put up with her highhanded, missish ways. What are you laughing at?" Sean scowled at the pair in the buckboard, pulling his horse up beside them in pursuit of explanation.

In the month since he had arrived, Maria had grown more fragile than before, if that were possible. In full skirts and petticoats she scarcely showed the burden of her pregnancy except to those who knew her. Her high breasts were fuller now, her waist thicker, and she no longer ran when she could walk. The color had never quite returned to her cheeks, and occasionally her eyes grew dark and impenetrable with some inner grief, but her ebullient spirit hadn't disappeared. When she looked up at Luke as she was doing now, her eyes sparkled like glittering gems, and her full lips curved in a delightful bow that made every man look twice.

Gazing at his friend, Sean felt a twinge of envy. The hard, cynical look had gradually faded from Luke's face. He still gazed upon the world with cautious eyes that revealed nothing of his emotions, but when he looked upon Maria—that was a different story. The warmth and understanding between them was almost tangible, and Luke's quickness to join her in laughter gave evidence of the changes in his life. Sean wished he could foresee the same future for himself. A warm, loving wife like Maria at his side would give him good reason to settle down, even if she were a volatile spitfire that could scratch his eyes out when cornered.

Maria's lips twitched at Sean's bemused expression,

and she ignored his plight as she leaned over to check on the safety of the little boy bouncing in the back. Pedro gave her a quick, shy grin and hugged his dog's neck. He wasn't the same carefree, rambunctious little boy of before, but traces of his old spirit flared occasionally now as he grew accustomed to his new home. He adored Luke, and Maria felt a profound relief that Luke treated him as one of his own. He had been the one to insist that Pedro stay with them despite the fact that he had a half brother and sister back in New Mexico. Pieta's senseless death had made it seem safer to keep Pedro here. Perhaps no one knew of the boy's parentage, but Luke had not been willing to take any chances. He had even invited Jose and Carmelita to join them, but they had lives of their own now. Maria tugged a lock of Pedro's hair and turned back to Sean's irate tirade.

"Luke, you had better tell him what happens to men who trifle with your sister. He seems to be under some illusion that he need only smile at her, and she will fall into his arms like all the others." Maria's eyes gleamed with mischief at the look of frustration on Sean's face. His courtship of Sara was not going at all well because neither of them would admit it was courtship.

"There's no harm in stealing a kiss or two!" Sean protested.

"There is when she wallops you on the jaw every time you try," Luke replied calmly, whipping the reins to speed their progress. "You'd think after a while your jaw would ache enough to remind you not to try again."

"Like I said, she's a cold, hard woman. I just think it's a waste to let all that beauty go untouched, but if that's what she wants, there's a few dark-eyed beauties here in town who won't be averse to my kisses."

Maria laughed at his peevish tone. "Those dark-eyed beauties are half the reason you're in hot water with Sara as it is. You're going to have to make up your mind, Sean O'Laughlin. If it's all the other women you see that you want, then you may as well forget Sara.''

''Forget Sara! I might as well forget my own name. By the saints, she even scolds me for a philandering Irishman in my sleep. The woman has a hurtful tongue, she does.''

Luke made a rude noise. ''Sara hasn't got the gumption of a church mouse. You must bring out the worst in her.''

''Gumption! Saints alive! The woman slugs my jaw, calls me names my own mother would cringe to hear, and you're complaining because she doesn't take a gun to my hide like your lovely woman here. Well, maybe I haven't got what it takes to be a Walker.''

''I don't think that's the question, Sean,'' Maria reprimanded softly. ''The question is whether you want a wife who happens to be a Walker. You better be thinking on that if you're expecting kisses from Sara.''

That settled the argument quite effectively. With an offended look Sean spurred his mount ahead and rode on into town. Luke hurried his horses after him, throwing Maria a sideways look as they rolled into the town's main street.

''If you and Sara are figuring on roping in a bronco like Sean, you picked the wrong man. I thought Sara had better sense than that.''

''Love isn't in the mind, Luke. You can't talk yourself into it or out of it. It just happens and you're stuck with it, come what may.'' Maria turned a blinding look up to her husband's sun-browned face. ''I don't know about you, but I certainly never pictured myself sitting beside the notorious Cheyenne Walker, fat as a roasting pig and just as frumpy.''

Luke grinned and started to comment on her pleasing plumpness, but Maria's face had gone pale as she clutched his hand fiercely. He felt his own face go gray as he caught her by the waist. ''What is it, Maria? Shall I call the doctor?''

She shook her head, dragging her gaze away from a spot over his shoulder and squeezing her eyes closed.

"Don't look. That man over there by the saloon. He used to work for Manuel. I know he did."

Luke clenched his teeth, but calmly drew the buckboard up to the hitching post. Climbing down, he caught a glimpse of the man disappearing into the saloon, and he bit back a whistle. The guns riding low on the stranger's hips told him more than the man's face.

Gently he extracted Maria from her seat while Pedro, unaware of the tension between the adults, scrambled from the wagon bed. Luke touched his hand to Maria's pale cheek, reading the fear in her eyes with a pain in his heart.

"Go inside Mrs. Bartlett's store. Take Pedro with you. Ask if you can go in her back room. The privy is behind the store and she will think that's what you want, but don't go out that back door until I come around and tell you it's safe. She won't notice where you are. Just stay put, all right?"

Maria nodded and, nervously biting her lip, took Pedro's hand and hurried into the mercantile store. She really shouldn't get so wrought up. The man might not even work for Manuel anymore. It could just be a coincidence that he had shown up here. But she and Luke had never made any effort to disguise where they were, and it would be easy enough to find them. She just couldn't imagine why Manuel would bother now that she was married.

The tall, stout, gray-haired lady behind the counter consented readily to young Mrs. Walker's request. The whole town had talked for weeks of the exciting match between the Walker boy and the lovely Spanish lady. Although there were those detractors who called Luke an outlaw and Maria no better than she should be, on the whole the town had taken the young couple into their hearts. Luke's anxiety over his wife's health and Maria's growing pregnancy had endeared them to every woman in town. Maria found herself welcomed warmly wherever she went, and she was grateful for their kindness.

Pedro did not understand when Maria led him into

the dusty, unlit storeroom and made him stand there, but she held a finger to her lips and he decided it made an interesting game. A few minutes later, when a loud voice and heavy feet sounded in the outer room and Maria clenched his hand tightly, he realized the game was more exciting than he had anticipated.

Mrs. Bartlett glanced up at the intrusion of the heavy-jowled stranger. His stained rawhide vest and stubbled chin indicated he was not someone's husband wandering in off the streets with a list from his wife. She knew all the single gentlemen in town, and he was not one of them. She frowned at the man's harsh words.

"Where's the woman that just came in here?"

It was a quiet day and no one else was in the store, so she knew who he meant. She just didn't think this was the kind of man the delicate Mrs. Walker needed to confront, and she certainly didn't intend to tell him she had gone to the privy. Stubbornly she glared at the stranger.

"There's no one here but me, as you can see. May I help you with something? Some laundry soap perhaps? I have a nice fresh batch in from—"

The man shoved aside a display of Lydia Pinkham's Vegetable Compound and advanced threateningly toward the counter. "I saw her come in here and I want to talk to her. Do I have to go through you first?"

In the back room Maria clenched her teeth to keep them from chattering. Luke had said not to leave without him, but she couldn't allow poor Mrs. Bartlett to be harmed for protecting her. Surely the man couldn't do anything too terrible in broad daylight in front of witnesses, and Luke should be coming soon. Releasing Pedro's hand and gesturing for him to remain behind, she moved toward the store.

A hand came from behind and caught her shoulder, spinning her back against the shelves as a shadow brushed past, blocking her passage. At the same time she heard Luke's voice in the front room, and her heart skipped a beat in fear.

Mrs. Bartlett looked up in surprise and relief as

Luke moved from the bright sunshine in the doorway to the shadows of the unlit interior, a rifle primed and loaded in his hands.

"Anybody asking for my wife goes through me first, not this here lady. What do you want, mister?"

The man whirled around, his hand reaching for his gun, but the deadly expression in Luke's eyes as he raised the rifle made him think twice, and he lowered his hand. "I've got a message for her."

"Then give it to me. She'll not talk to the likes of you." Luke edged closer, his rifle propped at a menacing angle as he sized up the stranger and read the hatred and fear in his eyes. Fear made a man do things he wouldn't normally, and Luke kept the shelf of iron pots between himself and the stranger.

"It's the little lady I want to talk to. Bring her out." Warily the gunman maneuvered himself closer to the back door and the old lady behind the counter.

Losing his patience, Luke gestured with his rifle. "Out. Get out now before this gun accidentally explodes in your face. I'll give you two minutes to clear town. If I see you anywhere near my wife again, you'll get no further warning. *Comprende?*"

In the back room, Maria gasped as the stranger reached for his gun, but Sean held a sturdy arm across the doorway, barring her path. His other hand rose to take aim, but Luke was quicker.

With seeming carelessness the rifle in Luke's hands went off, and the intruder gave a yelp of pain as the bullet grazed his gun hand. In rapid succession two more bullets spat at his feet and another flew above his head, all deliberately missing in such a manner as to make their intended target tingle with terror. The gunman raised his hands carefully away from his holster and began edging toward the front door. The icy look in Luke's narrowed eyes gave fair warning that the last shots in the weapon would do considerably more damage than a grazed finger.

As the stranger turned and half ran out the door, Maria collapsed against Sean's shoulder while Pedro darted between them to run after the gunman. Luke caught him by the back of his suspenders before he could get to the door, then glanced worriedly to the doorway, where Maria appeared leaning on Sean's arm.

Mrs. Bartlett's exclamations of anger and relief abruptly halted as another shadow stepped through the front doorway. Shoving Pedro behind him, Luke swung around, raising his rifle, but he just as quickly lowered it again.

"You're too late, Sheriff. I'm not disturbing the peace any longer."

Luke felt Maria come up beside him, and he circled her waist with his arms and held her closer while keeping a cautious watch on the tall man in the opening.

Broad, with a thick neck and a head too small for his shoulders, the sheriff had a reputation for being a slow man with a gun, but a hard man to beat any other way. His cold blue gaze looked Luke over, then he tilted his hat back in deference to Maria.

He didn't linger long over the pleasantries. "Luke, I'm going to warn you now. This here's a peaceful town and I aim to keep it that way. If you're going to make it a habit to shoot up strangers, I'll have to ask you to leave."

"Hell, Sheriff, that S.O.B.—"

"Luke!" In horrified tones Maria interrupted, disengaging herself and placing her hands on her hips. "Watch your language!"

In unadulterated astonishment Luke stared at the little witch who had cursed him and shot at him and never flinched an inch in the face of his wrath. Amusement mixed with incredulity at her femininely ruffled feathers.

"Hellfire and damnation, you're telling *me* to watch my language? Does that mean I get to wash your mouth out with soap the next time you call me an arrogant ass?"

Sean couldn't control his laughter at the look of outrage on Maria's petite features, and he staggered backward, out of her furious reach. The sheriff, too, struggled with amusement at the picture of the notorious Cheyenne Walker arguing with the little spitfire he claimed as wife. Her emerald eyes gleamed with angry fire beneath that heavy head of respectably arranged ebony coils, and the sheriff couldn't help but admire the way she held herself in the face of Luke's laughter.

Not understanding this scene, Pedro popped up between them to stand with arms crossed in front of Maria's skirts. "You can't wash Maria's mouth out with soap. She's a lady!"

That logic cracked a smile from even Maria, and she knelt to give the little boy a relieved hug, burying her flushed cheeks against his hair. She ought to wring Luke's neck, but the terror of earlier made it more likely that she would cry if she dare let herself go. It was better to be angry.

The sheriff relaxed and met Luke's gaze on a more amiable level. "You've got a right nice little lady there, Luke. We're proud to have both of you back. Just try to remember we've got law here already. You don't have to make your own."

"I just get a little irritable when someone harasses my wife, Jack. Except for that, you'll have no problem with me."

The sheriff nodded his understanding and, after exchanging a few polite words with Mrs. Bartlett, he took his leave. The shaken woman watched Luke with some trepidation as he helped Maria to her feet, but his gentlemanly behavior as he found his wife a seat and gathered up the items she wished to purchase relieved the elderly lady's fears. She tried not to think of the cold, hard expression of the gunfighter he had exhibited earlier as he smiled pleasantly and laid his purchases upon the counter. She had no desire to see his expression change again.

Word of the confrontation spread through the town on the wings of wind, and Luke's notoriety had many a young lady peering at him through modestly lowered lashes or giggling and blushing as he passed by. Maria held his elbow and tried to hide her irritation, but when a particularly brash young woman stopped in front of them to express her dismay that such a thing could happen here, Maria nearly slammed Luke's politely lifted hat back on his head.

When they extricated themselves from that encounter, Maria met Luke's amused expression with a glare. "You use your guns to show off. Now you'll have every damned woman in the town panting at your feet and every man wondering if he can outgun you."

"Such shocking language! You'll never make a proper housewife that way." Luke grinned at the look in tilted eyes made greener with jealousy.

"Even I know better than to use such language in front of Mrs. Bartlett. I want to be treated as a respectable lady, but they're just going to think of me as Cheyenne Walker's woman."

Luke caught her by the waist and spirited her into the narrow gap between the livery and the barber shop. His hands rested at her waist, no longer able to circle it entirely. His thumbs caressed the small bulge of her stomach admiringly as she looked up at him.

"You're more a lady than Caroline will ever be, and the people of this town aren't too dumb to figure that out. Now, what is really bothering you, *poquita?*"

He stood so straight and tall, skin bronzed by the sun, hair bleached in blond streaks, amber eyes almost golden as he gazed upon her. He was a temptation for any woman with half an eye in her head, and he had a reputation for accepting the invitations of any woman who offered. What would he do when she got too fat and ugly for his bed? Maria couldn't bear to think of it.

"Why was he here, Luke? What could he want of me?"

Luke caressed her cheek, not acknowledging the fear crawling in his belly. He had hoped Vasquero would give up when he found the ranch out of his reach. He should have known better.

"He's probably ready to make an offer, but he thinks he'll get it from you easier than from me. Don't worry yourself, Maria. We've got that deed so tightly tied up he'll never be able to touch it."

Maria held herself stiffly beneath Luke's caress, willing herself not to give in to any of the myriad fears rampaging through her mind. Her uncles and Luke had drawn up all sorts of papers tying up the ranch in a trust that would eventually be divided between Pedro and herself, or Luke as her husband, but she placed no reliance on pieces of paper. Only the deed could be filed at the courthouse, and that now had Luke's name on it instead of her own. Her uncles held the papers preventing his selling it and keeping Pedro's ownership secret, but such papers were meaningless unless her uncles intervened. Maria wondered if it would not be better to make them public, but they protected Pedro as well as herself, and she could not endanger him.

Sighing, she accepted his dismissal of the subject. The Vasqueros had little power outside of New Mexico. They could do nothing. "I know, Luke. I just worry. I feel so helpless. No one will let me do anything anymore."

Luke pulled her closer and pressed his lips to hers. He could feel the instant flame of her passion, and he pressed further, parting her lips and drinking deeply of their nectar before raising his head to gaze into limpid eyes. His palm covered the bulge of the abdomen beneath the full skirts.

"Don't ever tell me you're not good for anything. Carrying this child may occupy most of your time right now, but you're my life, Maria. I may laugh at you or curse you or I might even be fool enough or drunk enough to look at another woman, but you're the woman I want. Keeping me in line ought to be enough to keep anybody busy."

Luke had never said such things to her before, and Maria stared up at him in amazement. The warmth of his eyes burned a path to her heart, and for the first time since hearing of Pieta's death, joy flooded her veins.

7

By November Maria was well into her sixth month, although she gave small sign of showing it. Her eyes danced with joy as she moved through her new home, arranging her mother's antimacassars over the backs of the burgundy velveteen sofas that had once adorned the parlor at the ranch, sewing gauzy yellow curtains for the upstairs nursery, where her old rocking chair now waited for the child she would bear. In comparison with some of the grander homes in town, she knew these rooms looked almost barren, but she preferred the sunlight and space to the gloom and clutter of those fashionable abodes.

Maria wandered into the room she shared with Luke. She had not replaced the poster bed with her father's massive carved headboard, but that was the only thing she had not replaced. A polished mahogany clothespress now gave Luke plenty of room to store his shirts and hang his coats. The frilly curtains and dainty bedspread had disappeared, and in their place hung silver and blue draperies and a wedding ring quilt that Luke's mother had given them for a wedding present. Two solid wing chairs flanked the fireplace, and a small table with lovely carved wooden inlays waited for a breakfast tray or a game of cards in the evening. Luke's hat hung on a rack in the corner, and a shaving mirror adjusted to his height hung above the washstand. The room belonged to both of them now, and all traces of Caroline had disappeared.

The thought of Caroline brought a hint of laughter to Maria's lips as she remembered the hasty exchange with her mother-in-law just a few minutes ago. Letitia had just stopped in on her way to pick up a concoction at the doctor's that promised to ease the stomach and prevent vomiting. Caroline had been ill in the morning for the past month now, Letitia had informed Maria with a furtive laugh. It wouldn't be long before everyone guessed her condition.

Patting the place where a tiny foot kicked furiously at the swelling of her belly, Maria glanced at the calendar she kept on the corner of her dressing table. Today was her birthday. In another year one half the ranch would be hers to do with as she wished, but she had no mind for that now. She wondered if Luke remembered or even knew the date. He had said nothing when he kissed her and rode off this morning.

She felt a certain sadness at the loss of the people who had once shared this day with her, but she was determined not to let memories destroy this new life she had found. She had a husband she dearly loved, a child that would be born in a few short months, a little brother who filled her days with frustration and laughter, and Luke's family to share it all with. She could not ask for more.

She had debated asking Luke's family to spend this day with her, but selfishly she had decided she wanted to be alone with Luke. Letitia had agreed to take Pedro for the evening. Rosa and Mrs. Donleavy were preparing a special feast and had promised to disappear after it was served. Cleaning up would wait for morning. Tonight she wanted her husband to herself. That was all the birthday gift she required.

By evening, Pedro had been wrapped up in warm coats and rode off on his small pony beside Sean. The wicked Irishman had discovered it was Maria's birthday from the adoring Rosa and presented Maria with delicate gold hoops for her ears. They sparkled in the candlelight from the dinner table, and on the spur of the moment Maria abandoned her plan to wear one of the rich dinner gowns Luke had bought for her. Instead she unburied one of Pieta's loose blouses with the billowing sleeves and the too-big neckline that fell daringly low across her bosom. To that she added one of Carmelita's full skirts with red and gold cotton flounces and tied the waist closed with a blue sash. Luke had once called her a gypsy. She felt as carefree as one tonight.

When Luke arrived, he came in the back door, and odors of rich beef and pastry wafted toward him. His nose twitched appreciatively, and as he passed the dining room set with Maria's best china and crystal and candelabra, he began to grin. The little witch had planned her own party, but he had not forgotten the present.

Upstairs, he stopped in the bedroom doorway in surprise. After seeing the table setting he had expected to see Maria in one of her fancy gowns, wearing the ruby necklace she took out upon such occasions. Instead she stood before the dresser in her gypsy clothes with her long hair cascading down her back and curling about her hips. At his entrance she swung about and the lamplight glittered on the gold at her ears. Luke caught his breath at the beauty displayed just for him, and he strode purposefully into the room.

Maria threw her arms around Luke's neck as he swept her into his embrace, and the excitement she found in his kiss made this the best birthday she had ever had. Even though she had grown fat and unwieldy, he still found her desirable, and the pleasure of this knowledge filled her heart.

"Shouldn't I be the one surprising you, *brujita?*" Luke whispered against her ear, nuzzling her earrings. "Do I get to kiss you twenty times or would you prefer the traditional birthday licks?"

He had remembered! Maria smiled and pushed away so she could see the warm light of his eyes. "Kisses, please, after supper. Rosa and Mrs. Donleavy are waiting to serve us before they leave."

The amber lights of Luke's eyes grew brighter. "Then I will have you to myself? No Mrs. Donleavy asking you about tomorrow's menus or putting up jelly, no Rosa running in and out with washing and ironing, no boy and dog romping between our feet every time I try to kiss you?"

"You do not mind too much?" The question was half facetious, half worried. Their days had grown so hectic these last months, there had been little time for themselves. Sometimes she suspected he preferred it that way since she had grown so fat, but she could never tell with Luke.

Luke ran his fingers through the luxuriant strands of Maria's hair and smiled down at her. "Only if you promise I will get the same treatment on my birthday. Then I know I will have a little piece of heaven twice every year."

His kiss this time was more loving than hungry, and Maria reveled in the ecstasy of it. Luke made it so difficult to know him, but she was learning, and she knew she had pleased him tonight.

He didn't produce the package until after dinner and the servants had left for the night. While they lingered over the last of the coffee, Luke brought out a tiny, gift-wrapped box from his vest pocket and placed it beside Maria's saucer. Another, slightly larger box came from his inside coat pocket, and a third, longer box materialized from the outside coat pocket.

Maria stared at the gaily wrapped packages in astonishment, and tears filled her eyes as she glanced back to Luke. "I didn't think you would remember. You didn't have to get me anything; I didn't expect it."

"You want me to take them back?" Luke teased, reaching for the smallest.

Her hand instantly slapped over his and she pried the prize loose. "Not until I see what it is." Flashing him a laughing look, Maria eagerly tore through the wrappings of the small gift.

Inside the box sparkled a narrow gold band inset with tiny rubies and diamonds. Maria gasped as she drew the ring from the box and she looked at Luke with bewilderment.

"Luke, it's the loveliest thing I have ever seen, but shouldn't you be using your money to buy cattle and build that stable you wanted?"

Luke took the ring from her hand and gently slid it on the finger bearing the small gold band he had given her on their wedding day. "There wasn't time to find the right one before we married. I wanted something special just for you. You can't wear a cow around your finger."

Remembering the extravagant stone Caroline wore upon her hand, Maria had to smile, albeit with tears. Luke's taste had changed for the better over the years. This delicate setting suited her much more than a gaudy rock, but she wished he didn't find it necessary to buy her love as he had tried to do Caroline's.

"Thank you, Luke, it is so lovely I'm afraid to open your other gifts. Maybe I should let you take them back."

Luke gazed at her bent head and heard the tears in her voice with astonishment. Caroline and Peg had danced with joy when he had brought them expensive gifts. This one talked of cows and barns and cried. He did not understand, but he had no intention of taking the gifts back. He had worked long and hard at choosing just the right ones, and it had taken months to get what he wanted. She would wear them, and somehow he would make her enjoy them.

"Next time I will buy you a cow if you prefer, but not this time. You will have to suffer and indulge me." Without further warning Luke rose from the table and drew Maria from her chair. Piling the boxes in her hands, he swung her up in his arms.

Ebony hair spilled across his arm and trailed to the floor as Maria stared up at him in wide-eyed confusion. The warmth hadn't left his eyes, however, and she relaxed against his shoulder as he carried her toward the stairs with a determined expression upon his face. Her heart pounded in time with his steps, and her anticipation had little to do with the still unwrapped boxes in her hands.

Upstairs again, Luke gently lay his wife upon the bed, then sprawling on one elbow beside her he reached for the medium-sized box.

"Pretend this is a calf," he said mockingly as he pulled out a wide band of beaten gold and placed it around her arm.

Before Maria could reply he had opened the last box and drawn out heavy strands of intricate gold chains which he dropped over her head and arranged to his satisfaction upon the exposed skin of her throat and breasts. The brilliant metal glittered in the lamplight, sending dancing gleams along her tawny skin.

"That can be a stable if you like." With that nonsensical statement Luke pressed Maria back against the mattress and smothered any protest with his kiss.

Maria felt as if she were drowning. She threw her arms around Luke for safety and surrendered to the sensation. The gold burned warmly against her flesh, but she preferred the heat of his kiss. She would have followed him to the bottom of the deepest ocean had he requested it, but she was quite content to join him in his bed instead. As Luke peeled the blouse from her shoulders and bent to draw her breast into his mouth, she moaned with pleasure and forgot her expensive adornments entirely.

To Luke's immense pleasure, Maria wore nothing beneath her gypsy clothes to hamper his access to the satin of her skin. His fingers spread proudly over the bulge where his child kicked and played, then moving his hand beneath her, he drew her close to ease the aching heat of his loins. Somehow his clothes melted to the floor until nothing remained between them but the gleaming gold of his gifts.

They made love gently, reserving their passion for lips and hands, respecting the awkwardness and delicacy of Maria's condition. To have Luke inside her again erased all her fears and doubts, and Maria succumbed to the joy of it, giving all that he asked and more with pleasure. Curled into the curve of his body, she felt the explosion of his release deep inside her, and her body responded with shock waves of its own. Never would she have enough of this closeness he brought her.

The fire she had started in the grate earlier in the afternoon died to burning embers, but the heat of their bodies kept them warm as they lay wrapped about each other. Maria leaned her head back against Luke's shoulder and smiled as his hand rose to fondle her swelling breast.

"Is this sinful, Luke? Now that I've done my duty as wife, shouldn't I be insisting that we sleep apart?"

Luke chuckled low against her ear. "If this is sinful, you will have to confess it to your shocked priest every week, for I have no intention of sleeping apart from you. Perhaps I will have to ease my demands for a while, but you are going to lie in my arms every night for the rest of our lives, so get used to it."

He tempted the fates with those words, but Maria didn't believe in superstition and she snuggled closer to his heat. "I haven't thanked you for your gifts. The cow and the stable are very lovely, and I will treasure them always."

Luke laughed and Maria thrilled to the sound of it. He laughed more often now, with an easy abandon that made her heart soar. She turned to watch his eyes crinkle at the corners and touched her finger to the notch at the edge of his lips.

"I love you," she murmured, and the sudden blaze of warmth in Luke's eyes was all the reward she required as he bent to steal another kiss.

The pounding at the front door went unnoticed for some minutes. Only when it began to seem as if the visitor would break the door down did they take notice of the untimely intrusion.

In bewilderment Maria rubbed her eyes while Luke sat up and listened. She didn't know the time, but it had to be dreadfully late. The contentment of the evening's lovemaking still wrapped around her, and she didn't register any feeling of impending disaster until Luke rose and reached for his pants. In that instant all the terrible meanings of this late-night caller tumbled into her thoughts, and Maria gave a cry of alarm as she scrambled after Luke.

He caught her arm and handed her the nightdress thrown over a chair back. "Stay here. I will see who it is."

He might as well have told Moses to forget the Red Sea. When he took down his rifle, Maria jerked on her nightdress and reached for a robe. He wasn't going anywhere without her.

Not seeing any danger in an intruder who took the time to knock, Luke didn't argue. While Maria struggled with her robe, he strode out into the hall and down the stairs.

By the time he threw open the front door, Maria was standing at the top of the stairs looking down. She screamed at the glint of steel appearing at the open doorway, and screamed again when a broad man shoved aside the door and stalked in, followed by two other equally fearsome men.

With only the light from the small lamp in the hall, she didn't immediately recognize any of the intruders, but Luke apparently did. He lowered his rifle calmly and stepped back, sending an uneasy glance to the top of the stairs. Maria clung to the railing in terror, her long hair flowing loose around her white face as she met his gaze. She caught a fleeting glimpse of sorrow before his expression tightened and became unreadable. Then he turned back to the man she now recognized as the sheriff.

"It's a bit late for visiting, Jack. Is there anything I can do for you?"

The tall man had followed Luke's glance to the top of the stairs, and the regret in his eyes as he gazed upon her sent Maria scurrying down to stand beside Luke. She caught his hand and he clasped it tightly while the sheriff spoke.

"I'm sorry, Luke, I've got a man down at the office with a warrant for your arrest. I told him you wouldn't give us any trouble and made him stay there. I didn't cotton to his looks."

Maria bit her tongue to keep from crying out in fear. The grim set of Luke's jaw warned this wasn't anytime to interfere, and she held her peace, holding tightly to his hand so they could share their strength.

"On what charges, Jack?" Luke asked warily.

"Murder."

Maria felt Luke flinch. Panic clogged her throat and interfered with her breathing. She couldn't speak but stared at the sheriff's taut face with a terrifying fear. Perhaps she had heard him wrong. Maybe if they waited, the word would disappear, and they could pretend it had never been said.

Luke did not adhere to such a philosophy. With a wry drawl he asked, "Whose?"

"Dirk Jones. There's an assault charge for one Peg Owens, too, from Stockton. They're old warrants, Luke. You knew they were out there."

"Yeah, I knew. I hope the damned bounty hunter who dragged them out is well paid for his efforts." Luke released Maria's hand. His expression was stoic as he handed his rifle to the sheriff.

"Like I said, I didn't like his face, but the papers are legal. I got to take you in."

"Give me time to say good-bye to my wife. It's a heck of a birthday surprise for her." Luke didn't plead, simply stated a fact, man to man.

The sheriff gave him a cautious look, then glanced at Maria's face, wide-eyed with fear and nodded his head.

Luke twisted her around by the shoulders and steered her toward the stairs. His grip was tense and bruising, and Maria did as directed without thought.

Once he closed the bedroom door behind them, Maria woke as if from a bad dream. She flew to the window and looked down. It was a straight drop, but if they could tie the bed sheets . . .

"No, Maria, I'm not running." Reading her thoughts, Luke crossed the room and pulled her away. Taking her in his arms, he buried his face against her hair. "It's a hell of a time to tell you, but I love you too much to put you through that. I'm innocent, Maria, please believe me. I'll stand trial for it so I can come home to you when it's done. Will you wait?"

Tears spilled from her eyes as Maria twisted her head to look up at him. He said he loved her, and she could read the truth in his eyes. For once he looked upon her with all the pent-up emotion inside him, and she could see the tears in the corners of his eyes. He loved her! How long had she waited for that admission from a man notoriously tight with his feelings? How could he ask so foolish a question?

Throwing herself back in his arms, Maria muffled her words against his bare shoulder. "Let me go with you."

Luke ran his hands up and down her back, memorizing the feel of her soft curves, the scent of roses, the way her tears felt against his skin. That she did not question or condemn gave him the strength to do what he must.

"You must stay here and take care of Pedro and our babe. I'll have the sheriff send word to my father. Someone will be with you soon. Be brave for me, Maria. It will make it easier for both of us."

Maria wanted to scream, "I can't, I can't be brave!" and burst into a thousand tears, but she forced herself to remain silent. The way Luke held her told of how close he was to the breaking point, and she could not do that to him. He loved her because he thought she was brave, so she would be brave. For now.

She nodded against his shoulder, wiping away the tears with her fingers before looking up. "I'll find a good lawyer. Sean can help. There must be witnesses, people who can prove you couldn't do it. You'll be home before your son is born."

Luke's smile was grim, but he didn't argue with her. He didn't make any promises, either. Gripping her shoulders, he forced her to look up, and his mouth closed over hers with the heat of an eternity's worth of kisses.

When he walked out the door with the sheriff's men surrounding him, he didn't look back.

8

With all the tears she had cried, Maria didn't think there could be any more until Sean stopped in to see how she fared. Seeing the tense worry in his face brought it all back to her, and the tears flowed in a never-ending stream as she gestured for him to take a seat.

"Where are they taking him?" she managed to whisper, wiping ferociously at the moisture blurring her vision.

"To Stockton. Josh is going in to Abilene to look for a good lawyer." Sean didn't try to tell her finding a good lawyer was like looking for a needle in a haystack and twice as useless. The verdict could rely on the mood the judge was in or how drunk the jury was at the time. That was just one of the many reasons men took the law into their own hands in these parts.

Maria knew this as well as Sean, but she clung to the hope that a man like Joshua Walker could surely prove his son's innocence. She wouldn't rely on him for everything, however. Nothing could be left to chance. She began to catalogue all the measures that had come to her in the long, lonely hours since Luke's departure.

"Sean, I want you to take me into town. I want to telegraph my uncles. They might know of lawyers, too. And that man Luke worked for sometimes, the Wells Fargo man? My *Tío* Juan seemed to be impressed with him. Would he help? Could we telegraph him?"

"Mr. Hume?" Sean considered the prospect of wiring the educated California sheriff who had overseen the Wells Fargo guards these past few years. The man was more inclined to putter in his rose garden than to venture out in the wilderness, but he had a shrewd mind. There might be someone he could send, something he could do. "Why not? He seemed to like Luke. Let me go get the carriage and we'll give it a try."

Sean was back within half an hour with the Walkers' high-wheeled buggy. The canvas lid kept out some of the chill winter wind, and the fur blankets and warming bricks Letitia had piled in kept their feet from freezing. Maria would have preferred a horse, but even she had to admit she was in no shape to ride one now. She bore with the steady pace of the carriage as patiently as she could.

While Sean went to see the sheriff in the back of the general store to see if there were any new developments, Maria entered the telegraph office in the stagecoach station to compose her wires. It took all her strength to keep her hands from shaking as she scribbled the words to her uncles. She had to convince them that Luke was innocent and that this wasn't just payment for past sins.

The telegrams weren't easy to write, but she completed the task without crying and watched in awe as the young boy tapped them out over the wires. Somewhere, in faraway places she might never see, strangers were hearing her private words and writing them down. She didn't care what they thought of her impassioned pleas if only they passed them on to the recipients intact. It seemed difficult to believe such messages would arrive in St. Louis and California simultaneously, but the boy at the telegraph machine assured her they would.

With that task ended, she returned to the street to search for Sean. She needed to beg another favor of him, a large one this time.

The man strolling toward her seemed vaguely familiar, but Maria could remember no one who walked with such a noticeable limp or carried a Malacca walking stick. The gold watch chain over his burgundy brocade vest spoke of wealth usually not known on these plains, and she turned toward the sheriff's office before the sound of her name stopped her.

"Mrs. Walker, this is a pleasure!"

The man limped forward until she could see his face. She still had difficulty recognizing him. One side of his face seemed permanently twisted downward, and he no longer wore the full, gray beard that had hidden his weak chin. His eyes had a hard, faraway look to them, and Maria moved nervously backward a step or two as he approached.

Dallas! She didn't know how she pulled that name from her memory. The husky, healthy rancher she remembered bore little resemblance to this hollow-cheeked, twisted wreckage before her. Guilt struck her with a terrible pang. Had they done this to him? Sean had said he fell ill after the fire. Was this the result?

Trying to remain calm, Maria greeted him. "Mr. Dallas, this is a surprise. What are you doing here?"

A sly gleam leapt to his eye as his gaze swept over her awkward shape. "When I could not find you at your ranch, I met a gentleman who told me where your husband lived. A most considerate gentleman, Señor Vasquero, but he is not too fond of your husband."

Maria's breath froze in her lungs. If Luke's enemies had banded together, they could exert powerful sources and wealth, but surely they could do nothing here, out of their territory. She wanted to run and hide, but Luke wouldn't do that. He would stay and find out more. So would she.

"Luke tends to support the little people, Mr. Dallas. Señor Vasquero prefers to step on them. There are differences of opinion between them."

Dallas smiled, though the frozen downturn of his lips gave it an evil twist. "That's a pity, Mrs. Walker. It is not sensible for one man to stand alone against the power of many. I choose to believe you are innocent of his actions, but your husband must pay the price of his beliefs. My suggestion is that you return and beg forgiveness from Señor Vasquero. I will be glad to accompany you; my revenge should be satisfied shortly."

That sounded more like a threat than an offer, and Maria's fingers curled up in fists of fear and rage. Seeing Sean stepping from the general store down the street, she acted swiftly. This evil man would not be satisfied in seeking revenge just against Luke if he could have Sean, too.

"Then I will know whom to call on should anything happen to my husband, Mr. Dallas. I am not as fast with a gun as Luke, but I'm just as accurate. Good day." Maria whirled about and strode in the opposite direction of Sean, hoping he would recognize his enemy and duck into a doorway while Dallas still stared after her.

Sean did better than that. Not completely understanding the scene sketched before him, but realizing Maria had seen him and had deliberately walked the other way, he stepped into the saloon and watched as Dallas shrugged and walked off. Then he darted out the back door, ran down a side street, and caught up with Maria without being seen by anyone in the town's main thoroughfare.

Maria gasped as Sean caught her by the wrist and drew her down the narrow alley leading to the livery stable. Then she gave a sigh of relief as she realized what he had done.

"Thank goodness! I was afraid Dallas would see you. He's met the Vasqueros, Sean." Her green eyes grew dark with worry as she scanned the Irishman's square face. "He's talking about revenge and Luke and telling me to go back to Manuel. It sounds like he's not waiting around very long. I'm frightened, Sean. I don't think he's going to let Luke wait for a trial."

Worriedly Sean searched her face for signs of hysteria, but she seemed calmer now than when he had met her at the house. This was the woman who had coolly lured the rich rancher into revealing his dam while she buttered a roll. He would not mistake her judgment.

"OK, we're getting you back to the ranch. I don't think you ought to be alone with that *spalpeen* around.

I'll take you back to Letitia and Sara. Then Matthew and I and a few others will go after Luke. If there's going to be any trouble, it will be between here and Stockton.''

Maria ached to go with him, but logic told her that was impossible. They would have to ride like the devil to catch up with the sheriff and Luke, and she would only hold them back. She had hoped to ask Sean to take her to Stockton, but now it seemed she would have to do it on her own. She passively nodded acceptance to Sean's decision, and not knowing any better, Sean assumed she agreed.

The women at the Walker ranch enfolded her into the warmth of their protection. Pedro had remained there through the day, but finally finding a target for his anxiety, he demanded that Sean take him to find his Uncle Luke. Maria carried him away from the men and their worried faces, and even Caroline managed a wan offer to help entertain the little boy until the men had left.

After the first few weeks Caroline had taken her unexpected and unwanted pregnancy with remarkable aplomb. She played the part of expectant mother with great verve once she realized it meant everyone in the household would cater to her every whim. The intrusion of Maria upon her little party caused some confusion, but she rallied well to the occasion. Putting up with Pedro showed a certain maternal instinct, and it gave a good excuse for avoiding Maria.

Maria had her mind elsewhere than on Caroline's coolness. She paced the floor as the men rounded up horses and supplies and sent word to neighboring ranches for assistance. Joshua had insisted on riding out with them, too, and that cut the thread of one hope she had been harboring. Now she would have to find someone else who would take her after them, or do it alone.

Letitia ordered her to take a seat and drink some soup, but Maria couldn't sit still long enough to finish the cup. The child within her rolled and kicked restlessly, sensing her disquiet, and the impossibility of the task she had set herself dismayed her. Luke had ordered her to look after their child and she had every intention of doing so, but in the same town with Luke, not a hundred miles away.

Maria sat quietly as Luke's father and brother made their farewells. Sean bowed awkwardly before the room full of women, his glance sliding to Sara's tear-streaked face but not lingering. The sound of their horses galloping out a few minutes later riddled the cold winter air, and then silence fell. They were gone.

Letitia came and put an arm around Maria, offering solace even while she sought it for herself. The silence seemed to stretch into eternity, until Maria couldn't bear it any longer. She had been helpless when her father died. She had not even been there with Pieta when she was killed. She could not let them take Luke from her without doing something to prevent it.

As the other women began to stir and began speaking of fixing supper and other mundane matters, Maria steeled herself for the confrontation to come and approached Letitia with what she hoped was confidence.

"I want to go back to our house. Is there anyone who can take me?"

Luke's mother looked surprised and studied her daughter-in-law carefully. "If you need something, we can send someone back to fetch it. Maybe we should bring Rosa and Mrs. Donleavy back here. With the men gone, it might be better if we all stayed together."

"I would appreciate it if you could take them in. They can look after Pedro so he won't be as much of a nuisance, but I cannot stay. I simply cannot." Maria's eyes pleaded for understanding. She kept her voice low to avoid including the others, but she sensed Sara watching her from her place by the hearth.

"I don't understand." Letitia looked genuinely puzzled. "Is it Caroline? Surely you know she won't bother you while you're under our roof. I understand your animosity, but—"

Maria shook her head, tilting her chin stubbornly. "No. Your hospitality is welcome, but I cannot stay here while Luke is out there somewhere in trouble. If someone will take me back to the house, I can hitch up the buckboard and go after them. I am quite accustomed to looking after myself. If it weren't for the babe, I would ride, but I can manage the wagon quite well.''

Letitia opened her mouth to protest, closed it when she noted the dangerous gleam in Maria's eyes, and gazed in horror as Sara came up to stand beside them.

''I want to go, too, Mama. Anything could happen out there. And Luke will need our support. We can't let him suffer this alone. I'll see that Maria takes care of herself. We can take the buggy. It will be warmer and easier on Maria.''

''You are both quite mad!'' Letitia exclaimed, but not in a tone of horror. She appeared to be thinking swiftly, her soft, plump hands kneading the air. ''Maria, you cannot travel like that. Look at what happened last time.''

''That was not the travel. I feel fine. I will feel better when I can see that Luke is all right. I will make life here miserable for everybody by staying. I must go.''

''If there's trouble along the road . . .'' Letitia's thoughts traveled on without words. All her men were out there, and she, too, felt the frustration of helplessness.

''There won't be,'' Sara replied decisively. ''Sean and Matt and Dad will stop that. We just need to get to Stockton while Maria can still travel. Luke will need her there.''

That was what needed to be said. They could not combat Indians or outlaws or any of the terrors of the trail, but they could be there when Luke walked in front of that courtroom. To think beyond that to the verdict didn't bear considering.

And so it was decided. Instead of going alone, Maria traveled in the company of Sara and Letitia and half a dozen of the ranch hands Joshua had left behind to protect them. For the season, the weather was relatively mild, and the threat of a snow or ice storm to endanger the cattle was next to nil. They were needed more to ward off the dangers of the trail to the women than the weather to the livestock.

Caroline stayed behind with Pedro and the servants, much to everyone's relief. Maria wasn't given to complaining of her discomfort as the buggy bumped along the washboard roads, but Caroline had not stopped complaining since her pregnancy began. The tedious hours of travel went easier in congenial company.

Guides rode on ahead, securing resting places in stagecoach stations or isolated farmhouses along the way. Maria was grateful not to have to face a night under the stars in this condition. To find a comfortable sleeping position in bed was growing increasingly difficult, and without Luke beside her she slept little. During the day the effort of keeping a cheerful disposition kept her mind fully occupied, but at night all the horrors of her imagination leapt out to confront her.

With increasing diligence Maria counted her rosary and prayed. Each passing day made her more certain that Manuel and Dallas had joined together not only to revenge themselves on Luke, but to make it easier to gain access to the ranch. Manuel must certainly know by now that the land was in Luke's name and that Luke would never sell it to him. That meant the railroad would not go through the valley and all the land the Vasqueros had purchased would be as worthless as everyone had thought. Luke stood between them and riches or bankruptcy.

Her fears were confirmed when they met Joshua and Matthew returning. One of the guides had already encountered them and warned of the entourage following, but they still stared in disbelief at the train of wagons and one buggy traipsing across the plain. Spying Letitia beside Maria in the carriage, Joshua set his mount to a gallop. Matthew continued more slowly, his gaze sweeping the line of wagons in search of his wife.

"Lettie, what in hell is the meaning of this?" Joshua

roared as he came riding up. "My God, woman, I thought you had more sense!"

"Or that I was too old?" Letitia inquired mildly. "I'm not ready for the rocking chair yet, Josh, and if I hadn't come along, these two girls were determined to go anyway. We can't leave Luke alone at a time like this. Have you seen him? Is he well?"

Joshua anxiously regarded Maria's tightly composed features. She pretended stoicism, but he could see the white lines at the corner of her mouth and knew the source of the dark circles beneath her eyes. The unnatural brightness of those green eyes would haunt his sleep for many a night as she stared at him, waiting for his words. He cleared his throat and preparing his words carefully, he spoke to his wife, letting his daughter-in-law listen without need of maintaining her composure.

"Two days out they were attacked by a gang of bandits. The sheriff got himself and Luke holed up behind some rocks. The bounty hunter turned on them and they killed the b—" he cut off the word and found another—"the coward. That's when we rode in. The outlaws scattered before we could catch them. We got them to Stockton all right after that." His gaze strayed to the wagon with his daughter in it and on to the next laden with boxes and trunks. "You planning on taking up residence somewhere?"

"We're prepared to stay as long as necessary. Maria won't be able to travel back and forth, and the weather may worsen."

The matter-of-fact statements told all that was needed. They intended to put up a fight for Luke's life, and no court of law would stand in their way. Joshua hid the makings of a grin as he surveyed the women and their bodyguards. He sure wouldn't want to be in the shoes of that judge and jury when it came time for Luke to stand trial."

"Sean will be glad to see you. He and that fancy city lawyer I hired don't see eye to eye, so he's putting up pretty much on his own. Both them boys will be proud to see you." His gaze returned to Maria. She had relaxed enough to meet his eye with a small smile of gratitude. "You feeling all right?"

"Much better, thank you, sir. Will they let me see Luke?"

"Reckon so, but you gotta figure Luke'll be a mite riled to see you at first."

Maria smiled serenely. "It won't be the first time."

After a quick conference, Joshua decided to ride with the women, leaving Matthew to return to the ranch and Caroline. The men who had rode out with them had already returned to their homes, and Matthew took a couple of the cowboys from the ranch back with him. The trip from this point would be short and safe.

They rode into Stockton on the first of December, and Maria held her head high to hold back the tears as she gazed at the wooden city that hid Luke within its confines. Fortunately, the decent, law-abiding citizens around her couldn't read her mind as Maria cynically contemplated this hastily erected cattle town.

Keeping an eye out for the jail, Maria had already come to the conclusion she could burn the town down if needed to get Luke out of this place. They had better hope they had an honest judge.

9

The jail was little more than a tinder box with a few iron bars for looks. Unlike many of its kind, it connected to the back of the sheriff's office and thus shared some of the warmth of the potbelly stove.

Never having known a sheriff with the luxury of an office or familiarized herself with the interior of a jail, Maria did not appreciate these comforts. It took all her strength to keep the horror out of her eyes as she and Joshua were shown to Luke's cell.

He lay sprawled full length along a narrow cot, one hand propped behind his head while he stared at the tin roof. At the sound of the door opening, he turned his unshaven face in that direction without expectation.

It took a full minute before he registered that his father had returned with Maria. He stared at shiny ebony coils of hair above the delicate high-boned face as if in a dream, and only when she made some small sound did he rise and come forward to touch the bars separating them.

Maria's hands lifted to touch his cheek and caress the hair from Luke's forehead, proving his reality. At the burning look of love and anguish in his son's eyes as he gazed helplessly upon the woman beyond his grasp, Joshua discreetly removed himself from the back room. There were things being said here that other ears shouldn't hear.

Maria gave no hint of what went between them when she reappeared again, but the fire in her eyes was sufficient testimonial to her rejuvenated spirit.

"That room is positively icy, Sheriff. Luke will have pneumonia before he ever comes to trial. You will have to leave that connecting door open so some of the heat goes back there or install another stove. I'll be back shortly with some additional blankets and decent linen. Who is in charge of his meals?''

Joshua raised his hand to interfere, but thought better of it and waited for the other man's reaction. Beneath Maria's interrogation the sheriff grew nervous and began to squirm, assuring her with as much bluster as he could summon that the prisoner would receive the best possible care.

"I certainly hope so, sir. It would not merely be unfortunate if an innocent man died in your care, but it would leave his unborn child without a father and a provider. My uncles have some very influential friends, and I think the town would find itself sued for the worth of every resident in it should it occur. I merely state that as a friendly reminder, Sheriff. Sometimes one tends to forget that a prisoner could conceivably be innocent.''

With that amazing speech Maria swept out. The two men stared at each other over the desk, and Joshua shrugged his bulky shoulders.

"Better get used to it. His mother and sister are here, too.''

The sheriff sighed and settled his pudgy body farther into the chair. "I reckon I will. There are a few ladies in town up in arms about it, too. Never wanted to arrest the lad in the first place, but there are bigger men than me involved.''

Joshua nodded and kept that information to himself. Maria would not appreciate knowing there were other women out there unhappy about Luke's being behind bars. If he knew his son, Maria was the only woman he wanted to see.

The circuit judge wasn't expected for months or longer, depending on the weather. The lawyer the Walkers hired from Abilene acquired additional assistance when another arrived from Santa Fe and a third rode in a week later from St. Louis, compliments of Maria's uncles.

Sean settled on the man from Santa Fe, and the two of them spent many nights conferring, drawing up mysterious lists that they would not explain to Maria. Strangers came and went from the impromptu office the lawyers had established in a back room of the hotel. Sean made no effort to introduce them to Maria, although she haunted the office whenever she was not with Luke.

Luke's jail cell began to take on the ambiance of home as the women brought in clean bedding and linens, his shaving gear and mirror, books, and even his guitar. This latter he took with gratitude as Maria presented it to him and their gazes met with understanding. Here was a communication they could use even when they were not together. Luke smiled and kissed her cheek before the sheriff ordered her out.

That night the empty streets filled with the haunting melody of a Spanish guitar, and Maria slept more soundly than she had in weeks.

The arrival of James B. Hume caught everyone by surprise. Stepping off the stage one cold morning, he quietly located the sheriff without assistance and announced himself without ceremony. The sheriff gazed up at the imposing six-foot-two gentleman calmly removing his gloves and bowler, and wondered who the hell he was, although he could easily guess who he wanted to see.

Luke leapt to his feet in welcome as the gentleman entered. Even with the door open the back room remained cold, and Luke had taken to wearing his sheepskin coat for warmth during the day. His gloves interfered with his guitar playing, so the hand he offered was bare as the stranger took it.

"Mr. Hume, this is an honor. I don't understand—"

The gentleman smiled as he set his hat and gloves aside and gestured for the sheriff to open the cell door. "Your wife's telegram was very succinct. I hope you will be able to introduce us."

"That shouldn't be difficult. She's due in to harass the sheriff any minute now." Luke bent a crooked eyebrow to his jailer. "You better start pretending you're installing that new stove, Bill. Maria has one hell of a temper. Don't let that dainty disguise fool you.''

Since he had already suffered more than one polite tongue-lashing from the lady concerned, the sheriff snorted in agreement and locked the newcomer in with the prisoner. If the lawman had his way, women would be barred from entering the jail at all, but his one attempt at that had resulted in Maria's battery of lawyers shoving papers down his throat until he choked. He was beginning to feel sorrier for himself than the prisoner.

Luke offered the cot to Mr. Hume and lounged in the corner with interest. He had already been over his case a thousand times with the lawyers and in his own mind, but he could find no escape. Without witnesses or alibis, neither side could prove anything but motive, and that was certainly against him.

"Your wife claims you are innocent, Walker. Do I have your word on that?'' His piercing eyes focused on the prisoner propped against the wooden wall.

"The only thing I remember much from that night was walking out on the two of them, and they were very much alive then,'' Luke replied, remembering the scene with bitterness. "I went out and got very, very drunk, slept until noon, handed in my resignation, and rode out the next day. It may have occurred to me to kill Dirk, but I've never beat a woman in my life. At the time I had some foolish notion Peg was carrying my child. I'd not have laid a hand on her, drunk or otherwise.''

Hume touched the tips of his fingers together and regarded Luke calmly. "Then I guess we'll have to start looking for someone who would.''

The meeting between Maria and Mr. Hume took place that night over dinner with the rest of the Walker family and Sean present. He greeted Sean affably, as one recognizes a confederate; his words to Luke's family were polite but essentially indifferent. His attention focused wholly on Maria.

No one had thought to mention the fact that the intrepid, mettlesome young wife of Cheyenne Walker was seven months pregnant. Neither had they warned Hume that instead of the strapping Amazon he had expected, she stood scarcely to his shoulder and weighed no more than a hummingbird. Not until he took her hand and met the directness of her gaze did he begin to understand the strength of character that gave her the attributes others assigned her.

"Mrs. Walker, I have promised to notify your uncle at once if he is needed here. I suspect had it not been for his concern for your health, he would be here now putting you on the first stagecoach out. What would you like me to tell him?"

Maria liked this expensively attired gentleman at once. He could have written Uncle Juan behind her back, sent him careening down here to carry her off, but he had the honesty to admit he had been asked to spy on her. She smiled irrepressibly and offered him the same forthrightness.

"Tell *Tío* Juan that I am healthy and happy with Luke's family, and that Luke and I will be out to visit him after the baby is born, one way or another."

The man who assured the safety of Wells Fargo gold shipments read the steady gleam in Maria's eye correctly. He had dealt with numbers of criminals and desperadoes of all sorts in his years as sheriff and as head of the Fargo security forces. He knew determination when he met it, and he did not misunderstand Maria's. She was not optimistically blocking out the possibility that her husband could very well hang before the child was born. She intended to do everything in her power to circumvent it, legal or otherwise.

"Sometimes it is easier to say these things than to do them, Mrs. Walker," he warned.

"I'm not unaware of that, Mr. Hume, but you don't really think I'd watch him hang without doing anything, do you?"

The shocked gasps as Luke's family finally grasped the point of this conversation indicated it had never occurred to them what this pint-sized hellion meant to do, and Mr. Hume smiled. Maria was as much a person of action as Luke. He could count on her. He raised his eyes to Sean's and nodded approvingly.

Sean escorted Maria to the jail that night. He waited for her in the sheriff's office while she went back to visit Luke. The sheriff was a lousy card player and his deputy was worse, but it was a way of passing time and occasionally learning something. The news that Dallas had taken a room in town halted his shuffle momentarily.

"What's he doing here?" Sean began to deal the cards, hiding his interest.

"Don't rightly know, but I suspect it's to watch a hanging. He ain't making no secret of his dislike for our friend in there."

"Got anybody with him?" Sean threw away most of his hand, making the sheriff feel expansive.

"Couple of cowpokes all I can see. Why? You got a stake in him, too?"

Sean shrugged. "He threatened Maria, and I have reason to believe he was behind that attack on Luke coming down here. He's not much fond of me either, but for some reason he's pretending I don't exist. Not a pleasant party to have around, if you get my meaning."

The sheriff shot a wad of tobacco at the cuspidor, then studied his cards. "Well, there ain't enough of me to go around. You do what you like with him. Just don't get caught breaking no laws."

That gave Sean small relief. He wasn't a gunfighter; he couldn't scare Dallas out of town. He would just have to start working that angle along with all the others. Maybe Dallas knew something that he could use.

His main concern was to keep Maria out of it. She had enough on her mind as it was. Let her argue over stoves and meals and bed linens. That would keep her occupied without endangering the child she carried. She and Luke deserved this time together without the very real threat of hanging filling their every waking moment. Let them think everything was under control while they could.

10

Sara and Sean remained behind with Maria at Christmas. Joshua and Letitia made a quick trip back to the ranch at Maria's insistence so the rest of the family could be together and Pedro could have a small celebration. Maria spent the Lord's birthday on her knees at church, praying for Luke's release.

Word had already come that the circuit judge would be in before the end of January. The weather held and other than an occasional icy wind, there seemed no reason for delay. Fear began to form in the pit of Maria's stomach as the date of the trial drew closer. She had hoped some incredible new evidence would spring to light and free Luke before the public display of a trial, but as the days turned into weeks, that no longer seemed likely.

Because of the growing bulk of her pregnancy, she kept to her room much of the time now when she was not with Luke. Luke tried not to appear worried and worked at keeping her spirits up when they were together, but she had found a few strands of gray in the darkening gold of his hair that had not been there before, and the weathered wrinkles around his eyes grew deeper with each day.

The others watched with concern as Maria picked at her food and withdrew more and more into herself as the month of January ticked away. Mr. Hume had spent only a few days here gathering information, and the lawyers weren't saying what they heard from his operatives. Without any knowledge of the way things stood, Maria had to assume the worst.

It was in this frame of mind that Maria ran into

Dallas again. He caught her elbow as she left the sheriff's office and steered her in the direction of the hotel. She had felt safe running back and forth across the street alone in the middle of the day, but she felt her helplessness now as even an old man with a limp could maneuver her at will. She did not carry a gun and her awkwardness made it difficult to break free and run on a street pocked with frozen puddles.

To her relief he set her in a chair in a corner of the lobby behind a display of yellowed newspapers and magazines. They could talk relatively unnoticed, but she could scream for help and be heard easily.

"Mr. Dallas, I don't believe we have anything to say to each other." Coldly gazing at the reptilian features of the wealthy rancher, Maria remained calm.

"That is a mistake, Mrs. Walker. Much as I would like to see your husband hang until his neck snaps, I have other interests to keep in mind. I have come bearing an offer that you will have to seriously consider."

Maria meshed her gloved hands together, pushing at the fingers nervously. She knew better than to talk to this man. He hated Luke and would do nothing to help him, but she was desperate enough to listen to any suggestion. Somehow Dallas must be responsible for Luke's arrest. Maybe someway, he could undo this travesty of justice.

"You had best speak quickly, Mr. Dallas. I am expected upstairs."

"What I propose is very simple. You have something I want, and I have something you want. I propose a fair exchange, your land for Luke's freedom. Are you prepared to listen?" His cunning eyes watched her closely.

Maria had tagged along too many times when her father had bargained with other ranchers to fall for this simple solution. She offered none of the enthusiasm he may have expected. "The land is not mine and Luke will be free as soon as the jury confirms his innocence. I see no room for bargaining here."

"No jury is going to find your husband innocent, Mrs. Walker, I can assure you of that. There are too many powerful men interested in seeing him hang. This is the only hope you have of letting him walk away alive. Give Luke my message and persuade him to sign the deed. He will be free the next night.''

Maria started to rise. ''You expect me to believe that? I think you mistake me for a simpleton, Mr. Dallas. Excuse me, but I must go.''

He caught her wrist and jerked her back down, his lips twisting furiously. ''You are not listening, Mrs. Walker. You have a choice. Your husband will die or he will not. Do not doubt my word. Unless you are in a hurry to be a widow, you had better listen carefully.''

Maria jerked her arm away but sat back down, her green eyes glittering furiously. ''If you think me fool enough to sign away my ranch in exchange for a promise, Mr. Dallas, be assured my husband is not, and it is his name that must appear on the document.''

''If that is all that concerns you, madam, we can arrange that to your satisfaction. Luke may sign the deed after he is free. If he does not, we will kill him or send him back.''

Maria's fist knotted as she tried to keep the poisonous barbs of his threats from penetrating. Life was so cheap out here. It would not be at all difficult to do what he said. They had already tried once. It was only by mere chance that they had not succeeded. What worried her was who ''they'' were. And she had more than a suspicion that she knew.

''It sounds very much as if you mean to free him by other than honest means, Mr. Dallas. I can do that without your help. That jail is as worthless as a tin can. The only reason Luke stays is to clear his name. He'll not agree to your terms.''

''I repeat, he has no choice, Mrs. Walker. The jury will convict him, or we will kill him. Even should you break him out yourself, it is only a matter of time until we find him. We want that deed signed. If he will not sign it, he will die. It is that simple.''

''I think I have heard quite enough.'' Unable to control her fury and fear any longer, Maria stood up and marched away. This time he did not stop her.

Maria slammed the door to her room and burst into tears. She could not bear the tension any longer. It was just a wretched piece of land, not worth anybody's life, and already it had cost the lives of two of her loved ones. She would willingly sign it over today had it been in her hands, but it was not.

That night when she went to visit Luke, he read the signs of distress in Maria's face easily enough. Her normally luminous eyes were tinged with red and shadowed by dark circles, and her face appeared drawn and wan beneath the jut of high cheekbones. She wore her hair loose, caught in a simple ribbon as if the effort of brushing it and putting it back up again was too much for her. His heart felt impaled on his rib cage as he reached for her through the bars, and he threw the sheriff an angry look.

"Open this damned cage and let her sit down, Bill. It's not as if I were going to run away."

The sheriff shrugged. "Rules don't allow females consorting with the men prisoners, you know that."

"Consorting! Hell and damnation, you mindless coyote, she's eight months pregnant! I just want her to sit down."

Maria clasped the bars that had separated her from Luke all these months and sent the sheriff a pleading look. Just to be close to Luke again would be heaven right now. The sheriff scowled but reached for his key.

Luke caught her hand as she entered. When the door slammed closed behind them, Maria fell into his waiting arms, burying her face against the hard strength of his shoulders. They heard the sheriff slam the connecting door as he went out, and Maria lifted her face eagerly to Luke's kiss.

The pressure of his arms around her back held her upright as his mouth drank hungrily, desperately at hers. With no bars between them they could touch and cling and absorb all the sensations that had been denied them these past months. Maria's fingers caressed Luke's hair, slid down his cheek to his collar, then rested at the place where she could feel his heart beat strongest. The strong pulse of life throbbing through his veins gave her immense pleasure, and determinedly she vowed to do whatever was necessary to keep it that way.

Luke finally helped her to the thin mattress of the cot and sat beside her, pulling her head down on his shoulder as he leaned against the unyielding wood of the cell wall. Maria relaxed in the warm hold of his arm, and her fingers described patterns on the muscular width of his thighs.

"I love you, Luke. I think I've loved you ever since that first kiss. Nobody had ever kissed me like that before."

Luke grinned and ruffled her hair with his hands. "Nobody ever saw you in that red dress before, either, I wager. If they had, they would have swept you off your feet long before I came along. A man would have to be a blamed fool to let an opportunity like that get by."

"You're not sorry? I mean, if you didn't have to marry me and if I hadn't gotten sick, you wouldn't be here. It's all my fault."

Luke's laugh was low and rang with irony. "That's an easy excuse, but I'll not accept it. I'm here because I didn't face up to this earlier. Don't blame yourself, *poquita*. I knew what I was doing, and I'm not sorry for a minute of the time we've been together. You're the best thing that could ever have happened to me. Now, are you going to tell me what you've been crying about?"

He caught her by surprise, again. She ought to be used to his perceptiveness by now, but no one had ever taken the time to notice her as Luke did. She sighed and leaned back against his shoulder, staring at the water stain on the far wall. She didn't have the words necessary to persuade Luke to sign that deed. Perhaps if she just asked him to sign it without asking questions . . .

Luke tilted her chin up with his finger. "Tell me, Maria."

It was no use. In the semi-darkness of this cell his eyes lost their gold, and the hard ridge of his jaw spoke of his determination. She brushed the unruly lock of hair back from his forehead, and told him everything Dallas had said.

When she was finished, Luke's mouth had straightened into a thin line, and his eyes were cold and angry. Maria shivered as he stood up and restlessly paced the narrow floor. She would sooner be in a cage with a wild tiger than Luke when he was like this. If she had been Dallas, she would have been ripped into shreds of bloody flesh by now.

Luke halted, caught her hands, and pulled her to her feet. His grip was strong and his words firm. "Tell him to go to hell, Maria, then stay away from him. I don't want you going anywhere without an escort. *Comprende?*"

Maria jerked her hands from his and glared at him. "Don't I get any consideration in this? I don't want the damned land, I want you. The land can't raise a child or warm my bed or stand by my side when I'm alone. Sign the confounded deed, Luke. It means nothing to me. My uncles will honor your signature, and we can find some other way for providing for Pedro."

Luke grabbed her shoulders and squeezed them tightly. "The trade isn't worth it. I'll not have you spending your life on the run with me, with no home, no security, never knowing when a bullet will separate us, where it will leave you. That's what he's asking. Let them kill me if that's what they want, but dammit all, Maria, you hang on to that land until you get a firm offer from the railroad directly. The land they want is worth enough to keep you secure for life without selling the house or the barns. You can keep the prime acres or sell them for a fortune when people start moving in with the tracks. There will be enough for both Pedro and our son to get a good education and make something of themselves. I'll not sell their futures, Maria."

"You are! You are selling their futures, Luke

Walker! Money won't buy them. They need *you*, and why you're so damn hardheaded and stubborn not to see it, I'll never know. I don't want the house or the barns or the damned money! I want you.'' She tried to rip off the necklace he had given her that long ago night, but the clasp wouldn't loosen, and she burst into tears with frustration.

She turned to the cell door and started to pound on it, but Sean was already there, his face a wreath of concern at the sounds emanating from this room. His glance first went to Luke, who stood aloof, his face a grim mask.

''Take her back and stay with her. I'm counting on you, Sean. Keep Dallas away from her.''

Maria swung around to berate him for his insufferable attitude, but the words wouldn't come. When the sheriff followed Sean in to unlock the cell, she fled without a look back.

Sean warned the others and after that, Dallas had no further opportunity to approach Maria. His baleful glare followed her through the lobby as she hurried past with Sara or Letitia during the day, Sean or Joshua in the evening. Even Matthew showed up as the date of the trial grew closer. After talking to Luke, he had a brief encounter with Dallas, and after that, Maria saw no more of the rancher.

Instead of feeling relief, she began to worry. Manuel must want that land desperately to buy a man like Dallas to help him. They had already tried to kill Luke once; they would not hesitate to do it again. Even if she told them the land could not be transferred without her uncles' signature, it would not help. With Luke out of the way, she would be the only obstacle in their path, and Manuel knew her uncles would sign anything if she requested it. That left them little choice. Their next move now would be to see Luke hang or kill him as soon as he walked away from the courtroom.

On the way back to the hotel one evening after visiting Luke, Maria caught Sean's arm and made him halt before entering the lobby.

"Sean, you've got to tell me. Do they have any evidence yet? Can they prove Luke innocent?"

Sean stared down into her pale face and searched for words. He had dreaded this moment for weeks, but he had never perfected a reply. "They can't prove anything, Maria, I'm sorry. We've got other evidence, other witnesses to say his wasn't the only motive, but no proof. It could go either way." Briefly he explained the evidence the lawyers and Hume's investigators had uncovered.

When he was finished, Maria gave a weary nod. "No wonder Manuel wants to see Luke hung. That would settle any further questions. If only there were some way we could prove him responsible—"

Sean shook his head. "What do you think we've been trying to do? He covered his trail too well. The only thing we can do is hope the jury will believe our story and not theirs."

Despair darkened her eyes as she looked up to Sean. "Even if they find Luke innocent, Manuel will have to kill him. Is there no way we can protect him?"

Sean touched her pale cheek. "Give us some credit, Maria. We know the gunmen Dallas brought with him. I know all of Manuel's men if they show up. There will be more guns in that courtroom than in the rest of the entire town. If they try anything, we'll be prepared."

Somehow the thought of all those guns in one room did not reassure Maria. The one who needed them would be Luke, and he would be unarmed and handcuffed.

That thought did not bear thinking, either, and she turned back to the lighted lobby. Two more nights of torment before the judge arrived.

11

The morning of the trial dawned bright and sunny and crystalline cold. The air snapped when breathed and burned all the way down.

Maria lowered the window in her hotel room and, shivering, held her hands out to the small grate that was the room's only source of heat. She had needed the sunshine to lift her spirits, but the cold chilled the flesh.

When she appeared in the lobby warmly wrapped in her brown cashmere pelisse trimmed with beaver fur, her matching bonnet securely tied beneath her chin, and gloves in hand, the Walker men turned to stare. Sean looked resigned and stepped forward as she approached.

"You can't go, Maria, you know that. It's much too dangerous, and it isn't the kind of place you ought to be. There will be drinking and rough men and things you shouldn't hear. Go back upstairs until we send for you."

Maria straightened her bonnet over her coronet of braids, then began pulling on her gloves. "The only way you're going to keep me out of there is to shoot me."

Joshua and Matthew had come up in time to catch these words, and they exchanged despairing glances. Luke had not said anything about keeping her out, but common sense dictated that the women stay home. The town had no courthouse beyond the main room of the saloon. It was no place for women at the best of times.

Maria gave them no time to disagree. She knew where the trial was to be held, and she did not need an escort to reach it. Gloves on, she headed for the door.

Short of physically hauling her back to her room and locking her in, the men had no choice but to follow. Maria in full battle regalia made them feel slovenly in comparison, but it had never occurred to them to drag out coats and ties to attend a murder trial. All three wore holsters beneath heavy sheepskin jackets. The appearance of the frail, hollow-eyed lady in the midst of the rough frontier crowd caused a sudden silence in the saloon. Ignoring the stares, Maria's gaze swept the smoky room. The stink of liquor and half-full cuspidors choked the air, but she had been around these smells all her life. Her gaze found Consuela over in the corner with the lawyers, and she lifted the corners of her mouth slightly in greeting. Luke would not appear until after the judge. She wanted to be where she could see him. It looked as if the table in front of the bar would be the judicial bench, and she turned her feet in that direction. A murmur began to rise up all around her as she made her way through the crowd.

The lawyers politely stood up as she approached, Consuela grabbed her hand and squeezed it in sympathy and encouragement, and Sean hauled an empty chair from the back to sit on the aisle before the bench. For Luke's protection Joshua and Matthew found seats elsewhere to keep an eye on the crowd. Of little use in a gunfight, Sean had been assigned another task, and it now included keeping an eye on the lady at his side. He ws grateful she had not recognized the guns he wore beneath his coat. Retrieved many months ago along with Maria's possessions, Luke's six-shooters weighed like a ton of lead upon his hips.

Unaware of Sean's unlikely weapons, Maria settled into the hard-backed chair provided and prepared to wait. With all the lawyers in between, she could not speak to Consuela, but Sean had told her why she was here. Much of Luke's hope for freedom hinged on Consuela's testimony. As Sean had told her, the chance was slim, but if effectively done, it could sway the thinking of the men on the jury.

Her glance turned to the table, where the lawyer pointed out the members of the jury. Several men garbed in loose sack coats and narrow ties she recognized as merchants in the town, and one or two gave her uneasy nods of recognition. Several young boys in their best chambray workshirts and denims and high-heeled boots lounged uncomfortably with glasses of whiskey in front of them, pulled in off the ranches to do their civic duty in their fathers' places, presumably. Several trail-weathered cowboys numbered among the jury's ranks, and it was in these that Maria placed her hopes. They would know Luke, would know the kind of man he was, and they would not believe the lies any of the opposition raised.

There was bound to be some kind of opposition. Maria's gaze traveled in search of Dallas, figuring that would be where it came from. If the prosecution were left to the sheriff, the case would be cut-and-dried. Dallas had been too sure of himself for this to be the case. He must have bought witnesses or something to ensure a guilty verdict.

The child in her womb seemed to sink deeper as Maria found Dallas and his companions—Manuel and Señor Vasquero. She did not recognize the other man with them, but all four met her look with hostile eyes and she shivered. Señor Vasquero never lost. She didn't know how his influence could reach here, but the elegantly dressed man at his side might be part of the answer. She turned questioningly to Sean.

He had followed her gaze and understood the inquiry in her eyes. After conferring with the lawyers, he turned back to Maria. "He's a Santa Fe lawyer, one of Catron's men. He comes from these parts."

Since Thomas Benton Catron ran the powerful First National Bank of Santa Fe and was called boss of the Santa Fe Ring, Maria glanced nervously back to the dapper gentleman between Manuel and his father. Other than that first glance, he appeared not to know she existed, and tension knotted steel bands around her belly. If what Luke said about these men buying up the land between El Moro and Santa Fe were true, they had a vested interest in her ranch.

A stir in the back of the room indicated the judge had entered, and she turned back to face the bench. The hard chair made her back hurt already, but she scarcely noticed the ache as she watched the man who held life and death over Luke.

She found no hope in the rheumy eyes of the gray-bearded judge. Like many another lawman before him, he had been chosen for his imposing appearance and most likely his ability to speak assertively. He might even be able to read, since he carried a thick, leather-bound book with him, but Maria wasn't deceived by appearances. When he sat down and ordered a drink, she knew their hopes of a rational trial were small indeed.

They brought Luke in last. Maria bit back a cry of indignation at the ropes tied about his wrists. He strode in with the easy assurance of an innocent man, his gaze sweeping the room for friends and allies. He did not see Maria in the front row until the sheriff pushed him down into a straight-backed chair facing the spectators. His hands jerked automatically against the confinement of his bonds, and his face tightened with anger at her presence, but then his expression grew blank again, forced into line by his monumental self-control.

A murmur went around the room, and Maria could feel the gazes of many eyes on her back, but she sat proudly erect, facing the front without flinching. Luke was her husband and she belonged by his side. Let petty minds condemn her as they would. Just her appearance dared them to find him guilty.

The trial began without ceremony. The judge gulped his whiskey and pointed at the sheriff. "State your case, Bill."

The lawman's halting speech imparted nothing new, and the courtroom buzzed with dozens of bored conversations. Luke's lawyers stood up to present their side of the case, and Maria's heart beat faster as the jury began to take interest. They appeared impressed by the lawyers' erudite speeches and the series of character witnesses produced to establish Luke as a man of integrity, and Maria noted several of the cowboys nodding in agreement.

Luke refused to look in her direction, and Maria took Sean's hand for comfort as the lawyer stood to introduce the next witness. From the lead-in she knew this one would be Consuela, and she closed her eyes and prayed.

Just as Consuela rose to stand before the bar, a loud voice yelled in objection from the far side of the room. Maria felt an aching pain tearing through her middle as the Vasquero's lawyer refused to allow Consuela to come forth. This, then, was what they had planned. Consuela was their most important witness. It had taken time and money and much persuasion to bring her here. They could not deny her testimony now.

But they did. The judge took one look at Consuela's vivid beauty, and even disguised behind a respectable woolen gown of dove gray she fit the role the Vasquero lawyer condemned her to. The judge grinned and winked at Consuela's flushed, irate features and smacked his book against the bar.

"Only the testimony of respectable witnesses will be allowed in this court. Bring out your next one, boys."

The bottom fell out of their case after that. Pain washed over Maria as she watched Luke's unfathomable features while witness after witness stepped forth to prove that he and the dead man were in the same place at the same time, that angry words were exchanged, the the dead woman was Luke's mistress, and that the gambler and Luke's mistress were also lovers. Where the sheriff failed to make condemning points, the Vasquero's lawyers supplied the lack.

Maria refused to cry. She stared boldly at every witness who came forward. Some twitched and squirmed and looked nervously to Luke's cold features, others cut short their testimony and hurried out. Several men of the jury began to watch Maria with speculation and sympathy, and much of the crowd began to murmur in

ow undercurrents. Hands rested on ill-concealed guns
n several corners of the room, but the trial dragged
on.

By afternoon the crowd was worse for drink and
cries of "Lynch him!" erupted occasionally from the
back of the room. The jury looked hungry and bored,
and the judge had given up on the nicety of a glass
and swigged openly from the whiskey bottle. Maria
clung desperately to Sean's hand, but she refused to
leave the room, hoping some semblance of respectability would be maintained as long as she was here.

Not that it mattered a great deal in the end. Both
sides concluded their cases hastily under the growing
pressure of restless anger in the saloon. The audience
was tired of talk and ready for action, and even Luke's
city lawyers knew better than to speak at length.

The judge didn't give the jury much time to argue
among themselves. He rapped his book against the table and asked for a show of hands. Out of the nine
jurors they had rounded up, five lifted their hands for
the verdict of guilty.

Maria bit her tongue to keep from crying out and
turned terrified eyes to the soberly garbed lawyers beside her. Surely they could not hang Luke on such
little evidence and with little more than half the jury
believing him guilty? That could not be possible. That
made no sense. The entire proceedings had been a
shambles from first to last. Surely they could do something.

They tried. They raised their hands to object. They
shouted over the uproar for an appeal. They shoved
through the crowd to confront the judge verbally and
physically, but their logic died in the tumult.

Sean grabbed Maria and began to push her through
the crowd to the relative safety of a space along the
wall. Luke was lost in the throng of men near the
bench and bar. There was no way to get his guns to
him and little point. Even if his hands had not been
tied, he could not shoot his way out of a mob like this.
The guns would have served as self-protection had the
jury declared him innocent and Dallas tried to kill

him, but no one could help him now. Even Matthew and Joshua looked helpless as they tried to reach Luke before the sheriff led him out.

As cries of "Lynch him! Lynch him!" grew louder, Maria's face paled and she turned to grasp Sean's arm.

"They cannot mean to hang him now, can they?" Frantic, she searched his face for truth and found it in the nervous evasion of Sean's gaze. Her eyes followed his, and she swayed under the sight of a noose being swung in someone's hand. the moan that escaped her clenched lips could scarcely be heard above the uproar.

There would be no time to plan an escape, no delay while a gallows was built. Dallas and his men had seen to that. She should have foreseen it. She should have known they would not give the opportunity for escape when escape would be so easy. It was one of his men swinging that noose. She did not have to identify the others to know they led the shouts.

The judge didn't appear particularly interested in the how and where of the hanging. He staggered to his feet and wandered back to the bar for another bottle while the sheriff struggled to hang on to his prisoner. Too small to see any of this, Maria could only read it in the turmoil around her and in the grim line of Sean's lips.

"We've got to do something!" Maria shouted, pushing away from his hold and glancing frantically around.

"I could empty these guns into the crowd and it wouldn't do any more than get both of us killed. We've got to get you out of here." Sean tried to push her toward the wall and escape, but she resisted.

"Guns! You've got guns?" Maria's glance fell on the pistol handles nearly hidden by his heavy coat and her eyes lit with a fiery gleam that had no relation to joy.

"Give me a gun, Sean." She reached her small hand beneath the heavy weight of his sheepskin coat before he caught her wrist.

"Don't be foolish, Maria. You can do nothing with one gun in all this crowd."

Her eyes cold and hard as the gems they resembled, Maria shook off his grip defiantly. "Where will they take him?"

By this time Sean had maneuvered her to the empty space along the wall, and he could see Joshua shoving through the crowd to join them. Luke had to be in the center of the swirling crowd moving toward the front door, but Sean could only catch glimpses of disheveled tawny hair and the sheriff's furious features. The noose was being held high and preceding them out the door.

"The hanging tree, south of town. They built a platform under it when they wanted to hang a gang of rustlers in a hurry. It's still there, I reckon."

"Take me there. There must be another door in this place. We've got to get there before the crowd." No longer frantic, Maria's brain worked thoroughly and efficiently, searching for the only way out. She would not let Luke die for a piece of land.

"Maria, I'm not going to take you out there!" Horrified, Sean clutched her arm to prevent her from escaping.

"Then don't!" Curtly Maria turned to her father-in-law as he approached. "I want a rifle and I want to be taken to the hanging tree. I'll do it with or without you. Which will it be?"

Joshua and Sean exchanged glances over her head. Although garbed in the buttons and bows of a lady, Maria spoke like her father, and the same stubborn fury shone in her eyes. The fact that she was eight months pregnant and pale as a ghost hindered their decision.

Taking their silence for an answer, Maria shoved from their company and began easing along the wall to the back of the saloon. Some eager drunk had left his shotgun lying under the table and Maria's sharp eyes spotted it at once. This part of the saloon had nearly emptied out and she had no difficulty reaching the table, although stooping to retrieve the gun was another problem.

When she stood up, Sean and Joshua were beside
her. Their faces wore grim masks, but they didn't pull
the gun from her hands. When Maria ignored them
and continued making her way to the back of the saloon, they followed, one on each side, keeping spectators and curiosity seekers from getting too close.

Maria could hear the cries of the crowd as she found
the door she sought leading to the alley behind the
saloon. No sounds of a hammer and anvil echoed from
the blacksmith's on the other side of the alley. Everyone had apparently joined the lynching party in the
town's main street.

Without exchanging another word, the trio hurried
down the garbage-strewn back street. The smell of
cooking cabbage clogged the air as they approached
the residential end of town, but that was better than
the stench of the manure pile behind the livery or the
foul odor of sulfur behind the pill-pushing chemist's.
Maria felt her stomach wrench spasmodically, but she
did not have time to be ill.

Shotgun in hand, she nearly ran all the way. Her
side hurt and back ached and her breath came in short
pants, but nothing would stop her. The Vasqueros had
taken her father and Pieta. They could not have Luke.

The hanging tree was a broad, spreading oak that
would provide ample shade in the summer but appeared barren and ghostly in the midst of winter. A
crowd already milled under it in anticipation as the
barroom mob trampled through the street in their direction. Men on horses sat chewing tobacco and swig-
ging from flasks on the edge of the crowd while women
and children and unmounted men mingled in holiday
atmosphere around the weathered boards of the platform.

Maria refused to look at the hollow rectangle in the
platform underneath the low branches of the tree. She
knew how men were hanged, although she had never
heard the creak and thump of the trapdoor opening
beneath a condemned man's feet. Nor would she this
time. She would shoot Luke before she allowed him

to die such an ignominious death, but she would take a lot of other people with him.

As they grew closer to the actual faces in the crowd, Maria began to distinguish some who seemed more distressed than happy about the occasion. They were few and far between, but they were there. Luke's friends hadn't deserted him entirely; they were just outnumbered by the bloodthirsty sadists who knew nothing of Luke but enjoyed a hanging. Maria dismissed these latter as cowards who would not interfere no matter what happened.

As she and her stalwart bodyguards worked their way toward the platform, heads turned and whispers mounted. Curiosity made them stare, but no one stopped them.

Reaching a slight rise in the ground behind the platform, they could see two feminine figures racing down the hotel steps in the direction of the crowd. Maria could also see Luke now. They had thrown the noose around his neck and were parading him like a prize steer down the street, but she could not allow herself to be distracted by the overwhelming pain that brought. Instead she sought other targets and found them.

"There. That is Manuel and that is his father. You already know Dallas. Those are the ones we want. I want Manuel. Do what you want with the others." Maria pointed out her victims to her father-in-law, who gave her an appraising glance but nodded shrewdly.

Knowing more of this vendetta than Joshua, Sean picked his target without quibbling. If he had to hang, he couldn't do it in better company.

Maria allowed herself to breathe easier when she found the one other face she sought. Consuela's shrewd eyes had already found her, and she was working her way up to the platform, her eyes fastened intently on the gun in Maria's hands and a smile spreading across her full lips.

The shouting, drunken men approaching did not notice the three shadowy figures lingering behind the platform. People were everywhere; three more did not

stand out in the crowd unless someone was looking
for them, and foolishly, they weren't.

Not even Luke looked up as they shoved him toward
the stairs of the platform. Maria's hands clutched the
shotgun fiercely as another spasm of pain rocked
through her. She could not bear to look at the tight,
grim lines of Luke's jaw or the hard, cold glitter of his
eyes as he found his footing on the steps and arro-
gantly strode upward. The pain he suffered hurt as
great as her own, and the combination nearly bent her
in two.

The Vasqueros and Dallas remained on the ground
near the platform but in the background while their
drunken cohorts swarmed around Luke and the sheriff. At the top of the stairs the sheriff finally blocked
their passage with his girth and his rifle, allowing only
his deputy to pass with the noose and the condemned
man.

That was the moment Maria had been waiting for.
The rear of the platform was too high for her to climb,
but Sean and Joshua lifted her up without difficulty.
Intent upon the condemned man with the noose around
his neck and the deputy attempting to swing the rope
over a branch, few people in the crowd noticed the
addition to the performers on the stage. Not until
Joshua and Sean's large forms pulled themselves onto
the boards did tongues begin to wag and fingers point.

By that time it was too late. Maria had her shotgun
aimed at Manuel's heart and both Joshua and Sean
held six-shooters in their hands. The sheriff turned
around to stare at them in disbelief.

"My God, woman, have you gone loco? Get down
from there!"

Maria didn't take her eye off Manuel as she responded coolly. "I'll get down when the trial's finished, Sheriff. Try to remove me before then and three
men die."

12

The targets they had chosen began to edge uneasily toward the back of the crowd. Maria held out her hand to Sean, who slapped one of Luke's pair of Colts in her palm. The shotgun had only two barrels, but the Colts had bullets to spare. With her mouth pulled in the tight line that warned all who knew her to beware, Maria aimed the revolver and pulled the trigger.

Manuel yelped and slapped a hand over the burning hole in his coat sleeve, and people around him jumped as the bullet spit into the ground. Maria politely returned the weapon to Sean.

"That was just a warning. Stay right where you are, *señors,* or the next bullets will go through your evil hearts."

Cries of "Lynch him" again rang out from the back of the crowd, but the sight of a pregnant lady wielding a shotgun had captured the spectators' interest. The mob quieted to murmurs of speculation.

The sheriff still held his rifle and regarded the trio cautiously. "You can't get away with this, you know. He's been found guilty in a court of law. You can't run anywhere that I won't catch you."

"I don't aim to run, Sheriff. I just want the whole story told. You and your judge and jury have been railroaded." Refusing to look at Luke, Maria scanned the crowd until she found Consuela again and gestured for her to come up.

Hands tied behind his back and with his neck in a noose, Luke had no power to stop this demonstration. He stared out over the heads of the crowd while his fingers worked at his bonds. His gaze fell on his

brother standing protectively next to Sara and his
mother, and he cursed to himself that none of them
tried to stop Maria. He knew why Sean was up here
with her, but he couldn't believe his father had fallen
under the witch's spell. With furious determination he
continued to work on the bonds that had defied him
throughout the day.

Whistles and hoots followed Consuela up the stairs,
but no one made any attempt to interfere with her
progress. Although Dallas and the Vasqueros were
livid with rage, they did not dare signal their men to
put an end to this farce, not while three guns pointed
at their heads.

"Gentlemen of the jury," Maria found the men
whose faces she had memorized this day, "there is one
last witness you must hear before you can give a true
verdict. Consuela makes a living in the only manner
men allow her, but this does not make her any less of
a witness, not when we're dealing with the kind of
people that Peg Owens and Dirk Jones were. Consuela, tell these good people where you met Peg."

Luke had to admit that Maria handled it better than
he had expected. He had fully anticipated a fiery
speech laced with curses and threats, but other than
referring to Consuela's profession, she had remained
composed and almost ladylike. He guessed that he was
the only one who understood the control she exerted
to keep her hand steady, and his hands worked frantically at the loosening ropes as Consuela began to
speak.

"Peg Owens was a friend of mine, of sorts. She had
her own room above the saloon in San Pedro and a
rich boyfriend who bought her fancy gowns. She told
me she had gone to a mission school in Albuquerque
until her father died, and then Señor Vasquero asked
her to come back to San Pedro with him."

None of this meant anything to the crowd. They did
not know the Vasqueros or San Pedro, although several began to glance toward the handsome Spaniard
clutching his upper arm. The mask of fury on his face
served to start whispers of speculation.

''Peg liked pretty things. When the *patron* bought her a new gown and asked her to dine with his son, she agreed. When the son raped her right there in her new room, she did not go to the sheriff when the *patron* gave her gold to keep quiet.''

The crowd gasped and several of the women covered their ears or made gestures at running away from this obscene story, but fascination didn't let them go far. Consuela was an excellent storyteller once she decided to speak, and her eyes flashed with satisfaction at the effect she was having on her audience.

''Peg told me all this later. She found me on the street and brought me to her room and loaned me one of her dresses and introduced me to this *patron's* son. I did not understand why she would do this, and I did not understand for some time. The *patron's* son scarcely looked at me when Peg was around, and he always ordered me to leave after he arrived. Afterward, when he was gone and I returned to Peg, I would find her crying, and her nose was often bloody or her eyes blackened. I asked her why she did not leave, but she said she could not, he would come after her and kill her.''

Maria watched in satisfaction as Manuel's face darkened with fury. Consuela was endangering her life by standing up here and exposing his perfidies to the world, but he was helpless as long as Maria held a gun on him. He knew her aim and her temper too well.

''One day this Dirk Jones came to San Pedro. He talked fast and sweet and stayed for many weeks. I was his lover first and Peg was jealous, but when she was not with her boyfriend, she entertained Dirk in her room. When Dirk left, she left with him.''

Consuela's gaze shifted to stare directly at Manuel, and necks craned throughout the crowd to find the object of her wrath.

''It was then that the *patron's* son came to me. He beat me, trying to force me to tell where Peg had gone. He raped me, many times, all the time calling me Peg and swearing vengeance. This went on for many weeks. I could not escape. I had no money and nowhere to go and after Peg left, he placed guards in the saloon. Every time he came to me he would tell me what he would do to Peg when he found her. When he finally heard about Dirk, he went crazy. That night I learned he had men out searching for them. I wished to hell he had found them because he nearly broke half my ribs in his rage.''

The murmurs in the crowd grew to a low rumble as the spectators began to understand the direction this story took. From the corner of her eye Maria noted several respectably dressed ranchers pushing to the front of the crowd with their hands near their guns and their eyes on Luke and Manuel. The men she associated with Dallas were growing less vehement in their drunken cries for lynching, and the few who had come forward with ugly looks on their faces now retreated slowly. Consuela's story roused both the forces of good and evil, and a confrontation seemed imminent.

Consuela took an unconscious step in Luke's direction, putting herself between Luke and Manuel. ''All this happened many years ago. I was young and afraid. One spring this man, this *patron's* son came to me with an evil grin and said he had found them, he had found Peg, and he was going to fetch her. I was happy for me, but frightened for Peg. He is a large man and even a slap from his hand can knock a woman down.

''He was gone several weeks. When he came back, he did not bring Peg. I asked if he found her and he said he had, that he had gotten even with her and her new boyfriend, and he never wanted to hear their names again. And so I heard nothing of them again until a gentleman by the name of Mr. Hume came to me last month and told me Dirk Jones and Peg Owens were dead, that they had died that same spring when Manuel Vasquero told me never to mention their names again.''

Had Consuela practiced this speech for weeks, she could not have improved the response. Señor Vasquero seemed to explode from within, his leathered face falling into drawn wrinkles as his hand clutched at his chest. The vaqueros around him caught him before he fell, and they led him away, leaving Manuel to fend for himself.

Manuel grabbed for his gun and several of Dallas's men reached for theirs, but Luke's friends had already gathered in a ring in front of the platform. Manuel faced not only Maria's powerful shotgun, but the fury of men brought up to think of women as precious and fragile commodities not to be treated lightly. Consuela and Peg might have been whores, but they were first and foremost women. Men who beat women and then framed another man for their misdeeds did not live long in this environment.

Already the cries of the crowd began to roar for blood, Manuel's blood if not Luke's. The men who had been shouting "String him up!" of Luke had slunk away, but new voices took up the refrain.

Maria smiled triumphantly as she faced every member of the jury present. "Well, gentleman, would you care to vote again on the verdict?"

One of the merchants tugged nervously at his galluses and glanced at the sheriff while the crowd surged forward impatiently. "Bill, we can't do that, can we? Can we do this damned thing over?"

"If you hang Luke Walker now, hell, we'll hang that Mexican varmint over there and you with him, Bill Jackson! Get Luke down from there!"

Maria heard this bellow and the roar of other angry voices through a haze of pain. It was getting more and more difficult to stand upright, and her knuckles turned white as she clenched the shotgun. The roar of the crowd seemed to recede to a distance, and she could no longer focus on Manuel. She had to get to Luke, free his hands, but when she made a step in that direction, pain wrenched through her like all the brands in hell and she stumbled forward with a cry.

She didn't hear Sean's shouts or her father-in-law's running footsteps. The only thing she sensed as blackness closed in around her was Luke's hard arms beneath her and his warm curses blowing in her ear.

The sheriff had started forward when Luke broke free, but he halted as Maria collapsed in his arms. At the fiercely protective look on Luke's face he nodded, ''Take her back to the hotel, but remember you're still my prisoner.''

''I'll not be running while my child is being born,'' Luke replied scornfully. Already he could see his mother and Sara running toward the hotel to gather the necessities for a premature birth. His arms closed tighter around his precious burden as he walked down the steps he thought never to touch again. He could feel the wetness of Maria's gown against his arm, and he clenched his teeth against the panic rising up in him. He knew that wetness was blood, and he knew it was too soon. Tears misted his eyes as he nearly ran down the street after the women.

Even in the midst of uproar, the crowd parted to let the outlaw and his lady through before turning their furious attentions to the stranger in their midst. Cries of ''Hang him!'' continued to fill the air as Luke escaped, but their anger had found a different focus.

Matthew poured a tumbler full of whiskey and passed it to Luke to stop his pacing. The small parlor they had appropriated off the hotel's main lobby was not large enough to accommodate all that pent-up energy and emotion. It was akin to being caught in a cave with a wounded cougar, and he did not relish spending the evening in that manner. Maybe some good Kentucky bourbon would slow him down.

Luke took the tumbler and gulped the liquor as if it were water. Both Sean and Matthew stared at him in amazement, watching his gulps and waiting for him to fall flat on his face. When he only sat the glass aside to begin stalking up and down the threadbare carpet again, they both reached for their own drinks.

Joshua hurried in and all three men turned expectantly, but he merely shook his shaggy head. ''Nothing. They won't tell me nothing.''

Sean looked gray as another faint wail drifted from the rooms above, and Luke resumed pacing. Matthew refilled his own glass.

''Caroline would be screaming like a gut-shot coyote by now," he muttered to no one in particular. "I think I'll see how the weather is in 'Frisco when her time comes."

His father shot him a less than sympathetic glance. "Your mother went through hell delivering you. I almost swore off having babies after that."

Sean beamed an inebriated grin as he glanced toward Luke's pacing figure. "You should have stuck to your word, Josh. It would have saved us all a heap of trouble."

Luke swung around and pinned the Irishman to his chair with a glance. "You'd like that, wouldn't you? Then you'd have one more female to add to your harem. I ought to bust your bloody nose for you, but Sara would have my hide for hurting your pretty face."

That turned the tide from the anguished cries above, and with relief Matthew joined the fray. "He's right, you bastard. How much longer do you think you can dally after Sara without stating your intentions? We should have had you hog-tied and whipped and rode out on a rail a long time ago. When are you going to ask her?"

Sean looked frantically from Luke to Matthew to Joshua's stern expression and reached for his glass. Taking a reviving gulp, he appealed to Luke. "Tell them I'd make a lousy husband. Sara's too good for the likes of me. She wouldn't have me. I can't shoot, I hate cattle, I don't have any occupation she approves of."

Luke grunted implacably. "You got the first two right, but the rest is a lot of bull. Sara would take you if you were a bartender in the saloon. Why in hell don't you tell her you're rich as Diamond Jim and don't need no damn occupation?"

This statement dropped like a cannon shell in their midst, bringing Matthew upright and Joshua to stare at his younger son with a quizzically lifted eyebrow.

"When would the no-good son of a wild turkey get that kind of cash? Rob a bank?" Matthew reached for the bottle again. His dark hair fell in disheveled tangles across his brow much as Luke's did, and the whiskey brought a flush of heat to his weathered face.

"No, a gold mine. The bastard owns a piece of a gold mine. He doesn't work it, mind you," Luke sent his friend's slumped shoulders a disdainful glare. "He just collects a percentage of what they find in it. And even if they're cheating him blind, he's got enough to pave a pathway to heaven if he had a mind to. If he had a mind."

Sean seemed to take no offense at this slur on his character, but merely tipped back the remainder of his drink. Joshua settled his large frame in the sturdy chair by the stove and regarded his younger son speculatively.

"Are you on his payroll or is he on yours?"

Luke almost grinned at his father's perceptiveness, but the sound of Maria's scream from above turned his face ashen and he reached a trembling hand for another glass of whiskey, leaving Sean to answer for him.

"We share in the proceeds. They don't dare cheat Cheyenne Walker. He goes out there every once in a while and gives them that icy glare of his, and money comes rolling in for months afterward." Sean hiccuped and covered in his mouth in surprise. "Damn," he whispered under his breath and moved to set his glass aside until another scream echoed from overhead. He took the nearly empty bottle from Luke's hand.

Luke started for the door, but Joshua caught his arm and held him back with a warning look. "You can't help her now. Be patient."

Matthew in his besotted condition was more interested in the gold mine. "So that's how you two layabouts get by. Couldn't you at least indulge yourself in a new suit of clothes once in a while?" He sent Luke a suspicious glance. "And why does Maria keep worrying about having to sell those gewgaws you gave her to get you out of jail? Hell, with a piece of a gold mine, you could have bought the damn jail."

Luke didn't reply. It was possible he didn't even hear. This scream seemed to echo on forever, reverberating inside his head until it came to an abrupt halt and a deadly silence. No one tried to interfere as he dashed for the stairs.

The doctor stopped him at the door. Helplessly Luke stared over his shoulder, unable to glimpse Maria through the phalanx of women around the bed. The faint wails of an infant came from a far corner of the room, and he staggered slightly as the doctor shoved him back into the hall, stepped out, and closed the door on the occupants.

Luke caught himself and, clenching his fists, met the doctor's calm gaze with mixed panic and fury. "How is she?"

"Very brave. That son of yours could have killed her." The doctor studied the notorious gunman's face at these words. He didn't know Luke, had only heard the tales, and he judged him by his reaction now.

The liquor on his breath was unmistakable, but Luke held himself with remarkable steadiness at these words. An expression of pain briefly flickered behind his eyes, but he met the doctor's eyes without flinching. "I want to see them."

"Your wife's asleep and cannot be disturbed. Someone will bring the child out in a minute. I wanted to talk to you first."

Luke felt the fear rising in him. He glanced frantically at the door behind this bespectacled elderly gentleman, gauging the need to see Maria against his desire not to harm her. He just wanted to see that she was alive and well, that no one would take her from him, but the presence and finality of death kept peering over this man's shoulder.

"What is it? Why can't I see her?"

"She is much weakened by the struggle to bear your child. She needs complete rest." The doctor waited for Luke's full attention. What he was about to tell the virile young man would not be received lightly, he knew, but for the sake of the young lady, he would have it heard clearly.

When Luke's gaze veered back to him, the doctor finished. "You have a son. If you want to keep your wife, it would be better if there are no further children. Perhaps in a few years, if she is stronger, but not before then and maybe not even then. Do you understand what I'm telling you?"

Luke stared blankly at the white-haired gentleman telling him he would never share Maria's bed again. He had thought never to see her again, thought all of life lost to him, but Maria had given him this chance to see his son. To know she would live was more hope than he deserved, and Luke's eyes glazed with relief.

"I understand. I just want to know she will be all right."

The doctor could scarcely believe his ears, but he nodded hastily and stepped out of the way as the sound of crying came closer and the bedroom door opened. Luke appeared satisfied with this mute reassurance and turned eagerly to watch as his mother came out bearing the squalling bundle of blankets that was his son.

Letitia studied her younger son's face as he reached for his child. The past months has marked him. His smile did not appear as he lifted the bundle from her arms, and his eyes had a haunted, faraway look that nearly broke her heart. There were new lines etched about his mouth and a sprinkling of gray among the tawny colors of his sideburns, but the gentleness of his expression as he pushed back the blankets with his finger made her weep. He was a changed man perhaps, but not all of it was for the worse.

"Michael. We will call him Michael Connolly Walker. I think Irish would be proud of him." Luke touched his finger to the button nose, and the squirming babe seemed to quiet to study the sensation. The hank of fluffy hair brushed over his bald skull was dark, not so black as Maria's but a mahogany somewhere between his own and hers. Irish-colored, and Luke grinned at last.

The sound of footsteps on the stairs turned all eyes in that direction, and the sheriff reddened and removed his hat as he realized what he interrupted.

"Sorry, ma'am." He nodded at Letitia and glanced toward Luke. "A boy?"

"My son, Sheriff." Luke continued holding the child, reluctant to part with him even though he knew what followed. The sheriff caught his eye and looked away.

"There's a few things that gotta be cleared up before I can let you go, Cheyenne. You know how it is."

Letitia gave a little cry of anguish, but the doctor caught her shoulders for support. Silently she took the infant as Luke handed him over, but her eyes were wide with concern as she searched her son's face.

Without a word Luke turned toward the stairs, followed by the sheriff and his gun.

Luke stood up as the sheriff let Sean into the cell. "How is she?"

"Awake and asking after you." Sean watched to make certain the sheriff closed the connecting door. He turned back to Luke. "You know they're asking for a new trial."

Luke nodded, his eyes hard as he judged his friend's tone of voice. "Consuela is safe?"

"Consuela is on her way to St. Louis, where Maria's Uncle Patrick can figure out what to do with her. Her life isn't worth a plugged nickel out here anymore. Neither is yours."

Luke waited. There was no point in stating the obvious. While Manuel was loose and Luke behind bars, the advantage was clear.

"The women have been walking up and down outside with signs calling the sheriff and the judge some pretty rough names and demanding your release. They're a mite upset."

"Who? The women or Bill?" Luke sat down again, resting his head against the wall and sprawling his legs across the cot.

"Both. I told Sara it was the most unladylike thing I every heard of and I was glad she wasn't down there."

"And she went right down and joined them." Luke chomped down on a toothpick left from supper and didn't look at Sean. Sean was stalling for time, but he'd find out what he wanted to say sooner or later. "When are you going to marry that girl?"

Sean shrugged uneasily. "When she will have me. I thought it was all settled last night. She was all weepy-eyed over the baby and hugging me for standing up there beside you like a damn fool and well . . . I thought we came to an understanding.

Luke threw him a suspicious look. "You mean you finally persuaded her to kiss you and she allowed it and then some, and then you got so damn confident you didn't think it was necessary to ask. Now she's out there marching up and down with those other women and not speaking to you. I thought you knew better than that."

Sean ran his hand through his hair in embarrassment. "I didn't think Sara was like that. I just thought she'd understand."

Luke sighed and stared at the rough boards of his cell. "She understands, but she's going to make you jump through the hoop anyway. Are you going to do it before or after I break out of here? I'd kind of like to see things settled before I leave."

Startled by Luke's leaping to the subject he had tried to avoid, Sean stared at him. "I didn't think you would go. The sheriff would be glad to see the back of you. The women got the men all riled up and they're starting to talk election and that drunken judge has already left town."

"Kind of figured he was that kind. I'm going. I'm not doing Maria any good here and I'm tired of letting Manuel call the shots. What are you doing to do about Sara? I'd feel better if I knew you were settling down here and would be around to give Maria a hand if she needs it."

Torn between loyalty to Luke and love for Sara, Sean hesitated. "I've got your guns and your horse. It's just a matter of pulling down that back wall and persuading Bill to turn his back. Where are you going?"

"Does it matter?" Luke's steely gaze remained fiercely on the wall. "If I tell you, Maria will pry it out of you. I won't have her following. She's to stay here, where it's safe. Promise me that?" He turned and glared at Sean.

"She won't like it. I'll have to lie," Sean warned.

"Tell her whatever you need to, just keep her here.

Maybe someday I'll straighten this mess out. And don't let her sell the damned land. That's Pedro's.''

Sean muttered a string of curses that came strangely from his polished tongue. When he was finished venting his ire, he glared at Luke. "I'll pretend I'm you, hit Sara over the head and force her to marry me, then woo your lovely lady into complacency with your charm and wit. It should be a cinch. Are you ready to go?''

Luke turned his head to meet Sean's gaze. "Thanks, *compadre*. I owe you one.''

Sean cursed again and called for the sheriff.

Maria took the news of Luke's escape with remarkable aplomb. Holding her sleeping son close, she lifted her eyes to Letitia. "Is Sean with him?''

"No, dear, he swears he knows nothing about it. He's with the sheriff now.'' Worriedly Letitia straightened the covers.

Maria frowned slightly at this news, then remembering Sara, she smiled. "Of course. Are they sending out a posse?''

"I don't think so. I haven't heard talk of one. Josh is down there now trying to find out what's happening.''

"And Manuel? Have they locked him up anywhere?'' Maria touched her son's cheek. The jaw was Luke's. She couldn't wait to see what color his eyes would be.

"No, he's gone. His father died last night without seeing him again, the poor old man.''

Maria scoffed. "Manuel did just what his father would have done. They were two of a kind, only Manuel wasn't quite as discreet. Luke will catch him.''

That startled Letitia, but she said nothing further. Perhaps Maria knew something she didn't, but it would be better not to know. She desperately wanted to know Luke was safe, and if Maria wasn't worried, then everything was all right. For now she was just glad that rope still hanging on the tree was empty.

After a month Maria was not quite so content as that first day. She had insisted on being moved back to Luke's home, where Rosa and Mrs. Donleavy doted on Michael, and Pedro crowed with joy at her return. She woke each morning expecting the letter or the telegram that would tell her Luke was safe and where to meet him. Surely it wouldn't take this long to find a place where they could live together?

Sara and Sean announced their engagement, and Maria set aside her worries long enough to be happy for them. Defying doctor's orders, she arranged a dinner party in their honor and invited all the friends and neighbors who had stood by Luke through these trying months. It helped to have people around her, distracting her thoughts from continual worry about Luke's safety.

But one day in mid-March she could no longer bear the suspense. Spring was coming early. The trees already showed signs of green, and yellow jonquils pushed their heads up in the most unexpected places. It had nearly been a year since she had first met Luke, and her need for him now was great.

Maria watched sorrowfully as the wet nurse held Michael to her breast and the greedy little piglet suckled hungrily. She had desperately wanted to feed him herself, but her milk had never come in. The doctor blamed it on her earlier illness and the worry over Luke, and assured her next time she would not have the problem, if there ever were a next time.

She glanced at the mirror and frowned at what she saw. Her skin had faded to a dull ivory and there were dark circles under her eyes. She looked gaunt and worn and not in the least bit enticing to a man like Luke, who was accustomed to beautiful women. She had returned to wearing a corset so she could fit into the lovely gowns Luke had bought for her, but she knew she no longer possessed the youthful slimness that had made Luke compare her to a boy. Even if he should come home, he might not want to stay once he saw how unattractive she had become.

Her only consolation was that Caroline was now six months pregnant and bigger than Maria had ever been. With wicked glee she contemplated Caroline's face should Luke appear again, and she drew some satisfaction in knowing she was at least prettier than Caroline for a change.

Maria ran downstairs at the sound of a knock on the door. She knew that rap, and she greeted Sean with eagerness, drawing him into the parlor and finding him a seat.

"Did you bring the mail? Have you heard anything yet?" She reached eagerly for the letters in his hand. Even from here she recognized the spidery scrawl of Uncle Juan's wife on the top envelope, but the other looked promising.

Sean concealed his pain at the sight of Maria's eyes lighting up every time he appeared like this. He was beginning to despise himself and Luke for this deceit. Her hope that Luke intended to send for her had kept her content through her convalescence, but he sensed it was only a matter of time before she began to question him more thoroughly. He watched her disappointment as the mail didn't reveal the news she wanted and cursed himself for the thousandth time.

Maria held her chin high and bravely launched into a discussion of the wedding to take place in less than a month. Sean marveled at her pluck and felt even guiltier at deceiving a woman as fine as this. When he rose to leave, he felt no suspicion when she took his arm and halted him.

Luminous eyes turned up to him, and it was only then that he realized they were rimmed with tears.

"He's not going to send for me, is he?" Maria asked quietly, finding her answer in Sean's shame-faced evasion of her eyes.

"It's not a life for a lady, Maria, and certainly no life for an infant. He's a convicted murderer; there are U.S. warrants out for him now. It's not the same as before."

"Then why did he leave, Sean? We could have appealed the verdict. Everyone knows he's innocent."

Sean thought he knew the answer to that, but it was not his place to say it. He shook his head dolefully. "It would have been months, Maria, you know that.

He'd been as patient as any man could be expected to be for your sake. There wasn't any reason to wait longer. When he feels it's safe, he'll let you know."

Maria snapped her hand from Sean's coat and glared at him defiantly. "Well, I've been just as patient as I can be, too, and now I'm going after him."

Sean's sharp gaze swung back to her. "Don't be ridiculous. You have too many responsibilities here. There's Michael and Pedro and the ranch to think about now. And how in hell do you expect to find him if a U.S. marshal can't?"

"Because I know him and the marshal doesn't. Michael's too young to miss me, and Pedro is happy as long as someone feeds him. Luke hired men to look after the livestock and if he doesn't care how they do it, neither do I. I'm not putting a herd of cattle before my husband. He's been on his own too long, Sean. I'll not let him live that life again unless he looks me in the eye and tells me he prefers it to living with me."

Sean studied her for a minute, seeing the petite woman in velvet-trimmed skirts first, then conjuring up the little hoyden who had rode over the New Mexico countryside with only Luke and himself as companions. He read the determination in the flare of her green eyes easily enough, and he heard the love behind her words. He sighed in exasperation.

"All right, Maria, if that's what you want to do, I'll go with you. Luke's going to kill me either way, but Sara will have my hide if I let you go alone. I don't suppose you can wait until after the wedding?" he asked without much hope. He'd waited a long time to get Sara in his bed; the thought of postponing it once more made him gloomy.

"I'll bring him back for the wedding. I don't need you to hold my hand on the train. Thank you for the offer, though." Maria held her hand out in a businesslike gesture of dismissal, but Sean only stared at her.

"You're loco, just plain loco. Why in hell Luke hasn't turned you over his knee and paddled some sense into you is beyond my knowing, but so help me,

Maria, I'm not that shy. You try going out there alone and I'll come after you with a whip and a lariat.''

A dimple sprang briefly at one corner of Maria's lips and her eyes lit with laughter. "How will you find me?''

"I'll smell you. Roses in winter are a dead give-away. You get your things together and I'll find out when the next train leaves.''

"How do you know which train I want?'' The dimple disappeared.

"Because Luke is as loco as you,'' Sean responded tiredly. "He never leaves a job undone, and I reckon he figures there's a few loose ends needing tying down.''

He knew, too. Maria paused, unwilling to drag Sean away from Sara just before their wedding, but unwilling to wait a moment longer while Luke could be out there risking his life. Reluctantly she conceded to Sean's demands, since he already knew where she was heading. There would be no escaping without him following.

"Sara won't be happy about it,'' Maria pointed out in a last-ditch effort to persuade him to stay.

Sean offered a half grin. "Maybe she will be so terrified I won't come back alive she'll give me something to remember her by. I can always hope.''

Impulsively Maria hugged his neck and kissed his broad cheek. "There, now you will smell like roses and she will be so jealous she won't let you go at all. I'm perfectly capable of handling this myself.''

Sean hugged her, still not certain that maybe Luke hadn't got the better end of this deal, but his smile was genuine as he set Maria from him.

"You might handle Luke by yourself, or you might handle Manuel, but you aren't going to handle both of them with maybe Dallas thrown in, too. Just handle Sara for me and we'll be even.''

"Done.'' This time when Maria held her hand out, Sean shook it.

14

Maria didn't feel quite so confident when she climbed down alone from the stagecoach in San Pedro late that March afternoon. She had persuaded Sean to part company with her at the railroad station. While she arrived publicly, Sean would stay out of sight, her ace in the hole.

The stage ride hadn't been so difficult as those earlier ones, and Maria gave herself a mental pat on the back for that small accomplishment. Even though she traveled unaccompanied, she had fended off the unwanted overtures of her male traveling companions with more experience and assuredness than a year before. She smiled as she remembered the shock in her fellow passengers' faces when she had introduced herself to an overly friendly salesman as Mrs. Cheyenne Walker. They had stared at her elegant feathered hat and chocolate velvet traveling gown in disbelief until she casually mentioned that her husband wouldn't travel in stagecoaches because he couldn't draw his six-gun fast enough in one, but she managed quite well with her derringer. The gun had appeared in her hand at the same time, making believers of them all.

She was learning to deal with the outside world, perhaps, and even learning to control her temper much more effectively, but she was not at all certain what she would do when she found Luke. Luke didn't get angry often, but she knew of a certainty that he would not be pleased to see her. He had not disappeared without a word without reason, and Maria knew the reason. What he was doing was dangerous for him and more so for her. No, he would not be at all pleased.

Straightening her shoulders and touching a hand to
her hat to be certain it sat properly, she directed the
unloading of her small valise to the boardwalk in front
of the general store. Thanking the driver with a light
shake of her gloved hand and a silver coin, she proceeded in the direction of the general store.

Jesse looked up when she entered, and a slow grin
spread across his face as he recognized the elegant
lady in the doorway. "Maria Connolly! Or Walker,
now, isn't it?" He hurried out from behind the counter
as the idlers lounging about the stove lazily straightened to stare at the newcomer.

"Walker, it is, Jesse. I'm glad to see some things
don't change." She shook Jesse's hand and turned to
grin at the men at the stove. "If you're looking to hire
on at the Connolly spread, you're going to have to step
livelier than that."

"Maria!"

The cry came from the door behind her and Maria
swung to greet the scarecrow figure limping through
the doorway. "Charlie! You old dog, are you still
here?" She held out her arms and to the laughter of
all, hugged the old man's reddening neck.

"Maria, you ain't got no place coming back here
like this. Where's Cheyenne?" Charlie extricated himself and glared at her with as much sternness as he
could muster.

"That's a whole other story. I just stopped in to see
if Jesse would look after my bag while I go talk to
Father Díaz. How is everybody and everything, Charlie? How is Carmelita and her new husband? What are
you up to?"

"Ever'body's doin' just fine. Carmelita's expectin'
a young one soon. She'll be wantin' to see you. Where
you stayin'?"

"That depends on my talk with Father Díaz. What
about you, Charlie? Where are you bunking these
days?"

The laughter and crude jests behind her warned her
of the answer to that one, and she smiled at Charlie's
tongue-tied expression. "The Widow Stone's? It's a

wonder she can put up with the likes of you all week 'round.''

They joked and laughed some more, but Maria sensed the underlying tension. There was something they weren't saying, and they weren't sure how to say it or if they should. In her fancy new clothes she wasn't the same Maria they remembered, and although they talked and laughed with her, they refrained from sharing their usual confidences.

''You meaning to stock the ranch again? Heard prices are getting higher back East.'' Jesse finally raised the one question that would break the ice.

Maria's gaze swept the room as she answered quietly, ''That depends on a number of things, gentlemen. First and foremost, I mean to clear my husband's name, which means I'm not on mighty good terms with my neighbor. How many men around here are willing to go up against the Vasqueros?''

That silenced them. Her attachment to Manuel had made her an object of suspicion for some years, but out of respect for her father they had not closed her from their ranks. This declaration of war came unexpectedly.

''Manuel's been herding his cattle on Connolly land. Claims it's his,'' one man offered.

''Has he now?'' Maria asked calmly. ''Well, it's not and never will be. I don't sell to murderers. Jesse, will you look after my bag for a little bit? I want to catch Father Díaz before evening mass.

She left behind low-voiced murmurs of excitement and speculation. She had tried to plan what she would do when she reached San Pedro, but she had never been very good at strategy. It seemed much simpler to follow the current and strike out for land when it carried her where she wanted. She could feel the current now, but recognized a serious undertow. The town wanted Manuel out, but Manuel was the only one who could clear Luke's name. That did not make for easy planning.

Father Díaz welcomed her with open arms until he realized Maria meant to live alone in the small house next to the mission that Uncle Patrick had bought for Pieta. He protested immediately.

"Where is your husband? Surely he would not approve. A woman alone—it is dangerous. Stay with Carmelita or one of the others until your husband arrives."

Maria shook her head stubbornly. "The house is near the mission walls. Who would bother me there? Do not worry, Father, I will be quite safe." Besides, if Luke came, she wanted to be alone so no one knew he was here. The empty house and the empty mission yard would make it easy for him to slip in unnoticed. She had no doubt whatsoever that he would come sooner or later.

Father Díaz looked dubious but handed over the key, and soon her bags were carried from the general store to Pieta's small cottage and she was settled in, alone.

Her first visitor was Sean. Weary from the long journey and terrified more than she would admit of the loneliness, Maria had been about to carry the lantern into the bedroom and retire for the evening. The swift knock on the kitchen door startled her, and the lamp trembled in her hand as she walked unfamiliar floors to the back of the house.

At the sight of Sean she nearly wept, and only the lantern in her hand prevented her throwing her arms around his neck. Sean had good arms for comforting, and the concerned expression on his face made it easy to accept his sympathy.

"Where have you been? I've been worried about you. Have you eaten?" Maria hurriedly closed the kitchen door and pulled the curtain on the kitchen window.

"I'm fine, I've eaten. What about you? You look pale. Luke is going to kill me for certain." Sean propped himself on one corner of the kitchen table and rested his boot on the chair. His dark eyes studied her cautiously.

"I ate with Father Díaz. Everything is fine. I'm just a little tired. Where are you staying?"

"Since you've already turned the entire town on its

ear, I figured there wasn't any harm in staying at the saloon. What in hell did you think you were doing, Maria? They're talking about getting together a small army. We're talking range war here. It will be wholesale slaughter if that happens. You can't ride out after Manuel, Maria.''

"I hadn't planned to." Maria sat the lamp on the table and brought down the bottle of sherry she knew she would find in Pieta's cupboard. Cleaning a glass out with a towel, she offered Sean a drink. "If they're so desperate the arrival of one lone woman is enough to instigate a war, it's their battle, not mine. I just let them know whose side I'm on.''

"Maria, sometimes you're such a damned fool, you amaze me. To them you are your father. They think you'll do what your father would have done. They're waiting for you to lead the war, and they expect Luke to show up with reinforcements. They think they can *win*, for Pete's sake.''

"And can't they?" Maria asked quietly, leaning against the sink and sipping her sherry.

"Hell, no! Manuel has the meanest vaqueros this side of the border, and within the week he could have half the outlaws in the territory riding for him. You don't unleash trained murderers on a bunch of farmers. That won't solve anything.''

"What will?" Maria asked bluntly.

"Damned if I know. Let's just find Luke and get out of here. The railroad isn't going to buy land without a signed document. Manuel can pretend what he likes, but he doesn't own the Connolly ranch. His plans are shot. Let's leave it at that.''

"Have you ever heard of forged documents?" Maria surveyed Sean's reaction quietly.

Sean looked at her suspiciously. "Why?"

"Because my *Tío* Juan is quite certain that is how his parents lost their land to the Vasqueros. He cannot prove it. All the people were long dead, but he warned me of the possibility. Manuel need only file a forged deed in Santa Fe, where his corrupt friends will witness and certify it, and the Connolly ranch will be no more. I had never thought such things possible of Manuel before, but I can believe anything now. It is already war, Sean, whether you like it or not.''

''Damn.'' Sean drained his glass and looked glum.

Maria smiled as she read his mind. ''I told you to stay with Sara. Luke's been out here nearly two months and hasn't solved the problem. I don't know any quick way to put an end to it.''

Sean glanced up quickly. ''You've seen him already?''

''Of course not. I just know this is where he had to come. I only pray Manuel hasn't found some way to kill him, but I think he would have had the bounty hunters haul him in for the reward if he had. Then the case would be closed and Manuel would never face charges for those murders.''

Sean pushed away from the table. ''All right. I'll head out in the morning to see if I can find him. Just don't do anything foolish until I get back.''

Maria smiled but made no promises.

First thing the next morning, she gathered up Charlie and a few others and rode out to the Connolly ranch.

15

She rode out the next day and the next, and every night Sean came to the house to report his findings, or lack of them. There was no sign of Luke at the ranch or in the shepherd's cave on the ridge or anywhere else that might serve as a hiding place for a fugitive.

Maria stared at her coffee in despair as they sat in the darkened kitchen on the third night of Sean's dismal reporting. She had been so certain Luke was out there. Could she have been wrong? She would have to be wrong about everything, about Luke, about their marriage, about his love. She couldn't believe he would ride off and desert her like this. He had to be here.

"He must be staying with one of the other ranchers," she finally decided, looking up to Sean, daring him to disagree.

Sean shrugged uneasily. "That would be risky. Harboring a fugitive ain't looked on kindly. Maybe he's over on the reservation. Luke speaks Navajo."

She hadn't known that, but she should have guessed. He had cursed her in enough languages to confuse anybody.

"You try the reservation. I'll start on the ranchers. They all know me. Surely one of them has seen something."

Sean rose to leave and pressed a kiss of reassurance against her forehead. "If he's here, we'll find him. Luke's a complicated man. He might have taken a notion to tackle this from some angle we don't know about. Be careful."

He slipped out the back door and through the garden gate to the alley, and then he was gone. The yard was much too private to see his comings and goings, and so far no one had connected them. It might not matter, but it was best to be safe.

Maria slipped the bolt on the back door and, using the candle on the kitchen table, found her way to the bedroom. Wearily she stripped off riding clothes, chemise, corset, camisole, and pantalets and began to scrub the day's grime from her skin. Without someone to help her with fires and pumping and carrying water, she had about abandoned the luxury of a full bath. Simple scrubbing would have to be sufficient.

Only soap and water couldn't scrub away the ache that grew with every passing day, the loneliness and the hunger for emotional and physical companionship that Luke's absence denied her. Where was he? Damn him! How could he do this to her? How could he teach her the ways of love and then leave her to suffer the torment without him? She needed him—needed his touch, needed the warm look in his eyes when he gazed upon her, needed the hunger of his kiss. She needed more than that, but slapping the washrag in the basin, Maria refused to contemplate that.

Drawing on a flannel nightshirt as protection against the coldness of her empty bed, she blew out the candle. It was only then that she heard the sound of the casement opening, and she spun around to find a man's figure silhouetted against the window.

She started to scream, but he was already through the window and had only a step to take to cover her mouth, strangling the cry before it could escape. As callused hands covered her lips and a strong arm caught her waist, Maria went limp with relief. Luke!

When his grip loosened, she turned and threw herself into his arms, hugging him passionately, reaching to run her hand through his hair, assuring herself of his reality as she lifted her lips for his kiss. Instead he set her from him in disgust.

"What's the matter, Maria? Doesn't your new lover satisfy you?"

His scathing tones destroyed her faster than the words. Maria's arms fell to her side and she stared at him blankly, not certain what he had said or what she had done.

"Luke?"

He crossed to the far side of the room as if to put as much distance between them as possible. "What in hell are you doing here? Couldn't you carry on with your new lover just as easily back in Kansas? Or did you come here looking for my approval?"

Maria wished she hadn't blown out the candle. She could see nothing of Luke's expression in the thick gloom, but she could tell he had crossed his arms across his chest and barred the door with his frame. She didn't understand anything but the pain behind his words, and she groped uncertainly for the cause.

"Are you ill, Luke? Do you have a fever? Tell me what's wrong before I go out of my mind with worry."

"My God! You never were an actress, Maria. Don't try now. I've sat in that damned garden every night since you arrived, and I've seen Sean sneak in and out every night. Hell, I've seen you *kiss* him. Here I thought I was protecting you and like the damned fool I am, I'm guarding my best friend while he dallies with my wife! Maybe I ought to kill both of you and frame Manuel, make things even."

As the sense of his words finally began to penetrate, Maria shook her head with fury. Her hands clenched in anger, and she wished desperately for something to throw, something to stop the cutting, wrenching anguish of his hatred and distrust. She had nothing but her voice, and she unleashed it with poisonous accuracy.

"Do that! Kill us both! Then go back to your son and explain to him why he has no mother. Go back to Sara and tell her there will be no wedding. Then sit down and try to explain to yourself why in hell we would have risked our lives and happiness to come all the way out here to let you know we don't need you anymore. You've been a damned fool from first to last, Luke Walker, and I don't have to put up with your confounded thickheadedness any longer! Let them hang you, why should I care? You've stolen my love,

my life, my ranch, my *soul*, damn your miserable hide!
Why should I care about anything any longer?''

Tears choked her words before she could finish this
tirade, and in frustration she rushed for the dresser to
find the gun she had stored there. Luke caught her
waist before she could open the drawer.

''Don't, Maria. I'll go. I told you I wouldn't make
much of a husband. Just get the hell out of here and
back to Kansas where you'll be safe.''

Maria jerked her hand free and slapped his face as
hard as she could. Her movement was so swift and
unexpected, Luke had no time to prepare for it. He
brought his hand up to his cheek and stared at her
through the darkness. He didn't need a light to see the
furious flare of her eyes.

''What was that for?''

''For being a first-class jackass. For running off and
leaving me and not telling me if you were alive or
dead. For all those nights I've lain here alone while
you sat out there pretending I'm Caroline or Peg or
Consuela or whoever in hell you think I am that you
can say such things to me—''

Luke jerked her off her feet and, burying one hand
in her hair, bent her head backward, bringing the full
force of his kiss against her lips. Maria struggled in
fury, but she was no match for his strength and, in
truth, had not the spirit for it any longer. She was too
starved for his touch to deny it even when given in
anger.

It took only seconds for the fire to flare up between
them again. Luke's hands slid down her flannel-
covered back to find the sides of her breasts as he
lowered her to the floor again. Maria stood on her
toes, clinging to his neck as she eagerly drank his
kisses. His mouth traced the outline of her lips, lingering in the corners before exploring deeper, delving
into the depths he had been denied so long. Maria
moaned and bent into his embrace as they hurtled toward that precipice from which there was no turning
back.

Except Luke recovered his senses before they

reached the edge. Fingers digging into the soft, yielding flesh of her waist, Luke set Maria from him, his gaze hungrily devouring her silhouette in the darkness.

"I want you on the stage out of here tomorrow, Maria," he ordered firmly.

"Why?" She questioned his actions more than his words. Why did he set her aside? Why did he deny the love she offered? When all she wanted in this world was to hold him and be reassured of his presence, why did he pretend he felt nothing?

"You are too easy a target, Maria. Manuel has only to ride out and catch you while you're parading across the valley with your old men and cripples, and I will be powerless to refuse anything he requests. Get the hell home, Maria. I don't need any more problems."

Maria jerked from his embrace as if slapped. "Who do you think you are? Are you so much better than me that you can take care of Manuel and I can only cause trouble? Do I get no credit for saving your useless life? Do I get no credit for hanging on and praying for two solid months that you would regain your senses and leave Manuel alone? Do I have no choice in whether I am made a widow in fact or practicality? Who are you to tell me to go home?"

She was raging out of control. All the months of pent-up fury and frustration burst in a torrent of fear from behind the dam she had worked so hard to build. She swung away from Luke, fleeing the devastation he created within her, but he would not let her go.

Catching her by the waist, Luke shook her until her long hair snapped back and forth and caught on his collar. "It is because of all that that I send you back. How can I risk your life when you saved mine? I'll not be in a position to stand behind your skirts again. This is my job, and I will do it alone."

"We will do it together!" Maria yelled defiantly.

She brought out the best and worst in him, and they would destroy each other if he could not get the upper hand. Finally losing all control, Luke fell down upon the bed and dragged Maria across his knees. Before

she knew what he was after, he brought the broad
width of his palm down across her upended posterior.

The humiliation hurt more than the stinging slap and
Maria roared in rage, fighting to elude Luke's grasp.
He only hung on tighter, holding her down as he attempted to smack some sense into her. Only when her
struggles broke down into sobs of anguish did Luke
recover himself.

"Maria, don't!" He lifted her into his arms, cuddling her sobbing body against his chest. The scent of
her hair, the clean smell of soap, filled his nostrils,
and he was aware of his own pungent aroma. But more
than that, he was aware of the injury he had inflicted
on her vulnerable slenderness, and he despaired of ever
righting the wrongs he had inflicted on her. "Maria,
please, I'm sorry, but I can't let you stay. You have to
see that."

Maria shook her head stubbornly, unable to control
her sobs to reply. He could beat her all he liked, but
she would never leave his arms again. She heard the
love and pain in his voice and sensed the need in his
hands as they caressed her, no matter how much he
tried to deny it. He could not make her go.

Luke kissed the teardrops on her cheeks and stroked
her hair, rocking her back and forth as if she were the
child he had not held since its birth. It was not long
before his murmured apologies became sweet words
of love, and the comforting strokes of his hands drifted
to tender caresses.

As Luke's hand found the soft fullness of her breast,
Maria lifted her head from his shoulder. Their eyes
met, and a shudder ran through her as she felt the
pressure of his need. Without a thought she lifted her
hand to pull his head down to hers, and their tongues
met with the enticing rush of their breathing.

Luke groaned as Maria's tongue followed his and
traced sensuous swirls inside his mouth. His fingers
located the intoxicating thrust of the hard point of her
breast beneath the loose gown, and feverishly he ma-
nipulated it until he brought a low moan from deep
inside her. He wanted to touch her flesh, to feel the

silken smoothness of her skin against him, know the thrust of the soft curves of her body against those places of his that ached for fulfillment. His hand rode down over the valley of her waist and the full curve of her hip, lingering at the tender buttocks he had mistreated so cruelly. He felt her press against him and urgently he tugged at the long length of flannel.

Maria scarcely felt the rush of cold as the shift rode up her legs and tangled in Luke's lap. She felt only the rough caress of his chapped hands along her thighs and the healing balm of his touch on the bruises he had inflicted earlier. As his hand explored, his kisses plunged and invaded until she was on fire for the joining that their mouths only imitated.

When Luke touched her between her legs, she nearly exploded with her need for him there. Luke rolled her over against the mattress, his weight pressing her back as his mouth continued its travels down her throat to the untied front of her gown while his hand forced her into submission.

She wanted him inside of her; she wanted all of him, not just this maddening ecstasy that stole her mind and will and left her victim of her senses. Her hands pushed aside the cloth of Luke's shirt and spread across his hard, flat belly to the powerful width of his muscular chest until he impatiently ripped the material off and flung it aside. He did the same with her gown, lifting her to jerk the gown over her head until she lay naked beneath him.

Not until Maria moaned her satisfaction with this arrangement and reached for the fastening of his trousers did Luke finally remember the reason he had put this distance between them in the first place. With a groan of frustration Luke pushed away, hastily pulling the blankets around Maria as much to hide temptation as to keep the chill away. His own body ached too much to make a hasty escape, and he only succeeded in rolling from her reach while he waited for the throbbing to subside.

"Maria, I'm sorry. I didn't mean to say those things, I didn't mean to hurt you, and I certainly didn't mean to start this. Go home, Maria, before we both regret it. It's too easy for me to lose my mind when you're around."

Stunned by this rejection, Maria shivered but made no attempt to sit up. Luke was lying less than two feet from her, and she could not bring herself to increase the distance.

"Luke, I don't understand. Please don't do this to me." She couldn't help the tears in her voice. She had done everything she knew how to do to make him love her, and she had thought she succeeded. She could not live if she had been wrong. He was too much a part of her now to go on as only half a person.

Hearing her tears, Luke pushed up on one elbow and touched her cheek. "I'm sorry, Maria. It's been so long, and I've dreamed of you so desperately every night that I just didn't think. You're too precious to me to risk your life for just a moment's pleasure. You should never have come here. It's hard enough to keep my hands off you at any other time, but I need you so much—"

Maria gave a choked cry and turned to him, but Luke kept her at arm's length. She could see the pale outline of his bulging shoulder not inches from her, and she could not bear not to touch.

"I think you're mad. The sun or moon has robbed you of your wits. I am here. I need you to hold me. You said you loved me. Why can't you touch me? It's been so long, Luke . . ."

The blanket lay loosely over her breasts as she lay on her side, and Luke could scarcely keep his fascinated gaze from the sway of a woolen corner which revealed glimpses of pale skin with each breath. He had only to reach out his hand and the covering would fall aside. His hand literally ached to move.

"I can't risk losing you, Maria. Michael and Pedro need you. It would be selfish to endanger your life again. We don't need more children. I'll just have to learn to control these urges, but damn it, Maria, you don't make it easy. Where did that blamed gown of yours go?"

Luke sat up to search the floor, but Maria threw aside her blanket, distracting him totally with the pale gleam of her breasts in the moonlight.

"I want more children, Luke, but if you're not in a hurry, I can wait. Just don't use that as an excuse to send me away. Do you still think that Sean and . . . ?"

She wore the gold necklace he had given her, and it gleamed wickedly between her breasts, drawing his fascinated gaze to the twin peaks begging to be caressed. Luke shook his head groggily.

"I'm sorry. It's easy to imagine things when you're alone. Maria, for the love of Pete, cover yourself."

Understanding that he could not even look at her without the need to touch, Maria moved provocatively closer, touching her fingers to the *V* at the base of his throat and drawing them downward. "I have missed you terribly, Luke. Why will you not love me, *querido?*"

The endearment went straight to his head, and Luke caught her against him, reveling in the heat of her soft breasts against the aching cold of his chest. "The doctor said it would hurt you, Maria. I almost lost you with Michael. I cannot take that risk again. I love you too much to lose you through my own selfishness. You're putting me through hell, little one. Go home."

Luke heard Maria's soft curses mixed with loving endearments in both Spanish and English, but mostly he felt the path of her hands as they once more reached for the fastenings of his trousers.

"Do not believe all the doctors say. I am fine. I am healthy. I will bear more children, but they will wait. I want to hold you, be close to you, to feel you in my arms again. Do you think I know less than Caroline or Consuela? For you, I will go to the *curandera* and obtain the salves. And you will have to ask Sean to buy those things from the bartender at the saloon that men use. And there will be no babies until you are ready. Just do not make me wait to hold you until then."

"Witch," Luke whispered as her hands succeeded

at their task. Any other woman would have used th
excuse he had provided to escape the duties of th
marital bed, but Maria had never been any othe
woman. Her need for him was no pretense, and wit
this knowledge his desire grew to painful proportions
He would not hurt her, but he would not risk her lif
either.

Maria cried out as Luke stood up, but when he onl
stepped out of the remainder of his clothes and re
turned to her side, she sighed with satisfaction.

Not until his lips had drunk their fill until her breast
ached and then moved lower did Maria understan
what he was about. She caught his hair and cried ou
in protest, but she was beyond fighting the sensation
sweeping over her with the powerful current of pound
ing tides. It was not what she wanted, but her bod
was beyond her control and in his complete possessio
now.

As the tides crashed and carried her to the brink an
over, Luke grinned in satisfaction. His wife might hav
the temperament of a witch, but only he had the abilit
to reduce her to a whimpering kitten. He would neve
ask for more.

16

Dawn had not broken when Luke kissed her awake. Maria responded languorously, moving closer to the source of heat in her bed and fitting herself to the curve of his body. Contentment stole through her veins as Luke's hard arm wrapped around her waist and locked them together, but his persuasive whisper against her ear gradually woke her consciousness.

"Do that again and we may both spend the day in bed. What will your friends think when they find the lady in bed with an outlaw?"

"That she has exceptional taste, and if they are any friends at all, they will leave us alone and mind their own business." Maria kissed his throat. He smelled of dust and sweat and masculine musk, and she loved it all.

Luke reluctantly rose from the bed. Wrapping the blanket around her, Maria sat up and pulled her knees against her chest as she watched Luke move silently around the room.

"Where do you go? How can I find you? Will you come back tonight?"

Picking up his trousers, Luke moved in front of her, offering a half grin as she bent her head back to meet his gaze. "I'd better send Sean shopping at the saloon before I come back."

Maria blushed and buried her face in the blanket over her knees. There was enough light to see the expression on his face, and the look in his eyes was enough to melt icicles.

"You will see Sean and then come back? I will get

the makings for a meal if you will tell me when you'll come.''

The rough growth of several weeks' beard made him look the part of outlaw and more, and she was grateful she had not been able to see him clearly last night when he had been angry. She would not have been half so brave.

Luke lifted her chin to read her eyes. ''You'll not go back, will you?'' It was more statement than question. They had already had this argument.

Maria shook her head. ''Not without you.''

Luke dropped his hand and began pulling on his pants. ''All right, if you're determined to make Michael an orphan, we'll have to draw Manuel out of hiding.''

''That should not be so difficult,'' Maria shrugged casually. ''I need only show myself at the hacienda. He will be out to murder me before you have time to draw your gun.''

''That is precisely why I would send you back to Kansas, little fool.'' Luke glared at her with mixed love and exasperation. ''Do you think I have sat outside your window these last three nights because I enjoy making myself miserable? Once he knows you are here, he will come looking for you.''

'I am not afraid of Manuel,'' Maria said. ''What will you do with him?''

''That is my concern. Your concern is to stay out of his way. He has taken to rustling to raise the cash for all the land the railroad has not yet paid him for. His men are moving out tonight. I will tell you what to do if you promise to go stay with Carmelita for the evening.'' At her eager nod, Luke described his plan.

Maria memorized his every word. Luke thought quickly to come up with a plan like this overnight. It seemed flawless, as far as it went. She frowned when he finished. ''Manuel will be behind bars where he belongs, but what about you? How will you prove your innocence?''

Luke caught her hair in his fingers and drew her up

beside him. "Just do what I say, *poquita*. One step at a time."

His kiss leeched away the questions and arguments, and she was left standing drained and empty long after he had gone.

The sheriff stared at her as if she had lost her mind when Maria marched into the saloon later that morning in search of him. Wearing a lightweight woolen gown of rich green pulled back over a striped underskirt that rustled satisfactorily beneath her fashionable bustle, Maria look entirely out of place in the smoke-begrimed saloon. She wore her hair stacked in smooth curls on top of her head to add inches to her height, and the foolish piece of frippery she had perched on top held his fascinated gaze as she approached.

"Sheriff, I need a word with you." At this hour the bar was nearly empty, but Maria felt the few men listening straighten their shoulders and take heed. One even doffed his hat, and that had never happened before when she was just Connolly's tomboy daughter. She was rather beginning to enjoy her impact as a woman.

The sheriff obligingly led her outside. It had been a day much like this when he had first seen Cheyenne Walker ride down that hill. A lot had happened since then, but nothing had really changed. Vasquero and his cohorts still had a strangle hold on the valley, and though the old man was dead, Manuel was expanding operations. A new feed and general store has just opened on the outskirts of town, and the Vasquero tenants had been forced to transfer their business from Jesse. Before long Jesse would be broke. It didn't take a blind man to see how that could happen to every business in town.

"Sheriff, my husband says you can be trusted. That's a mighty strong compliment coming from him, and I'm relying on his faith. Don't let me down."

Sheriff Jack Stone was a tall, broad-chested man in his mid-forties. He had done a lot of things in his life, some of which he was ashamed, but he had settled

here and made an honest name for himself, and he
had enjoyed Irish Connolly's friendship. He looked a
Irish's daughter now and saw the green eyes of his
friend staring back at him.

"Don't get uppity with me, Maria. I knew you since
you were wet behind the ears, and that fancy gear don'
impress me none. Tell what it is you're needing and
I'll see what can be done," he drawled calmly.

Maria breathed easier at this sensible reply. "Manuel and his men have been rustling cattle from over in
the north valley and riding them through that pass on
my land. Word is they're going out tonight. I want a
band of men to cut them off and put them behind bars
I'd say twenty would do it. I can round up most of
them if you'll get the rest."

Stone stared at her in disbelief. She looked just like
her mother, all high cheekbones, big eyes, and luxuriant hair, but damned if she didn't talk just like her
father.

"You've been back here less than a week. How in
hell do you know a thing like that?" Even as he said
it, the sheriff knew he had asked a stupid question.
The wanted poster for Cheyenne Walker was lying with
a stack of other neglected mail in a box that sufficed
as his desk.

"I think you can take my word for it." Maria calmly
pulled on her glove and began to button it. "I'll ride
out with you, if you want. I have an interest in seeing
Manuel Vasquero behind bars."

He didn't doubt that in the least. He kept out of
other people's business; it was the best way to stay
alive out here. But he kept his ears open, and he knew
what went on. She hadn't pressed charges that time
Manuel beat her, neither had O'Laughlin, but Stone
knew about both of them.

"You and a hundred others, I reckon. You'd better
give me the whole story, Maria. I ain't riding out there
empty-handed."

Maria gave him a shrewd look and decided he deserved an explanation. Stone nodded as her story cor-
roborated what he already knew and tilted his hat

backward as he stared at the hills when she was finished.

"Your husband's a wanted man, Maria. You know I got to take him in with the others if I see him."

"I don't think you'll see him unless you let Manuel escape. Just don't let anything happen to Manuel, Sheriff. He's our only hope of clearing Luke's name."

"He's not going to be mighty cooperative behind bars." Stone lifted his hat and scratched his head idly.

"That was my thought, but I'll not argue with Luke. He usually knows what he's doing."

"That's about all any of us can say. All right, Maria, I'll see what can be done. Am I taking O'Laughlin with me?"

Maria grinned. "He's as brave as any man I know, but unless you're dealing cards instead of guns, he'll not be of much use. Luke thought Sean might keep an eye on the Vasquero ranch in case Manuel slips through the net. He'll know what to do if that happens."

"Will do. I'd rather you stayed with friends tonight. It'll be easier on you."

"Thank you, Sheriff." Maria smiled and walked off with no intention of heeding his words any more than she had heeded Luke's in this.

As the mantel clock struck eleven, Maria made one last check of her derringer and slipped it in the pocket of her riding skirt. It would be cold on the range this time of night, but her small valise held a limited amount of clothing and a heavy mantle wasn't among them. The coat of her riding outfit would have to do.

Luke would kill her if he knew what she was doing, but she knew Manuel better than he did. Manuel wouldn't be out on a night like this for the menial chore of rustling a few cattle. No, he would be in the warm comfort of his home with whatever poor maid he had enticed to his bed, safe from any criminal charges should his unlucky men run into trouble. She would simply have to confront him and come to some understanding.

She had her gun, and Sean would be there. Manuel

couldn't do much harm surrounded by witnesses. Men
had the irritating habit of acting first and talking later
when a little talk might save a number of lives. She
would just have to step in to fill the gap. There had
been too much killing already.

Slipping out the rear door to the garden, Maria
breathed deeply of the cold night air. Tonight she
would put an end to this warfare once and for all, one
way or another. Then they could go home.

Sean cursed as he watched the tall Spaniard leave
the hacienda and head for the stables. Why in hell did
the bastard have to choose tonight to go alley-catting?
Luke would be furious at this change in plans. With
another expletive as he hurried through the grounds to
his horse, Sean signaled to a small figure waiting in
the shrubbery. The boy raced to join him, and minutes
later, one set out after Manuel and the other rode off
into the hills.

Maria exclaimed in surprise as a tall shadow loomed
out of the alleyway as she opened the garden gate. Her
first instinct was to run, but this was Manuel, the man
she wanted to talk to, and running wouldn't solve anything. She glanced around uneasily for some sign of
accompaniment, but he appeared to be alone.

"It's late to be out walking, isn't it?" Manuel solved
her dilemma. Slamming open the gate, he strode in,
and without permission he caught her elbow and
steered Maria toward the back door.

"Manuel, you're forever hurting me. Let go." She
jerked her elbow from his grasp and reached for the
door. All of a sudden she was very certain she had
done an insane thing, and her thoughts flew to means
of escape. The door had a bolt, if she could only . . .

Manuel grabbed the door before she could shut it.
Shoving her inside, he followed and carefully closed
the door behind him. A lamp burned over the sink,
and in its flickering glare he could see the shadowed
hollows of Maria's cheeks and the haughty tilt of her

chin. It was time he stripped her of some of that arrogance.

"I'm going to talk, Maria, and you're going to start saying yes. I'm tired of playing games. If you had just done what you promised, none of this would have had to happen."

The Spaniard advanced into the room and Maria stepped backward, keeping out of his reach. She didn't like the way his eyes glittered as he looked at her. He had looked at her with disdain before, and he had looked at her with desire, but never had she seen this expression of cold, calculating fury. She had been very wrong about Manuel, and her fingers slid to the pocket of her skirt.

"Take off your coat, Maria. The fire's still burning and you won't be needing it."

He kept moving toward her and she kept backing away. The house had only three rooms, all in a row: the kitchen, the bedroom, and the front room. She stopped in the doorway of the bedroom, and Manuel started around the kitchen table after her.

"What did you want to talk about?" Her fingers closed around the handle of the derringer as he moved toward her.

"You and me and some land that should have been mine. The coat, Maria."

Maria choked back a gasp as a revolver appeared in Manuel's hand. He gestured with it, and, releasing the derringer, she did as indicated. She removed her riding coat.

Manuel smiled and looked her up and down, his dark gaze lingering on her breasts, then sliding over the trim curve of her waist and flare of her hip. His gaze came to rest on her boots, and with a certain amount of relish he gestured with his gun again.

"The boots, Maria. They can't be very comfortable. Take off your boots."

"This is ridiculous, Manuel. Can't we just sit down and talk like two normal people without your waving that gun? I don't want my boots off. There's coffee on the stove. Let me fix you a cup." Refusing to believe he would harm her, Maria stepped toward the stove, bravely pretending everything was normal.

Manuel caught her shoulder and slammed her back against the wall. The gun waved inches from her nose. "The boots, Maria. Go in and sit down on the bed and remove your boots. They got in my way last time. I'll not have that happen again."

It was then that she understood. Maria stared at him in horror and disbelief. It did not seem to matter that she was married and had just had a baby. He meant to take her as he had tried before, only this time he had a gun instead of his hands to beat her into submission.

"You'll not get my land this way," she warned, searching frantically for some escape. The gun in her pocket was a last resort. She had only two bullets to his six, and his was already in his hand. The odds were not in her favor.

"I already have your land, Maria. What I want now is you. Be good to me and I might let you live. You're even better-looking than Peg when you fix yourself up right. I might even arrange for you to stay at the hacienda now that I'm the master of the house. Take off the boots."

He had her back against the bed, and Maria sat down abruptly, staring at him in disbelief. He really believed he could do anything he wanted. She could see it in his eyes. He thought he could take her and her land just as he had taken everything else he wanted. An icy edge of horror began to form around her heart as she thought of Luke. What had Manuel done to Luke that he felt so confident of getting away with this?

Maria bent to remove her boots. "You won't get away with it, Manuel. I have friends and family. They won't bother with the law this time. They will simply hang you."

Manuel shrugged and leaned against the door frame as one slim, stockinged ankle emerged from the boot. "They will have to reach me first. I'm not easy to get to, as your husband has already discovered. I daresay he's out there chasing shadows tonight, hoping one will be mine. It should be amusing when our honest

Jack Stone locks him behind bars while I dally with you. That will even the score somewhat for that scene in Stockton, don't you agree?''

Maria jerked her boot off and flung it at him, but Manuel moved to one side and it landed uselessly in the kitchen.

''Haven't learned to control that temper, have you? That should add a little pepper to the broth. Life has been dull recently. *Mi madre* insists that I marry and provide heirs, and she has chosen a very proper and bovine cousin of mine. It would have been much more interesting with you running the household, but she is right, of course. Carlota is much more suitable. She will breed a passel of brats and not complain if I keep a mistress or two. The skirt now, Maria. If you're going to learn to please me, you will never wear one of those unfeminine abominations again. You should wear red, like Consuela.''

Maria seethed. Fear fled as rage took over. ''Do you really think I will play the whore for you like Consuela and your Peg? Why don't you just shoot me now and make it simple? Isn't that what you are good at, Manuel? Shooting unarmed men and beating helpless women?''

''But I can't kill you yet, Maria. Not until Luke is behind bars where I can watch his face when I drag you down to see him hang. I didn't kill Peg, either. I just tried to teach her a lesson. It was the brat she carried that killed her.''

Manuel stepped forward and grabbed the collar of Maria's shirt, jerking it downward. The buttons flew off and the linen fell open, revealing the lace of her chemise and the swell of her breasts above her corset.

Maria's hand flew to her pocket. He was too close. She couldn't even stand without stepping on his toes, and his towering presence frightened her. Just a blow from his hand would render her helpless; she had learned that lesson. The gun was her only hope.

When he reached to rip her chemise, Maria lifted the gun in her pocket. She couldn't aim it. She didn't have a chance of getting it out without him seeing it.

But she wouldn't sit here and let him do this. She dodged his hand, rolling across the bed out of his reach.

Manuel dived for her, dropping his gun in the process. He caught the back of her shirt and pulled it down her back. Maria freed her arms and almost made it to the other side, but his fingers gripped her shoulder and she cried out as he wrenched her back against the bed.

Turning her head, she viciously bit his knuckles, then kicked with her bare toes at his crotch as he tried to straddle her. She missed, but the blow caught him off balance and the bite loosened his grip. He cursed as she jumped from the bed.

Both of them leapt for the gun. Manuel was closer and his hand closed over the grip before Maria could reach it. Instantly she moved away from the bed and jerked the derringer from the pocket of her skirt. Manuel caught her movement and turned the barrel of his weapon at the same time as she drew hers.

Both guns flashed and twin echoes bounced against the thin walls.

17

Sheriff Stone held his mount still as they sat on the ridge watching the roundup below. The rustlers had rode right into the ambush as planned, but there was no sign of the arrogant Spaniard among them. He waited, not with any hope of catching Manuel, but of seeing the outlaw he knew hid somewhere in the rough terrain around them.

His vigilance was rewarded, although not with the sight of Cheyenne Walker. The movement of a young vaquero and his pony on the other side of the ridge held his attention. The boy hadn't been among the men who had responded to Maria's call. In the darkness he couldn't recognize the lad's silhouette, but he recognized the type of saddle and stirrups. Manuel's vaqueros clung to the old ways, but this one looked a bit young to be of the old breed.

Quietly he rode down the rise and behind the ridge, following the pony at a distance. The boy seemed to have little interest in the cattle milling in the brush pen below or in the curses of the rustlers being roped like steers underneath the guns of his hastily appointed deputies. One would almost think the boy knew about the outlaws and the ambush.

The pony stopped near a fall of boulders and the boy got off, slipping down into the rocky rubble and disappearing into the gully. The sheriff dismounted and tried to approach quietly, but the man he sought apparently had ears like a prairie dog. Luke stepped out from behind the boulders before Stone could reach it. Frightened now, the young boy stopped just behind

Luke, his eyes wide and frozen as he stared at the sheriff's drawn gun.

"It's all right, Juan. Go on to your pony and ride back to the ranch. Just keep your eyes and ears open."

The boy scurried back to his mount and Luke shrugged at the question in Stone's eyes. "Pieta has a very large family. They are eager to revenge her death."

The sheriff nodded understanding. That was how Luke had been surviving out here in the wilderness. "Manuel's not down there. What are your plans now?"

"I didn't think he would be, but the bastard moved faster than I anticipated. He's gone after Maria, Jack. You're a good man and I don't want to hurt you, but I'll not let any man stand between me and Maria. Manuel isn't going to win this one."

"That's where he is, with Maria?" The sheriff's tone sharpened.

"I don't know where else he'd be heading this time of night. You with me?"

"For now."

With a whistle Luke's stallion raced from the crevasse, and within minutes the two men and several of the newly appointed deputies were speeding across the plain in the direction of San Pedro.

The derringer flew across the room and Maria cried out in pain as blood spurted from her grazed fingers. She didn't linger to examine the damage, but tried to stand and make her escape before Manuel recovered from his surprise. The damned derringer had done no more than burn a hole through the shoulder of Manuel's expensive shirt, taking a little skin with it as it went. She hadn't had time to aim, but she had hoped for more damage than that. It was too late now. She wasn't going back in that bedroom to find it.

As she raced for the doorway, Manuel was upon her. All his control had fled, and he snarled as he caught the band of her skirt and jerked her back against him. Maria flung herself backward with all her weight, catching him under the chin with her head and throwing him off balance. They both staggered backward, Manuel refusing to release his grip even as he fell.

He hit the bed first and Maria tried to jump clear, but he rolled over at once, capturing her beneath his weight against the edge of the mattress.

"You're not getting away, Maria. You might as well begin to enjoy it."

His hands were everywhere, tearing her chemise and reaching for the fastening of her skirt, mauling her breasts and bending her farther against the bed until she thought her back would snap. She clawed his face, maneuvered her knee between his legs and brought it up as hard as she could, but he was too tall and too strong and her futile struggles only made him laugh.

Maria could feel the hardness of his arousal through his tight breeches as he pressed against her belly, and for the first time real panic set in. Her fingers throbbed with pain and she could scarcely bend them to fight off Manuel's invading hands. Her position made her legs useless, and his greater weight and strength made it impossible to get free. She was tiring quickly, but she continued to bite and scratch every time he brought his face and hands within her reach.

She blessed her corset and riding skirt. The heavy twill once more defied Manuel's attempts to rip it, and he would have to release his weight to pry it loose from her hips. He apparently had little experience with ladies who wore corsets, and he struggled with the strings and hooks, seeking the secrets of their release.

Manuel gave a cry of triumph as he succeeded in ripping open the front corset hooks, and he ground his hips against Maria's belly as his fingers slid beneath the whalebone to discover the softness of her breasts. A moment later he gave a frustrated growl as his hands encountered the camisole beneath the corset.

"Why in hell do you wear so many damn clothes! I'll keep you naked once I get you back to the ranch."

Lifting his weight to one side so he could strip off the corset and camisole, Manuel gave her the opportunity for which she waited. With her good hand Maria made a fist and aimed it for that male part of him with which he meant to hurt her.

Manuel yelped and momentarily released her, but she was not strong enough and the angle was not good enough for a damaging blow. With a vicious curse he swung a blow at her jaw, but Maria turned her head and he only grazed her chin. That was sufficient to make her head spin, and she scarcely noticed when the kitchen door slammed open.

At the sound Manuel immediately jerked Maria in front of him, trapping her throat with his powerful arm as he reached for the gun beside him.

Maria's scream of terror stopped the men rushing through the kitchen. Cautiously the sheriff appeared in the doorway, his gaze quickly taking in Maria's torn clothing and the gun in Manuel's hand. He gestured for the men behind him to halt.

"What is the meaning of this visit, Sheriff? Has it become your job to spy on lovers now? You know there is talk that you will lose the next election, Jack. I do not think this new proclivity of yours will win you votes." Calmly Manuel stood up. He kept Maria in front of him, making a show of caressing her breast as he trained the gun on the man in the doorway.

"Maria, are you all right?" Sean shoved the other men aside and the sheriff made room for him.

"No, I'm not all right! Sheriff, I want him arrested for assault. And he has admitted the beating of Peg Owens, so you know Luke is innocent. He wants Luke to hang for his misdeeds—"

The arm tightened around her throat, cutting off her words. Manuel shrugged carelessly. "She talks too much. That is why I would not marry her. But she's always been my woman and you have no right to interfere."

He backed toward the doorway to the front room, dragging Maria with him.

She tore at his arm, gasping each word with every breath. "It won't work, Manuel! The land's not mine, it's Pedro's. You've wasted your time. You killed my father and Pieta for nothing."

"I didn't kill your father. He meant to tell you about me and Consuela; you know that, don't you? He didn't want me to marry you. He was a sick old man. He had to die soon. I cannot help it if bandits ended his life a little earlier than planned."

"And Pieta? Was she sick and old, too?" Sean asked with disgust. He did not dare advance against Manuel's weapon, but the scoundrel would not get far with Maria. He kept him talking.

"The Indian?" Manuel scoffed. "She was nothing. None of you are anything. The land is mine. The woman is mine. Now leave before I take exception to your intrusion."

Maria attempted to jerk free of his hold and screamed in pain as Manuel brought his hand up sharply to jerk her head backward. That scream was his undoing.

Unable to contain his fury any longer, Luke kicked open the front door and advanced into the house with his guns drawn. Maria sagged to the floor as Manuel swung around to confront his enemy. Before Manuel could grab her again, Maria rolled behind the wall, but she knew who had entered without need to see him.

Luke's voice rang out with murderous hatred. "This is the only warning I give you Manuel. Drop the gun or I'll kill you."

Manuel laughed. "With the sheriff watching? I'm no fool. Jack, I believe this man is wanted dead or alive?"

Manuel raised his gun, aiming it at Luke's head. The explosion that followed echoed through the small house, but it was not Luke who crumpled to the floor. With a moan Manuel fell not inches from where Maria lay, and his eyes were incredulous as he lifted his bloody hand from the wound in his side.

"Get me a doctor," he gasped, turning from Maria's frightened eyes to stare up at the men crowding around him.

One of the men turned as if to obey, but Luke halted

him with a wave of his gun. "Nobody touches him. Maria, where are you?"

His amber eyes hardened as Maria staggered to her feet and Luke saw the bruises forming on her tender skin. He caught her with his free arm and glared down at the wounded man. "Let him die, Sheriff. They can't hang me twice. I might as well get the benefit of the crime for which I'm wanted."

"Jack! *Madre de Dios,* call a doctor! He is a madman. Maria, tell him, tell him he cannot do this . . ." Manuel's breaths began to come in painful spurts.

"If my husband is to hang for your misdeeds, Manuel, I will just as gladly watch you die for his. You've robbed me of everyone I loved. Don't expect my sympathy."

Luke's arm tightened protectively around her, and Maria was grateful for the support. The blood spilling from between Manuel's fingers was a painful sight, but this was their only chance. She would spit on Manuel's grave if Luke had to die for his sins.

"Is there something you want to say before you die, Señor Vasquero?" Sean asked laconically from behind the fallen man. "Maybe Cheyenne would let us fetch a doctor if you give him some reason to think he need not hang."

"Jack, do not let them get away with this! I will have your job! Jack . . ." Muttered curses were cut off as a spasm of pain shot through him.

"You'll not have anybody's job, boy. Just tell me who killed Dirk Jones and I reckon the doc can be fetched. Most of us can testify Peg was your whore, and the little lady here's already said you admitted to beating her half to death. Just give us what we want and we'll see what we can do."

The pain was beyond bearing now. Manuel turned a deathly white as he tried to speak, and Maria had to bury her face against Luke's unforgiving shoulder to keep from watching.

"I did it, I killed the bastard. He drew a gun on me. It was self-defense. Now for God's sake, go get the doctor!"

The sheriff gave his nod of consent and silently one of the men headed out the door. The others bent to lift the injured man from the floor.

Gathering Maria against him, Luke stepped out of their way.

As they passed, Manuel threw Luke a look of pained fury. "I will get you for this!"

"Before I'm done, you're going to be bankrupt, Señor," Luke assured him. "And I wouldn't ride through any lonely deserts if you get out, either. The score's not even yet."

The sheriff came between them, hurrying his small posse out the door. Maria clung to the safety of Luke's arms and didn't look up again until the house was quiet. Luke's ragged breathing gradually slowed to normal as he gently ran his hand up and down her back.

"I should have killed him," he muttered through clenched teeth as the door closed.

"He's not worth it. Someone else will do it for you, sooner or later. I just thank God you're safe." Maria pushed her hands against his chest and looked up at Luke's lined and weary and incredibly handsome face. She lifted her fingers and touched his jaw with relief.

Luke grabbed her bleeding hand, then gazed down at her disheveled state of undress with growing anguish. With her shirt gone and her corset unfastened and her long hair streaming in tangled strands across her uncovered breasts, she created a picture of temptation for every man who had just been in this room, and the urge to kill Manuel grew stronger.

"What in hell happened here?"

Before she could even try to explain, Sean reappeared in the doorway. For the first time they noticed his dust-coated clothing and the painful limp he used to carry himself through the room. Maria gave a cry of dismay and started toward him until Luke growled and jerked her back. She turned and looked at him in disbelief while Sean swayed in the center of the floor, his dark eyes meeting Luke's contemptuously.

"Go ahead, Walker, blacken my eye and loosen a

few teeth. I might as well look like you did when I walk to the altar. But don't ever, ever ask me to keep an eye on this woman of yours again. I'm getting too old to take it anymore.''

Luke's tired scowl began to fade, but his voice remained gruff as he demanded, ''Where have you been?''

''If you're not going to knock me down, may I sit?''

This time when Maria pulled away from his arms, Luke let her go. She grabbed a blanket to cover herself, then headed for the kitchen, turning a kitchen chair around for Sean to collapse in. She reached for the kettle of hot water hanging over the dying embers of the fire, but Luke grabbed it from her. With a worried look at her hand he poured some into the wash bowl, and then filled the coffeepot.

''No wonder your brew stinks. You're supposed to use cold water.'' Sean lowered himself into the offered seat with a groan. He watched as Maria washed her hand in the bowl and grimaced at the unsightly wound across her slender fingers. ''I'm sorry, Maria. I should have got here sooner.''

''I'll second that motion. I thought that was the whole point of your following Manuel.'' Luke slammed cold water in front of Sean. ''Will you tell me why you weren't?'

Maria held out a hand to steady him, but the two men were glaring at each other again and neither took notice of her.

''Dallas was waiting for me outside of town. I wasn't on Manuel's list of things to do, but I reckon Dallas hadn't forgotten me.'' Sean splashed the hot water in his face and wiped at it gingerly. ''Lucky he only brought one of his bully boys with him, but they slowed me down some, I admit.''

''Oh, Sean, you could have been killed! What happened?'' Maria hurried to pass him her cake of soap.

Sean grinned at the scent of roses wafting up to him from the soap, but he boldly plunged it into the water. ''Pieta's family came to the rescue. I don't think Dallas will venture back here again too soon.''

Luke's ominous silence caused Sean to look in his direction. "Any more questions?"

"Like why in hell did you let Maria come out here in the first place and why were you sneaking in her back door at night? There might be one or two others, but I suspect Maria can answer them. Who are you walking to the altar and when?"

Luke's abrupt change of subject left both his listeners gaping, but Sean recovered rapidly. "Who the hell do you think is crazy enough to walk in front of an altar with me?"

Wrapping her fingers with a piece of clean linen, Maria watched the two men in her kitchen with affection: Luke, tawny and lean and dressed as if just back from a three-month cattle drive, and Sean, dark and broad and garbed in frock coat and linen. They had nothing in common but friendship, but it was good to know they had the strength of character to remain loyal to each other all these years. It bode well for the future.

Mischievously Maria walked up behind Sean and began to play with his dark curls while smiling at Luke. "Aren't you going to guess, Luke? Do you really think I'd settle for the title of mistress?"

Sean groaned and covered his face with his hands. "Don't, Maria. I want to be alive for my wedding night. With any other woman it would be amusing, but not you. I never knew he had a jealous streak a mile wide and long until you came along. May the saints preserve me, Maria, but I'll not die for you."

Maria laughed and lifted her eyes in silent challenge to her husband. The need for slaughter had left his eyes, replaced by a look of desire she knew well, for it matched her own.

"I think I need to make a visit to the saloon."

Maria colored at the suggestive tone of Luke's voice, remembering the conversation of the night before.

Sean looked at him as if he were crazed, but seeing the way Luke looked at his wife, he shrugged without understanding. "By all means. It seems the thing to do."

"I think I'll accompany you. The room overhead should still be unoccupied." Maria came out from behind Sean and took Luke's arm.

The saloon would be better than returning her to the scene of chaos in the bedroom, and Luke grinned in appreciation. "Are you planning on wearing the blanket?"

"What else would a lady wear?" Maria inquired with great dignity. "Sean, you may have the house tonight. You'd better get some rest if you're catching the stage in the morning." She never took her eye from Luke as she spoke.

Sean stared at them both in disbelief, but he said not a word as Luke swung his barefoot wife into his arms and carried her out the door.

Maria undressed, washed hastily in the tepid water in the bowl, and slid between the clean sheets before Luke returned to the attic room. Consuela's taste in color had been vivid, but the bed was luxurious. The mattress was soft and the linens cool and smooth against her skin. It was a good thing no other woman had come along to fill her place. It seemed a shame to waste such luxury on the unappreciative.

The door opened, causing the candle flame to flicker. Maria smiled and sat up wantonly, allowing the covers to fall from her shoulders as Luke entered. "Did you get them?"

Luke eyed his eager wife with a mixture of lust and admonition. "Anybody could have walked in and found you like that."

"No one would be that stupid." She held out her arms to him. "Are you going to join me?"

"Did you have any doubt?" Throwing off his shirt, Luke fell down on the bed beside her and scooped her into his bare arms. As he pressed kisses along her jaw and throat, Maria arched against his chest and he groaned with impatience. "Maria, I'll not hold out for long if you keep that up," he warned in a low whisper.

"What do they look like?" she asked impishly as Luke stood to finish undressing.

Luke looked down at his amazing wife in astonishment laced liberally with love. "Maria, sometimes you are downright embarrassing."

He blew out the lamp, and she never did find out that night.

Downstairs the bartender poured another round of drinks for the customers regarding each other with more than the satisfaction of Manuel's imprisonment. With grins they lifted their glasses to toast Cheyenne Walker and his lady.

About the Author

Patricia Rice was born in Newburgh, New York, and attended the University of Kentucky. She now lives in Mayfield, Kentucky, with her husband and her two children, Corinna and Derek, in a rambling Tudor house. Ms. Rice has a degree in accounting and her hobbies include history, travel and antique collecting.